PRAISE FOR
CHARLIE N. HOLMBERG

THE SPELLBREAKER SERIES

"Romantic and electrifying . . . the fast-paced plot and fully realized world will have readers eager for the next installment. Fans of Victorian-influenced fantasy won't want to put this down."

—*Publishers Weekly*

"Those who enjoy gentle romance, cozy mysteries, or Victorian fantasy will love this first half of a duology. The cliffhanger ending will keep readers breathless waiting for the second half."

—*Library Journal* (starred review)

"Powerful magic, indulgent Victoriana, and a slow-burn romance make this genre-bending romp utterly delightful."

—*Kirkus Reviews*

THE NUMINA SERIES

"[An] enthralling fantasy . . . The story is gr   he start, with a surprising plot and a lush, beautif   Holmberg knows just how to please fantasy

—   ushers Weekly*

"With scads of action, clear   w supernatural elements function, and appealing charac   mart backstories, this first in a series will draw in fans of Cassan   Clare, Leigh Bardugo, or Brandon Sanderson."

—*Library Journal*

"Holmberg is a genius at world building; she provides just enough information to set the scene without overwhelming the reader. She also creates captivating characters worth rooting for, and puts them in unique situations. Readers will be eager for the second installment in the Numina series."

—*Booklist*

THE PAPER MAGICIAN SERIES

"Charlie is a vibrant writer with an excellent voice and great world building. I thoroughly enjoyed *The Paper Magician*."
—Brandon Sanderson, author of *Mistborn* and *The Way of Kings*

"Harry Potter fans will likely enjoy this story for its glimpses of another structured magical world, and fans of Erin Morgenstern's *The Night Circus* will enjoy the whimsical romance element . . . So if you're looking for a story with some unique magic, romantic gestures, and the inherent darkness that accompanies power all steeped in a yet to be fully explored magical world, then this could be your next read."
—Amanda Lowery, *Thinking Out Loud*

THE WILL AND THE WILDS

"An immersive, dangerous fantasy world. Holmberg draws readers in with a fast-moving plot, rich details, and a surprisingly sweet human-monster romance. This is a lovely, memorable fairy tale."
—*Publishers Weekly*

"Holmberg ably builds her latest fantasy world, and her brisk narrative and the romance at its heart will please fans of her previous magical tales."
—*Booklist*

THE FIFTH DOLL

STAR FATHER

ALSO BY CHARLIE N. HOLMBERG

The Star Mother Series

Star Mother

The Spellbreaker Series

Spellbreaker
Spellmaker

The Numina Series

Smoke and Summons
Myths and Mortals
Siege and Sacrifice

The Paper Magician Series

The Paper Magician
The Glass Magician
The Master Magician
The Plastic Magician

Other Novels

The Fifth Doll
Magic Bitter, Magic Sweet
Followed by Frost
Veins of Gold
The Will and the Wilds

STAR FATHER

A NOVEL

Charlie N. Holmberg

Published by 47North, Seattle

www.apub.com

Amazon, the Amazon logo, and 47North are trademarks of Amazon.com, Inc., or its affiliates.

ISBN-13: 9781542034289
ISBN-10: 1542034280

Cover design by Micaela Alcaino

Printed in the United States of America

To my niece Liesel.
Never fear the journey;
anticipate the destination.
You will reach it.

PART 1

I'm not happy with the statue.

None of the others agree with me. The stone is meant to show only an approximation of the god, not His actual face, as none of us have ever beheld it, and the priest claims His radiance would burn our eyes from our skulls if we did. But it feels wrong to create something like this without a face. I can't help but think the piece will forever feel unfinished.

CHAPTER 1

Daylight winked out at a quarter past noon.

Cloudless thunder ripped across the sky, as though I stood in the middle of a collapsing building. It rattled in my ears and zipped across my skin, raising gooseflesh in its wake. The animals in the barn erupted into a frenzy, bucking and bleating and crying out sounds I'd never heard in all my thirty-four years. Vine's hoof whipped by my jaw, close enough that I could feel the air compress around it. The cacophony was almost as violent as the thunder itself.

And then everything went dark, as if the world were lit by one candle, and it had been snuffed. No gradual setting of the Sun, no closing of lids. Only darkness.

If the utter black that consumed the barn and the farm outside of it weren't terrifying enough, the animals hushed just as swiftly, so silent I would not have known they were there if I couldn't smell them.

I had dropped the shoeing nails balanced on my lap but didn't stoop to pick them up. I was lucky Vine's half-shod back hoof had missed me in the commotion. I backed away, stepping on my skirt, fingers grazing across packed soil and scattered bits of hay. For a minute, the shifting of my body was the only sound in the barn. My crawling and my breathing, which grew heavier the longer the darkness held.

By the gods, what has happened? I found my feet and felt my way to the door. I'd been on my grandmother's farm long enough to know my way about, but my limbs trembled with every step regardless of my attempts to soothe them. The barn door groaned as I pushed it open.

Soft, weak light poured over the fields of corn, hay, and oats. Relief stirred in my chest at the sight of the stars, and I realized that in a wash of fear, I'd expected the sky to be as dark as the barn ceiling. So many stars pocked the night sky, more here than in the city. But that relief was quickly squashed when I recalled the time.

A quarter past noon.

Stepping away from the barn, I scanned the sky. No Sun, no moon. Only stars and a smattering of distant clouds.

Even scripture had never depicted such a thing. No matter how long I stared, I couldn't wrap my thoughts around it.

"Ai?" My mother's voice called from the house. "Ai!"

"Here!" I called back, hugging my arms around myself, needing something sturdy, as I hurried toward her. I took care with my step; the last thing I needed right now was a twisted ankle. "I'm fine! Kata?"

"She's fine!" My mother, Enera, bustled out from the house, her light linen clothes making her easier to find in the dark. The shuffling of her skirt and legs seemed so loud in the night—which gave me pause. Turning, I strained for other sounds. No crickets, no birds. My mother, my grandmother, and I lived a good way from the closest village, and far from the capital. I was used to the quiet.

Yet there was something distinctly wrong with this quiet. Something that shivered in my bones and made my fingertips itch, almost like when I had an excellent idea for a painting but couldn't get away from my chores to execute it. Except instead of frustrated anticipation, dread curled in my middle like a tired cat.

My mother closed the gap between us and grabbed my shoulders. "Did you see?"

I shook my head. "I was shoeing Vine—"

The grip tightened. "Are you hurt?"

Trying to smile, I put my hands over hers. My mother was a worrier, even when the cosmos behaved itself. "Missed me by a hair."

My mother released me. She was shaking badly, and I picked up her hand to offer comfort. "They heard it clear to Helchanar, I'm sure." She swallowed. "The gods are angry with us."

"The gods are angry with each other," I whispered, glancing at the sky. There had been rumblings of late, stories from far away about strange storms and flashes of light—evidence of another war in the heavens. It was hard to know what was speculation and what wasn't. It had been hard to pay it much heed, when our own country was in the midst of a human war.

Both had seemed very far away, until now.

"Let's go inside." I spoke a little too loudly, but I needed to ensure my voice didn't quiver or shake. My pulse beat wildly beneath my skin, moisture had fled my mouth, but I needed to be my mother's security. I needed to be the stake that held down the tent against the wind. Enera's soft heart could bear only so much.

My mother nodded, and we walked back to the house, my gaze continually darting from one end of the sky to the other. Every time I blinked, I expected the day to return. Expected to wake up on the barn floor and discover it all had been a dream. Surely only that could explain the sudden onset of night.

Yet my ears still hurt from that terrible cracking sound, like the sky itself were made of thick, shattered glass.

My skin grew cold.

Candles were already set up in a circle on the kitchen table, half a loaf of bread and my grandmother's wedding ring at its farthest point. Kata knelt on one of the benches, hands clasped together in prayer. Her hair was entirely gray, and if she lasted another decade, it would surely bleach white. She had a small frame, smaller than mine or my mother's, and she lost a little more weight with every year she defied the grave. As though her skin and her skeleton were lovers and sought to unite, pushing everything else away. The thinness emphasized her nose and her knuckles, which seemed all the more severe in the dim light. In truth, my grandmother's slowly weakening body was the only thing that made me feel useful on a farm that had run just fine without me during my time in the capital.

I gestured my mother to the nearest seat before saying, "The pleadings of one woman won't bring back the light."

Kata opened one dark eyelid. "Neither will blasphemy."

I let out a long breath. Rubbed my hands together. The cold was seeping into muscle. "It will pass. Tomorrow morning, the Sun will rise and this will pass."

My grandmother raised her head. "And can you explain it?"

I shook my head. "It won't matter, if it passes. The ways of the gods aren't for mortals to understand." I started repeating that over and over in my mind, hoping to wring some sort of comfort from it.

Kata frowned, then dipped her head again.

Enera leapt from her chair. "We'll need firewood. I'll get firewood." She scrambled back the way we had come.

I held my stomach, taking deep breaths to keep myself calm. My mother was prone to panic, and my grandmother prone to sharpness. My role was to be the balance between them. "It will pass."

It did not.

The next morning—what I determined to be the next morning by frequently checking my grandfather's old pocket clock—was just as dark as the long night. I stood at the kitchen window after offering pleading prayers, watching the stars. My mother had been right—despite it being late summer, we needed firewood. It had grown cold. Not cold enough for ice, but cold enough that the small hearth blazed, and I feared the temperature might drop further. Feared for the crops, and for us. I had brought a decent sum with me when I fled Algeron, but the savings were nearly spent. The crops were crucial for our survival, and we had but a few precious candles for light.

I pressed my hand to the glass.

"The moon." Kata hobbled in, stiff from sleep.

Ducking to better see the sky, I searched for the moon, but it was behind the house. Slipping outside, I walked toward the hayfield, then turned around.

My lips parted in surprise. The moon—I'd never seen it so large. It hung in the sky like a vibrant pearl, if the world had shrunk to the size of an oyster. From my vantage point, it was so large I had to lift both hands to cover it, surely as large as the Sun and His rays together. It glowed white, brighter than an opal, and the light highlighted the many scars across it. Across *her*. Still, she wasn't nearly bright enough to make up for His loss. While the Sun's light illuminated all of the Earth Mother, the moon's beamed a soft silver that burnished the sky and merely softened the shadows of the world beneath it, gleaming against puddles, metal, and pale stones, never truly penetrating the darkness of the night that cradled it.

Surely the gods' war had come to Rozhan, for the moon to be so brilliant. I had always thought the moonlight lovely, its light pure and unassuming, highlighting the world in a way that changed it entirely—something any artist would appreciate. But never had I beheld such intense majesty from the demigoddess. I could never hope to copy such a spectacle on canvas, or any other medium. Perhaps a mosaic of obsidian and diamonds would come close.

My hands trembled when I came inside, but I picked up my sketchbook and took it to the closest candle, choosing a stick of charcoal to begin. The off-white of the paper would have to suffice.

I began sketching the silhouette of the horizon. I'd drawn it so many times I didn't need to see it with my eyes. Memory was enough.

My grandmother clucked her tongue. "What good is drawing going to do?"

She had never understood anything that didn't put food on the table or hay in the barn, so I ignored her. I shaded in the horizon, pressing hard to make it dark, then drew a near-perfect circle in the sky, filling in the page around it. Added scars with flicks of my wrist.

Drawing helped me think. Painting helped me think. Sculpting helped me think. And I direly needed to think.

"Perhaps the Earth Mother has moved," I whispered, filling in shadows.

"The Earth Mother sleeps," Kata argued.

"Have you never moved in your sleep?" My hand stilled. There was only so much of the scene's majesty I could depict with a dark setting and a nub of charcoal. I set the stick down. One of the first lessons I'd learned as a budding artist in Algeron was knowing when to stop. Yet I did not want to. It felt strange, that such a simple picture represented such a complex problem.

"Where's Enera?" I asked after my mother. My grandmother preferred the use of her first name, and as I aged, I'd adapted it to my mother as well.

Kata hobbled to the table and sat, but didn't light the candles of her makeshift shrine. She was devout, but she was smart, and it would do us no good to waste our sources of light. "Feeding the animals. They still eat, you know."

I pressed my lips together. "I should help her." With the daylight stolen away, I might actually be useful to this place. A selfish and petulant thought, but I had it all the same.

"Perhaps the gods compromised," Kata speculated.

I swallowed. "Perhaps the Sun is dead."

"The Sun can't die. Gods can't die."

"Perhaps they can if killed by another god," I whispered, stomach tightening. But the moon was only a demigoddess—still immortal, still powerful, but not as great as the Sun and Earth Mother. That was why her presence was so much less than Theirs, even now.

After grabbing my apron and tying it on, I stepped into the dark, not bothering with a lantern. The moon was brilliant enough that I could see my way, though the fields loomed like black iron bits standing on end and shadows along the path stretched thick as tar. I offered another weak prayer in my mind before reaching the barn, the doors and windows open for more light.

Animals of the day remained quiet; I'd not heard the call of a songbird or buzz of a bee since the sky darkened, but the skittering of mice had increased, as had the rhythm of crickets and calls of owls. The sheep didn't bleat, but they fidgeted, restless. Should I take them to the fields? But how could I keep an eye on all of them, without daylight? Were the wolves prowling, or had they curled up in confusion, waiting for the endless night to pass?

My mother worked, forking hay into stalls; I heard it more than saw it. Enera was a shadow against shadows, a slip of moonlight from the doorway touching her shoes and nothing more. I didn't ask the question about the sheep. My mother was working against fear. I wouldn't interrupt that.

We would wait. The sheep were safe in the barn, for now. We would wait, and the dark would pass. In all the stories, the heavens' battles never lasted long. It would pass.

I had never been so diligent in winding my grandfather's clock as I was during that time of darkness. After the end of the second day, I kept it on my person, winding it when my hands were empty, winding it when I couldn't sleep, winding it when my mother wept into a blanket so Kata wouldn't hear her.

On the eve of the fourth night, I held the pocket clock tightly in my left hand as I ate with my right; bread and beans and rabbit roasted over the constant glow of the hearth. My palms were blistered from splitting firewood, but we needed as much as we could get, even if the walk to the trees was a long one. Even if I could barely see the log in front of me. There was so much work to be done. There had always been so much work to be done, especially without a man to help, yet as the rest of the world slowed down in the shadows, it seemed there was more.

"I wonder how Danika's brood is faring," Enera whispered between bites of bread. No butter—that was a task I could finish. Churning the butter. If I could even find where we'd left the churn.

"I know the road. I could find my way to the village," I offered.

"She'll be fine," Kata snapped. The darkness had begun to make her ornery, like the rain did. "She's looked after."

Danika was my aunt—my mother's sister. She lived in Goatheir, the nearest village, which was half a day's walk away. Unlike my mother, she had married. Most of her eight children had stayed nearby, including Zyzi, my cousin and best friend, who was six years my junior.

"Zyzi will handle it well." I spoke quietly. I didn't have to, but something about the perpetual night demanded quiet.

Kata drained her small cup and said, "We need water."

I ran my thumb over the face of the clock. "I'll collect some tonight."

My mother shook her head. "Not in the dark. Wait until—" Then she caught herself. *Wait until morning.* But what if the morning didn't come?

What if it never came again?

"I'll go with you," she amended.

"We need more firewood," Kata protested, plunging her fork into a piece of meat. "All our extra time will be spent chopping firewood. Not moping. Not sleeping. Not drawing." She eyed me as she muttered that last one.

I didn't respond. It did no good to rile my grandmother, who had never gotten me under her thumb as she had my mother. Probably because I'd been swept away by a man and spent the better half of my life away from the farm. Working there as an artisan—an *acclaimed* artisan. I may never have left if mining disputes hadn't driven Belat's armies over Rozhan's borders, and thus driven me to the safety of home.

The conflict had raged for years, and from what little news reached us here, in the sparsely populated plains, there was no resolution in sight. Until the battles ended and people had money in their pockets again, my work would never sell, no matter how acclaimed it might have been.

But I couldn't simply *stop* creating, even in the countryside. Even when the Sun didn't rise. My grandmother might as well have asked me to stop breathing.

Kata was simply angry that, at seventy-three years of age, she couldn't do what she had once done. Her body was too frail. She had to rely on her daughter and granddaughter, and Kata hated relying on anyone.

I understood that, more than most. It was easier to depend on yourself. I'd never fully given myself to anyone, even Edkar. Never understood how so many could. I had never . . . *felt* that depth of romantic attachment toward another person, though there was something that called to me in the songs and works of art depicting effortless and endless love. Like a riddle I couldn't answer.

Then again, it might have been safer not to.

"Bandits are probably holing up, as we are." I offered my mother a smile. "It's not far to the river. And I'm a fast runner, just in case."

My mother wasn't happy about it, but it needed to be done. That, and Kata had asked her to get the firewood. In the five years since I'd returned to the farm, I'd never once seen her act against my grandmother's will.

We finished dinner in that same stifled quiet—a quiet that would surely drive me to insanity if it lasted much longer. I collected the dishes and set them next to the washbasin for Kata; dishes were a task she could still do, and she got livid if anyone took that away from her. Then I slipped into my room. The farmhouse had two bedrooms, and my mother had kindly given me hers when I returned from Algeron. She'd moved in with my grandmother, and the two slept in the bed Kata had once shared with my grandfather. I shook my hair out from the tail I'd put it in this morning and recoiled it. My mother and I both had thick black manes we wore long, simply because long hair was easier to pull back, and the coarseness of the strands complied better. The rest of me might as well have come straight from my grandmother—I had her taupe eyes and darker complexion. I'd been told I had my father's lips, but I'd never met him. Even my mother barely remembered him. He was a useful mistake, and little else.

I pulled on my coat, the weight of it still strange, as days ago it had been summer. I didn't bother with gloves, but I took a lantern outside with me, along with two empty pails and a yoke. The river ran past the oat and hayfields. It would have been easier to take Vine; she could carry far more than I could. But if our only horse—who still was not fully shod—broke a leg in this darkness or startled and ran off, we would feel the loss sorely. Better for me to do it alone, until the Sun returned.

The moon hovered near the distant mountains in the west, a range so minute it was barely discernable from the plains. Half her face was covered by a cloud, which appeared entirely silver from her increased light. I watched that light for a moment before blinking and turning my gaze toward the well-worn path to the river. It was smooth and sure, but I'd best pay attention, regardless. That, and I would hurt my night vision if I stared too long at the unnatural brightness of the moon.

I passed the fields, which had taken on a heavy and strange presence in the endless night, pocked with the slow song of crickets. Together, they made the night more dreamlike.

At least the river didn't hush beneath the oddity of the heavens. It babbled readily as I approached, lazy with the season, meandering between shallow banks. The reeds along its edges looked tired, and I feared again for our crops. Surely they would die if the Sun did not return soon. The new brilliance of the moon might slow their withering, but it would not be enough to nourish them in the long term. And we needed those crops to sustain us.

"Gods help us," I murmured as I knelt at the bank, setting down my lantern. I uttered a prayer to any god, demigod, or even godling willing to listen, asking for the day cycles to be restored so we might be spared. I filled the first pail with water and hefted it ashore, then filled the second. As I strung the yoke through the pails' handles, I begrudged the walk back. I hadn't been sleeping well. The endless night confused my mind. My skin and mind craved Sunlight. Even before the consuming dark, I'd always craved Sunlight. It was, perhaps, the most pious thing about me.

Another prayer flowed through my thoughts as I reached for my lantern, but I was too hasty, and my foot kicked it, sending the glass lamp sprawling along the bank. Hissing, I darted after it, snatching it before it spilled oil or, worse, toppled into the river. Letting out a breath, I held up the light, checking for damage.

Something gold glinted at the edge of the lantern's gleam.

I paused, squinting. Held the lantern higher. Curious, I approached quietly, my footsteps swallowed by the sound of the river to my left. The shimmer of gold darkened, expanded—

Into an arm.

Chin dropping, I hurried forward until the full brunt of my light fell upon him. A man, lying on his stomach, one arm curled under him, the other extended as though reaching for something. His feet hung over the bank. His clothes were of strange make, drapey and pale, but my focus remained on his skin, which was such a deep shade of gold it was almost brown. A trick of the light?

Kneeling beside him, I shook his shoulder. "Sir! Sir?"

His skin was feverish. But he was alive.

Setting the lantern down, I shook him harder. "Can you hear me? Are you hurt?" I checked him for injury. I didn't *see* any, but he was obviously ill. His skin was hot as the lantern's glass, and he wouldn't wake.

There was no way I could carry him back myself. He was too big, and I cursed myself for not bringing Vine. "I'll get help," I whispered, snatching up my lantern. "Don't worry—I'll get help."

I took off down the river, swerving toward that well-worn path, no longer caring for the safety of my ankles.

I only hoped we could get back to him before it was too late.

I wonder what His face looks like, and if I would even recognize Him, if I ever saw it.

CHAPTER 2

I stopped first at the barn, then rushed in a frenzy to the farmhouse. My mother had thankfully not yet left to chop firewood; one look at my face and she was on her feet. I explained on the way, telling her that I'd found a feverish man passed out by the river, a stranger. Our closest neighbors were miles away, and I'd met all of them at least once. He was not of their ilk.

We risked riding Vine for better speed, though she made our lanterns sway violently and shied away from every shadow, the silence bothering her even more than it did me.

I slid off when we reached the river, searching frantically. For a moment, I feared the man had slipped into the river or moved just enough that I'd never find him, but I followed the current, and there he lay, just as I'd left him. Enera ran up beside me, panting, and wailed, "That is a *lot* of man!"

We tried again to rouse him—it would be so much easier if he could mount Vine himself. My mother cupped handfuls of water and doused his face. I shook him, shouted at him, but he didn't stir. The only movement was the expanding of his rib cage with each slow breath.

"He's so warm," Enera remarked once we'd determined we had to move him on our own. "Too warm. He won't live through the night."

"We must try." I gripped him under one arm, my mother took the other, and we heaved.

He certainly *was* a lot of man.

We lugged him mere inches at a time, dragging his feet from the river. Enera coaxed Vine to relax while I muttered things like "I wish you'd wasted away a little with this fever" to the poor soul, who was heavy as a cow. I'm not sure how long it took us to finally get him onto Vine's back—Enera had to make the poor mare kneel—but the night had never felt longer. My shoulders and arms tremored with the effort.

The way home was a little easier.

"What is *this*?" Kata crowed when we brought Vine right up to the door. She was a plow horse, thickly built, so we couldn't lead her into the house. I slid the stranger off her back, and his weight brought me to my knees. My mother quickly shuffled around to his other side to lighten the load.

"Found him . . . by the river." Awkwardly sidestepping into the kitchen, I avoided my grandmother's gaze and focused on keeping my back straight. My room was closest, so we stumbled into there and plopped the man onto my bed.

Most of him made it.

Five years of farmwork had done nothing to prepare me for this. Energy drained from my body, but I scooped up his legs and hefted them onto the mattress, too. My shoulders were hot where he had touched me, his fever seeping from his skin into mine. I wiped sweat from my brow. My mother hurried from the room, probably to get water—reminding me that I'd left the pails at the river—and Kata came in, holding a candle high.

I gasped at the same time she inquired, "Who is he?"

I didn't answer. My grandmother's candle was bright; combined with the other little lights in the house, it gave me a good look at the man's face for the first time. It was . . . mesmerizing. Striking. Like nothing I'd beheld before. His features were broad, almost regal, and strange as it may sound, there was a sort of lionlike quality to them. It had been no idle fancy of mine that his skin was gold. It lacked metallic shimmer, but it was so deeply gold it made me wonder if his muscles, organs, and bones shared the same hue. His hair, which was unbound and shoulder length, was similar in color, with a few darker strands running through it. Loosely pleated fabric hung from his shoulders, pinned there with unmarked medallions. The folds draped over his chest, tied around his waist, split over wide pants. I had never beheld such a fashion before, but the truly odd part was the material. In my trance, I leaned forward to pinch it between my fingers. Definitely not cotton, wool, or linen. It was almost like organza, but it was too soft to be that, either. My mind listed every material on this side of the Earth Mother, and none of them matched.

But strangest of all . . . I felt a soft tugging in my mind, like I *knew* this man. But I also knew I would never forget that face, so the inkling had to be wrong.

Kata slapped him.

"Kata!" I snapped. She'd struck him far harder than necessary.

The man didn't stir.

"Not Telorian, but that's my best guess." Kata leaned so close she risked dripping wax on the man's skin. She pushed a thumb into his eyelid and lifted it, but his eyes were rolled back.

Enera came hurrying in with a bowl of water and several rags. She wrung out one and put it on his forehead, then another on his chest.

"Not Telorian." My agreement was a meager whisper. His skin *might* have passed for Telorian tan in different lighting, but most Telorians were thin and lanky. I would have had little struggle getting a Telorian onto my horse.

Shaking myself, I backed away. "I-I'll get some nettle tea." It would help lower his fever.

My grandmother scoffed. "With what water?"

Nothing slipped her notice. But I left the room anyway, heating some of the water we still had on the meager stove, seeing the stranger's gold face behind my eyelids every time I blinked. I shook myself. Took deep breaths to ease the tension growing beneath my breastbone.

I don't know him, I told myself as I crushed thorny leaves with a mortar and pestle. *I would never forget a face like that. I would have drawn it.*

And despite my sore limbs, weariness, and confusion, I itched badly to do just that.

I woke sometime later with the edge of my simple bed frame imprinted into my cheek. I'd offered to keep vigil over the stranger, and I'd fallen asleep leaning against the bed. One of the candles had burned out, so I moved another closer to get a better look at him.

Unchanged. His chest rose and fell with the rhythm of deep sleep. I took the rag from his forehead, noticing its heat. Pressing my palm to his brow, I flinched. His fever seemed to have worsened.

He won't live through the night, my mother had said. I fished out my grandfather's pocket clock to check. Five in the morning. The moon's courses were not like the Sun's, and we couldn't depend on them to gauge the time. Some days she crossed the sky from midnight to noon, only to reappear again at three and vanish at four. As though she couldn't fathom the expanse of her newly grown kingdom. Or as though she was looking for something.

The stranger was still alive, but not improved in the slightest.

Sitting on the edge of the bed, I patted his cheek, which was covered by a short, well-trimmed beard. "Sir, wake up." I whispered not for his sake, but because Enera and Kata were surely asleep in the next room. "You have to wake up long enough to tell me your name."

He didn't stir.

Biting my bottom lip, I took the candle with me to the kitchen and rummaged through the cupboards, finding more nettle and some elder-flowers my mother had dried in the spring. Foraging for herbs would be difficult with the heavens dark, I realized . . . assuming they'd continue to grow. I didn't have the sort of stores my cousin Zyzi kept, and now I was regretting it. I made another tea, stronger than the last, and brought it to my room. Lifting his head in the crook of my elbow, I helped him drink. A few drops at a time, but they went down steadily enough.

Goodness, he was pyretic. I'd never seen a fever so bad.

"You're in Rozhan, just outside Goatheir," I murmured to him. "You're safe now." He must have been traveling, though I hadn't seen any bags near the river. Perhaps they'd been swept away. Perhaps *he* had been swept away, and used the last of his strength to climb that bank. "We'll help you in any way we can." I glanced at the dark window. "Though you're not missing much."

Sighing, I set the cup aside and studied him. He really was remarkable. I leaned closer. "If you don't wake, I'll give you a terrible nickname, and it will stick, mark my words."

The threat didn't rile him.

Frowning, I held the candle closer to his face. Feeling a little foolish, I lifted my free hand and ran it down the length of his strong nose. I could carve that nose in marble. Those eyes, though I wondered what shape they would be if they opened. Round? Downturned? Hooded?

He had a strong jaw and prominent cheekbones. Full lips. He would be amazing to sculpt. Of course, Kata would lose her mind if I tried chiseling stone in the house, not that I had stone to chisel.

I checked the pocket clock again.

Stretching out my arms—the soreness was settling in well—I crossed to my tiny closet and pulled out my easel. I still had some canvas, though I hoarded it, usually using paper instead. It was less expensive, although neither was cheap, which was likely the real reason my grandmother disliked my art. I chose a smaller piece, set it up nearby, and brought in two more candles, lighting them so I could see both Goldy and my work.

I smiled. "See? I told you you'd get a terrible nickname."

I worked with a graphite pencil, gently sketching, wishing for more light, but I would not waste more candles on a whim, and I knew my hand well enough to see what the shadows tried to hide. I sketched the outline of his bust in loose shapes before going in and adding detail, occasionally glancing at him to better shade the tilt of his nose or dip of his upper lip.

I left his eyes for last. I didn't want to sketch them closed, but neither did I want to guess at their appearance and get it wrong. With a frown, I drew him as he was, deeply resting, delicate eyelashes splayed.

He was beautiful. Later, when the Sun rose, I would paint this, though I doubted I'd be able to get the colors just right.

Setting the easel aside, I returned to the bed. Felt his forehead. Tsked. "These herbs are doing *nothing* for you." Wetting a rag, I drew cool water over his features, down his neck, and across his collarbone, pushing his strange robe-like shirt aside to moisten his chest. By the time I returned to his forehead, the water had evaporated.

My heart sank like a scuttled ship in the sea of my stomach. Sorrow, sharp as a sickle, sliced through me. I felt oddly invested in Goldy's welfare. In his story. "If you don't wake, I'll never know the shape of your eyes," I said. Leaving the rag on his brow, I reached down to pick up his large hand. It was tough, like a workingman's hand, yet without any specific calluses, and I wondered what his occupation could possibly be. "The very least you could do to repay me for my efforts is show me your eyes."

He didn't move.

"Stubborn as an ox," I growled.

"Perhaps he's a bandit."

My grandmother's voice startled me. I dropped Goldy's hand and turned toward the doorway. "He hardly looks like a bandit."

She cocked a near-white eyebrow. "And you know what bandits look like?" She shuffled in, stiff from sleep, leaning on her cane. "All shapes and sizes, bandits." She eyed my easel. The wrinkles around her mouth deepened.

"He didn't have anything with him, that I saw." I glanced back to his serene face. "I should look again when I retrieve the pails. He might have lost his things in the river."

"Maybe a pirate."

I rolled my eyes. "We're not near enough the ocean for a pirate."

"And why should a pirate be limited to the ocean?" She scowled at him. "Why not be a river pirate? Easier to port, harder to sink."

A dry chuckle caught in my throat. "If you say so."

She came close enough that her knees touched the bed frame. "He's not a babe, Aija. Don't treat him like one."

"He's an invalid. Very much the same. Should I not cater to you next time your knees swell?"

My grandmother grimaced but didn't respond. She snapped her fingers. "Mercenary. Look at those shoulders. He's a mercenary."

I did look at his shoulders. Touched one and groaned inwardly at the fever boiling beneath his skin. "Don't mercenaries wear armor?"

"Not if they have to swim. Not if they're escaping the fold." She considered. "Deserter, I'd bet. We should tie him down, just in case."

I shook my head. "He won't wake anytime soon. His fever has gotten worse."

Kata motioned for me to rise. I did, and she took my place. "You need to be more liberal with the water. Fetch me that balm, then go get the pails."

I did as she asked, taking Vine to the river.

I didn't find any of Goldy's belongings, nor any sign that he had ever been there.

I decided on clay.

We all took turns watching over Goldy as his condition worsened, enough so that his breathing took on a rasp and his lovely skin paled. We tried everything we could. My mother took out a lantern to forage for herbs and check on the crops. I halfheartedly took care of the animals while my grandmother smeared Goldy with balms and chided him for every evil path his life might have taken.

By the third day of his care, seven days after the night had swallowed the world, I decided to sculpt him from clay.

I enjoyed working clay. It gave the art more depth than a sketch or painting ever could, yet it was more forgiving of mistakes than stone. I brought in a hunk of dark clay I'd mixed myself, and even Kata didn't complain, because we all needed something to do while we tried to keep our stranger alive. So I sculpted him, delicately inlaying every hair, realizing as I carved his hairline that he didn't sweat.

What kind of fever kept a man from sweating?

Halfway through my work, I paused to give my fingers and arms a break. "Perhaps you're a famous cartographer," I tried. "And you *have* sailed, but you're not a pirate. Your skin is too clear and your gums too healthy for that."

Yes, I had checked.

"A renowned cartographer from the other side of the world"—I studied my eyeless bust of him—"but you grew up poor. You worked on a farm, not unlike this one. That's why you don't look like a scholar. And your father . . . *he* was a mercenary, but he fell in love with your mother one fateful night and decided to renounce his old ways and settle down.

"But his wanderlust was in your blood, and you wanted to see the world." I stretched my back. "You wanted to remember every curve of coastline and point of mountain. You wanted to explore and make something of yourself. But you don't boast of it." I paused and studied the face that had become so familiar to me. "Well, you do in private, among friends. And in your published works, though they're penned by someone else, of course. I wonder, do you speak many languages, or have you hired a translator to bring your story to a wider public? If so, where is he?"

Goldy was not amused by my story. He drew in a rasping breath.

Abandoning my sculpture, I returned to his side and pulled off hot rags from his forehead and chest. Wound and checked the pocket clock. He was due for more medicine, so I went and poured him a cup from what Enera had made that morning. It might do him well to have it served cold. When I returned, his breathing had quieted.

I paused before lifting his head for the tea. "Why are you breathing better?" I asked, and lowered the cup. He'd only grown worse since my mother and I had brought him here, despite our best efforts. I wondered if we had gone about his fever wrong. If it was somehow different from all the others I'd seen and experienced in my lifetime.

There was only one way to tell.

I set the cup aside and brought the bowl of rags back into the kitchen.

For now, I would simply let him rest.

The darkness wormed into our minds a little more every day, if "day" even existed anymore. It fed my mother's fright and shortened my grandmother's temper. It made me anxious and sharp tongued. My dear mother, upon relieving me from my vigil and seeing my sculpture, teased me about falling in love with Goldy. I practically bit her head off in response.

"Don't be ridiculous," I seethed. "I've never been *in love* with anything."

I'd stormed past her, and it took less than a quarter hour for regret to loosen my muscles. When I returned to apologize, both Enera and Kata were in the room, crowding it with the two kitchen chairs they sat on, murmuring with their heads pressed together.

I strained to listen but couldn't quite make out their words. "What?"

Kata's taupe eyes whipped to me, while my mother's gaze drooped to the floor, making my guilt all the heavier.

"Luthas stopped by while you snoozed." My grandmother jerked her chin toward the thin pallet on the floor where I had dozed off during my vigil. I had not slept in a bed since finding Goldy. "Says there've been bandits lurking around Goatheir, taking advantage of the darkness. With the cover of night, they can rob us twenty-four hours a day." She spat.

Enera's gaze crept toward the man in my bed. "What if they're looking . . . for him?"

"Are bandits so loyal?" I folded my arms, my irritation climbing my spine like a ladder. "Or perhaps he's in more danger than we are."

When my mother's soft eyes found mine, I dropped my hands. "I'm sorry about what I said."

She simply smiled and shrugged.

Slipping behind Kata's chair, I returned to Goldy's side and pressed a palm to his forehead. "He's still burning up, but his breathing has been easier. I haven't given him any medicine or cool cloths, just some broth to drink."

Enera stood to replace my hand with hers. "Odd. But if it's working . . ."

She glanced at me and shrugged.

Letting out a long breath—I was tired—I dropped onto the edge of the mattress, shifting Goldy's body slightly. "I wouldn't worry about bandits. We're in the middle of nowhere. That's a ways to travel for little gain."

Kata narrowed her eyes at me as though I had insulted her farm—and I supposed I had. "Crops dying, no Sunlight . . . the food in that mill will be worth more than gold soon enough."

The mention of gold brought my attention back to Goldy's peaceful face. I still itched to capture it, not satisfied by the sculpture or the many sketches I'd already made. It seemed I could only capture a fraction of his essence in each piece of art, and it would take thousands to truly illustrate what I saw.

"Should be colder," Kata added.

For a moment I thought she meant Goldy, but her nose pointed toward the window and the ever-night beyond it. She was right, I supposed. With no Sun, each night should grow colder. And yet the air seemed to dance just before the line of frost. Perhaps it was the moon, which was so much more present, so much larger and brighter.

Was this how the world would be from now on? Would mortals simply die out, or would we find robust plants and skinny animals to fill our bellies?

I rubbed my forehead, trying to alleviate my worry. We needed Sunlight. I *craved* it.

Perhaps detecting my thoughts, Enera whispered, "The Sun is dead."

Logic pushed up my throat. "Gods can't die." It was not the first time I'd stated such.

My mother considered this a moment. "Perhaps the war has been taken away from Earth Mother, and the Sun went with it. Or some other god of darkness has rested here."

Leaning my elbows on my knees, I said, "Say your theory is true . . . It's unlikely some new god is looming over us. There are far more demigods and godlings, and they wouldn't have the power to consume all of the Earth Mother at once. What if the affliction has only struck Rozhan? Perhaps there is light elsewhere."

Godlings were the weakest celestial beings, though still far more powerful than any human could hope to be. Although not immortal, like gods and demigods, they were very long-lived. Hundreds, if not thousands, of years. It had been a long time since I'd leafed through scripture, and godlings were not spoken of often. Indeed, none of us had ever seen one with our own eyes. They may have been the most plentiful of celestial beings, but that did not make them numerous. I'm not sure I'd recognize one even if it poked me in the nose.

My grandmother smacked her cane into the floor. "I will not run from my home. Chase the light without me."

I exchanged a glance with my mother. This was not a battle worth fighting. It was only speculation. But trapped in the dark as we were, speculation was all we had. No scientist or king's messenger would come riding our way with news. Information would trickle down slowly, from the richest to the poorest, eventually making its way on the lips of a bard or merchant passing through Goatheir, and then, most likely, Danika or Zyzi would make the trip out to inform us.

I tried not to wonder if we would all die out here, alongside my well-rooted grandmother.

My stomach hurt.

Enera touched my elbow. "Take my bed, dear. We'll be up for a while yet."

Up. I checked the pocket clock. It was four in the afternoon. My body had completely forgotten its rhythms already. Or my grasp of time was wavering, and it was four in the morning, but I was fairly certain—

My mother pinched my arm. "Go."

Nodding, I made my way to the second bedroom, not bothering to light a candle to find my way.

I didn't even remember falling asleep, but I woke sometime later, staring at shadows on the ceiling made from the faint glow filtering down the hallway from the kitchen hearth. I lay diagonally on the bed that smelled like leather and sage. I'd slept, but my eyes still felt gritty. I rubbed my knuckles into them and sat up slowly. My stomach growled for nourishment. I wondered if anyone had thought to cook.

Fortunately, as I meandered into the hallway, I heard the clanking of a spoon on an iron pot. Enera was dozing on a chair in my room, so it had to be Kata in the kitchen. Gently shaking my mother's shoulder, I said, "Trade with me."

She patted my hand with gratitude and slipped into the hallway.

After stretching, I pulled the chair my mother had occupied closer to the bed and took up my sketchbook. "What shall we do today, Goldy? Perhaps I should start at the other end and sketch your feet."

I turned my sketchbook to the next clean page, then picked up a nub of charcoal.

When I looked up again, Goldy's eyes were open and locked with mine.

The Sun seemed a little brighter today.

CHAPTER 3

His eyes were like mother-of-pearl. That was the first thought that broke through my astonishment. The opalescent vibrancy of mother-of-pearl—the inner part of the shell, where the light hit and reflected—warmed by the slightest hint of gold. Edged with a darker outer ring reminiscent of the outer shell. They were deep set, slightly hooded, and vertically narrow, with a faint upward tilt on the outside corners.

My second thought was *He is awake!*

I nearly dropped my sketchbook, but caught its edge just as it slipped off my knees. The charcoal was not so fortunate. It hit the floor and rolled beneath the bed.

I lifted off the chair, not quite standing. "How are you?"

He stared at me in the uncomprehending way of one who's woken from a deep slumber—their body awake but their mind slow to follow. His bizarre, breathtaking eyes shifted from me to the wall behind me, then his bed, then the ceiling.

"You're in the countryside, not too far from Goatheir," I tried.

He sat up violently, his blanket dropping to his hips, his strange clothes tightening around him.

Both my hands flew up like I was calming a startled horse. "In Rozhan. But . . . surely you know that, right?"

"Ai?" My mother's voice floated down the hallway.

I swallowed, ignoring it. "My name is Ai. Aija. I found you unconscious by the river. You've been here five days."

Confusion burrowed into lines between his brows and tugged at the edges of his lips. An entirely new expression to sketch—but now wasn't the time to dwell on that. Shifting away from me, he pressed open palms to his chest and stomach before lifting them and holding them before his face, turning his hands over like he was seeing them for the first time.

I wondered what sort of dream had haunted him for its hold to be so firm.

I stepped back. "L-Let me get you some water—"

"Rozhan?"

I would have expected his voice to be gravelly from slumber, but that single word punched the air in a deep baritone that played at bass. The sound of it raised gooseflesh on my arms. As though his speaking somehow made him real.

He still stared at his hands. "Rozhan, you said?"

I nodded, but since he wasn't looking at me, I murmured, "Yes."

Enera appeared in the doorway and gasped. "You're awake!"

I held out my hand, staying her, not wanting to overwhelm him . . . though surely my grandmother had overheard us by now, and she would not patiently wait for answers.

Goldy fisted his hands and slowly lowered them to his thighs. "I see."

Exchanging a glance with my mother, I asked, "Were you not . . . traveling . . . in Rozhan?" Our farm was nowhere near the border. I could not believe a man would be swept all the way downriver to our lands and survive it.

He let out a breath, and it felt like a summer wind swept through the room. Shifting, he swung his legs over the edge of the bed.

I hurried toward him. "Don't stand straightaway. You're still recovering—"

Before my hand could reach his shoulder, he twisted back, avoiding my touch.

I froze, gawking at him. He stared right back at me.

Confused, mouth dry, I struggled to reclaim my last thought. "Y-You're still recovering." Though he looked hale. "You should take it slowly. Eat something."

Harsh whispers in the hallway announced Kata, but my mother seemed to be arguing with *her* for once. Hopefully asking her to wait so we didn't startle the poor man by bombarding him with too much attention.

Besides, there was the possible danger to consider. He was unknown to us, and however much I loved drawing him, however sick he may have been, he could easily overpower the three of us if he wanted to.

His gold-tinted brows drew together as he stared at me.

"We have soup." My mother's timid voice sounded from the doorway. She held a candle in one hand and a wooden bowl in the other, padding carefully toward the two of us. "Please, eat. You'll need to regain your strength."

The added light of her candle pressed between us, making Goldy's eyes even brighter. His brows relaxed.

"I know you," he whispered.

My entire body went slack. A shiver coursed down my spine and back up again.

Had I not had a similar inkling?

"How?" I asked.

His gaze shifted up to my forehead, then down to my chin. "Aija. The cathedral . . . Rozhan. Algeron."

I nodded slowly, but my confusion only mounted. The new cathedral in the capital had been finished ten years ago. I was one of the artisans who'd helped beautify the building and the grounds—specifically the great sky mosaic and a sculpture of the Sun God. Had he been there?

But I would have remembered. I know I would have. I could not fathom how, in this world or the next, I could forget a face like his.

My mother stood motionless, bowl still extended in her hand. I felt my grandmother's presence in the doorway.

I took the soup from Enera and held the bowl between my hands. "What's your name?"

His mouth pressed into a line. His eyes shifted away from mine. Then he went very still, so much so that air ceased to fill his lungs.

I followed his line of sight. He was looking out the window. At the dark everything.

"It's been like that for nine days," I offered.

Several seconds passed before his lungs worked again, drawing a deep breath into his body and releasing it.

He stood suddenly, and I nearly dumped the soup onto my shirt in my haste to back away and give him space. His height had been hard to gauge when he was a lifeless sack of man, but standing, he appeared to be a few inches over six feet. He strode past me and my easel, to the window, and peered out into the darkness.

He stood like that for a long time.

"You're welcome," Kata spat.

He turned from the window. "My apologies. I thank you for your service to me."

Stiff silence filled the room. Eager to break it, I set the soup down and gestured to the doorway. "This is Kata, my grandmother, and Enera, my mother."

He nodded slowly, gaze passing over each of them. When it returned to me, he said, "Aija."

I nodded.

He wiped a hand down his face. When it dropped, he noticed the easel, his sleeping face sketched upon the canvas. Suddenly embarrassed, I sidestepped to throw a blanket over the half-finished clay sculpture. Not that I should have been. The least he could do while taking up a bed in this house and demanding our constant care was model for a bust.

Enera said, "You can stay as long as you need," to which Kata gave her a hard glare. But where else was he to go? Despite his knowledge of our language, it was obvious he was far from home. My mother was easily the most generous among us; I wasn't surprised she made the offer, asking nothing in return. And while I felt in my gut that Goldy wasn't dangerous, I doubted my grandmother wanted to keep him. Not without something in exchange.

"Do you remember how you got here?" I tried.

He didn't answer.

"Do you remember your name?" I tried again, fighting my own impatience. The man had been severely ill, after all. He still was . . . or was he? He seemed in perfect health—another oddity to add to the list. "I doubt you want to continue going by Goldy."

His brow twitched, and those fantastical eyes found mine again.

He hesitated.

"No one else knows you're here," I tried, in case my grandmother's theories were correct, but I had not yet finished the last word when he spoke.

"Saiyon," he said, soft and careful. "You may call me Saiyon."

Saiyon.

That was not a Telorian name. It wasn't a name I'd heard before, anywhere.

The syllables danced over my tongue, tempting me to voice them, to taste the strange yet lovely word. But the wanting irritated me. It was only a name. He was only a muse. The manner in which even the smallest aspects of him entranced me felt like barbs in my skin. When he had slept, it was an innocent game, but now that he was conscious and animated, it was foolishness.

Asserting myself, I said, "You seem hale, but your fever isn't one we're familiar with. It would be best for you to rest and eat." I gestured to the bed. "I can attempt to make inquiries for you, but it will be hard with the darkness."

He hesitated, like he was debating whether to accept the invitation. But he made no attempt to push past the door and abandon the farmhouse, so wherever it was he had been traveling must not have been urgent. With a stifled sigh, he returned to the bed, though he merely sat on the edge of it, forearms on his knees, hands clasped.

Kata stormed away, muttering something about ungrateful mercenaries.

Picking up the bowl of soup, I offered it again to him. He waved it away. "No, thank you."

That irritation pushed a little deeper. "Sir. You've had little more than drops of water and broth for five days. You need to eat."

"Have I?" His voice sounded far away, but there was the slightest tweaking of his lips. I might not have noticed it had I not been drawing his face so often in the last week. But it looked distinctly like amusement.

What, exactly, did this stranger have to be amused about?

Setting the bowl aside once more, I reached forward to feel his forehead. Delaying his treatments seemed to have helped him improve, but the fever had shown no signs of breaking—

Like before, he cringed from my touch. When my hand followed him, he put up his arm to block me.

Irritation breaking free, I smacked his wrist aside. "Stop it."

The look of shock on his face was nearly comical. What was he, some long-lost prince who'd never had the switch in his life?

I pressed my palm to his forehead. Just as hot as before. I didn't understand it. He *seemed* fine, but . . .

Pulling my hand back, I was about to say something, but his fingers caught mine, and my mind wiped clean, leaving me dumb as a babe. Seconds ago, he'd avoided my touch, but now he clasped my hand, those fascinating eyes looking at my fingers the same way he had studied his own upon waking. The shock still widened his features, but it was different now. Not agape at being disciplined, but surprised at being . . . what? Touched?

Surely a man such as he had been touched before, and I'd only done so to check for fever. Yet that expression was utterly genuine, and the longer he held my hand, the more his heat seeped into my skin and traveled up my arm, simultaneously creating and casting off shivers.

I know you, he'd said. But we didn't know each other! The confusion was so intense I could have wept beneath the weight of it.

My mother was still in the room, watching us silently. His grip loosened, and I pulled my hand free, hugging it to my breast like it had been burned. Flustered, I thrust the soup bowl into his hands.

"Sleep," I ordered, barely louder than a whisper. "Gods know the rest of us haven't."

Desperate for reprieve, I turned and stalked out of the room, my heart racing as if the space between the bed and the door had grown ten leagues. I found refuge in my mother's bedroom, and in the farthest corner where no candlelight could reach, I pressed my face into the junction of the wooden walls and let myself say it.

"Saiyon."

My grandmother riddled Saiyon with question after question, most of which he evaded. Where was he going? How did he end up in the river? Where did he hail from? What was his occupation? When was he going to leave?

His dialect was peculiar. Algeron bustled with people of many nationalities, but I'd never heard someone speak quite like he did. Even under Kata's scrutiny, he was formal, which made me believe he was well educated and likely from a high class. His vowels were long—another sign he couldn't be Telorian—his consonants soft, his lilt smooth and even, like someone had taken the most beautiful sounds from every accent and language on the Earth Mother and combined them to form his dialect. I think even my grandmother was entranced by it, because her interrogation grew soft too soon. Her forcefulness eased, Saiyon's answers playing like a lullaby teasing her to sleep.

I listened as they reached a temporary agreement; Saiyon would work the farm in return for food and board, until either the Sun returned or we could find him better lodgings in Goatheir. He agreed to every one of my grandmother's demands—he'd sleep in the barn, cut firewood, muck stalls—and made only one request of his own: that he might complete his tasks in the order of his choosing. A strange ask, I thought as I eavesdropped in the hallway, but Kata hesitantly agreed, and that was that.

Though my mother needed rest, she lingered in the hallway as well, occasionally mouthing things to me or tapping her full lips with her finger.

Saiyon mentioned the war, but we were a long way from the north border and from Algeron, where the battles were the heaviest. He was not Rozhani—not a native, anyway—and he certainly wasn't from Belat, our neighbor to the north, which had started the combat. The Belatites were pale as milk and dark haired. Which lent to the mercenary theory, but again, I had trouble believing a mercenary would be as well educated and mannered as he was. Perhaps Saiyon was a general of some sort, and he *had* deserted, or had not yet made it to the battlefront.

Kata apparently came to the same conclusion, for she outright asked him. Saiyon merely thanked her for her concern, neither confirming nor denying the theory.

Finally, Kata asked him how long their deal would extend, to which Saiyon replied, "I apologize for any trouble I have caused you, but I cannot leave at this time." He paused, and when I peeked into the room, he was gazing at the window. The enormous moon hovered near the horizon, casting the sky silver. "I will do all the work you ask of me. I have little monetary substance with me, but I will give you what I can." He touched the gold medallion on his shoulder. Was it *real* gold?

"What we need is work." Kata's sharpness returned.

He nodded. "Then allow me to work. I will do anything you ask, but if it is outside these walls, I must wait for the moon to be down."

That gave me pause. Was that why he wanted to control the order of his tasks? To time them with the uneven cycles of the moon?

"Down?" Kata repeated the word like it was a slur. "Why on the Earth Mother would you want to work in the dark?"

Again, he evaded the question. "My strength is well enough. Show me what I can do. She'll descend shortly."

Stepping away from the door, I slipped into the kitchen to peer out the window at the strange and half-faced moon. I wondered if Saiyon was religious, of some sect I didn't know. Or if he simply feared someone seeing him in the moonlight. But no one frequented these parts. It was only my grandmother, my mother, and me.

And now, Saiyon.

Unsurprisingly, Kata set Saiyon to chopping firewood.

I was quickly reminded of the unfairness between sexes, for Saiyon, being a man, could split far more logs in an hour than I could in a day. He worked without complaint, as though he'd never been sick a day in his life, and soon our fuel stores were quite impressive.

Fearing for his health, I came out to him, a lantern on my arm and a cup of water in my hand. I offered it to him, and this time he drank. When he finished, he said, "Aija."

"Ai is fine."

The night was dark, but in the glow of the lantern, I thought I saw that subtle smirk once more. Or perhaps I only wished to see it. I wished to sketch it and wondered whether I would have the chance.

"I am indebted to you." He turned the cup over in his large hands.

"Not at all." I pulled my shawl closer. "I consider us even."

He paused. "What do you mean?"

I pushed through sudden sheepishness and shrugged. "Your unexpected arrival gave me something to do." That sounded strange. "That is . . . well, I was concerned about your welfare. It was . . . nice . . . to have someone to take care of." *Someone who* needed *me, if only for a little while.* I cleared my throat. "I'm relieved to see you so well recovered."

He considered me. "Does your grandmother not need your care?"

I snorted. "For a few things, but she would never admit it. Anything Kata can do herself, even if it takes twice as long, even if it hurts, she will do herself."

He nodded. "You two are alike, that way."

Straightening, I asked, "Are we?" and retraced our interactions since Saiyon's waking, wondering what headstrong thing I had done to earn the comparison. Before I could put a finger on it, Saiyon spoke again.

"If you will not take the debt"—he ran his thumb along the rim of the cup, his gaze locked on it—"then take my gratitude. I am . . . not used to being cared for. Not in this way."

I lowered my brow. "Not cared for? Is your family—or your employers—so harsh?"

"I do not have an employer. Not in the typical sense." His lip quirked again.

"Then in what sense?"

He considered that a few seconds too long for a natural answer. "You could say I am a sort of overseer. A manager."

I reeled back. "Of slaves?" Slavery was outlawed in Rozhan, but not in Belat. One of many reasons our country and theirs never had peace.

His face slackened. "No. Of many things, but never that."

"Households?"

He took a sip. "You are very inquisitive."

"And you are very elusive."

"I am," he agreed, lowering the cup again. "And I fear I must remain that way." He glanced out over the farm. "I hate to ask more of your—"

"Ask."

He regarded me, his eyes glimmering like opals in the darkness. "I am in need of a few things. There were . . . friends with me, and they may still be in these parts." A look of alarm must have crept onto my face, for he put up a staying hand. "Gentle folk. Neither I nor they wish you any harm."

I nodded, but my neck hesitated to comply.

"Do you have anything that I could use to build a trough?" Setting the cup beneath his arm, he gestured with his hands. "Something shallow and long that won't burn if lit?"

The request took me aback. "Uh . . . so metal or ceramic?" I glanced toward the barn. "The gutters are metal. You can use those, if it's so important. As long as you nail them back when you're finished." I was hardly worried about rain at this point.

I pulled my shawl closer against the chill.

He followed my gaze. "That might do. I don't suppose you have any . . ." He paused, twirling his arm about like he was trying to find the word he wanted, though he was perfectly fluent in Rozhani. "Perhaps quartz. Or granite?"

I shook my head. "Not unless you want to trek to the mines." I gestured to the very distant mountains in the west.

He frowned. "Embers will have to do. I hate to take wood from you, but if I could cut down enough—"

"You're welcome to the resources, so long as you replace them," I said.

He paused. This time he *did* smirk.

I eyed him. "What?"

He merely shook his head and offered me the cup. "Thank you."

I didn't take it. "You must answer *some* questions, stranger. Our imaginations are vast and prone to whimsy. If you're not ready to tell us why you're here, you can at least explain why you smiled."

He considered me for a moment, and I felt bashful beneath the stare that looked like gold coins in the lantern light. "I am merely not accustomed to being interrupted."

I blinked. "Surely you weren't born a respected manager, traveling in the middle of nowhere with questionable friends."

He held out the cup, not rising to the jab. "I will finish this task for your grandmother. Then—" He gestured to the barn.

I bit the inside of my lip. Took the cup. Started back inside but paused. "I won't tell her you're after the gutters," I said over my shoulder. "It will be our secret."

His soft chuckle touched the back of my hair like a caress of summer.

I managed a few steps before he said, "Aija. Ai."

I paused.

"I did not think you could improve, but you have."

I turned to face him.

He picked up a half log and set it upright. "The likeness of me on the easel. It's very good."

Feeling heat in my cheeks and fearing I would say something stupid, I simply nodded at the compliment and continued on my way, squeezing the cup so tightly in my hands I was surprised I did not break it.

Saiyon worked tirelessly for two days. I'm not sure when he rested. Though Kata had consigned him to the barn, I left my bed empty for him the first day, but he didn't come inside to rest, so I slept in it the second "night." He let Kata boss him around constantly, which reminded me of her dynamic with my grandfather, who'd behaved much the same way, so long as she provided him a hot meal before bed and her warm body in it. When it was my turn to cook, I sat in the open back door, plucking a chicken, murmuring with my mother.

"He still hasn't told us who he is," she hummed, peeling a carrot. She'd picked it from the garden on the side of the house. Its leaves were wilted and brittle, its body like rubber, and still there was no promise of daylight.

"He might not remember." It was a defense I only half believed. "There might have been trauma, before I found him. From the war or something else."

Enera pinched her lips and nodded, considering.

We both paused when we heard footsteps on the roof.

"What is he doing?" my mother asked, staring at the ceiling as if she could see through it.

I thought of the gutters. "I could check."

She nodded, but after I set down the mostly plucked fowl, she grabbed my hand, turning it so the side faced our shared candle. Charcoal was smeared along it.

"Always drawing," she said with a small smile. "Even when the world is ending."

"It's not ending," I assured her, pulling my hand back. But I *had* been sketching. I'd filled page after page with images of Saiyon, trying to capture his eyes, but it was as difficult as capturing the brilliance of the moon in that first rendering I'd done after the Sun winked out. They were simply too brilliant for rudimentary tools to mimic.

He'd said I'd improved. From my work at the cathedral?

Every time I tried to piece together our history, I got annoyed by his refusal to tell me anything. When I found our ladder propped against the back of the house, I climbed it heavily, frustration leaking from my every step, a lantern swinging from the crook of my elbow.

I nearly forgot my temper when I saw what Saiyon had done. He'd bent and cut the metal gutters to form a symbol I didn't recognize, at least not from this vantage point. Soft red embers glowed along most of it, and he was lighting kindling at its base to create more.

Multiple questions pressed the inside of my skull, but one claimed victory. "How do you know me?"

He glanced up, his eyes seeming to glow of their own volition, again making me think of a lion. Crickets sang from the shadows.

His gaze returned to his work. "I saw you in Algeron, at the cathedral."

I stepped onto the roof, careful with my balance. "I would have remembered."

"Would you?"

I grabbed a fistful of braid. "Of course I would have. You're . . . memorable." I refused to be embarrassed at the word.

He didn't answer for a moment. "I am not the same now as I was then."

I stared at him, trying to understand. Trying to picture him with shorter hair, or a leaner build, perhaps clean shaven. My memory refused to comply, but if I could study him anew in the light—

"Do you not trust me?" I asked.

He paused but did not respond.

I sighed. "Of course you don't, you barely know me . . . except perhaps you do, and my memory isn't nearly as infallible as I believe."

He shook his head. "It is not a matter of trust."

"Then what is it?"

He did not answer, and we both knew it was because he couldn't. But Saiyon . . . he seemed such a gentle man. What scenario could be forgettable enough to slip my memory yet so unthinkable he felt the need to hide it?

Finally, a faint breath passed his lips. "If you will open your soul to me, Aija, perhaps I could do the same for you."

I choked on that response. I had expected a change of subject, more terse silence, or perhaps an apology. But not an offer like this—one I couldn't accept.

Because lying was not an option. I knew, even then, that he could see deeper than skin. If I were to hide any of my truths, he would know—which meant I could not possibly undertake such a bargain. I could not tell him I missed my prominence in the city, my art, and that I would never feel fulfilled shoeing horses and harvesting oats. That I craved but had never truly experienced romantic love. That I wished to have children to carry on my name, because my mother's line stopped with me. That I wanted so badly to mean something *more* to another person. To be their entire world, even just for a few years before they outgrew it.

I couldn't tell him I'd lost my passion for life when war came to Rozhan, and something about *him* had begun to rekindle it. Something that went beyond his strange beauty and bright eyes. Something that sang down to my bones.

I was quiet for too long, the unaccepted bargain falling to ash around us. Instead, and without malice, he asked, "Would you bring that light, please?"

I stood my ground for several heartbeats before climbing over to him. "Only because you asked nicely," I muttered. I lifted the lantern high to illuminate his work. "Why would a soldier be at the cathedral?"

"Are soldiers not allowed?"

I met his eyes. "Then you *are* a soldier, in addition to an overseer."

He paused. "I am many things."

I considered this, picking away at him like he was an apple to be peeled. "They *are* allowed, but—"

"I believe your war had not yet started."

I licked my lips. "*My* war."

He lit the fire. I didn't see him use flint and steel, but I wasn't exactly focused on his hands. I wondered if he'd meant that as a hint or if he wasn't adept at lying. Or . . . not lying, but masking.

I waited several seconds. "You're not a soldier for Rozhan."

He hesitated as well. "No."

"Or Belat."

"No."

I settled down on the shingles, still holding the lantern high. "But you will not tell me who you serve."

This time he met my eyes. "No."

Sighing, I set the lantern down. "And your friends? The ones this monstrosity is for?" I didn't know how they would see it, on the roof.

He shook his head. "It is better to spare you."

"Spare me? You said they won't harm me."

"They will not."

"So you think me too daft to understand." I didn't want to broach the subject of *trust* again. Not yet.

His movements paused. He met my eyes. "I would never make such an assumption."

Hugging my knees, I looked out over the black expanse around me. The moon was tucked away again, surveying the other side of the Earth Mother, but the stars were bright and numerous, twinkling without a care in the world.

"We're farmers," I muttered.

I felt his gaze on the side of my face like the heat of the Sun.

"I'm worried about the crops," I added, pulling out my grandfather's pocket clock and tilting its face toward the light. Winding it, I said, "I don't know how much longer they'll survive this."

He nodded. "Her light will slow their deaths."

"Her. The moon?"

Another nod.

I leaned back on my elbows. "I wonder where the Sun has gone. If He cares that we might starve without Him."

Saiyon grew very still.

I sighed. "We'll make do with what we have." I offered him a smile. "My grandmother thinks you're a crook, and my mother might, too, but perhaps you're a blessing. You've already stocked more fuel for us in two days than I could hope to manage in two years."

"I doubt that."

I shrugged. "Still." I searched for constellations. "Are you worried for your family?"

He didn't answer.

I rephrased. "Do you *have* family?"

He pulled his hands back from the gutter. "That depends on what you mean by 'family.'"

My brows drew together. "What I mean? How many definitions are there?"

He glanced up to the sky, as though the stars could answer for him. When he dropped his gaze, it landed somewhere beyond the farmhouse, peering into the darkness.

"Ai." My name sounded so reverent, so perfect, in his smooth voice. "Hm?"

"You said it is only you, your mother, and your grandmother." His bright irises slid toward me. "There are no brothers or other men on this farm?"

I sat up straighter. "No. Why?"

He let out a breath. "Because I see one entering your chicken coop."

I zipped to my feet, heart launching into my throat. "What?" I glanced toward the coop, but it was too dark for me to see anything. The man's light must have slipped behind the gate.

Cursing, I rushed for the ladder, shouting for Enera and Kata both.

I had been wrong.

We *were* susceptible to bandits.

I felt the Sunlight in my hair today, even through the clouds. Like a friend leaning in to tell me a secret.

CHAPTER 4

"Enera! Kata! *Bandits!*" I kicked the kitchen door open but didn't enter the house. I ran toward the barn, my lantern swinging so wildly its light was barely any guidance at all. I burst through the doors, Vine hoofing the ground in protest, and spied a dark figure darting from the doors on the other end. I grabbed a pitchfork so swiftly a sliver bit into my thumb.

We'd had "bandits" once before, though I still believed they were hungry travelers desperate for a meal and too timid to ask. Thieves were less common here than in the capital, but harder to deter. One couldn't simply lock the door to an entire farm.

"Get back!" I barked, chasing the dark figure. I screamed as loudly as my lungs would allow. There was a reason thieves lurked in the dark; they were cowards. Most of them, anyway. I could only hope this one was no different. "I'll hang your hide from the rafters!"

I burst back into the cool night, lantern light swinging, the flame almost dousing itself in its own oil. From behind me, back near the house, the ear-grinding noise of iron striking a metal tin ripped through the air. No doubt my grandmother's contribution.

The chickens flapped and shrieked. I bolted toward the henhouse, wielding the pitchfork's spikes ahead of me.

Chickens scattered over the ground, bobbing and flapping in terror. The moon peeked over the horizon, highlighting the silhouette of a man shoving live birds into a sack.

"Drop them!" I bellowed, just as a silver glint came streaking up the path. My mother, armed with a shovel.

When the situation demanded it, she was as daring as a fox.

A second body whisked out of the coop and darted by me, taunting me, heading back toward the barn. Chickens were one thing, but we couldn't lose our larger livestock. Though bandits would have a hell of a time outrunning me with a sheep in his arms, if they got Vine—

We couldn't lose Vine.

I spun on my heel and darted back the way I'd come, lungs working. I could just make out the shadow slipping between the barn doors I'd left open. I swept after him. Sure enough, he was at Vine's stall. If he rode her out, I'd never catch him—

But I could make it harder for him to get out. My mind returned to the sheep. Stopping hard, I swung my pitchfork around, slamming the handle into the lock keeping the sheep penned. Sheep were easily startled creatures, and that action alone prompted them to bolt.

Their fluffy bodies filled the barn as they bounded for the door, bleats piking the air. One tripped the bandit, slowing him.

I pushed through the panicking bodies, lifting my pitchfork, ready to remove the thief's head from his shoulders.

Forgetting Vine, the dark-clad man spun around and pulled a long knife from his sheath.

They weren't all cowards.

He dodged my blow and struck out at me in a wide arc; he might have hit me if an old ewe hadn't scrambled between us. The pitchfork was a heavier weapon, far slower than the knife. When he struck out again, I had to drop it or lose a finger. My lantern flew from my wrist, landing in the straw scattered over the barn floor. Glass cracked. If the straw lit—

The man said nothing, only advanced. Raised his arm to strike—

A hand caught him just above his elbow. The lighting was poor, but there was no mistaking Saiyon's golden skin in the lamplight. Relief surged through me as he yanked the man's arm back. But this wasn't a common thief. From the way he moved, he'd obviously had combat training. Perhaps *he* was a true deserter—

The two men fell back into Vine's stall. The shadows fought; I screamed as the knife plunged into flesh. Scooping up the pitchfork, I ran to intercept—

The bandit's knife fell to the ground half a second before he did, his body dark and still.

I drew up short. Panted. Gripped the pitchfork in my hands. Stared at the bandit. I was sure he was dead. Snapped neck? Too dark to tell.

"Th-Thank you," I breathed, and barely perceived Saiyon's nod.

Remembering my mother, I turned back for the door.

"She is chasing him out toward the river," he said quietly, toeing the still body on the ground. He sounded regretful.

So one was a coward, at least. Lowering the pitchfork, I picked up the lantern, glad it hadn't caught anything on fire. Saiyon stepped away from the stall, his hand pressed to his chest under his collarbone.

I gasped. "You're hurt." I hadn't been mistaken. He'd been stabbed.

"It is nothing."

"Nothing?" I closed the gap between us. "It's a knife wound! It needs to be cleaned—"

He stayed me with his other hand. "I am fine."

Admittedly, he seemed fine, but men could be stubbornly stoic. "If it's fine, then let me see it."

Saiyon turned like he was going to leave.

I stepped in front of him. He was a head taller than I and far broader, but I'd never let a man's size intimidate me before, and I was hardly going to change my mind now.

He sighed. "Aija, please. Grant me this."

"No." I held my ground and grabbed his arm, trying to move his hand, but it didn't budge. "Let me see."

He shook his head.

Gritting my teeth, I pinched the inside of his thigh.

He startled, either from the gesture itself or from the pain, but it was enough for me to wrench his hand back and shed some light on the—

On the—

I nearly dropped the lantern again. It wouldn't have mattered if I had. Because Saiyon . . . Saiyon was *bleeding light.*

"Gods," I whispered, and set the lantern down. The knife had stabbed through his shirt and into his upper pectoral, an incision two inches across. It didn't seem deep. But I didn't know how to measure it. I didn't know . . .

He was *bleeding light.*

Even Saiyon seemed a little fascinated by it, from the way he examined the liquid light on his fingers. Like he'd never seen his own blood before. If I could even call it blood.

Entranced, I lifted a hand toward it. Hesitated. He didn't move. Carefully, reverently, I touched the edge of the wound. Light kissed my fingertips.

My tongue was half-numb, but I managed to whisper, "Does . . . it hurt?"

Saiyon shook his head. I barely registered the movement from the corner of my eye. I couldn't take my gaze from the light.

Drawing back my hand, I ran my thumb over the pads of my fingers. His blood—if it was even blood—glowed of its own volition. Like white-hot iron, but it was too thin for that. It didn't burn me. It didn't—

It slowly faded from my fingertips, like the day would fall away at Sunset.

My head weighed a thousand pounds, but I drew my focus back to Saiyon's face. "Who . . . are you?"

Saiyon did not say. Neither did he look away. His gaze bore into mine. It may have been the only thing keeping me rooted in reality.

Several seconds passed before I gathered my wits. What sort of creature might bleed like this? Was he a godling? But . . . surely godlings weren't so *human*. And he'd been sick for so long. Celestial beings wouldn't fall ill to mortal afflictions.

Yet my mind couldn't wrap around another explanation.

I swallowed. "Perhaps don't . . . tell them about this . . . either."

Saiyon picked up the lantern. Took my cold hand in his feverish one and wrapped my fingers around its handle. I tried not to be, but I was still stupefied. I had the forethought, at least, to take off the scarf holding back my hair and drape it over his shoulder, masking the incredulous wound from sight.

"I-I'll treat it," I managed. "A cut is a cut . . . It might get infected . . ." I shook myself. "Wait for me in the house. I have to get my mother."

Saiyon merely nodded. My knees were slow to bend, my gaze obstinate, like my eyes had been sewn to him. But I forced my stubborn body to move, grabbing the pitchfork and running toward the river. "Enera!" I shouted, scanning the shadows for her or any other lurking bandits. It wouldn't be hard for them to hide in the dying fields. "Enera!"

His blood glows like Sunlight.

My steps slowed, my lungs burning. The Sun vanished, and days later I found a stranger passed out on the bank, wearing strange clothes and bleeding light . . .

I shook myself. I didn't believe Saiyon was mortal, after what I'd seen. But the Sun God was something else entirely. He was Ruler over All, the greatest light in the heavens. He was no man.

Gripping the pitchfork, I kept running, staying to the center of the path, which would be the smoothest. "Enera!"

"Ai!" My mother's voice called ahead of me, and I let out a tremulous breath. Her shadow appeared heartbeats later, the shovel still in hand.

"Are you hurt?" I called.

"No. He ran off!" She sprinted to me—she had no light. She'd pursued the bandit in the dark. "You?"

"I'm fine. Kata should still be in the house, with Saiyon." I swallowed. "The sheep are loose. Saiyon's hurt, but not badly—"

Bleeding light.

"I'll get the sheep. You see to him," she said.

We jogged back to the house together, our blood running too fast for walking. My mother took off toward bleating in the oat field, and I hurried to the house, spying my grandmother hale in the doorway, thank the gods. I noticed, before I slipped inside, that the moon was peering out from the horizon.

And I wondered why her face bothered him so much.

Kata fretted over the both of us, and I told neither her nor Enera about the dead bandit in the barn. Gods, the bandit . . . I'd have to drag his body out to the river in the . . .

Not in the morning. Morning no longer existed. But sometime soon, before he started to stink. My stomach shriveled at the idea of a dead man in the barn, but I was not so naïve as to regret the loss of his life. He would have killed me and Saiyon both if given the chance.

Saiyon had tucked himself away in my room. I gathered our healing supplies and sequestered myself in there with him. Lit two more candles. The wound wasn't bad, but I needed to treat it. I needed to do *something* familiar. I needed to root myself.

I needed to think, which meant I ached to sketch, but now was not the time.

I set the basket of bandages and balms on the bed and made him sit next to it. He did so without a word. I glanced over his shirt, not sure how it worked.

"Off," I said.

He hesitated. "It will pass."

I rolled my eyes. "Now there's something we have in common. Unwillingness to let someone help."

His brow ticked.

I pressed my lips together and sighed through my nose. Calmed myself. "I already saw, Saiyon," I added quietly. "Your secrets are safe with me."

He held my gaze then, his pupils piercing. A shiver coursed up my arms and down my back.

Obedient, he unhooked a clasp under the medallion on his shoulder and pulled the gauzy material over his head. It had been evident during the treatments of his fever that Saiyon was a strong man, but seeing the majesty of his bare torso was a different matter. I might have blushed or ogled if I were in my right mind. I wasn't. But I was a woman who noticed men, and I was impressed, nonetheless.

I wet a rag with some spirits and pressed it to the wound, which now merely shimmered with faint yellow light. He didn't so much as flinch. "You must be a very dedicated soldier and a very hands-on overseer."

His eyes locked on mine. "Why do you suggest that?"

I pulled the rag away. The wound glowed softly, not a hint of red to be seen. "Because of your physique." I returned to the basket for some healing balm, which I spread on gingerly. "Only very physically enthusiastic men look the way you do."

He finally tore his gaze from my face, deciding instead to examine the basket.

I was nearly done wrapping the bandage when I heard my mother's and grandmother's voices in the kitchen. They stomped their shoes, probably trying to loosen mud caked on the soles. I let out a long breath, cool relief winding through me that they were here, safe. Then I scanned the bedroom, ensuring there was no trace of golden blood to be seen. I'd meant what I said. I wanted Saiyon to trust me.

I wanted to trust him, too.

Tucking the bandage end in, I dropped onto the bed beside him. "You still feel feverish."

He placed a hand over my ministrations. Again, with that strange air like this was a first for him—the bandaging, and the process of being cared for—that was, while he was conscious. "I am well."

But you shouldn't be. His skin was too hot, always, and while that wound was superficial . . . it was less than a splinter to him. *Godling, godling . . . Where can I get information on godlings?*

My grandmother's scriptures, perhaps, but I didn't recall it going into depth about the long-lived creatures. Would Goatheir have anything? The only library I knew of was in Algeron.

I was very warm, sitting beside him. Heat wafted from him like it did from desert sand. His well-sculpted shoulder was very close to touching mine.

Searching for distraction, I picked up his shirt and examined the tear. The light from the wound had already faded from the material, just as it had from my fingers. The strange fabric pooled in my hands like water. "I'm not sure how to fix this," I admitted. "I can try, but it won't look right—"

He placed a warm hand over mine. Heat raced through my wrists and elbows and planted itself in my shoulders, making my pulse work harder to keep me cool. "It is fine."

I met his eyes. Would I ever be able to draw them? To re-create them on paper the way they looked in reality? The *way* he looked at me right now . . . I couldn't even put it into words, let alone into graphite or charcoal or paint.

And why did I want to, so badly? I'd been inspired by people before, but something about him stirred me . . . differently. Like I'd only just discovered I was right-hand dominant, when all this time I'd been drawing with my left. It confused me. It . . . scared me.

Because he's interesting, the thoughts in the back of my mind chirped, trying to mend my fraying thoughts. *How many portraits have you seen that look like him? Maybe you could sell one, war or not.*

And yet I had lived long enough to recognize the justification as feeble. It was not so simple. But what was it that I wanted? To master the marvel of his features before he moved on to wherever he was going? To outfit my little shed by the barn with enough images that I might not notice loneliness when he left?

Why was it that a stranger who'd been here only a week made me feel it so keenly?

And I *wasn't* alone. I had Enera and Kata. I had Zyzi and extended family in Goatheir. I had plenty. I didn't *need* anything else, however misplaced I might have felt. However unnecessary.

I tore myself from the draining thoughts. "Thank you for helping me."

"I have a debt to repay," he answered.

I tilted my head. "And if you didn't, you'd have let him stab me?"

He drew back, and the alarm on his face made me laugh. A short laugh, but a purifying one. It made me feel like myself again. Made me forget, for a moment, that the sky was dark and this man bled light. I hadn't laughed in . . . how long? Since before the Sun vanished.

He wasn't how I'd imagined godlings, in as much as I'd tried, but how many godlings did I know? None. Yet I didn't want to ask now. He was so guarded about his identity. Perhaps when he trusted me more, he would reveal his truths.

Clasping the torn shirt in my hands, I stood, taking in a last eyeful of him. "While I hardly mind the sight, I think I might find something of my grandfather's that will fit you."

He blinked at the compliment, again with that subtle surprise. Surely such comments were not unusual for him! Or did he travel with such robust people that his own form was easily ignored?

Biting down a smile, I slipped out of the room, stopping briefly to recount to my family what had happened in the barn, which already felt like it was weeks ago. I told them of Saiyon's intervention—he could benefit from Kata's sympathies, especially—but said nothing of his blood. Or of borrowing one of Grandfather's shirts, though she'd discover that soon enough. My grandfather had been dead twenty years, but Kata was protective of his old things.

I found the widest shirt I could, searching by the light of a single candle, and brought it in to Saiyon. He stood as I approached; I shook out the garment and handed it to him.

As he slipped his arms into the sleeves, he said, "What happened to him?"

I shook my head. "He died when I was fourteen. My grandmother is hard as iron, but she's kept most of his things." I smiled to myself. "Kata will never die. She is far too stubborn."

The shirt fit well enough—Saiyon was able to get it buttoned, at least. "I see a lot of her in you."

I laughed. "So you've said. I don't know if that's a compliment or an insult."

"A compliment. Those with the strongest wills are far more likely to achieve their highest aspirations. It has always been so."

He met my eyes then, and that need to draw—sculpt, paint, *any-thing*—burned in my hands. I needed an outlet for my confusion, my frustration, and this other annoying thing that had brewed in my chest ever since I'd dragged this man's body into the light.

Man. If I could even call him such.

Reaching forward, I touched his arm. Gently. "Will you not tell me who you are?"

His gaze softened into an expression that was too beautiful to ever re-create. "Not yet, Ai." His hand came up to grasp mine. "I would never willingly change the way you look at me, or speak to me. You are one of a kind. You always have been."

After the bandit attack, Kata made no more mention of mercenaries or deserters, or any unkind statements about Saiyon whatsoever. He'd proven himself not only a diligent worker, but much-needed protection in a time of darkness and uncertainty.

My art began to change.

I lost sleep dedicating time to it, for I wouldn't shirk my duties to my family so I could scratch an itch.

I hadn't been so dedicated to my craft since leaving Algeron. I hadn't felt the *rush*, the sort of bottomless urge creatives get when they have an idea and crave a release. But it was as if I'd bottled up that urge for the last five years and Saiyon had uncorked it. Night after night I set up by the kitchen fire to save candles, working out pieces of it in fine graphite lines or black ink, desperate to find where the path ended.

I drew Saiyon. Sometimes I feared I was obsessing, and I'd try sketching my mother or the moon, or even Vine. But the muse pulled me back from every attempt at distraction, urging me to create what I wanted to create. Reminding me that Saiyon had a life outside this farm, and he would not always dwell with us. That I should embrace the inspiration he lent me while I could.

I drew him. I drew his eyes over and over and over. I drew his portrait, his body, his expressions. I drew his strange shirt and his subtle smile, like he was too embarrassed to grin. I drew him before the fire and at the table, doing a variety of menial chores around the house without a single complaint on his lips. I drew him with his head bent as my grandmother halfheartedly berated him. I drew him pretending not to notice my mother watching him, wondering.

I drew him bleeding light.

And my art began to change. How it changed is hard to describe. It took on a new life. Incorporated an intangible element that hadn't been there before—an element that I was sure would fetch a high price, were I still in the capital and the war only a glimmer in the back of our king's mind. The difference was in the depth of the sketches, the colors of the paint, the strokes of the pencil. Like I had somehow managed to draw beyond Saiyon's clothes and skin. Like I had found a way to capture his spirit—his kindness and wisdom, his patience, his illusiveness. At least, that was what *I* saw, when I beheld my finished pieces.

Even my mother, slipping by at midnight to use the privy, commented on it. "I forgot how skilled you are, Ai," she whispered, one hand pressed to her breast.

"It's different," I mentioned, a fortnight after the Sun winked out.

She nodded. "It's more alive. More . . ." She looked at a finished sketch on the floor beside me, this one of Saiyon looking up at the dark sky, his forehead tight. "More passionate," she said so softly I barely heard it.

My shoulders stiffened at the compliment. Something about that word—*passionate*—bothered me, and I couldn't determine why.

I picked up the sketch and examined it long after Enera returned to bed. My old art had not lacked passion. I would never have made a name for myself in Algeron were that the case. And yet . . . my mother was right. I wasn't afraid of the feeling—I was too old for such hesitance. But it had been a long time since true *passion* had been part of my life, and I wondered what it meant that Saiyon had lit it within me, even as he slept from a supposed fever. Even before he ever opened his eyes, though I hated how shallow that sounded.

The tune to an old bard song hummed in the back of my thoughts, but I couldn't recall the lyrics.

I would have remembered him. What was he not telling me? And would I believe it if the truth finally surfaced?

I remained vigilant in winding the pocket clock, so I knew it was evening when we all pulled pillows and chairs around the fire in the kitchen, Saiyon included. We'd all gotten used to him, so much so that Kata hadn't remarked on mercenaries or pirates for a full three days. Saiyon continued to burn his strange signal on the roof when the night was black—Kata was convinced it was a plea to the gods, just as her candles were. The darkness was not any colder, thankfully, but that night itself seemed to seep between the walls. The crops had one foot in their grave, and we still hadn't sorted out what we would do if this was our new normal, indefinitely.

None of us wanted to dwell on that.

My grandmother went on about the story of how her grandparents— my great-great-grandparents—met, which was a tale I'd heard often but never tired of, especially because Kata embellished different things with each telling. I always listened closely to find what she would change. It had been a time of war—there was always war, again with Belat—and my great-great-grandmother had dressed as a boy in order to fight for Rozhan. She and my great-great-grandfather were both taken as prisoners. They shared a cell, where her secret came out. Needless to say, my great-great-grandmother was pregnant with my great-grandfather before the two of them were released.

"They set up a maypole when the war finally ended." Kata had the most comfortable chair, and she adjusted her frail body in it. "Twice the ribbons, five times the dancing. It was a celebration."

"A maypole in winter," Saiyon commented. I could tell it was more to himself than to us, but despite her age, Kata had keen hearing.

"April is well into spring," she argued.

Saiyon straightened upon getting caught. "The War of Doves ended with the treaty signing on January 17—"

"It was April!" Kata snapped. "What do you know? You're not Rozhani."

Saiyon bowed his head in acquiescence. "No, I am not."

I studied him, wondering. He knew, or at least appeared to know, the exact date a century-old conflict had ended. Was he a historian? But that was hardly something worth hiding. Unless he'd been alive then . . .

The thought sobered me. I glanced at him. He looked to be about forty, perhaps forty-five, if he'd aged well. I'd yet to ask about his age. Godlings lived for centuries, so if that theory were correct, he could easily be older than my ancestors' story. Which made me wonder what other sorts of things he had seen, experienced, heard.

Reaching over, I placed a hand on his knee. He smiled at me—that warm, hesitant smile that sparked fire behind my breastbone. "Why don't you tell us a story?"

I thought he would turn down the invitation, as he was loath to speak of himself, but he considered it awhile, rubbing a hand over his short beard. Although I had never seen him trim it, it was the same length and style as the day I had found him, the same lovely shade of gold.

"A long time ago, there was an island," he finally said, eyes on the hearth. I hadn't moved my hand, though, and his ring and pinky fingers wove through mine. "—some distance from here, called Soolo. It was made from a great undersea volcano, a sore on the goddess's side that caused Her great pain—"

"What's a volcano?" My mother's soft voice wove into the tale.

Saiyon paused. "It is a great mountain full of liquid rock, too hot for mortals to touch."

Kata's brow skewed, but my mother merely nodded. I waited for the story to continue, yearning to hear his voice. To keep his fingers in mine.

"Soolo came from that great sore," he went on. "The liquid rock struck the sea, and Tereth, demigod of the sea, cooled it to soothe his love. Explorers from a southern continent found it sometime later and settled it, making it beautiful.

"The volcano slept for centuries, until its belly began to rumble once more. And if it broke, if the Earth Mother bled again, all the people of Soolo would perish. For though the island had been settled by seafarers, the people of the island had lost those ways, and they did not have time to relearn them, nor to harvest trees and build enough ships to bring them to safety."

My grip on Saiyon's fingers tightened. His bright eyes found mine, kind and reassuring. Something about them made me think of Edkar. Didn't he used to look at me that way?

My mind was playing tricks on me.

"They pled to Tereth, begging his aid, but he could not stop the volcano from exploding, only help Earth Mother heal once it did. But he whispered to them, on the waves lapping against the shore, of a godling who nested at the top of their highest peak. His name was Krognik, and he was born of the Earth Mother's fire. Though a temperamental creature, he might be more capable of help.

"The people of Soolo sent their strongest men and women to climb the mountain. It was a treacherous journey, and the mountain was filled with wild cats. Many lost their lives. But one woman reached the top, where a great nest of igneous rock sat, and in its center was a large godling with a hard shell like a turtle's. When he rested, he looked like an egg or nut. When he stood, he appeared as a dragon.

"But the woman, Taylain, did not fear him, for all her fear had been spent over the great volcano that would kill her people, and she had none left to give. She pled to Krognik for his help. But Krognik was lazy and did not want to bother with mortals. So Taylain appealed to his pride, promising her people would worship him if he saved Soolo. Being a young godling of little importance, this persuaded him."

"And what did he do?" Kata asked, as though Saiyon would dare leave out that part of the story. I rolled my eyes at her, cheeks pinching in mirth.

"He rolled down the mountain with Taylain in his grasp, for he had to preserve her so she could fulfill her promise. Then he dug to the heart of the island, where the awakening volcano burned. Just before it erupted, he jumped into its maw, plugging it with his great shell. The energy of the volcano shook the ground and imploded, devouring most of his mountain, and the lava bled beneath the sea—creating a bridge of molten rock that connected Soolo to the mainland. Krognik's efforts also carved out a black-rock basin right in the center of the island. It swallowed part of the people's village, but most of them were spared. And at the center of the basin lay a smooth, round rock that looked like a nut, or perhaps an egg. Taylain named it the Seed of Soolo, for from Krognik's sacrifice would her people grow. Every sixth day the island people climbed down to the seed and laid out offerings upon it—or they did, until the island sank."

I straightened. "Sank? After all that?"

He nodded. "The people lived on it a very long time, before the Earth Mother shifted and Tereth swallowed the land. But because of Krognik's bridge, the people were able to migrate to safety. Some still worship the Seed of Soolo—those who remember."

I let out a long breath. "What a story."

"I've never heard that one," Enera said.

Kata hummed beneath her breath.

Turning to better see him, I asked, "But was being worshipped worth sacrificing his life?"

That subtle smile returned. "You suppose Krognik to have died."

"You said he was a godling," I protested. "Godlings are not immortal."

Saiyon nodded. "Perhaps. But every sixth day the people brought him offerings, and by the next sixth day, the offerings were consumed, as though Krognik had taken them into himself." He lifted his free hand. "Where he went or how he passed on after that is up to the listener."

I pondered this. The ways of gods and godlings were too complex for me to grasp, but I didn't say as much. Saiyon seemed to appreciate being treated as any normal man, and I did not want to sully that.

His grip on my hand suddenly slackened, and he pulled away, leaving my fingers cold. I reeled them in, pressing them to my chest, wondering at the threads that seemed to cinch my hand to my ribs.

He tensed like a deer might upon hearing a snapped twig in the wood, but he covered it quickly. "If you will excuse me." He stood and strode toward the back door, opened it, and paused in the frame to scan the sky before slipping out into the darkness, without so much as a lantern.

Enera and I both watched him go, but while my mother seemed content to remain by the fire, my heartbeat quickened, and the curiosity that had been building for days sent shivers over my skin and tightness into my throat.

"My neck hurts," Kata complained.

I stood. "I'll get some oil and rub it for you," I offered.

Kata nodded, which was her way of showing gratitude.

I headed into the hallway, opposite the direction Saiyon had gone. And while I *would* get the oil and aid my grandmother, I first grabbed a lantern and lit it, then slipped out the front door. I doubted Saiyon was going to the privy. Just as I'd never seen him trim his beard or eat without being prompted, I'd never once caught him going to or from the simple outhouse twenty paces from the back door.

Shielding the lamp with my shawl and clenching my jaw so my teeth wouldn't chatter, I walked around the house on light feet, searching for him, wondering where he'd gone.

I didn't have to wonder long, for I heard his voice not far off, in the direction of the hayfield. Blowing out my lantern, I peeked around the corner of the house and squinted in the starlight.

I saw him a little ways off, but he wasn't alone. With him were three other personages, silhouettes tinged silver with starglow, murmuring one to another. I immediately wondered if these were the men he'd been signaling, though how Saiyon had heard their approach from within the kitchen, I didn't know. The man on the far right shifted, allowing me to get a better visual of his shape, and one of his companions.

My breath caught in my throat.

These were no men.

These were godlings.

Today I went to the poppy fields north of the capital and lay in the grass, pretending I was a child with no other cares in the world. It made me miss the farm, but my time here isn't finished yet.

Even with the nostalgia, I feel most at peace on balmy days like this, when the Sun is full and there isn't a cloud in the sky.

CHAPTER 5

A startled gasp squirmed up my throat and ballooned in my mouth, where it died a silent death. I was not familiar with godlings, but I knew that's what they were. That's what they *had* to be.

One of them had horns. Tall horns that sprouted from the top of its head, almost coming together at the top like praying hands. Another was taller than Saiyon by about a hand, but it hunched forward as if its neck had been misplaced from its shoulders. The third, revealed when the first shifted, had a normal enough silhouette, but its skin glittered where starlight touched it. It was a mirage-like quality that made me think of heat rising from city streets on hot summer days.

I pushed forward, as close as I could get without leaving my hiding spot, craning to hear what they said, wishing the echoes of my thunderous heart didn't make it that much harder.

"—may be compromised," Saiyon was explaining. "She . . . out when . . . attacked."

"—take you back," said the shortest, the one with the glimmering skin. "But . . . your state . . ."

"You'd . . . limited . . . go," the horned godling said softly, and I cursed him for not enunciating more clearly.

Holding my breath, I set down the lantern and put my hands around my ears, trying to enhance my eavesdropping.

"—palace is broken," the tall godling said, its voice even lower than Saiyon's, yet I got the distinct feeling she was female.

"I will stay on the Earth Mother," Saiyon responded. "That will make me a smaller target, harder for her to find. If you must post guards, make them few. I do not wish to bring attention to . . . or the mortals helping me." He paused. "It is too risky for me to travel."

He said *mortals* like it was something *other*. I had suspected he wasn't, but the confirmation tingled beneath my skin like too much liquor.

"Too much moonlight," said the horned creature, or I was fairly certain that's what he said. I let my breath out slowly, quietly, before holding it again.

"I am concerned for the welfare of the mortals here," Saiyon repeated.

I thought of his two fingers laced through mine mere minutes ago and couldn't help but wonder, *How concerned?*

The glimmering godling spoke, but he was so hushed I couldn't pick out a single syllable. The response was equally unintelligible.

Determining I would gather no more information, and not wanting to be caught, I carefully backtracked, taking my unlit lantern with me. I wandered out to the cornfield, slipping into the faint shadows between its rows.

The cornstalks could hardly stand straight. Were the night unaltered, they'd already be dead, so I suppose I couldn't complain. But the moonlight wasn't enough to sustain them. Cradling a limp leaf in my hand, I sighed. *Could your war not have waited until harvest time? Then we'd be able to salvage something.*

Thoughts of war had me glancing over my shoulder, back to where Saiyon convened with celestial creatures, though they were far from my sight now.

Was he a soldier in *that* war? Perhaps thrust down from his heavenly chariot? But then why could he not return to wherever it was celestial creatures lived?

I shook my head. Why was it the more information I got, the more confused I became?

I mulled over what the godlings had said, not wanting to forget any of it, before passing through the corn to the barn to check on the animals. I lit my lantern there, and Vine whickered, throwing her head back and forth.

"I know, I know." I ran my hand down her long face. Enera should have exercised her today—what little exercise we could risk in the dark, which was no more than a walk to the river and back. The poor mare was anxious. All the livestock was.

Saiyon had mucked the stall earlier today—the idea of a godling mucking stalls should have been comical—so I just checked the animals' food and water and whispered a few reassuring words to them. One of the ewes let me rub the fleece atop her head.

"The light will return." It was an empty promise, but we needed *something* to hope for. "It can't just be . . . *gone*."

My hands stilled. I pulled back, rubbing my fingers together, remembering blood like light vanishing from their tips.

The light.

I glanced toward the barn doors. Saiyon certainly wasn't *that* light, but light flowed through his veins—possibly the reason he was so radiant, so golden. Then what was he? A fallen star? I'd never heard of such a thing, but the last fifteen days had been nothing if not educating.

I rubbed soreness from my neck, which reminded me of Kata, so I ventured back around the house, not bothering to hide my footsteps. I blew out the lantern and retrieved the grapeseed oil from my grandmother's room, finding it by memory in the dark.

Kata and Enera were both in the kitchen still, sitting before the fire. "Did you take a nap on the way?" Kata snapped.

I apologized by slipping behind her and warming oil in my hands, then delicately working out the knots in her neck and shoulders. She said nothing else on the matter.

The front door snicked as I finished. I wouldn't have noticed it, had I not been listening for Saiyon's return. A silver hue on the window told me the moon had peeked out from behind the mountains again.

That Saiyon chose to spend his time in the house with us instead of in the barn with the animals was assuring.

My mother stifled a yawn. "I'll start the tea," she said, rising from her chair. A tea of sleeping herbs, which we'd been taking the last week. Even keeping to a regular schedule, none of us were resting well. Our minds and bodies grew depressed in the dark. The resulting insomnia was what had allowed me so much time to draw.

I glanced at the small table, where the dinner pot still sat. "Did Saiyon ever eat?"

Enera shrugged.

Grabbing a bowl, I scooped out the leftover pottage and sliced a piece of bread before venturing down the hallway. The front room was empty, and Saiyon had never once stepped foot in the one Kata and Enera shared, so I pushed into my bedroom. Sure enough, he stood by the window, staring out into the sky without so much as a candle. Though Kata had given him the barn, he kept to the house when the moon was out, and no one complained about it.

I set the food down on a small table by the bed and lit a nearly spent candle. "How well do you see in the dark?"

He glanced back. I didn't think he'd heard me come in, though I hadn't attempted silence.

"Well enough," he answered. Spotting the food, he added, "I did not ask for this."

"Sometimes asking isn't necessary."

Again, that awed expression came over his face. "Thank you."

"Evasion." I folded my arms. "How well do you see in the dark, Saiyon?"

His shoulders relaxed, though he was anything but. "Very well."

I gestured to the bed. "Sit."

He obeyed.

I touched his shoulder, the one above the stab wound. "How is it healing?"

"Well enough."

I scoffed. "Do you have any other answers?"

He regarded me a moment, then the dress sprawled on the narrow dresser, laid out to dry. "I do not mean to appropriate your room."

I shrugged and undid his first button. He didn't stop me. I undressed him out of petulance, but only because I would not let myself dwell too long on the physicality of it. "So what if you do?"

"I do not want you sleeping on the kitchen floor."

I smiled then, which confused him, if his risen eyebrow was any indication. "And how do you know I sleep on the kitchen floor, when you're supposed to be tucked away in the barn?" I sounded confident, but in truth I tried to recall if I'd left any of my drawings visible.

Then I realized I had not seen Saiyon sleep since he woke from his fever.

I undid the last button and pulled his shirt over his bandaged shoulder. He endured my ministrations easily, quietly. Loosening the wrap, I peeked beneath them.

There wasn't so much as a scar on his hot, golden skin. But it seemed nothing about him could shock me. Not anymore.

"You won't be needing this." I pulled the bandage out from under his arm, coiling it around my hand as I unwrapped his shoulder. He watched me as I worked, and I let him, unabashed, because why should I be?

When the last of the bandaging came free, he ran a hand over the unmarred spot where, only three days ago, a bandit's blade had pierced him. Not so much *unable* to resist, but refusing to, I did the same, running my fingertips over the unblemished skin.

"I sleep in the kitchen by choice," I finally answered. "It's warmer in there, besides." I smirked at him. "If you weren't so broad, we could share this bed."

I didn't surprise him with the flirtatious comment—I think he was growing used to me. But amusement glittered in those pearlescent eyes of his. Eyes I still couldn't perfect. Not with the mediums available to me. Just one more frustration brewing around my bones.

Crossing the room, I turned the handle on the door so it would close quietly. Set the bandages aside. Sat next to him on the bed. Looked into those beautiful eyes but refused by sheer willpower to be hypnotized by them. If this darkness continued, I would surely grow too weak to withstand their spell, but the heavens had not beaten me into submission yet.

"How much of your past do you remember, Saiyon?"

His expression softened. Lifting a hand, he slid a strand of hair behind my ear, leaving a burning trail in its wake. I tried not to be embarrassed at the warming of my cheeks, for so few things got such a reaction from me. "I remember."

I nodded. "But."

"But." He lowered his hand. "I cannot go home."

I grasped his hand and squeezed it. "Why?"

He looked away. I gave him time to think—I could muster enough patience for that. "I should not be here. But neither can I leave."

I bit my lip. Ran my thumb over his knuckle. "You don't have to."

He hunched over, one elbow on his thigh, and squeezed my hand. "Everything is dismantling, and I can do nothing but wait. And yet a riotous part of me . . . a part I have worked tirelessly to make insignificant . . . is glad."

Glad, he said, yet he sounded miserable. I released his hand, and he wiped his palm down his face.

"I am ashamed of it," he confessed. "But I am glad. I . . ." He shook his head.

"I will hardly judge you." I smoothed his hair. I wanted to take fistfuls of it in my hands, bring him closer to me, feel the true extent of his heat . . .

I squelched the thought immediately. What did I want, to end up like my mother, burdened with a child and abandoned by its sire, judged by the local villagers and deemed wanton? I had gone without a man for a long time. I didn't *need* a man. All I needed was my art. I would funnel my emotions and frustrations through charcoal or pen or paint, and I would be fine, and when the *human* war was over, I would return to the capital, and it would be as though I'd never left.

And yet . . . I had lusted after men before, but this wasn't the same. Yet I dared not dwell on how, or why.

He let out another long, summer-wind sigh. "I am a being who cannot be selfish. I can*not* be," he emphasized, leaving another maddening clue for me. Then, so quiet I could barely discern it, "But I cannot go home, and I am glad."

Leaning forward, I took his chin in my hand so he would look at me. So I could see his face. So I could better understand. "Where is home?"

He took my hand in both of his. "Far away from here."

I tried to think of the farthest place I knew, tracing rivers and borders on a map in my mind. My thoughts raised heavenward, to the endless night sky, and I again thought of fallen stars and wondered what they would look like, in the shape of a man. My mind couldn't wrap around it—*wouldn't*—and I blinked the question away to examine at a later time.

I swallowed, considering how brave I really was. Several seconds passed before I said, "This can be your home. For as long as you need it." I rolled my lips together. "Even if you aren't mortal."

He made no response—no sign of surprise that I knew. Neither did he correct me.

Who was this man who burned like a furnace and bled light, who spoke so kindly and berated himself for enjoying peace? I had only pieces of answers, but one thing was certain.

I would never be content to only sketch him.

Winter is still months away, but today's rain made me think of it, and somehow I'm already missing summer.

CHAPTER 6

I was groggily stirring in front of the hearth, the fire mere embers in what should have been early morning hours, when I heard a distant call outside. While the songbirds had kept quiet even beneath the cool light of the moon, the voles and crickets were alert, and it took me a moment to recognize a human voice among them.

"House Beldun! Are you well?"

Beldun was the name of my grandfather.

Blinking, I righted myself and halfheartedly dropped a log onto the embers. It would catch soon enough. I reached for the pocket clock, which had fallen from my pocket during my sleep. Just past the seventh hour.

"House Beldun!"

Alertness slammed into me. "Zyzi?"

Throwing off my blanket, I rushed to the kitchen table, where I'd left my lantern, and struck a flint far harder than needed to light it. Grabbing it and forgetting my shawl, I raced outside, the cold lapping at me and needling through my clothes, raising all my skin like I was a newly plucked pheasant.

Down the narrow dirt road that passed between the house and the oat field and led all the way to Goatheir, I saw a pinprick of swinging light.

"Here!" I bellowed, waving my lantern. Some clouds had dared to cross over Rozhan, and they blocked out a large portion of the moon's light. "Here!"

The swinging of the distant light grew quicker, and soon the pounding of footsteps accompanied it. Laughing, I ran toward it, holding my light high.

I knew it was my cousin, but seeing her face come into view thrilled me, nonetheless. We collided, a tangle of arms and trembling flame. I laughed into her wild unbound hair, which fell around her shoulders in uneven waves, dark brown against my own black. Pulling back, I lifted my lantern to better see her, and she did the same, and we smiled at being of one mind. She looked hale, her russet skin unblemished, her umber eyes bright. She had a small, straight nose and wide lips, and stood at equal height with me.

"You traveled at *night*?" I chided her.

She snorted. "There is no other way to travel, Ai." Her expression grew serious. "The others . . . ?"

"We're all well and accounted for. Yours?"

"Besides my hysterical mother, who has burned so much incense I'll smell like lavender and sandalwood for a week?" She sniffed her arm for emphasis. In truth, she *did* smell like sandalwood. "Those of us who stayed in the village are well." She bit her lip. "Our hunting party is still in the Furdowns."

My heart snicked. Two of my cousins—Zyzi's brothers—always went with the hunting party to the Furdowns, the thick forest two days south of here, where game was plentiful. "They're experienced," I assured her. "They'll be fine. With the moon so bright, they could find their way back. Perhaps they're using the cover of darkness to bag more game."

She nodded, as though she'd tried to reassure herself of the same thing often. Pulling forward a satchel at her waist, she said, "I brought you a few things. Herbs for sleeping droughts, more joint balm for Kata, and a few prayer rolls."

"Thank you. We need them." Zyzi was all but the village wise-woman for Goatheir, though until Yunka, the healer in the next town over, died, she would be treated as an apprentice. Zyzi knew more about herbs, barks, tinctures, and medicines than I could ever hope to learn, and she'd taken to the religious aspect of her studies as well. As she'd said, it never hurt to beseech the gods when one was ailing.

Pushing the satchel back and slipping past me, she peered toward our crops. "The farm."

I swallowed a frown. "There is little to be done for it." And no point dwelling on what couldn't be saved, for the gods had never been moved by mortal misfortune. I hooked my arm through hers. "Tell me what's happened in the village." I pulled her toward the house.

"Families are losing their godsdamned minds," she said. "Half of them have taken to worshipping the moon. As if doing that will bring the Sun back. The council meets every night even when they have nothing to say."

"Any word from the capital?" It was a slim chance, but I had to ask.

She shook her head. "Why would they care about us in a time of crisis? We have to care for ourselves." She pinched the underside of my arm. "We've been so worried about you."

"We did have bandits."

"Bandits!" She slowed her step and looked me over. "I take it you gave them hell."

I smiled. "Something like that." I tried not to picture the dead body in the barn. Ultimately, Saiyon had disposed of it. I hadn't asked where, or how.

Zyzi sighed. "Us, too. Not our home specifically, but in the village. Though I don't think they're outsiders. I think a few greedy men have decided to take advantage of the dark—" She stopped walking entirely. "Who is that?"

I turned and held my lamp high. Saiyon was walking toward the house from the direction of the hayfield, a bundle of quartered wood on his shoulder. He glanced our way.

"That"—I ignored the prickles in my belly—"is a man I found by the river."

Pulling her arm from mine, Zyzi gave me a peculiar look. "A man you found by the river. Who is chopping wood for you?" She took a few steps down the road, holding her lamp to the side. "Fine-looking man, from here. Far as I've ever been able to tell, anyway."

I nudged her with an elbow.

"Telorian?" she guessed.

"More or less," I said, which earned me another confused look. "I'll explain over breakfast." As much explaining as I could afford, that was.

It felt wrong to disclose Saiyon's bizarre secrets, even to one as trusted as Zyzi.

Zyzi settled in as though she'd lived on the farm all her life. With the distance to Goatheir being substantial and the darkness making travel that much harder, she intended to stay for a couple of weeks before venturing home. Enera embraced her like a long-lost child; Kata acted aloof, like Zyzi had been expected, though I detected relief in her countenance when she averted her gaze. Not so long ago, back when Zyzi had fought her parents on the topic of marriage, Kata had taken the side of my aunt and uncle, but enough time had passed for such battles to be forgotten.

Saiyon, unsurprisingly, did not join us for breakfast. I allowed my mother to explain how he had come to be with us so I would not have to mask what few truths I knew. I learned more of Goatheir and my extended family there, and we speculated yet again on the war in the heavens, if and when it would end, and what we would do if the darkness persisted. How it had impacted Rozhan's fight with Belat up north—whether men still slaughtered each other in the dark, or if the gods had finally struck enough fear into their hearts to stay their blades. Being so far from the battlefront, and from any major city, we would not hear for some time.

There was work to be done, however, so reminiscing was brief. I ate quickly and put on a knit sweater to exercise Vine and bring water from the river, while Zyzi brewed the assembly of herbs she'd brought. The moon was high by my second trip, so I blew out my light to save fuel. She lit the path well enough, though the crops cast shadows across it, so I kept Vine to the middle of the way.

We harvested what little we could. We couldn't spare the fuel to try to nourish our garden with firelight, though my mother potted a few plants to bring close to the hearth, in hopes they might get enough light to survive. With the moon out, Saiyon took to indoor chores. He patched a leak in the roof and swept ash out from the hearth, gathering it in a sack to be deposited outside.

When I came in with my last bucket of water, Zyzi was watching him closely as she worked bread dough on the table. I watched her watching him. Saiyon gathered up the large sack of ash, nodded briefly to her, and went on his way. I caught one of his subtle smiles as he passed, and that itch to draw tickled my fingers yet again.

I'd been inspired by faces before—family and friends, strangers on the street, people at worship—but one or two works always fulfilled that creative need in me, and I moved on. With Saiyon . . . the more I sketched him, the greater the need became, like a gaping void within me. Like I fed only on hay, and it couldn't nourish me.

I pressed my lips together until they hurt—until I got ahold of myself, though my fingers trembled so slightly, only I would notice. Like I'd been burned. Like I'd taken a drug and my blood craved more of it. And it was foolish—*so foolish*—

"Never seen a Telorian like him." Zyzi's comment scissored through my thoughts, though her attention was on the bread. "He certainly would put fine stock in a woman's belly."

My cheeks warmed, since I knew she made the comment for me and not herself. Zyzi had never been interested in men, women, or anyone in between. I set my jaw. It was a truth—someone as virile as Saiyon would not sire frail offspring. But I hated the way the thought niggled at me, like my bones were termite-eaten wood. I didn't like the feeling of weakness these pestering emotions left in me.

Zyzi paused. "I'm sorry—I didn't mean it that way."

It took a moment to understand her, and then I shook my head. "I didn't take it that way."

I had wanted children, once. Wanted them badly. But it hadn't been in my cards, and I'd never found another sire I wished to share them with. I'd accepted the fact. Truly, I had. Still, to this day, I never sketched the young.

Later, after lunch, when I left to check on the chickens—we'd lost three in the bandit attack—and collect eggs, I noticed a faint light around the door to the little shed where I kept my art. Curious, I crossed over and peeked inside, finding Zyzi there with a lantern, studying the pictures I'd stowed away, the canvas I'd pinned up to dry, the half-finished bust sitting in the corner.

Many of the pieces were of Saiyon.

She was not at all embarrassed to have been caught. I'd never made an attempt to hide my art before, and it wasn't like I had locked the door. My cousin's eyes were slow to find me, and when they did, she said, "Your art is changing."

Just like my mother had told me.

I rubbed a chill from my arm. "For the better, I would hope."

She nodded. "For the better." She stepped closer to a canvas of Saiyon, only half-finished, and held her light close. "But it's not just your art, Ai. You're changing, too."

I scoffed. "You've not been here even a day—"

"I can tell." She lowered her light. "I know you well enough to notice. You're changing." She tipped her head toward the painting. "And I think I know why."

I bit my lip. Glanced behind my shoulder, as if the local judge might be standing there, ready to drop his gavel. I stepped into the shed, letting the door close behind me. "I . . ." I couldn't finish the sentence.

"I wouldn't dare say you love him." Zyzi smirked, a canine poking over her lower lip. "I'd like to keep my head on my shoulders. But you're certainly"—she turned, her light cascading over the bust—"*intrigued* by him." Reaching out, she touched the still-soft gray clay. "You should finish this."

"I didn't know what his eyes looked like," I whispered. Sighed. "I don't have time to finish it."

"You're making time." She gestured to the other pieces, and she still had not seen the many pages of Saiyon filling my sketchbook. Her gaze softened. "You never make time for frivolous things. So these must have meaning."

Hugging myself, I begrudgingly dipped my head in agreement. "There's a depth to him I've never beheld in anyone else. Like I could fall into him and never hit the ground."

Zyzi didn't answer right away, but studied another portrait.

"He says he knows me, from Algeron," I continued. "He's remarked on my journey, on my progress. There's something familiar about him." I leaned against the doorframe. "But I can't place him. I would never forget a face like that. A man like that."

"Perhaps Edkar—"

I waved away the name that hadn't been spoken aloud in years. Edkar's passing wasn't something I enjoyed dredging up. "It was after that. At the temple."

"The new one?"

I nodded.

She worked her mouth. "Be careful, Aija."

"I always am."

"Be careful," she repeated, regardless.

She squeezed my shoulder, then stepped back into the endless night, taking her light with her. I lingered too long—long enough to be scolded by my grandmother, were she to catch me—and stared at my art. Thumbed through my older pieces, some from my time in the capital, and pulled a few out and compared them to my new work. Then I tucked my thoughts away just as I did my paintings, making sure to latch the shed door when I left.

The moon had slid behind the clouds again, so I held my light high as I walked to the chicken coop and collected only a few eggs; the birds struggled to lay, but from the darkness or the scare from the bandits, I couldn't be sure. I scavenged a few oval rocks and stuck them in their nests to encourage them. Checked on the animals in the barn, though Enera had done that this morning.

I started back for the house, but I spied Saiyon up the path between the oat and hayfields that led to the river. He'd donned one of my grandfather's beaten hats, pulled down nearly to his brow, like he was trying to disguise himself. He stared heavenward, where a sliver of the enormous moon's silver light peeked between clouds.

I walked to his side. "She is lovely, but I miss the Sun."

A low hum in his throat was his only response.

I watched with him until the clouds shifted and covered the light. Despite the cool air, Saiyon radiated heat. My sleeve brushed his elbow. "What did you do before you were a soldier?"

He glanced down, his eyes flashing as if lit from within. "Why do you ask?"

I twisted my lips at such a question, and did not miss that his gaze dropped to them. I pressed onward so I wouldn't dwell on it. "Because I want to know. What other reason is there for asking?"

That small smile tweaked his mouth. I wondered if his lips were soft, or if they were rough from work, travel, and the Sun. I didn't think I had a preference.

"What did you do before you were an artist?" he countered.

I lifted my basket of three eggs. "I farmed, what else?"

He nodded. Turned back to the sky. "I was a law keeper."

Not an answer I'd expected. "How did you get into that?"

He seemed to shrink, like I'd settled a heavy yoke on his shoulders. "It was not something I chose." His face turned back to me. "That is an amazing gift you all have." He gestured to the house. "Agency. Something easily taken for granted."

"You mean mortals?"

He nodded.

I stepped in front of him to better read his expression, though I kept my lantern at my side. "Can you not . . . choose?"

He hesitated. Lifted his hand and studied it. Ran his fingers over his palm. "Like this? I am not sure."

Setting down my basket, I followed the path of his fingers, tracing the lines on his palm. *Like this.* Was this not his normal state?

His hand closed around mine, his touch driving back the coolness of the night. "Why do you not use your full name?"

He so deftly changed the subject, but I allowed it. I shrugged. He meant my full given name—Aija. I knew some, like the Belatites and Telorians, had family names as well, but the Rozhani had always been designated by geography. Aija, or *Aija of Rozhan*, was the only name I had. "People have a tendency to shorten names. It's done out of fondness. Or perhaps laziness."

"It's like you're always speaking in the third person." Amusement lit in his eyes. "Ai did this. Ai did that."

I swatted his arm. "And what of your name? Saiyon. I sighed and I yawned. I've never heard of such a name."

He nodded. "It is very old."

The simple statement cooled my mirth. "How old?"

He looked out over the oat field. "Very old."

How long could godlings live? About a millennium, give or take, wasn't it?

That *was* very old. And it got me thinking.

"Your earliest memory," I said. "What is it?"

He glanced to me. Shook his head.

"I haven't told them," I whispered, turning to better face him. "About the godlings you spoke with. About the . . . light."

He didn't answer. Only watched my eyes, like he could see the truth behind them. Like he knew I'd eavesdropped.

"Even if you're a deserter, or a mercenary, or a . . . pirate"—I smirked—"I don't mind. Well, that's not true. I might mind a little."

He withheld a smile, which only broadened mine.

"But you can trust me," I finished.

He closed his eyes, like he was thinking. "My first memory . . . I've never been asked that question."

"All the better to keep you on your toes."

"It was . . . darkness." His voice was wind in ripe, green leaves. "And then light."

I considered that. "I suppose that's the case for all of us, isn't it? Any . . . details?"

"I do not mean to be obscure." He looked skyward. "That was it. Darkness, and then light. A ring of white light across the sky, and then my own."

I peered up, tracing the cluster of stars that separated one side of the heavens from the other. "That?"

He shook his head. "No. Another light entirely. A light I cannot express. A light that cannot be seen from here." He paused. "What was yours?"

I hesitated. "I . . . also have never been asked that." I tapped my chin, wondering. "I remember the smell of cut grass."

He waited for more, and I shrugged. "That's it. Just the smell of it."

The soft turn of his lips warmed me. "Here?"

I nodded. "My mother has never lived anywhere else."

We stood there in companionable silence for a long moment, me thinking of the summery heat seeping through his clothing and the smell of grass, until a chill encompassed me.

Saiyon had stepped away and was running his hand across the plants. They should have been waist high, but they bent and drooped, curving back toward the ground from which they came.

"How much will it hurt you, to lose these?" His voice was low, soft.

"We have storage that should see us through the winter. I have a little left in my savings, but . . . it will hurt." There was little point in sweetening it. "We won't have anything to sell or trade. We'll need to ration. Perhaps sell or slaughter more animals than we should, because we won't be able to feed them." I shrugged. "Everyone will suffer. And I can't do much. The desperate don't want art, and these people were desperate even before the Sun vanished."

He nodded. "I have some power to help." He glanced skyward again, but the moon was veiled in clouds and half-set in the horizon. Then he glanced toward the house. Toward the hay- and cornfields.

We must have been alone, for he stepped between the rows of plants, wilting leaves brushing his thighs. I didn't follow, only watched him, curious, a tight feeling constraining my breaths.

He went to the center of the field, where I could see just the silhouette of his head. I stood on my toes to get a better view.

He began to glow.

My hands flew to my heart, pressing against its threat to escape my chest. Soft, warm light radiated from him, rippling over the oat field like it was suspended in water. I reached out as the glimmer of light reached the edge of the field, and it waterfalled from my hand and dissipated, not unlike Saiyon's blood had.

The plants drank in the power, their stems gradually straightening, their leaves broadening. I gaped, chill after chill shivering across my limbs even as splashes of warmth tickled my skin. Tiny threads rose from him and vanished as they reached for the heavens, pulled taut like some eternal puppet master loomed among the stars.

I stepped between the rows, following the same path he had. The waves of light lapped around me, cascading down my dress in bright whispers. The oats grew stronger with every step, drinking in the nourishment, bending slightly toward Saiyon, as though trying to get a better look. My pace quickened, my eyes locked on his glowing form, on the light that his clothing could not contain.

He began to dim as I reached him, his power fading, his features tired. But I'd gotten close enough to see something that stilled my very soul.

They were not threads, those delicate beams of light that reached to the stars.

They were chains.

It's the first week of spring, and yet today felt like the middle of summer. The Sun beat down so intensely, like all His attention was on the growing cathedral. Perhaps He is pleased with it.

CHAPTER 7

When he slumped forward, I caught him, arms around his shoulders. I wasn't strong enough to keep him on his feet, so I knelt and helped him kneel with me, the two of us disappearing among stalwart and healthy plants.

My heart beat like Vine's hooves when I let out the reins. "Saiyon?" I swept hair from his face. He didn't perspire. He still burned with that inhuman heat. He took in a slow, deep breath.

"I am well," he answered after a moment. "I am . . . not used to this."

"To using your power?" And what power!

But he shook his head. "To feeling weak."

I recalled what he'd said to me earlier, when I'd asked if he could choose his own path.

Like this? I am not sure.

Like this.

Was *this* not truly Saiyon?

I took his face in both my hands, his heat sucking the cold from my fingertips. "Saiyon. *Who are you?*"

He looked into my eyes, tired and . . . something I feared to assume without a lantern to better discern. Something that made my blood pulse as hot as his did.

But he didn't respond.

"Why?" I pleaded. "Why won't you tell me?"

He let his head droop, but his jaw remained firmly in my palms. "Because I cannot lie."

I gaped. "Can't lie?"

"It is eternal law"—he sighed another summer wind—"and from law was I made."

I mouthed those words. *From law was I made.* I didn't understand the way of celestial creatures. I couldn't grasp his full meaning. But when I blinked, I saw those golden chains engraved on my eyelids.

No agency. Law. *Chains.*

"I do not want to tell you," he continued, quiet as a hummingbird's wings, "because I do not want you to look at me as others do."

I lowered my hands. Touched his chin so he'd meet my eyes again. "What do you mean?"

His luminescent gaze penetrated me, like I was naked. Like I was more than naked. No clothes, no skin, no bones. Only my soul. He was looking right through me to my very center, and I quivered from the vulnerability of it.

Pressed between rows of oats, we were very close. Sharing his heat. Sharing our breaths.

"Because you see me as a man, Aija." His whisper enfolded me in Sun and silk. "As a soul. And *no one* has ever seen me as such. None have been able to."

I didn't respond. My ability to speak had toppled to the dirt beneath my folded legs, and I had no urge to dig for it. Saiyon's hot fingers traced my cheek. I leaned into the touch involuntarily, my heart reacting before my mind could discipline it.

"I can speak with you as I cannot with anyone else," he continued.

I covered his hand with mine. Intertwined our fingers. "Saiyon," I pleaded. "How do you know me?"

He searched my gaze for a moment before exhaling. A sound that whispered surrender. "I watched you at the cathedral in Algeron. I watched you shape and place the tiles of the mosaic. I watched you plan and talk and draw. I watched you sculpt my image into stone with deft fingers. You were so dedicated, so talented, so beautiful. I could not look away, except when the skies turned and forced me to wait. You mesmerized me, and when the work was complete, I mourned."

My lips parted a little more with every sentence. My body rooted itself with the oats. Despite the heat of his nearness, chills crept up my back with the legs of centipedes.

I shook my head, understanding and yet not. He was there, every day, but I never . . .

The heat of his hand reminded me of something. Of Sunlight against the back of my neck as I spread grout. As I assembled patterns. As I lifted my chisel.

Sculpt my image.

"But I . . . ," I murmured, tongue heavy.

I had sculpted the Sun God.

I felt as though the Earth Mother Herself had slammed me to the ground. The heat, the gold, the *light*, and the way the plants had bent toward him. His confusion when he woke. His avoidance of the moon. The darkness.

I had known, and I had dismissed it as impossible.

"You're him." I nearly wept with the words. "You're . . . *Him.*"

He nodded as a dying man would.

I shook my head. "I . . . How? How are you *here*?" I stared heavenward. "*Why* are you *here*?"

"The moon was not always as you know her." He followed my line of sight. "Millennia ago, she stole a portion of My light. And she has always wanted more. We have battled ruthlessly since losing Twilight."

My mind rushed to piece together his meaning. "Twilight?"

He shook his head. "He is a being you would not know. A demigod who stretched between our kingdoms, who acted as a shield. His . . . is a long story. I regret My part in it in many ways.

"My armies have always kept Moon at bay . . . but she's grown in strength and cleverness. Her forces broke through and stole much of My power. I fell from the heavens and landed here by happenstance."

I stared at him. "Then . . . when I found you in the river . . ."

Four days. It had been four days after the sky had darkened.

"She does not have the ability to harness that power," he continued. "And the universe would never allow her to. She cannot be *Me*." He worked his hands together. "I am the one who bears its chains. I am the only one who can."

I slouched, taking it all in. Trying to imagine . . .

I had that itch to draw, but what could I possibly draw?

"You asked Me," he went on after a silent minute passed, "if I had family." He gestured to the sky. "They are My children, though they cannot be in the sense mortals have children. The law . . . forbids it. Even now, the chains pull."

He swallowed, and from the effort of it, I could tell his throat was tight. To be the bearer of so much, and to fail. To have children but never be with them. To be a man but—

I do not want you to look at me as others do.

And I didn't want to. I believed him, but I could not fathom that he was the Sun. That he was a god. *My* god. That *this* was the reason he'd seemed so familiar to me, because I'd seen his face every day as it crossed from horizon to horizon. I'd basked beneath it, but it had been too brilliant for me to comprehend its features, its soul.

I clasped his shoulder. "Saiyon—"

"Ai?" My mother's voice called over the farm. "Aija!"

I bit my lip.

Taking me by the wrist, Saiyon pulled my hand from him. "I am nearly recovered. Go, and I will follow."

My heart twisted. There was no other way to explain the painful stretching in my chest. "Saiyon—"

"Ai!"

He gave me a soft, sad smile that threatened to crack my ribs. "Go."

Rolling my lips together, I got my knees under me, then pressed a kiss to his forehead. "I do see you," I whispered against his brow. "I see you, Saiyon."

He grew very still.

Finding my feet, I hurried down the path between rows.

And left the lantern and eggs behind.

Everyone remarked on the oats. My mother noticed them first, then showed Kata and Zyzi. They couldn't explain it. Perhaps the moon *was* strong enough, they speculated. But then why did the hay and corn still droop?

I couldn't say anything. I couldn't betray him by telling them what happened, and I wasn't sure I could find the words. It felt . . . sacred. A *god* had touched our field to make it thrive. To help us.

To help me, because I wasn't fool enough not to realize he'd done it first and foremost for me. It blossomed such strange, too-large petals in my chest—of pain, of hope, of yearning, of confusion, of *need*—and the bloom refused to shrink. I knew what was happening to me. It had been described to me all my life. But to *know* it now, so deeply, so intimately . . . it terrified me.

Feigning illness, I slipped into my bedroom and closed the door. Didn't light a candle, just dropped into my bed. Lay there in the perpetual night, though it wasn't yet evening, per the pocket clock.

I watched you at the cathedral in Algeron.

Watched me from the sky. Watched *me*, out of the hundreds of other mortals building that site of worship. Out of the tens of thousands who lived in the city. Out of the millions, if not billions, who lived on the Earth Mother.

You were so dedicated, so talented.

He'd told me I had improved.

So beautiful.

No amount of rest or deep breathing could calm my heart.

You mesmerized me, and when the work was complete, I mourned.

He had mesmerized me from the moment I first brought him into the light. He mesmerized me still.

Because he was a god?

No. I hadn't known. I *hadn't known.*

But I knew now.

I had more or less confessed the truth to my cousin when I told her that I could fall into Saiyon and never hit the ground. I hated it—I didn't like *wanting* someone so badly. I didn't like the idea of something outside my control controlling *me.* I fought it. Reasoned with it.

And yet I knew, lying there in the dark, that I wanted Saiyon more than I had ever wanted anything in my life. Despite his revelations, his truths. *His* truths, with a capital *H*, but I couldn't think of him that way, write him that way. Because if Saiyon could stay him, and not Him, then maybe . . . maybe I could embrace this horrid, astounding, consuming feeling eating me alive.

I hated being afraid. I always have, ever since I was a little girl. When another child cried at a spider, I'd crush it under my bare foot, my body shaking with swallowed fear as I did. When harsh winter winds whipped through the farm, I'd open my windows and scream back at them, as if doing so would expel my own trepidation. When rumors of war came to Algeron, I'd shrugged them off and continued painting, refusing to notice the tremor in my hand. I'd stayed until the last moment, even when all my customers had fled, a paintbrush in one hand and a chisel in the other, until the city guard had banged on my door, telling me I had two options: leave or face the Belatite soldiers.

I didn't know how to outwit this kind of fear. How to pretend it didn't affect me. How to mock it. How to shrink it.

Did I have the courage to face it?

I pressed my palm against my racing heart, then touched my cheek, where the imprint of Saiyon's touch lingered. Perhaps I was too like Kata. Too stubborn. Because despite the fear, despite the *truth*, I still wanted him.

And yet I had a sinking feeling that Saiyon was someone I could never have.

It was no surprise that I couldn't sleep.

I took dinner in my room, continuing the guise of illness, because I needed to think. Saiyon didn't take dinner; I heard him outside chopping wood again, and I wondered if there would be any trees left on Earth Mother by the time he was done. I tried to spy on him through my window, but the chopping stump was on the south side of the house.

So I started painting.

My mind was getting tired of sketches, so despite the poor light, I set up one of my last canvases—gods knew when I would be able to purchase more—and selfishly lit four candles for better light. I mixed paints until I had the colors I needed, though none of them were the *right* colors. But I could not paint with light and gold and summer, so I made do.

I painted Saiyon. I painted him without sketching anything first. Just freehand, from memory. At first I thought to paint him in the oat field, glowing and brilliant, but that was our secret, and I didn't want to explain it to my family, should they come across the piece. So I washed the idea from my mind and painted with little thought whatsoever. Like I was in a trance. Like I was dreaming.

Taking my smallest brush, I dipped it into my brightest yellow and whipped it up the canvas once, twice, three times. Again, and again, drawing the threadlike chains binding Saiyon to the universe. Then I took a thicker brush and went over them, making them stronger, harder.

I added more. They curled around his arms, legs, and neck. Restraining him. Suffocating him.

Then, with a tear running down my cheek, I took black and cut through every single one, destroying with such violence I panted with the effort, until there was nothing left to break.

Exhausted, I set my brushes down without washing them. Wiped my palms across my cheeks. I hated crying. I hated it more than I hated being afraid. I blinked several times. Worked my lungs like quiet bellows. Stopped any further tears.

After blowing out all the candles but one, I grabbed the still-wet canvas and the light and snuck out of the house, wanting to tuck it away in my shed before anyone else saw it. Before they could question me or merely wonder if I'd gone mad.

I regretted not grabbing at least my shawl. The air felt especially cold tonight. Perhaps because the moon still nestled on the other side of the world. A gentle breeze danced around my candle, but a sharp look dissuaded it from doing anything more, or so I liked to think.

Approaching, I again noticed a faint light around the door of the weathered shed. Did Zyzi also struggle for sleep? I hadn't seen her by the hearth, but perhaps she had made a pallet in my mother and grand-mother's room, which immediately made me feel guilty for taking the second bedroom all for myself. With an apology ready on my tongue, I reached for the door, left slightly ajar—

And stopped.

It was not Zyzi in the shed, but Saiyon. Saiyon, standing before all my art from the last five years, so many of the pieces portraying *him*. He saw straight to my spirit for the second time in a day. My joints turned to lard.

Holding my breath to be quiet, I watched him study the pieces. He drew close to some, examining them carefully.

Letting myself breathe, I pulled the door open. He didn't even look back; he'd known I was there.

"Much improved," he murmured, studying the same portrait Zyzi had remarked upon earlier that day, of him sleeping. His voice carried a hint of something hoarse and distant, something that sounded like straw underfoot. "These are remarkable."

I set the new painting down, its face turned away, carefully leaning it against others so the paint wouldn't smear. "Thank you."

"I've seen many artists over the years," he added, laying his hand on a stack of canvases against the wall. "You truly have remarkable talent. And for one so young."

I scoffed. "I'm thirty-four."

But I supposed that would be very young for an eternal god.

He thumbed through the canvases. He paused at one in the back. Pulled it out. "Who is this?"

He held a square canvas, eighteen inches by eighteen inches, dusty on the top. The portrait was of a man not quite as dark as I was, with sharp hazel eyes and short-cropped hair. Clean shaven, oval faced, broad shouldered. I had forgotten about that painting. It had been so long since I'd seen his face that it startled me.

He didn't look the same in my memory as he did on that canvas. But was that a fault in my memory, or in the artwork?

"That's Edkar," I said, drawing the shed door shut. "He was my husband."

Saiyon glanced my way. "You were married?"

So the Sun God didn't know everything. I took heart in the fact. "When I was twenty. It was an arranged marriage, but I liked him well enough. He's the reason I went to Algeron, initially." He'd been kind, hardworking, loving, even. Everything a woman—I—could need. "He died in our first year of marriage. Something in the stomach—a cancer, perhaps. The doctors weren't sure. I stayed after he passed and put my efforts into my art. Made a name for myself. But war came, and I fled."

Saiyon nodded, studying Edkar's face. "Did you love him?"

Hugging myself, I leaned against the doorframe. "No." I'd wanted to. Tried to. I'd been convinced the poems and songs and conversations among women were all hyperbole, or that my heart was too hard. "Maybe I would have, in time. I think I would have. He was a good man."

Saiyon set the picture down. "I loved a woman once."

"I would hope so"—I offered the smallest smile—"as old as you are."

He chuckled in his throat. Moved to an old sketchbook.

"Who was she?" I asked. The way he said *woman* made it sound like a mortal. Like me. "A . . . star mother?" Everyone knew the Sun was the father of stars—godlings who had to be born of mortal mothers. Yet all star mothers perished in birth—I'd never heard of their noble lives ending any other way. It would be terrible to love one.

Yet something niggled at the back of my mind. A story I'd heard in passing in Algeron. A song I couldn't quite remember the tune to, and lyrics I might not have believed.

His shoulders drooped. "I have never understood that law. Why stars must be formed so."

"With mortal mothers, you mean."

He nodded. "Who never survive their births." An anvil might have hung from his neck, for how heavy, how *bitter*, those words sounded. He took his hands from the sketchbook. "But yes, she was a star mother. She lived, unlike the others. And she still lives, but not in the manner you do."

That surprised me, and I wondered where on the Earth Mother such a woman might have existed. Far away, for I would have known her otherwise. And yet perhaps I *had* heard her tale, perhaps strummed on the lute of a traveling bard, and easily dismissed it. My mortal memory was too faulty to recall. Saiyon spoke so reverently of her I couldn't bring myself to be envious. "In the heavens?" Then, dreading the answer, "With . . . you?"

He shook his head. "Not with Me." He glanced my way. Noticed the painting I'd set aside.

I stepped in front of it.

His gaze met mine. "Have I embarrassed you?"

I dipped my head. "No."

He crossed the floor. The boards creaked with his weight. The aura of his heat radiated around me. The heat of a domesticated Sun.

I didn't meet his eyes again, but after a few heartbeats, I stepped aside and let him take the canvas.

He studied it in silence. I caught a hitch in his breath.

Wax dripped down the sides of my candle, pooling in its brass holder. I set it aside.

"You are a passionate artist, Ai," he whispered. "You have learned to pull into your creations what is not there to be seen with the eye."

I don't know why that made me angry. Looking back, I think I simply couldn't stomach the vulnerability. The idea that I'd been stagnant those five years, until he appeared. The idea that I needed a man, *him*, or anyone in any way. I was terrified of the new and tumultuous feelings pushing against my breast. I needed a defense. "What do you mean?"

He lowered the painting, slow to take his gaze from it. "You did not *see* this." He didn't mean the chains. "There is such feeling—"

"There's plenty of *feeling* in my life," I snapped. "I live with people who love me. Free from the whims of others. I chose to come back here."

He was unfazed by the outburst. "Do you think I do not know the difference?" He gestured to an older painting of mine, one of the trees on the south side of the farm—a pretty picture that was a mere copycat of what the Earth Mother made, nothing more. Then he tilted his head toward the wild, angry, glistening painting on the canvas in his hands, full of chains and breaking and *him*. A rendition that wasn't truly visual. Like both I and that image had been turned inside out.

Quietly, patiently, he asked, "Why do you paint Me, Aija?"

Tears burned my eyes. "Why shouldn't I?"

He turned back to the painting, scrutinizing it, but I ripped it from his hands. Nearly threw it across the small shed, but I couldn't bring myself to destroy it. Instead, I shoved it by my candle.

Jaw set, I said, "I don't *need* passion."

His gaze bore into me. "Your art says otherwise."

I tilted my head back, if only to stall tears. I blinked rapidly. Breathed deeply. Forced my fire to dim. He said nothing, and I couldn't tell if that made it worse or better.

After what felt like a week, I murmured, "Only with you. This"—I gestured feebly to the new painting—"only happens with you."

He stepped in front of me, reassuring hands clasping my upper arms, though in my state of frustration, his touch made me feel too warm. "You, your art, is astounding because it is a window to your inner fire. A fire that burns brighter than the stars."

A sharp lump formed in my throat. I forced myself to look at him.

"That is why I noticed you then," he continued, gentle and sure. "Why I was enraptured. You stood out among artisans. Among mortals. And I have known many."

His visage blurred through my unshed tears. His golden skin, mother-of-pearl eyes, gilded hair. I tried to imagine him burning as brightly as the Sun once had, tried to imagine him a god in truth, and I couldn't do it. Which was for the better, given what I was about to do.

Standing on my toes, I kissed him.

He startled against me, but he hesitated for less than half a heartbeat before lifting his hands to the back of my neck and pulling me closer, his touch pouring heat into my blood. I pushed into him, demanding, coaxing his lips to part beneath mine. They did, and I drank fire. I *became* fire, a red-hot ember stoked to white-hot flame. I felt I would burn alive, but I didn't shrink from the heat. My fingers tangled into his hair, my body arched against his, and I took what I wanted, heavens and hells be damned.

Tenrick spoke to me at length about his home and chil-
dren today. He's usually a reserved man, but he was
forward with me. His house needs a mistress, and his
children need a mother. But if Edkar, with all his fine
qualities, could not spark that desire in me, then Tenrick
certainly cannot.

I feel terrible. But my heart is simply too hard for
love.

CHAPTER 8

I lost myself in the way Saiyon kissed me. Like I was the fuel to his flame, the air to his lungs. Like *he* was the artist, and I was his creation, painted in the dead of night with strokes of remembered passion.

I had kissed a few men. None compared to this.

It was one kiss or it was many. Either way, I cannot be precise about how long we embraced in that shed, exploring each other, burning to ash only to be reborn as a pyre. He smelled of summer skies and the hackberry wood he'd been chopping. He tasted of sage and cayenne. He felt, and responded, like a man. His energy fed the pressure in my chest until it split me in two over and over, and in those moments all the songs and poems made sense to me. *Art* made sense to me, like I understood it with the mind of a goddess, not a mortal.

My body felt like it had run all night, but my spirit was vibrant enough to light the sky all on its own. Our attentions to each other slowed, and when he bent down to kiss the side of my neck, I let out a breath of everything that I was, fears and passions alike.

"How is it," he murmured beneath my ear, "that you make Me want to promise everything to you?"

I ran my thumb across his bearded jaw. When he pulled back enough for me to meet his eyes, I said, "You don't have to promise me anything."

He touched my face, my lips. I pressed my cheek into his palm, wondering at the sadness filling his expression. "They would be promises I could not keep."

Those words sank into me. I touched my lips delicately to his, testing to see whether his sorrow would draw him away. It did not. "Do your laws forbid you from . . . associating with mortals?" I whispered, allowing a small flicker of hope into my voice. "Outside of star mothers?"

He searched my face, though I couldn't determine what he was looking for. "No, they do not."

I licked my lips, tasting him there. I stood at the edge of something I did not want to examine too closely, for fear of losing my balance. "My life is but a breath to you, I imagine."

That sorrow deepened. "I can only touch you, *be here*, because of her."

He meant the moon. Because of what she had taken from him.

What his armies fought to win back.

I didn't know what to say to that. I didn't fully understand his meaning. And how could I have? I was a mere mortal. So I leaned my forehead against his collarbone and stood with him in that dimly lit shed until my candle burned to nothing.

It only occurred to me later, as I dragged myself back through the impregnable night for much-needed rest, that I had kissed a god.

I didn't draw that next day. Even if I'd had all the time in the world, I didn't know *what* to draw. I had exhausted my talents on that canvas, and they needed time to recuperate.

I hoped Saiyon had tucked the painting away. I did not have the energy or patience to explain myself to anyone who stumbled upon it.

Zyzi and Enera both worried over my quietness, but I told them I was simply tired, which was true, and helped them complete the daily chores. I rubbed balm into my grandmother's joints and walked Vine to the river and back. I fed the sheep and mucked the stalls—the moon was bright and high, and Saiyon tried to stay away from her watching light. I wondered if she'd noticed him, when the bandits attacked, or if she'd managed to peek around the clouds when he'd pushed his light into the oat field. If she'd recognized him.

He remained heavy on my thoughts. I took a brief nap an hour after noon, and I dreamed of him. Though the images were nonsensical, they made my heart hurt. Later, I smiled at him doing laundry, at Enera showing him how to properly scrub the clothes. If my mother discovered the truth about Saiyon, she'd shrink into nothing. Perhaps black out. Maybe lose her voice for a year or two.

When the moon dipped away, I found him on the roof. He'd returned the rain gutters from his crude structure, now that his godling soldiers knew where to find him. I climbed the ladder and sat beside him in comfortable silence, leaning on him for warmth.

After some time, I asked, "Where is she now?"

"Hm?"

"The star mother who lived. The one you loved."

He scanned the sky. Pointed to the stars forming the little bear. "There."

I wondered how a person could live in a constellation. "Why is she there, and not here?"

"Ceris's story is unique." His voice was low, soothing. This was the first time I'd heard the woman's name, and I was not surprised that it was lovely. "She was . . . misplaced in time after she survived our first star's birth. The life she knew was lost to her. She found companionship in the one responsible."

Sifting through the information, I looked at him. "The one who . . . misplaced her?"

He nodded. "He was a fugitive, but she helped pay back the time he had stolen. She paid it at My side, and when the years had passed, they returned to the Earth Mother. Had a mortal family before joining their celestial one."

I looked back at the seven stars forming the Little Dipper. *Celestial family.* Star mother. Then those stars were hers. Multiple stars. But stars could only be born of the Sun . . .

My jaw slackened. "She chose him over you."

Saiyon rubbed his chin. He was so calm, so reposeful.

I was not. I could not fathom *anyone* choosing *anything* over this man, this *god*, who worked so quietly without expectation of gratitude, who spoke so truthfully, who loved so fervidly. And there she hung, glittering in the sky, looking down on us as if to make a mockery—

"How?" I didn't hide the edge in my tone. Indignation leaked from my pores. "How could she choose a fugitive over you?"

He answered without so much as drawing a breath. "Because she loved him."

I might as well have jumped into a winter-frozen trough, the way his answer doused my anger. I gaped at him, waiting for a slip of cynicism, a jab of cruelty. But none came. He looked at what we had called the North Star, gratified.

And there, so easily, I saw his age. His centuries, his millennia. For only someone so ancient, so experienced, could relate such a heart-rendering truth with such acceptance, understanding, and maturity. For the first time, I felt small beside him, and saw all the things I was not.

I licked my lips. Picked at the hem of my shawl. Studied him studying the sky, until those breathtaking eyes shifted toward me.

Little more than a croak, I asked, "Can love be so great?"

His lips turned up in that modest smile. Reaching forward, he ran his hand down my braid. That one simple gesture made the worth of my soul spark back to life. "Love is the one eternal thing all beings are capable of creating. It has more potential than anything else—literature, stonework, folklore. Mortals, more than any, know it intimately. It lingers in the universe long after their bodies have moved on."

And what happens when my body moves on? I wanted to say, but my throat was getting thick, and I did not want to sound weak to him. Or more exactly, I did not want to sound weak to myself.

I was mortal. My body would age and die, and my spirit would join the hereafter. But Saiyon . . . Saiyon's fate was to elude death forever. There was no place of rest for him.

In that, more than anything, we were fundamentally different.

He stiffened suddenly, and I wondered if I'd said something wrong, but when he placed his thumb against my lips in a signal to be quiet, I knew it was something else. The lines creasing his forehead, the way his eyes scanned the night, seeing what I could not, had fear tickling the dip of my spine.

Saiyon stood, drawing me up with him. "Go inside," he whispered.

I grasped his forearm. "What? Why?"

He scanned the sky. His muscles were hard as stone beneath his skin. "Her warriors are coming. They do not care for mortals. Keep your family inside, and you will not be harmed."

My stomach dropped. I whirled around, trying to see what he saw.

A great serpentine shadow passed over the stars.

My body spiked cold and hot at once, creating thunder within my bones.

Pulling me toward the ladder, Saiyon made me face him. "Protect them."

But who will protect you? Reminding myself of what he was, even with his powers diminished, I nodded dumbly and scurried down the ladder, missing the last two rungs and stumbling over the dark ground. Pulling my shawl tight, I ran around the house to the kitchen, heart pounding, breath straining. The hearth was burning bright, a cook pot over it. My mother peeled potatoes. Kata put herbs away.

"Zyzi," I gasped. "Where's Zyzi?"

My mother's hand stilled. "What's wrong?"

"Where is *Zyzi?*"

"She's collecting eggs—"

Hairs on the back of my neck stood on end. The chicken coop was on the other side of the barn—

I ran back to the door, feeling light-headed and full of ants. "Bar this behind me. Don't open it for anyone but me and Zyzi—"

"What is wrong with you?" Kata snapped.

"It's here." I wrenched the door open. "The gods' war is here."

My mother's eyes widened large as Vine's. My grandmother looked at me like my sanity had finally slipped.

Enera began to say something, but a loud and distant *crash!* muted it.

We stared at one another for a moment, packed in silence.

"Stay *here*," I warned them, and dashed outside.

Hugging the house, I darted toward the barn and choked on a gasp. Part of the hayfield had been decimated. I spotted Saiyon immediately; his skin glowed, though not as brightly as it had when he'd revived the oats. Beside him was one of the godlings he'd spoken to days ago, the one who'd shimmered with early morning stars.

In the hayfield loomed a great . . . I didn't know what it was. A *dragon*, made of shadows. Shadows that sucked in the light around it. It was the blackest black I'd ever seen.

It lunged forward, and my bowels nearly gave way.

So many things happened at once. Another godling, the one with horns, zipped up from the north, holding a brilliant sword in his hands. As he swept down, a burst of light emitted from Saiyon, stinging my eyes. I blinked away spots of color. Heard another *crash!* When my vision cleared, I spied the third godling, the tall blue female, entangled in a shadowy tentacle. It whipped and threw her into the darkness. I didn't hear her land.

Zyzi's name built up in my throat, but I dared not shout it and draw attention to myself. I reached the barn and took the long way around, trying to avoid moonlight—

The dragon charged. I bit my tongue to hold in a scream. These beings moved so quickly my mind could barely keep up with them, especially in the dark. Saiyon's light vanished, although I told myself he'd done it on purpose to make himself less of a target.

The horned godling's sword struck true, and the dragon keened an un-Earthly sound. If one could *hear* poison—

Oh gods, what if Zyzi had been caught in the field? What if she was already . . . I couldn't stomach the thought. My skin *hurt* at the possibility that she might be dead.

A flash of glitter pulled my attention skyward. The first godling, the one who shimmered, fought with something not attached to the dragon. They flew beyond the house, out of my line of sight. The dragon charged, forcing the others that way—

I turned around the corner of the barn and nearly screamed at the nearness of a body that was distinctly not human—a creature taller than I was, with four arms and a tiny head, turned away from me—

And then a shriek as it seized its prey, a woman who must have been desperately trying to make it to shelter.

Zyzi.

Rage and worry burst like a festering sore within me. I had no weapon but myself, but I charged and leapt, grabbing the godling around its thick neck. My weight hauled it backward. One of its hands released Zyzi, who fell to her knees—

One of its other hands reached over its shoulder and grabbed at me. I hissed through my teeth, squeezing tighter to choke it, but its neck was hard as bone and didn't give. Its gnarled fingers clamped onto my hair and pulled—

A sickening cry sounded from its mouth, and its hold eased. I looked up to see Zyzi huffing before it, fist closed around the hilt of a knife embedded in the creature's midsection. She wrenched it out and stabbed again.

I jumped away, releasing the godling. It fell to its knees as Zyzi stabbed it a third time. Jerking the knife free, she stumbled back into the barn wall, shaking.

Running to her, I grabbed her shoulders. "Are you all right?"

The Earth rumbled beneath our feet. Tears streaked her cheeks, highlighted by the moonlight, but she nodded. She didn't sheath the bloodied knife. I didn't blame her, but we couldn't stay out here. I pulled her toward the barn and eased one of the doors open, wincing at its creak. We slipped inside.

Darkness swallowed us.

"We have to get to the house." I tugged her through the black to the opposite doors. "Saiyon thinks we're in there. He'll protect the house."

"Protect it from . . . what *are* those?" she cried, but she didn't resist me. I eased the opposite doors open, blessing a cloud sliding over the moon. It was a straight sprint to the house.

"Godlings," I whispered, turning toward her. Squeezing her shoulder. "Stay with me."

She nodded again, not surprised, exactly, because what else could they be? She still trembled, but not as badly. "I'm here. I'm . . . here."

As I readied to take off, my hand clasped tightly with Zyzi's, something flashed like lightning and sounded like ten thousand cracking walnuts. My mother screamed from within the house. My chest vibrated like a hummingbird's. My palms sweated lakes.

Saiyon. Where was Saiyon?

My gaze whipped back and forth until I saw streaks of violet light giving way to the silhouette of a godling dragging its long legs across the Earth. Not one of the messengers I'd seen before, but one of *hers*. But the light wasn't power—it was blood leaking from cuts smattering his skin. He must have been injured earlier and left behind, but he was still alive. Still able.

He was close to the barn, moving toward the hayfield. I didn't think we could run past him without being spotted.

Something smashed against the barn roof; I bit my tongue, trying not to scream, and a deep cry pulsed in Zyzi's throat. My thoughts turned and twisted. We needed a distraction—

A high-pitched scream rent the air, vibrating in my skull. My hands flew to my ears. That would do.

Palms pressed to the side of my head, I elbowed Zyzi forward, urging her to run. Blessedly she did, taking off toward the house. The bleeding godling didn't notice her over the horrid screeching.

Zyzi was nearly to the house's back door when the awful scream cut off. Saiyon's glimmering godling returned, and I knew, somehow, that he had killed one of the moon's soldiers. That *it* had made those noises as it died.

Zyzi would realize I wasn't with her. Yet she wasn't foolish—she'd go inside. I held my breath, waiting for the back door to open. Enera and Kata would know her—no attacking monster would bother knocking. *Open the door. Don't wait for me!*

The glimmering godling lunged for the dragon. I averted my eyes as another burst of light—a disk of fire—erupted from the hay, bright as Sunlight. Saiyon.

The dragon snarled.

Now. I had to run now—

But as Saiyon's power illuminated the night, I caught movement from the corner of my eye; the injured godling from before—half man and half bear, with heavy crystalline tusks—had changed direction and crept through the darkness toward Saiyon. One of its large hands clutched a dagger not unlike the other godling's sword.

The blood froze in my veins.

Was Saiyon still immortal in his present form? Did the moon's soldiers have the ability to hurt him, kill him?

The others didn't see the tusked godling's approach.

It began to run toward them. Toward Saiyon.

I dropped my shawl. Sprinted.

"No!" I screamed, bursting into the fray, cutting off the assassin's path.

Light erupted behind me. The dragon keened. A spiral of darkness edged my vision.

They'd heard me.

The tusked godling reared and hissed, angered by the sudden impediment in its path. I tried to strike its ugly face, but my hand passed right through, as if it were a ghost.

The dagger flashed. Pain sharp as an operatic note bloomed from my gut and tore up into my shoulders. Then light—so much light. Blinding light. My eyes watered from it, but I couldn't move. I just stood there, my body not quite mine. I weakly registered a gritty wail from the creature before it vanished entirely. My knees hit the soil. Warm wetness coursed over my pelvis and down my legs.

A scream. Zyzi?

And then stars. So many stars above me. Why had I never noticed how many stars there were? Millions and millions of them.

Coldness bit into my limbs like serpent fangs. Light grew around me. Warm, golden light.

My name. Someone was saying my name.

Mother-of-pearl eyes loomed over me. Saiyon. He was *safe*.

I smiled. Tried to reach for him, but my arm wasn't mine anymore. It wouldn't obey.

The stars started winking out, just as the Sun had over two weeks ago. Dark, darker . . .

I fell.

It wasn't like normal falling. I didn't feel a rising lump in my chest or a thrill beneath my skin. Just a descending, almost like the world rose around me all at once, and in that act lost its color and shape and became nothing. The pain, the cold, even the heat and light vanished. I fell, and I had this strange, instinctual feeling that when I hit wherever I was going, I wouldn't get up again.

Far away, at the highest peak of sky, a single star lit into being, whiter and brighter than any I'd ever beheld. I focused on it. Watched it spark and grow. Watched it reach for me. It grew four fingers and a thumb.

The darkness didn't like it. The darkness sucked against it, whirled and complained. But that bright hand fought it. Pulsed against it, glowing so radiantly it should have blinded me, but I wasn't seeing it with my eyes.

I fell faster, no wind stirring my hair or caressing my skin, but still that hand reached for me. It pulsed and reached and plunged into my chest. *That* I could feel, like a hot brand against my ribs, like a phoenix rebirthed in my very soul. Grabbing me, it heaved, slowing my descent. Stopping it. Gradually, inch by inch, it pulled me up.

I blinked, trying to understand. Stared at the hand and arm of light pulling me. Delicate chains wrapped around it, digging into it, piercing it until even brighter light leaked from its form. Still, the hand drew me upward.

I didn't want it to let go.

I surged upward. Suddenly the stars returned in all their numbers. The world was not black but indigo, blue, and violet. I could feel myself again, all four limbs, my chest, my stomach, head. The hand of light released me, and the cold night struck me all at once, more painful than the dagger had been.

Saiyon loomed over me, his light winking out, but not before I saw those chains wringing and choking, digging into his flesh, strangling his neck and seizing his arms, trying to stop him from whatever he had done.

My mind snapped into place last, and I knew. Somehow I knew that Saiyon had done something he was not meant to do. Something celestial law forbade him from doing, but in this mortalesque state he had managed to overpower it, at the risk of unwinding his own existence.

The descending darkness had meant to claim me entirely. Saiyon had stopped it.

And as I gasped breath into my lungs, he collapsed.

I massaged my hands as I walked home, sore from a day of holding a hammer and chisel. The festival had started that morning, blocking off the main road, so I wound back to the roads behind the bakery, thinking it fine since the Sun had not yet set. But the shadows cast by the close-quarter buildings seemed to be enough for ruffians, for two approached me, eyeing my bag.

"It's only art supplies, gentlemen." I held my ground, trying not to let my hands shake.

If spent oil could smile, that was the expression they gave me. "We'll see for ourselves, miss. We'll take the bag, and the dress."

Cold fear spiked up my center as they approached. I retreated, wondering if I could outrun them—

They stepped into a strip of light, and their smug expressions suddenly melted as they peered at something behind me. I turned to see what horror had caught their attention, but there was nothing beyond the alley and the blinding, setting Sun.

When I turned back, the men had run the other way.

CHAPTER 9

The glimmering godling rushed to Saiyon's side as I sat up. "Satto." He grasped Saiyon's shoulders. "Satto!"

My heart wedged into my throat as I studied Saiyon's unconscious form. "What happened?" My voice shrunk with the plea. "What happened?"

I pressed my ear to his chest. His heart still beat. He still breathed.

"He should not have done that," the tall godling said in her low voice. She regarded me with both animosity and curiosity.

The glimmering godling pressed a hand to Saiyon's chest. Soft light emanated from his fingers and rippled across Saiyon's chest, but there was no change in his condition.

"I don't know." The horned godling finally answered my question. He turned around, listening. "There may be others."

"Go," said the glimmering one. "Go and check. He will survive this."

The other two godlings lingered only a moment before obeying and darting out into the night, too quickly for my eyes to follow.

"He'll survive?" I repeated.

The glimmering godling regarded me with interest, though I could not see any eyes on his face. "He is a god. But I have never beheld something of this kind before"—his head turned toward Saiyon—"and not the breaking of that law."

I clung to Saiyon's still form. "What law?"

"Death cannot be reversed," he said matter-of-factly, like he was surprised I didn't know. "One of the great four."

The confirmation that I had *died* slammed the breath out of me.

Beholding my stupefied state, the godling said, "I will carry Him. You must shelter Him. We must take Him away from her face."

I nodded, numb. "O-Of course." *My family* . . . but Zyzi had already seen the spectacle outside, and surely she'd told my mother and grandmother. If not, they would have to learn of it now.

The glimmering godling pulled Saiyon's limp form up with far more strength than a human could muster. As he slung Saiyon's arms over his shoulder, I remembered myself and ran to the house. Zyzi stood outside the front door, shaking, and grabbed my shoulders. "A-Ai?" she muttered. "But you . . ."

I squeezed her hands before pulling free. "We have to make room for him." I hit the door five times, and when I heard it unlatch, I pushed it open, startling my mother.

Enera, Kata, and Zyzi all stared, bewildered, as I led the glimmering godling through the house.

He set Saiyon on my bed, where he'd lain for days while recovering from his "fever." He seemed so still, so comatose. The luster was gone from his skin and hair. I wondered how long it would take him to wake. If he even would. Yet the godlings seemed so sure.

I was still grasping at seeds on the wind.

The godling moved to the window. Although it was much too small for him to use as an exit, somehow I knew that was what he intended. "Wait."

He paused, glittering skin shifting as he regarded me.

"What should I do? How can I help?"

He shook his head. "Your ways will do nothing for Him. You must wait for the universe to decide His fate."

"The universe?" I knelt beside him. "But—"

"There is nothing more to do." He turned to leave.

"Your names, please," I begged. "He hasn't told me. You've served him so well, and you watch over my farm." Names were important. Names had power, even if only in the heart. "Tell me your names."

The glitter of his flesh shifted again. "I am Pree. He was Sai'ken, and she was Kalanakai."

Then Sai'ken was the horned godling, and Kalanakai was the tall one. Such strange names, but I repeated them, forcing my strained mind to remember. "Thank you."

Pree glanced down to his sleeping god, then back to me. I wished he'd speak his thoughts, but he didn't, instead warping through the wall and window like it was not there at all.

Kneeling by Saiyon's side, I grasped his large hand in both of mine. "Wake up," I whispered, tears pricking in my eyes. I would pray to the gods, but whom could I possibly pray to besides him? The moon was our enemy, and Earth Mother had slept for as long as our scriptures recounted.

A creaking floorboard told me my family was in the doorway. Pressing my cheek into Saiyon's knuckle, I turned just enough to see all three of them watching me, features hollow and unsure.

"Bring him some water," I said, "and I'll explain everything."

When I told them the truth about Saiyon, my grandmother called me a liar, my mother nearly fainted, and Zyzi stormed from the room.

But they had seen a good portion of the battle with the shadow dragon. They had seen Pree, who appeared to be formed of the deepest night sky, carry him into our home. They saw Saiyon bleed light on my bed, for he'd not come through the fight entirely unscathed.

So I continued with my story, telling my grandmother and mother all I knew of how the Sun had come to be at our farm and why he couldn't leave. Zyzi returned partway through the tale with some sort of tincture for Saiyon. I doubted it would work on a god, but I thanked her anyway. I neglected to tell them only that I was in love with him and of the intimacies we'd shared, and that if . . . *when* he did go, a torn and bleeding piece of me would follow.

I might have wept then, had my family not been so close, so uncertain and confused. But their presence forced me to be brave. Forced me to pretend Saiyon was just a wayward man asleep with fever, though he was so much more than that.

He had saved me.

I stayed with him that night. On the bed, not the floor. It was a tight fit, but I needed to feel him breathing against me. I needed to hear his heart beat. And it did, just like a man's.

Around one in the morning, Saiyon went cold for the first time.

I was awake; I'd only slept in fits. I'd been winding the pocket clock and wondering how much longer the single lit candle would last. Then, suddenly, like a fire doused with a full washtub of water, his body turned cold as the moon-cast night.

I sat upright and grabbed his face. Gods were immortal, they couldn't die!

And he was not dead. But his face tensed, and when I brought the candle closer, it highlighted dips and lines of pain across his features. His jaw clenched. His breath grew sharp. And against his arms, neck, and chest, I saw fine indentations—those delicate, invisible chains constraining, suffocating, punishing.

A sound like that of a trapped animal stopped halfway up my throat. I tried to claw at the chains, thinking I might feel them even when I couldn't see them, but they were as intangible to me as that assassin had been. Saiyon was being scourged by some otherworldly power. From within or without, I couldn't tell.

Death cannot be reversed, Pree had said. It was one of the four great laws.

And in my head, I heard Saiyon whisper, *From law was I made.*

"It was my fault," I whispered, unbuttoning the front of my dress. Glancing to the door, but I had shut it when the others turned in for bed, and no one had tried to open it since. "Why, Saiyon?"

And it would not be just me who suffered should he perish. All the world would die with him. Surely the universe understood the consequences. Surely those powers had mercy.

Pulling the front of my dress open, I lay atop him, hoping my body might warm his. His skin made me shiver, but I pressed close, slipping my arms under his shoulders, nestling my head in the valley between his neck and shoulder.

"You're not alone. I'm here," I whispered to him. "It will pass." It had to. The godlings had seemed so sure he would survive. Saiyon himself had said no one else could be him. And if that were true, the universe *needed* him.

I don't know how long it took. I didn't check the pocket clock. But eventually, gradually, Saiyon's muscles relaxed. His forehead smoothed. His heat returned, so much so that I grew too warm against him and had to shift away. I made myself modest and stroked his hair, murmuring assurances and gratitude.

I would have died without him.

It took two days for him to wake. Two days of sleeplessness, two days of story retellings, two days of bartering with my grandmother, who I know believed me but didn't want to. I was exhausted and scared and snapped at dinner that she couldn't turn out her own god, and she didn't speak to me again.

He stirred at midnight. I was nearby, grooming my nails, and rushed to his side. I hadn't drawn the entire time he slept. I couldn't have if I'd tried.

"Saiyon." I smoothed hair back from his face and waited for his eyes to focus on me. "Saiyon."

He blinked, and in his eyes flashed a tortured and morose soul. It struck me to my core, and I shuddered to think what horrors he had endured—

But then his gaze focused on my face, and he *smiled*, banishing the agony, filling his countenance with warmth that split me like cold glass placed in a fire. His hand swept over my cheekbone and cupped my ear. "You're here."

"Of course I'm here, you buffoon." My eyes misted. "Why do you think you've been useful as a sack of rocks the last two days?"

"Two days," he repeated, and glanced up toward the window, limned silver by the high moon.

I let out a long breath. "Pree, Kalanakai, and Sai'ken are watching the house. I haven't seen them since . . ." I waved my hand. "But I know they're there." I pressed my lips together and looked him over, searching for signs of pain. I didn't see any physical ones.

"Ai," he murmured.

I kissed him, soft and brief. "Death cannot be reversed," I whispered.

His chest deflated, filling the room with summer wind. He moved to sit up, but his recovery wasn't so immediate this time. He struggled. I looped an arm around his and helped.

"You broke a law," I said.

He shook his head. "I *bent* it. You were not dead yet."

I clasped my hands tightly in my lap. "Almost."

His eyes met mine. They looked like quartz at Sunset. "I did not think I would be able to." He clenched and unclenched his hands. Rubbed the tips together like he was trying to coax feeling into them.

"You did not think at all."

"I have existed since before your kin walked the Earth Mother," he said. "I knew what I was doing."

My throat tightened again. Blast this man, this god, this *whatever*, for making me weepy. "And how long will you suffer? Or is it done?"

"That I do not know," he whispered.

"You were in pain."

He didn't reply, only got a faraway look in his eyes.

"How long will you suffer?" I pressed. "How long will you suffer for *me*?"

Placing his hand on my thigh, he said, "Yours is a light I will not let diminish. Not before its time."

A stark reminder that I was mortal, and he was not. Everything that had happened the last few weeks reminded me of that, like the universe itself refused to let me forget.

To hell with the universe.

I placed a kiss on his temple, seeking distraction. "What are the other laws?"

He winced and touched his head.

I bit my lip. "You should rest—"

"A god's reign cannot be inherited"—he stuck out a thumb—"only conquered, claimed."

Perhaps his place *wasn't* guaranteed.

His index finger. "Time cannot be altered." Middle finger. "Death cannot be reversed." Ring finger. "Mortals cannot be forced to do a god's will, only convinced."

Eternal laws. I wondered how many smaller ones existed, and how many of those were unjust or outdated. Were they as convoluted as man's laws? Did they remain forever unchanged?

I kissed his temple again, then his cheekbone, lingering so his heat would warm my lips. When he turned toward me, I kissed his mouth, and when I pulled away he watched me like I was a puzzle he'd just finished, only the pieces didn't make the picture he'd been expecting.

"Ai," he murmured.

"You're right." I hadn't smiled for two days, and it felt good to do so now. "It is confusing. I can't tell if you're saying my name or merely starting a sentence."

I was rewarded with that subtle smile, but I wanted his full one, the one he'd given me when he'd first awoken. Like I was the only thing in all creation he wanted to lay eyes on.

Even Edkar had not looked at me like *this*.

I leaned toward him, coaxing him, letting him come to me. His mouth wasn't as fervent as it had been in the shed; he was still recovering from his ordeal. Yet it sparked fire in my breast and blitzed thoughts into my head.

Pulling back, he leaned his forehead against mine. "I cannot stay here."

If happiness were a vase, mine had cracked from lip to foot.

His hand ran up my arm and across my collarbone. Perhaps he sensed the break and was attempting to mend it. "Before . . . My messengers have alerted Me that the tide has turned. My armies will advance and prevail. Once Moon's stronghold is broken, My powers will be restored. She knows this. The attack was a foul attempt to fabricate victory."

I wondered how many godlings had come to report when I wasn't looking.

"The moon cannot win. It is against the workings of the universe." His fingers trailed back down my arm. "And yet in vain she tries. She has always been a selfish being. But either way, it must end." He pulled back and met my gaze. "Mortals are dying in the darkness. If the Earth Mother would wake, if She would ally with Me . . ." He shook his head. "She has slept too long."

I swallowed to keep my throat open. "Then let us make the most of the time we have, if the tide is turning." I pressed my palm to his heart. "If I have you for a week, I will take you for a week. For a day, I will take a day. For an hour, I will take an hour."

That look returned. Like I was the only thing he could possibly look *at*. But this time it was edged with a sorrow so deep my heart chilled. It was the kind of sorrow only a being who has lived for millennia could carry. A being who has been hurt and betrayed again and again, who bears scars no balm could heal.

I wanted so badly to heal them.

I thought back to his story of the star mother, Ceris. At the time, I'd struggled to believe any force could be powerful enough to compel a woman to leave this man, this god. But love *could* be that great. Because I was utterly in love with Saiyon. I couldn't deny the rising pressure in my chest, the knots in my gut, the *need* that threaded me to him like a thick leather patch. No one had ever churned such feelings in me. Such hope and sadness. Such longing and desire. Not even a renowned poet could adequately relate the push and pull inside me.

I kissed him, letting out a little of that lusty fervor. I climbed into his lap. Let my hands fall like rain over his shoulders.

"For a minute," I whispered, "I will take a minute."

His mouth slowed against mine. Hands grasped my elbows. "I will hurt you," he murmured.

"Not like this," I assured him. "Not if the sky isn't missing a star." Without his full godhood, without the need for a star in the sky, he was little more than a man. I wouldn't meet the fate of the star mothers. I could have all of him, and he all of me.

The candle sputtered out, but we didn't need the light. His skin glowed faintly beneath my touch, and mine *felt* luminescent. Saiyon's fingers and lips traced lines of the sweetest flame over my flesh, and I drew promises over his, sketching him onto my bones, my heart, my soul. With him I discovered true passion, too bright, too colorful for the finest paints to capture. We forged it again, and again, until our bodies were too weary to continue, and I fell into blissful slumber in the crook of his arm, shocked at how whole I felt, for I'd never realized I'd been anything less.

After that, dangerous reveries inflicted my thoughts.

They were the kind of fancies that I hadn't allowed myself since I was an adolescent. Fancies of a cottage on a hilltop, or an apartment in the city, decorated to my whims, with garlands on holidays and portraits on the walls. A man I loved whittling or doing some other pastime by the window, and little children brown as me running about, learning their letters and how to hold a pencil.

I say *dangerous* because they were impossible phantasms. One does not build a mortal life, a mortal family, with a god. And certainly not a god whose place was in the sky, whose very existence all of humanity depended on.

But I struggled to remember he was one.

During the day, when I was busy, I could . . . not *forget*, but push that knowledge and my fears for the future aside. Focus on farmwork. Pretend the eternal night didn't whisper against the back of my neck. But I worked hard, because the harder I worked, the more time I had with him, and as he had reminded me, that time grew shorter by the second.

But I was happy.

My mother, even my grandmother, remarked on my disposition, sometimes with awe, sometimes accompanied with a roll of their eyes. Zyzi, too, but her smiles never reached her eyes, for she understood the ephemeral nature of our relationship. But I smiled, and they smiled, and even Saiyon smiled. Just like before, he took to the life of a farmer as if he'd been born into it. He avoided the moon's light, for his godlings had created an illusion to suggest he'd moved on—or so he whispered to me one night, before I dragged him into the hayloft and made love to him like it would be our last time.

It wasn't our last, but near to it.

My mother knew. I don't know how she couldn't have. But she never scolded me for my lack of matrimony, knowing what Saiyon was, and she herself had never married. Instead, she let me be happy. She, Zyzi, and Kata all let us be happy, and I loved Saiyon with all I had in me, with facets of myself I hadn't even realized I possessed, and those dangerous daydreams floated in and out of my mind, building up hope and sharpening it like a knife. At night, when I lay against him and told him all the things I never let anyone see, that hope scared me, because I knew how deeply it would cut, eventually.

I had asked Saiyon for one minute. He gave me one week.

Later, I would wonder if he'd somehow known that night would be our last. If that was why he made love to me so fervently, why he whispered poetry into my hair, why he worshipped me like I was the deity, not he. But my heart knew better. Because if Saiyon had known, he wouldn't have held on to me so tightly while I slumbered.

Because it was then, while in the depths of a dream, that a searing, blistering pain tore me apart.

I started awake like someone had shaken me, but I was alone in the courtyard, surrounded by cut tiles and dry mortar.

Clouds had filled the sky while I slept. Fortunately, I made it into the nearly finished cathedral before the rain fell.

CHAPTER 10

Consciousness slammed into me. My face was pressed to the floor—I'd leapt out of the bed. Searing agony pulsed through my middle, burning in an acidic ring around my torso. I could barely breathe. Breathing hurt. Not breathing hurt. The pain encompassed my thoughts, leaving little room for anything else. Never had something so excruciating racked my body. Even death had not been so unbearable.

I blinked back sweat and tears. Smelled smoke. *Fire.* Gritting my teeth, I lifted my head to witness flames licking the walls of the room. Consuming the bed. Rising toward the ceiling—

For a heartbeat, the pain dulled, giving way to shock. It was not fire that reached the ceiling, but a god, bright and burning. His skin was made of flame, and his hair billowed with its heat. His eyes glinted as diamonds.

His hands flew out, and the fire eating the room sucked into itself, leaving behind ash and smoke. His own splendor dimmed, like he was trying to hold it back for my sake but couldn't contain it all.

That's when I recognized him, and the agony lit anew.

Saiyon.

His glory had returned.

"Ai!" The door slammed open, and Zyzi's voice cut through the room. She collapsed beside me, blocking my view, nearly touching me but not. "Oh gods, oh gods," she whimpered. "Enera! Water!"

The water would do no more than any herbs Zyzi had with her. The burns were severe, coiling from my back, over my side, and just under my breasts. Where Saiyon's arm had been draped when his godhood returned.

I hissed between my teeth as a new wave of agony overtook me. Darkness edged my vision. *Please,* I begged my body. *Please wait. I need to think.*

The light brightened around me. Saiyon drew closer. His feet didn't touch the floor. I had a distinct impression that he *couldn't* touch the floor, or it would incinerate just as the walls and bed had.

"Stay back! You'll hurt her!" Zyzi snapped. "You've already hurt her!"

"No," I protested, but it came out as a mew.

A new hand touched my neck—my mother. She murmured things to Zyzi I couldn't discern. *Focus, Ai.* I tried to push my seared body from my thoughts. Craned to look at Saiyon.

The sight of him broke me.

He hung there, unable to interact with my mortal world, utter misery on his face. It warped his beauty so much that he no longer resembled the dozens of paintings, sketches, and sculptures I'd made of him. He looked as though he bore the burns himself. As though his own heart were pumping and bleeding out on the floorboards and he could do nothing to return it to its empty cavity. He reached forward, straining as if there were whole canyons between us.

And that made the convulsing wounds burn even more.

"Satto." Pree was suddenly in the charred bedroom, kneeling on one knee not far from me. "We must hurry."

New fire scraped my spine. I screamed. Zyzi grasped my shoulders to hold me still, and it was then I realized my mother was smearing medicine on my wound. The room was so bright from Saiyon alone; I peered down and saw the wreck of my skin, red and bubbling and charred. The sight of it churned bile up my throat.

"See to her," Saiyon whispered. "Please."

Within seconds Pree was beside me. Zyzi was hesitant to let him touch me, but neither did she want to touch *him*, so she moved aside.

Pree's hands clasped my shoulders, and blessed coolness flowed beneath my skin. It did not heal me, but it took the edge off my suffering. Gave me a chance to untangle my thoughts.

Even while he attended me, he said, "Satto."

I pushed Zyzi away. "It won't kill me," I groaned, but even with Pree's aid, I hurt so fiercely I half wished it would. I met Saiyon's eyes. The way he carried himself, his shoulders slack, his head bent, his spine curled, he looked like half the being I knew him to be. He did not meet my eyes.

"Look at me," I demanded.

He did. Were I in a better state, his brilliant visage would have awed me. But there was no room in my mind or broken body for awe.

"Take me with you," I ground out.

"Aija." My mother's ministrations froze.

I pressed on, trying so terribly hard to ignore my scorched skin. "Take me with you. Make me a star mother."

The guilt in Saiyon's countenance gave way to shock, even anger. "No."

He might as well have slapped me with his fiery hand. "How dare you—"

He hovered as close as he could without hurting us. "A star must die before another is made. And even if there were a need . . . you would *die.*" His voice was quiet, but it was hard as the granite in his Algeron Cathedral. "Second." He paused. The halo of celestial light surrounding him wavered. "Second, I would hurt you." His gaze shifted to the mess of my back. "I would hurt you more than I have. I cannot stomach that." He dimmed. "I could not bear for you to look at Me the way star mothers do. I could not bear to scar your spirit."

"But—"

"Aija." He said my name so gently it pulled tears into my eyes. "Of all the laws that bind Me, the compulsion to make mortals star mothers is the one I hate most."

My body trembled. From the burns, from my breaking heart, from my yearning soul. So quietly I could barely hear myself, I asked, "Do you not want me?"

He came closer, his heat, even though he restrained it, strong enough for Zyzi to back away. The coolness pouring from Pree's hands intensified until my teeth chattered with it. Enera held her ground. Saiyon crouched on air, still not touching the floor, despair tilting his eyes and lining his mouth. "I cannot have you."

A tear fell against my cheek.

"Every time I have loved, I have lost." His voice was as a dying ember, the last of its kin, sputtering in a sea of ash. "Such is My existence."

A sob curled up my throat. I reached for him, though my burns splintered when I did so. But I could not even get within a hand's width before his aura burned my fingertips. Instinct forced me to recoil.

Saiyon dropped his head. Delicate flecks of gold leaf wafted from his face. I noticed before he did. He caught one, floating on the air, and studied it just as he'd studied his hands the day he'd first awoken in my bed. Like it was something he'd never seen before.

Like he hadn't known he was capable of crying.

"Satto," Pree urged.

Saiyon withdrew, leaving a trail of golden flecks twirling on the air. Watching my face, he wound his fingers together, pulling his own light into a spiral until it solidified into a golden ring. He let it float onto my half-burnt nightstand.

"We will always be connected, Aija of Rozhan." His tone was dying, nostalgic, regretful—it was every tragic thing a poet could write, or an artist could paint. "I will always watch you. When you feel the Sun upon your face, know that it is Me. It will always be Me."

More tears poured down my face, and not because Pree had finally released me. "Saiyon, no. Please."

But what else could we do?

He bowed his head. A blinding flare left dark spots dancing in my eyes. When they cleared, Saiyon and Pree were gone.

PART 2

He traced his thumb down my spine and his lips down my neck, murmuring something in a language too beautiful to understand.

But it sounded like a promise.

CHAPTER 11

The Sun rose again.

It had risen every morning for three weeks. As if it had never left.

But he did leave. And I'd yet to feel his light, his warmth, shining down on me. I'd yet to step foot outside.

Saiyon had hurt me badly. In every way imaginable. It was not his fault. I did not blame him, even in the heights of my despair, my pain. Even when I dearly wanted to.

He had wanted to stay. He'd been ashamed of it.

And thinking of his radiant, anguished expression as he looked at me one last time before winking away felt like a newly forged sickle tearing me from collar to stomach, every time.

It hurt worse than the burns.

They were terrible burns. Utterly sickening. Burns I should have died from, but Pree's ministrations had healed them enough that I would survive, unless I succumbed to infection, but Zyzi had smothered me with so many herbs that I didn't believe such a thing possible. Still, the burnt skin was like cracked soil in a drought, red and blackened, scaly, oozing.

Our medicines and Zyzi's ministrations could do only so much. There was no balm for something like this. Saiyon must have known our limitations, because three days after he left, he sent Tyu.

"Tyu" is the closest I can get to pronouncing her name, which sounds more like a newborn lamb sneezing than anything else. Yet the simple name absolutely encapsulated her. She was a godling unlike any other I'd seen before. Only the length of my forearm, she had no face or humanoid body parts; she was a triangle atop which floated a circle head with a sideways crescent cut from it, like she wore half a halo. She was so thin she looked like a drawing. Her body felt like paper but sturdier. Her color was somewhere between pink, lavender, and white, all at once and yet . . . not. That was the closest I could get to describing her.

Tyu administered to me, flitting around the room, carrying things far larger than herself. Water, bowls, blankets. She would vanish for hours at a time and return with strange ointments and elixirs, always from a place I'd never heard of. When Zyzi was with me, she always insisted on carefully examining these gifts before allowing them to touch me, but the godling never expressed any impatience or haughtiness. When I asked after Saiyon, Tyu merely chirped, "I've been assigned to you, L'Aija."

Even after three weeks of bedridden healing, even with the aid of my family and Tyu, it still hurt to lie down. It hurt to do anything, even breathe. In truth, the only thing that kept me from crying constantly was the terrible ache that accompanied it. I'd ripped more than one scab giving in to despair.

I could move a bit now, but I had little motivation to rise from my pallet on my bedroom floor. My bed had been unsalvageable.

My family was patient with me, of course. They recognized the blood and pus that stained my bandages. That, they could and did handle. But they could not see, and likely did not understand, my inner torture. And in truth, were I in my mother's shoes, or my grandmother's shoes, I would not have understood it, either. Saiyon had not been with us long, and Aija of Rozhan was not a woman to go moon eyed over a man and pin all her happiness to him. She was not so weak.

And yet Saiyon was more than a man. I had truly bathed in the depths of love. Like I'd been a blind woman allowed to see for the first time, only to have the vibrancy of the world ripped away again. I had never felt so hollow. Not when my grandfather passed. Not when Edkar died. This . . . This was a pain I could not control. A pain I could not adapt to.

I was glad that Tyu did not have a face. Glad that there was one being on this farm that did not look at me with pity.

Even with the godling's dedication and the return of daylight, Zyzi stayed on, pulling my weight on the farm and treating me alongside Tyu. I blessed her for it. She, Enera, and Kata took turns tending to me, following Tyu's instructions, changing my bandages, cleaning my wounds, filling my belly with food and medicine.

The crops would survive, the oats most of all.

As the Sun climbed up the sky, I lifted my left hand to stare at the golden band on my middle finger, lined around the center with amber. If I twisted it, the band turned black. I kept it on amber. Saiyon had given it to me with the promise that we would always be connected. I didn't entirely understand, but if this ring was part of that, I would never take it off. Often, when I was left alone to rest, I whispered to it, wondering if he could hear me, feel me. I never heard or felt anything in return.

I blinked rapidly. I was so weary of tears. My eyes were always dry and swollen.

Tyu noticed and flew over with a handkerchief, which she held with invisible hands. I took it from her, and she perched on the foot of my pallet, tilting her head to the side like a parrot's.

"Visitor," she chimed seconds before a soft knock sounded at my door.

I knew everyone by their knocks; the quick, light, two-beat rap was Zyzi's. She stepped in, and I grabbed the edge of my makeshift mattress to haul myself up, gritting my teeth as my skin strained. Tyu flitted behind me, pushing on the base of my neck to help.

Zyzi eyed the godling before setting down her bowl of supplies and rushing over to assist. "You'll hurt yourself."

"Give me the dignity of sitting up." I drew in a slow breath. Slow, easy breaths hurt the least. "Tyu, some privacy, please."

The geometric godling winked out of existence.

Zyzi had been my confidante these past weeks. I'd told her every last detail about Saiyon, including my intimacy with him. My feelings for him, when I could think of words to put them into, which I often couldn't. My cousin and I had always been friends, but that wasn't the only reason I felt more comfortable speaking to her than my mother. She would go home, eventually, and take any judgments with her. In the meantime, she listened quietly, unassumingly. I thought it was out of pity, but then, I was truly pitiful.

"A rider came from Goatheir yesterday." Kneeling beside me, Zyzi gently unrolled a layer of bandaging. "The war is over."

My breath caught. "What?"

My mind went first to the heavens, so when Zyzi explained, it took me a moment to understand. "The darkness put a complete stop to the action on the battlefield. Many of the armies withdrew. I imagine they thought judgment was befalling them." She moved carefully as a piece of bandage stuck to a scab. "I'm sure details will follow soon enough, but when the Sun rose again, Belat and Rozhan agreed to a treaty. It's over."

I stared at my feet, processing the information. The war between Rozhan and Belat, the war that had driven me back to the farm, had raged for nearly six years. It was over.

I could go back to Algeron. Back to the capital.

The information passed over me like a cool wind I couldn't feel.

"The infection is all gone," Zyzi said as she gingerly poured calendula-steeped water over my back, catching it in a towel. "That's good."

I nodded dumbly, considering the life I had left behind. My recovery would not be easy, nor short. But the option was there. I could go back. Maybe even to my same apartment, my same studio. Back to the life I'd made for myself, where I had felt useful and valued—

Why wasn't I more excited at the prospect? Why did my heart feel as charred and dead as my skin, when only two months ago I would have leapt and sang at the opportunity?

"I'm going to wrap you a little tighter so you can lie down without chafing anything." With the touch of a feather, Zyzi smeared balm across my back—one of the many potions Tyu had brought in from elsewhere. It smelled terrible.

Maybe I just needed to heal first. I wasn't myself, as I was. I wasn't ready for good news.

She bound me snugly and helped me lie down. Slow, easy breaths. She set a book at my bedside, one I'd read a dozen times but hadn't picked up in years. I might be well enough now to hold it up.

She kissed my crown before departing.

I slept for a time. I looked forward to sleep, now that my dreams had ordered themselves. They'd been akin to nightmares the first week. Sometimes, I even had dreams that didn't involve Saiyon. I both cherished and despised those dreams.

I dozed on and off throughout the day—less than I did at first—and woke from another nap sometime in the evening. The room was empty; no family, no Tyu. I didn't have the pocket clock on me. I hadn't seen it since fire had eaten up my bed and left black scars on the wall. I wondered if my scars would look like those once my skin finished restitching itself. If it ever would.

Sunlight poured through my window, which was cracked open to let in the breeze. It stretched across my floor, highlighting charred lines in the wood. Dust motes twirled in its rays.

Carefully, I wiggled one leg out of my blankets, stretching it toward the Sun-warmed floorboards. I wore only my mother's dressing robe, something light and easy for tending my injuries. Pointed my toe. I could almost reach the edge of it—

The light brightened, like it did when a cloud moved away from the Sun. And yet it had already been bright.

I wanted to feel it on my skin. I needed to. He'd promised me he would be there when I did.

Grabbing my mattress again, I held my breath and sat up. The tighter bandaging helped with the strain. Scooting carefully, trying to keep my back straight, I pushed my foot into the band of light. Subtle warmth caressed my skin.

More damnable tears. I should stop drinking water altogether.

And yet I scooted a little more, letting the light climb up my ankle, my calf, my knee. I inched forward until I could reach my hand into it.

The hairs on every inch of my body stood on end. Not like I was cold, but . . .

Swallowing, I inched to the table that Tyu had dragged in from Kata's room. Winced as I gripped it and hauled myself upright, careful not to pull at my wounds.

There, in the distance, just past the corn, I saw a body of light.

A shiver coursed down me so suddenly it hurt. "Saiyon," I whispered. It had to be him. Who else could it be?

My body moved before my mind could think. I was in the hallway for the first time since Saiyon's touch blistered my skin. One hand to the wall, I stumbled for the front door. Heard my grandmother call, "Zyzi?" as I stumbled outside.

Pain shot up my right shoulder blade and rippled through my ribs as my breathing quickened. The Sun in the sky drooped toward the horizon. Could Saiyon be both here and there?

He was a god—surely he could do that and more.

I came around the corner of the house and dragged myself toward the cornfield, one arm wrapped around my middle in hopes I could hold my cracked skin together by sheer will. I didn't see the light anymore. I didn't see anything. Had I been hallucinating?

But I had *felt* him. Desperation took hold of me like a well-used drug. A thorn bit at my bare foot.

I kept moving. Into the corn rows, hissing when one batted at my burnt side. I moved as fast as I could, but it wasn't fast enough. I was limping. When had I started limping?

A searing ache burst from my shoulder blade, and I knew I'd torn something. Heat and wetness bloomed. Sweat beaded my forehead.

Keep going, keep going. I knew what I had seen. I hadn't lost my mind. Not yet. My left hand formed a fist around the ring he'd given me.

Finally, achingly, I emerged on the other side of the cornfield, faced with wild stretches of yellow-tinged prairie grass. I spun around, sending another jolt through my shoulder.

"No," I pleaded, that sickle digging in once more. "No, you were here. You were here." My eyes rose to the heavens, as close to his brilliant body as they could get before instinct made me look away. "You were here."

Did insanity slip into a mind so easily, like oil slicking the surface of a pan?

I dropped to my knees, feeling another tear beneath my breast. I set my jaw and tried to control my breathing, but a strangled sob pushed through, sending another flare across my torso. I pressed the meat of my palm between my teeth and bit down, trying to bear it.

You were here.

"Aija."

I started. Looked up.

He was there—nine, maybe ten feet from me, not quite touching the ground, less luminescent than I remembered him being. Like he wasn't entirely here. Like he was a ghost, a projection. I tried to push myself up, but an agonizing wave shocked across my back, filling my stomach with nausea, and I collapsed.

"Please. Please do not." His voice was so quiet, so strained, mirroring the desperation blazing in me like a fever. He reached a hand toward me, then dropped it. That hand was what had caused these injuries, however unintentional. "I should not have come." Again, quieter, "I should not have come."

As if to punctuate his words, I heard a faint rumble of thunder, though there were no storm clouds in the sky. Was a battle underway even now? Was he losing it to see me?

"Why, then?" I pleaded, hating the tears in my voice.

He seemed so small. How could a paramount being seem so small?

"I—" His voice was hushed like the rustling of wheat, barely discernible. "I had to know you were well." His eyes dropped to my torso. "As well as you could be, after I—"

I tried again to stand. Hot agony stabbed through the burns. Saiyon begged me to stop. But I dug my feet into the Earth and forced myself upright. Paused as light-headedness encompassed me. Moved my tongue around to moisten my mouth. Blinked perspiration from my eyes.

"It isn't over, your war." The words were mostly breath.

He shook his head. "It will never truly be over. I . . . I cannot stay." He glanced at himself—at the Sun in the sky. "It weakens Me when I divide like this." He swallowed. "But Tyu is tending you . . . ?"

I nodded.

He relaxed a hair. "Good. Good." He turned to go—turned with his shoulders, but his feet didn't follow. Like he'd been rooted in place. Like he really, truly, did not want to leave me.

My heart felt raw, like a butcher had removed it, sanded it, and shoved it back into its swollen cavity. A spark, a piecemeal idea that had until now tempted me only in slumber, began to surface in my thoughts. I pushed it forward, for he was leaving, and I did not know when, if ever, I would see his face again.

"Saiyon."

He looked at me like a beaten dog. A bright, majestic, beautiful hound.

I managed a half step forward. "Do you love me?"

His light dimmed, a bonfire threatened by rain. "I love you, Aija of Rozhan."

The thunder roiled once more.

The sickle pierced deep.

I thought of Saiyon's chains, which I couldn't see in his current form. I thought of my painting, the shapes of which had limned my dreams night after night. In the painting, I'd broken his chains, but that was only a fancy. Saiyon's bonds could not be broken, least of all by me.

But was there another way?

"You can't be mortal." It was a fact. He could be little else than what the universe had made him. I kneaded my mind like bread dough. Sweat stung my burns. It took monumental effort to stay on my feet.

I was mortal. I was *changeable*. What was mankind if not ever changing?

"And I will not be denied," I pressed. Even in sick agony, my grandmother's stubbornness thrived in me. "So *I* will become immortal."

His face opened like that of a child's. I'd shocked him. I'd shocked myself, though the forced humility of my physical state masked it. His diamond eyes softened for a brief moment before drooping to mirror that expression that was burned into my mind, the one he'd worn right before he'd flashed away to Pree, abandoning me in my half-burnt room.

A look of sorrow. Of defeat.

"To obtain immortality"—he floated closer until I felt the heat of his presence on my face—"is not possible. If it were, men would have achieved it before."

I refused to be moved. I stayed the blade of that sickle with my hands, refusing to let it dig further. "But the star mother, Ceris—"

"Even she is not immortal." Ember red coursed over his face and chest. "And her story is not repeatable."

Another rumble, a little closer. We both looked up. Both felt the threats time laid on Saiyon's shoulders.

"But if I were," I pressed, "I could touch you. I could live up there." I glanced skyward.

For a moment, I thought he would not answer. Then, gruffly, he said, "Immortality would change your body, so yes, but—"

"I won't give up so easily."

He looked so mournful it brought new tears to my eyes. "Do not sacrifice for Me, Aija. You need to live your life, live—"

"I don't want that life," I spat, my words made venomous by the pain lancing my skin and soaking my bandages. "Not if you're not in it."

His brow lowered, and he turned away. "If I could . . . I would change you, Aija. I would give you a body unimpeded by time. Or flame. But it is not in My power to do so. I would . . ." He paused. Perhaps even gods' throats swelled with emotion, for it edged his next words. "I would scour the universe for the answer. But if I abandon this war, My people will fall, and all of mortality will fall with them. Even if we are victorious . . . by then, it will be too late."

I strained against a thorny lump in my throat. "Then I will do it myself."

His countenance tensed like I'd stabbed him. "You cannot."

"You are a fool, Saiyon."

His gaze widened. I wondered, later, how often someone dared to insult the Sun God.

Yet I had not known him as such.

"I have never lived the way I lived when you were here," I croaked. I took a step forward, but it was more of a stumble, and I was forced to shy back from the power of his aura. He shifted away instantly. "I have never given myself so fully to anyone or anything, including my art. And if love like that isn't worth sacrificing for, what is?"

He shrunk before me, flames of blue passing over his limbs. "Aija." His voice was so taut, so weak. "Aija. I cannot do for you what you wish to do for Me. I am begging you to stop. To heal. For yourself, if not for Me. You must . . . forget Me. Find your own happiness."

But I pursed my lips. Shook my head.

Saiyon had said he'd loved and lost. Such was his existence.

He did not understand how sore of a loser I was.

A soft whistle, almost like a wind chime, zoomed over the cornfields. Tyu swept before me, her strange, flat head bowing. "Forgive me, Satto."

No more explanation than that.

A fourth rumble sounded overhead, but this time Saiyon froze. Cursed—or what sounded like a curse. It was not in my language. "Aija, please." He turned back, ignoring the godling. Without quite looking at me, he said, "I should not have come. Tyu, take care of her. She is your queen until further notice."

Tyu bowed even lower. Then, like before, Saiyon flashed away in a burst of brilliant light.

My knees buckled, and I fell to the Earth, gasping as pain radiated from my shoulder. I licked my lips and tasted sweat. My chest heaved, despite the strain of it. Tyu squeaked and flew circles around me, her touch featherlight as she examined my reopened wounds, as though she could see them through the robe and bandages.

I didn't know how I'd get back to the house, let alone accomplish *immortality*. But I was no quitter. And I was no liar, either.

I would find a way to heal both our scars.

My breathing was just starting to even out when a rustling caught my ear. Peering over, I saw Sai'ken, the horned godling who had fought the dragon in these very fields. Tyu hovered away from me, giving him space. Kneeling beside me, he gave me a sad, faint smile.

"He asked me to be His hands," he murmured, and lifted his palms.

Gaping at him for a moment, I nodded, and the godling carefully pulled me into his arms, holding me as if he knew exactly where my burns started and ended, carrying me as if I were a porcelain doll. I slumped against him, my energy spent, as he cradled me through the corn, Tyu flitting about nervously but keeping her distance.

"Sai'ken."

He glanced down at me.

"How does one become immortal?"

He shook his head. "I do not think it's possible, dear one. Even my kin and I are not eternal."

I closed my eyes, trying to focus more on the swaying of his gait than the erupting agony of my injuries. I considered what he'd said for half a second, at best.

Surely nothing was impossible. Surely the powers that sustained the gods in the heavens and made the Earth Mother turn could extend life and robustness to a mortal. Surely we were not all born here merely to die.

I would find a way. Somehow, I would find a way to hold Saiyon in my arms, to claim the love he had given me. I would accomplish it. I would succeed.

Even if I had to do it alone.

"I never realized how cold I was, before you."

CHAPTER 12

For the first few months, I still watched for Saiyon.

I knew, deep down, he could not come. He was not of my world, and war consumed his own. He'd stated clearly his desire for me to move on. At times, I agreed with him—he shouldn't have returned. But most of the time, I was too one minded to dwell on the rekindled hope that laced my internal and external pain like acid.

I had so much healing ahead of me, especially since I had aggravated my injuries in my run. While abed, I pestered Tyu for information. Asked her about immortality. Asked her about the worlds she'd seen. Asked her for lore and stories about immortal creatures.

Like Sai'ken, she didn't know much. She might have hidden truths from me, but . . . Tyu seemed too naïve for something like that. After all, she was only sixty-four years old. Which, I had learned, was very young for a godling.

So I leaned on Zyzi. She scribed letters for me without complaint, though I had yet to reveal my intentions to her.

"Write to the head priest in Algeron," I said. "He owes me a favor. Ask him for transcriptions of the sacred scrolls.

"Write to the scholar in Mayon. Tell him my name, and that I can give him an eyewitness account of the heavenly war, if he's interested. I will trade information for information.

"Write to your mother in Goatheir and ask if I might borrow her family copy of the scriptures. It's an older edition than Kata's."

I pored over Kata's tome while I waited for responses. And however much it chafed, I stayed in bed, took all my medicines, and held back complaints when Tyu poked and prodded me, or when my grandmother's hand was too harsh in applying topical treatments. I had to heal as quickly as possible. I needed to be myself again. I needed to work.

I did not write to my landlord in Algeron, or to my studio, or to my fellow artisans. I made no plans whatsoever to return to the capital.

My sketchbook quickly filled with notes and transcribed scripture. I received Zyzi's family scriptures first, and compared them to Kata's, noting any changes, particularly anything that spoke of gods, of immortals, of eternal life. I cross-referenced everything with my grandmother, who was the most familiar with the religious texts. The questions made her cross—she still hadn't reconciled that the stranger who'd taken shelter in her home, who had worked the farm, was her god. It had made her jumpy and quicker to anger. Still, she approved of my renewed interest in religion, and at least the questions gave us something to discuss, though she was at a loss for words around me lately, knowing the connection I'd had with the Sun.

I heard back from the head priest at the capital next. He sent me transcriptions for half the scrolls and promised the remainder after winter. I studied them relentlessly, until even my mother complained I was not resting enough and eating up all their candles.

I received the last of the transcriptions in the spring, as well as correspondence from the scholar. By this time I was on my feet again, writing letters myself, exchanging information. I asked the scholar for everything he knew about star mothers, godlings, and immortality. I'm sure he thought I was a crazed woman, but when I sent him accounts of the moon's attack on my home—leaving out Saiyon's involvement—from both Zyzi and Enera, he caved and posted copies of his own research, though only after making me sign an agreement that I would not publish any of it myself.

I had no interest in publishing.

In his notes, I discovered a name familiar to me: Ceris Wenden, of Endwever. A name that had passed Saiyon's lips more than once. The star mother who had lived. The priest had three separate accounts of her story that conflicted with one another, dates that were seven hundred years apart, as well as a drawing of a tapestry of her lineage. While Ceris's tale was interesting, Saiyon was correct—I could not follow her path, whichever of the stories proved true.

I networked through these men, bullying their contacts as best I could with the written word. By summer, the scholar stopped responding to me. Zyzi finally went home to see to her wisewoman duties, leaving me to my normal routines—the tasks assigned to me before the Sun ever winked out. By fall, I'd exhausted everything I could glean from Algeron.

"Time heals all wounds" is a popular expression, and one that my mother had shared with me on numerous occasions. I was not sure how I felt about proving it wrong. About being as flayed and fresh a year after Saiyon's departure as I was the night it happened.

Saiyon's words in the field haunted me: *To obtain immortality is not possible. If it were, men would have achieved it before.*

I started from the beginning, in case there was something in the scriptures, scrolls, and research I had missed. And I did it outside in the cooling autumn air, where I could feel the Sun on my face. I *did* feel him in it, but like he was very far away, and I peered through a spyglass that barely distinguished him from the prairie. But he was there, and sometimes, though it may have been only my imagination, I felt the amber-limned ring on my finger warm.

Soon enough, when the leaves had just begun tinting and harvest was nearly complete, Zyzi returned with her mother to visit, to spend some quality time with family before winter made traveling difficult.

She found me on a milking stool outside the barn, the Sun warm on my face as it made its slow descent into night, papers arranged all around me. Though I was able-bodied again, Tyu had not left my side. And while I tried not to be dependent on the godling, I was grateful for her presence. Not only for her friendship and frankness, but because she was a symbol of Saiyon. A symbol of his love, his worry. His hands, in a sense.

Zyzi's family, of course, knew nothing, and believed I'd been hurt in the bandit attack. My cousin had spun a story of a lantern being thrown at me by one of the thieves. The burns, she had said, were from the oil. And so, whenever Danika was around, Tyu stayed out of sight.

Now, the dainty godling perched on the handle of the butter churn, twirling atop it like a child. Zyzi crouched before me and said nothing for a long while. When she picked up my notes, I did not stop her.

Because I needed help.

Long minutes passed before she spoke. "Why do you care about this, Aija?"

I glanced up at her, frowning.

Sighing, she set down the book. "You mean to chase Him."

"I do not need to chase what is already mine." I turned a page of transcriptions.

Zyzi laughed. "You mean to own our god?"

Our minds must have connected, for we both glanced to the ring on my finger. We had both been in that room after Saiyon's glory returned, leaving me cracked and bleeding on the floor. She'd heard the exchange between him and me. And she knew everything else, too.

Swallowing down a lump in my throat, I said, "Why would the universe create us so differently, and in such absolutes? What is there to be *gained* from it?"

My cousin shook her head. "I don't know. Tiers, classes, castes . . . they seem eternal."

"They are not law." And I knew the laws. "Surely the gap can be crossed. He cannot cross it, so I must."

Zyzi waited until I met her eyes. "When was the last time you drew?"

Pressing my lips together, I took up my sketchbook and flipped back seven pages, to a tiny portrait of my mother in the corner. She'd been worrying after me constantly, but I couldn't let guilt distract me.

On the opposite page was a similar drawing of Saiyon.

"Is this all worth it?" Zyzi gestured to the copious notes. "All of this, for a *man*?"

I closed the book. "Do you really think that's what this is? An infatuation?"

She didn't answer.

Setting my work aside, I leaned onto my knees. "I'm nearly thirty-six years old, Zyzi. I've been married once already, and I didn't love him. Saiyon . . . he reached into eternity and wrenched my soul back into mortality at the cost of his own being. Is it so much to ask that I read a few books on the subject?"

She shifted. "You'll do more than read books, Ai. I know you."

Tyu's twirling paused. Although she didn't have eyes, I felt her regard me.

That drew a small smile from me. "There is . . . such a sadness about him. A weight that never leaves his shoulders."

"'Every time I have loved,'" Zyzi whispered, "'I have lost.'"

It shocked me that she remembered his words, spoken in my smoldering bedroom. Had they struck her the way they'd struck me? "'Such is My existence,'" I finished.

We sat in silence a long moment before she said, "Chains."

I studied her face.

"I saw them in your painting, in the shed," she confessed. "Chains around Him, broken in anger. It's your most bizarre creation . . . and yet the most beautiful, too." She shrugged. "I haven't seen the ones in Algeron."

The lump returned. "Thank you," I squeezed around it.

She picked blades of grass from the Earth, one at a time. I watched her for a few minutes before gathering my notes.

"There is," she said, but her voice cut off, like she didn't want the words to come out. I paused, wondering if she had come to berate me, or to pass on concern from her family in an attempt to straighten me out. "There's a rumor. And it's *only* a rumor." She glared at me as though I had already done some unspeakable thing. "My brothers mentioned it after they returned from that hunting trip, after He fell. Of . . . Of a godling that lives in the Furdowns."

I had not expected that. My spine straightened tick by tick, pulling on the tight skin hidden by my dress. Since my recovery, I always made sure to dress and bathe alone, for I knew the sight of the hideous malformation on my torso brought my mother to tears. I suspected it did the same to Kata, but she was far better at hiding her emotions.

"A godling," I repeated, and Tyu flitted over, landing on my knee with the weight of a butterfly.

The way Zyzi nodded made her head seem heavier than Vine's. "It's only a rumor . . . but a rumor I have heard from more than one source. All this correspondence . . . it doesn't go unnoticed. People talk."

I worked my mouth but didn't reply. *Another godling.* I had asked Sai'ken and Tyu about immortality. Neither of them had information, but they were creatures of Saiyon's court, not the Earth Mother's. This godling might be able to fill in the blanks in my research. I had learned everything I could from mortal men. Perhaps I needed to seek knowledge by celestial means.

"Then I must go," I said.

Zyzi winced. "I knew you would say that."

Tyu leapt off my knee and hovered in midair. "I do not advise traveling!"

Zyzi tore a blade of grass into smaller and smaller pieces. "Ai, it's only a rumor . . . and winter is coming."

"The Furdowns are south. The farther south I go, the warmer it gets. I could make it in four days if I travel hard."

Tyu buzzed with anxiety.

Zyzi glanced up at me. Glared at me. Sighed. "If *we* travel hard."

The offer gave me pause. "I couldn't pull you away from your family, Zyzi. Or your wisewoman duties."

"And I can't let you travel to the Furdowns unaccompanied."

"I'll have Tyu."

The godling chirped.

Zyzi tilted her head and frowned, like I might as well have claimed the company of a rag doll.

I clasped my cousin's shoulder. "Thank you, but I know the way. It's been a while, but—"

"I'm coming," she pressed.

Her insistence buoyed me, but at the same time my stomach sank. Glancing at my notes, I murmured, "You've already done so much for me."

"Aija." She waited for me to meet her eyes to continue. "You paid my bride price. Do you not realize how much *I* owe *you?*"

A shiver coursed through my shoulders. Words abandoned me.

Years ago, shortly after Edkar passed, Zyzi had written to me in Algeron, desperately detailing the struggle she was having with her family, her mother, especially. Her parents wanted her to marry and had a couple of suitors in mind. Marriage was Zyzi's utmost nightmare. Her studies would be ended, she'd be taken from Goatheir, and she'd be bound to a man she could never love, for the Earth Mother had made her different than those around her, and love such as that was abhorrent to Zyzi. Not knowing where else to turn, she'd reached out to me.

I'd traveled harder than I ever had before, moved by her plea and the kinship we'd shared since childhood. I'd arrived just as Zyzi's marriage contract was being set, and argued with her family *and* mine for two days before signing it myself and giving over the entirety of my and Edkar's savings to my aunt and uncle—the cost of Zyzi's hand. And while the signature held no legal standing in Rozhan, the price had been paid in coin and in tears, and Zyzi's parents finally loosened their white-knuckled fists, allowing her to live her life however she saw fit.

We had not spoken of it in years.

I swallowed, my throat thick, and nodded. "Though I can't take Vine from my family," I squeezed out. "So perhaps six days."

Tyu flashed bright pink. "You're not ready, L'Aija! You've been outside too long already. Let me see you back to bed—"

"Hush," Zyzi snapped, and a glimmer of blue coursed over Tyu. To me, she said, "I want you to know where I stand."

I watched her, waiting.

Zyzi stood. Brushed off her pants. "I don't like this. Any of this. I think you're pursuing a lost cause and that you'll only be more hurt for it."

An echo of pain, of that scythe scraping my skin, rang through me. "Then it would be better for me to hear the same from this godling. Perhaps he will give me the permission I need to give up."

I would never give up.

I sensed Zyzi's thoughts warring with one another. Her arms tensed and relaxed. Her cheek flexed as she ground her jaw. I waited, patient, hope burning.

"I don't understand your drive," she went on, barely loud enough for me to hear. "But you helped me when you didn't understand mine. That's why I told you." She planted hands on her hips. "And that is why I will go with you. On one condition."

I fought against a smile tugging on my lips. "Anything."

"*You* get to tell the others. I won't deal with them, least of all Kata."

I grinned so broadly my cheeks ached, and I realized I did not remember the last time I had smiled.

No one was happy about Zyzi's and my sudden trip, our mothers least of all. As promised, I took the brunt of the scolding and explaining, but I bent to none of it. Kata, Enera, and my aunt knew I would not bend, but they would make for poor family if they did not at least try to dissuade me. Tyu's accompaniment did little to assuage their concerns.

We took a day to make our preparations, Tyu buzzing in my ear the entire time, pleading with me not to go.

"It isn't safe! You're still hurt!"

"I've been doing my chores for two months now, Tyu. Walking and lifting and shoveling." I shoved a pair of undergarments into my bag.

Tyu landed on the lip of the bag, as though she could keep it shut, but the fabric barely bent under her weight. "Satto will not be pleased!"

Bending so my face was level with her, I said, "Then why don't you go tell him?"

She squawked and flew two circles around the room before landing on my shoulder. "I do not report directly to Him, L'Aija! I could only tell one of His stewards."

I shoved a skirt in. "I'm not stopping you."

She flashed lavender, her papery body wilting. "Do you not require my assistance anymore?"

I paused and looked at her. "No, I don't."

A hint of blue passed over her half halo.

"But I want your company," I added, and she brightened. "We may disagree, but you've been a good friend to me. I . . ." I paused, sighed. "Perhaps I do need some help. Will you help me?"

She shimmered, considering. Saiyon had sent her to care for me as he couldn't—her presence alone reminded me of that. Reminded me of the sound of his voice, his touch, his love. I ran a thumb over the golden ring. I *didn't* want Tyu to leave. And surely she would have a better chance tracking a godling than Zyzi or I.

"You are my queen," she chirped. And it was decided.

The next morning, Zyzi and I headed south on foot, with Tyu nestled in my hair like a flower. I would have liked at least one man to accompany us, to guard us against the dangers of the country, but we had none but he who shined down from above, warming my dark hair and skin and lighting my way. I wondered where his face was turned. I wondered if he knew, and what he would have said. As far as I knew, Tyu had *not* tattled on me, and I wasn't sure if that pleased or saddened me. Even if my journey riled Saiyon, perhaps it would tempt him to come down and scold me again.

At least then I could see his face.

But that was a selfish thing to want. I thought of Sai'ken, Pree, and Kalanakai. Three soldiers entrenched in his war. Did I want them, and others like them, to perish, all so I could see the being I loved? A being I couldn't even touch?

Besides, Saiyon might not come. Perhaps he already knew this was a pointless venture. He was the most powerful being in the universe—at least, the fraction of it I was familiar with. And if he couldn't . . .

I tried not to dwell on it. I tried to choose hope.

I spoke to him sometimes, when Zyzi hiked off-path to search for herbs or had yet to rise in the mornings. When Tyu flew ahead to scout the road. He couldn't reply, but I spoke to him anyway.

"I've been to the Furdowns twice," I murmured to the dawn. "Once as a child and once as an adolescent. My grandfather would hunt there every fall. They'd take a wagon, he and his friends from the village. I imagine you've never seen that forest from down here. They're lush and piney and thick."

I wanted to paint a picture of the trees in the snow, when I returned. The only art supplies I'd brought with me were a sketchbook and some pencils, and I needed to preserve those in case I needed to remember something or take notes.

"I miss you," I whispered on the fourth day of travel, when we were close. I cleaned up breakfast, and Zyzi was putting out the fire. I touched my sternum through my clothes, tracing bumps of uneven flesh. "Do you still think of me, Saiyon, or am I really doing all of this for naught?"

His beams felt warmer, suddenly. I feared it was only my own imagining until Zyzi wiped her forehead and said, "It's damn hot for mid fall."

I smiled, and clung to hope.

Later that day, Zyzi pointed ahead of us, to a sparse copse of trees bordered with pale stone. It was slightly off course, but we ventured toward it anyway, curious. Even when we reached it, I didn't recognize the structure. A small circle had been built of pale rock among the trees, utilizing two boulders that looked to have already been here. They were unmortared and seemed recently laid.

Tyu hissed, a sound I'd never heard her make before.

"What?" I asked.

She flashed a deep purple. "They built this for the usurper."

Zyzi stiffened at the other end of the copse, touching a carving in one of the trees. "This is a shrine to the moon."

I pinched my lips together. Zyzi had mentioned that even in Goatheir, men's hearts had turned during the darkness. I couldn't entirely blame them; when all the world was falling apart, it seemed wise to reach out to the god—or demigoddess—most likely to listen to your beseeching.

But the Sun had returned, and—

"These prints aren't old," Zyzi added, coming closer to me. She pointed at footprints in the soil.

I swallowed. "Best we be on our way before Sunset." Those who had built this shrine might be peaceful, but I wasn't eager to find out. Not with the Sun's ring on my finger and his servant perched on my shoulder.

We said nothing more about the discovery, although we stayed up around our campfire later than usual once night settled, watching the shadows and listening for other travelers. Fortunately, none disturbed us.

Outside that small adventure, we trekked hard, Zyzi complaining only once when she got a blister on her heel, which Tyu quickly mended, and arrived in the Furdowns after a six-day journey.

Pines and shaggy firs composed the majority of the forest. Many had begun shedding needles and cones in a variety of sizes and colors. Broad, ancient branches provided shade from the Sun, which saddened me, but I had work to do, so I trekked on without hesitation. Tyu flitted ahead like a hummingbird, and I couldn't tell if she was scenting like a hound or merely curious about the wood. Before she'd been assigned to me, she'd spent little time on the Earth Mother, and many things here were still unfamiliar to her.

It took nearly two hours before she returned and said, "There is magic here." And pointed east.

We'd packed ribbons, string, and painted rocks to mark our way. There were a few paths through the wood. We followed them the first two days, heeding Tyu's direction. Soon we stepped off-path, ever searching, scanning the sentinel trunks and sniffing the air. Here and there, we left offerings and prayers at upturned roots.

By our fourth day of searching, I began calling out for him, or her, or it—whatever the godling might be. Our food reserves were limited, and I feared having to turn back home empty handed, driven by hunger. We never separated—that would have been foolish—but we searched restlessly from Sunup to Sundown, sometimes fetching kindling and firewood in the dark.

By day seven, the last day we could linger if we wanted full bellies on the return trip, I heard rustling in a nearby bush after Zyzi finished a third round of worship songs, hoping to draw the godling to us. I'd been fooled twice already, both by deer, but this time the creature that emerged was not a common animal.

It walked on all fours, with pigeoning legs and pointed toes. Its heavily armored back was rigged with uneven spikes, all of which looked like otherworldly glass. It had a short, stumpy tail and brilliant ruby eyes. It only came up to my mid thigh.

It looked nothing like Pree, Sai'ken, or Kalanakai, but it was undoubtedly a godling.

My heart leapt. "Hello, my name is Aija." Names had the power to dismantle fear. They made strangers more real. "I've come seeking—"

The thing growled at me and charged.

Instinct took over. I darted away, dropping my heavy pack. The creature's short horns banged into the pan within when it struck. I bolted around a tree, trying to keep something between me and it. Tyu lunged for it with the bravery of someone ten times her size, but the creature slammed into her, knocking her into a nest of pine needles. I choked on a shriek, but the animal didn't continue on my trail. Instead, it spied Zyzi some thirty paces away. She'd drawn the knife on her belt and gripped it in pale-knuckled hands.

"W-We just want to talk," she stuttered.

But I had the distinct impression this godling was not intelligent, and my hopes shattered around me as fear pumped through my veins. My gaze flashed to Tyu, whose colors shifted from white to pink to white as she zipped around us, trying to distract the godling as it stalked Zyzi, but the creature disregarded her just as it ignored the dragonflies darting overhead. We were in a small glade, and Zyzi had little to dash behind, but she slowly sidestepped toward a pine. That wouldn't save her, though; I needed to think fast.

A tree with limbs low enough to climb was ten paces from me. If I could draw the creature's attention and gain altitude, I could give Zyzi a chance to run.

Unless this thing could climb, but I had little time to debate.

After tying a knot in my skirt, I bolted for the low-limbed tree. "I'm here! Get *me*!"

"Ai!" Zyzi barked.

But the godling spun, red eyes locking on to me. It gave chase.

It was *fast*. I didn't know if I could climb swiftly enough to—

My toe caught on a root. I fell forward, elbows and knees slamming into the Earth.

Zyzi screamed. I looked back as the godling leapt—

And a staff soared downward into the center of its skull. The monster puffed into slate-and-ruby smoke and dissipated into the air.

I rolled over and gaped at the staff's wielder. Godling. He was short, perhaps a head shorter than myself, with skin the shade of dying leaves after the color had left them. He had a flat skull; a long, protruding nose that bent soundly in the middle; and long, leathery ears on either side of his head similar in shape to his nose. His back had a great hump in it, but his body appeared to be molded that way, as opposed to weakened into it.

Through a dry mouth I managed to say, "Th-Thank you," and crept toward Tyu, who alighted on a nearby root.

Surely *this* was the godling from the rumors.

Zyzi, knife still in hand, approached with caution from behind. I scooped Tyu into my hands and picked myself off the ground inch by inch, treating this creature as a hart that might startle at any sudden movement.

The godling's eyes found Tyu first, then me; his gaze was glassy and reminded me of a turtle's. "Were. It. Anyone. Else," he said slowly, overenunciating each word, "I would. Not have. Answered."

I stood fully, allowing Tyu to perch on my shoulder. "Anyone else?"

He dipped his head toward my hand. I lifted my ring, still limned amber.

I swallowed. "He sent you?"

The godling shook his head like it was mounted on a rusted nail. "No. But only. One special. To Him. Would wear. Such a thing." He tilted his head to Tyu. "And keep. Such. Company."

I wondered if Saiyon had known others might cater to me if I wore the token he'd left behind.

I began to lower myself to kneeling, Zyzi doing the same, but the godling waved his hand. "No."

I straightened. "I've come seeking answers. Will you help me?"

He glanced to my ring again. "I will. Listen."

Zyzi, giving the godling berth, walked around to my side. "What is your name, holy one?"

"Ist."

"Ist," I repeated. "Thank you, again, for helping us."

He nodded toward where the creature had perished. "Little. Gremlins bored. With the. Passing of. Summer." He shrugged, which seemed a monumental effort. "I only. Mean to. Rest. Until. The time of. My passing."

Tyu hummed in my ear.

"Passing?" I repeated. Godlings, while celestial, were not mortal. "Might I ask how long you've walked the Earth Mother, great one?"

"Great. One." He released a puff of air meant to be a laugh. "No. Not great." He rolled his head to one side, cracking his neck. "I have. Passed. Eight. Hundred. Twenty. Four years. I have seen. Many. Mortals. But none. With such. Adornment." He blinked, eyelids like slugs. "What is. It. That. You've come. To ask? Hollering. Through the wood. Like children."

My cheeks pinched with a smile. "I've come to ask you about immortality." I raised both hands to stall his response. "I do not seek it for power, only so I might share life with my beloved. The one who gave me this ring."

His eyes widened a little, another sluggish blink closing over them. "Beloved."

I nodded. Licked my lips. "He fell from the sky near my farm. And now he cannot touch me. Nor can he leave his war. *Her* war."

Ist adjusted the grip on his staff. "Mmm. Yes. The sky. Was dark. For long. Interesting. He should take. With a. Mortal." His gaze roamed from me to Zyzi. "Two lovers?"

Zyzi's hands sliced through the air as if to destroy the assumption. "No. I'm just . . . helping."

Ist nodded. "But. Immortality. Is not just. Found. In a. Forest." He did not walk as slowly as he spoke, thankfully. Digging his cane into the Earth, he began moving west, and Zyzi and I fell in step beside him. Tyu regarded him with interest but remained quiet.

"All I know of the celestial realm is from scriptures and scrolls." My statement rang more like a plea. "I know you are not immortal, but you've spoken with those who are, have you not? You've lived upon the Earth Mother. Surely you know some—"

"Earth Mother. Sleeps."

I nodded. "Of course. But I have tried for a year to find a way to him." I glanced up through the canopy. "He cannot come to me."

"No. He. Cannot. Must not," Ist agreed. He paused and looked at me. "I believe. Your tale. I see. Your scars."

My hands shot to my midsection. I was fully clothed.

"We see what mortals cannot," Tyu whispered, sounding ashamed. "I have always been able to see the marks, even when not tending to them. They are etched on your soul."

I wasn't sure how to digest that.

Zyzi sidestepped to retrieve my bag.

The godling sighed, and his deep exhale seemed to make him shorter. "I have. Been. Around a long. Time. I do not . . ." He paused, working his mouth. "But maybe."

Hope sparked. *Maybe* was a lot further than I'd gotten before.

He cocked his head to the other side, eliciting another *pop* from his neck. "The only. Way I. Can see. It being. Done is. Bartering. With those. Dark ones."

Tyu shuddered and tucked herself behind my ear. Her tiny body was cold, and her touch raised gooseflesh on my neck.

"Dark ones?" Zyzi croaked.

"Demons." He looked pointedly at her, then at me. "Wayward. Creatures. That feed. Off. The energy. Of. Celestial beings. Like. Myself. The. Earth Mother. And her." He gestured toward Tyu. "But. They are. Protective. Of. Their stolen. Powers. Will only. Barter. With. Clever. Deals that. Never. Favor. The other. Party. Or so. I think." Scratching the side of his large nose, he added, "I do. Not. Particularly. Associate. With demons. Once but. Many chords. Of time have. Played since then."

"I've never seen any," Tyu whispered, and I would not have heard her were she not pressed up against my ear, "but I've heard tales."

Zyzi grasped my arm. "*Demons*, Ai." Her expression was slack, her eyes bright with fear. "Even *He* isn't worth demons."

My chest constricted like my burns were fresh. "But—"

"*Dark ones,*" Zyzi hissed, "never make deals that favor the other party. It isn't safe." She looked to Ist. "Tell her it isn't safe."

He blinked. "Have I. Not. Said so?"

"Tell her again," Zyzi pleaded.

Ist rolled his shoulders, issuing more *pops*. "I. Would not. Recommend. It. They are. Dark ones."

"Not safe," Tyu said, loud enough for Zyzi to hear.

I felt made of wood, lit hours ago, crumbling beneath devouring flame. All this way to find a godling, one who would actually answer my questions, only to be told my one hope was too dangerous to contemplate?

I couldn't bring myself to speak, so Zyzi said, "Are there more of those things around here? Those . . . gremlins?"

Ist shook his head. "Not. For now."

Zyzi tugged at my arm. "Ai. Aija. Let's go home. Please."

Chewing the inside of my lip, I sought out Ist's face again, hoping to find encouragement there. But his expression was blank, his large eyes matter-of-fact, and I let Zyzi pull me and Tyu from the forest without protest.

By nightfall, I'd pieced my shattered hopes together with the glue of my own stubbornness. Worked out my thoughts. Caressed the ring on my finger.

As far as I could see, I had only one option.

I put extra wood on the fire beside which Zyzi and Tyu slept, letting it burn bright. I needed to be able to find them when I emerged. Then, fashioning a torch, I crept back into the wood, keeping an ear out for predators. I was about half a mile in when I called for him.

"Ist. *Ist.* Please come to me. I must speak with you."

He did not make me wait long. I'd called for him for less than a quarter hour before his shadow emerged between the trees, his eyes luminescent as a predator's. Eyes that, for the briefest moment, made me think of Saiyon's, which only bolstered my decision.

"How do I find them?" I asked, keeping my voice low, though I doubted anything but nesting songbirds and mice would overhear. "These demons?"

He walked in a three-step pattern toward me, his shuffling feet plus his staff. "You still. Wish to see. The dark ones."

"Where can I find those who would make the fairest deals?"

Ist hummed deep in his throat. "I don't know. If any. Trustworthy. Dark ones. Exist. But then. Again. I don't. Know many. Of their ilk."

"But you know where I can find them. And you know they might be able to make me immortal."

He clicked his tongue. "Find them. Yes. All things. On the Earth. Mother. Leave an. Impression. On Her," he said. "Her body. Is formed.

By them. By us. We must. Follow the. Patterns. They leave." He considered for a moment, rubbing his flat chin. "If any. On Her face. Can do it. I would think . . . yes."

I closed the space between us. Hunched to his eye level. "Ist. Please. Come with me. Be my guide."

He shook his head. My burns itched. "I only. Want. To die. In peace. Here. In my wood. Mine. Is not. The way. Of mortals."

Hope and desperation pressed against my skin, trying to escape through my pores, making me feel at once too full and too light. "What is the point of dying alone in this dark place? I will do whatever you ask to prove myself to you. To be worthy of your help. I'm an artist, I can—"

"I care. Not. For mortal. Arts." He shrugged.

"Then care for *me*," I begged. "As he does." I held out the hand with the Sun ring on it. "As Tyu does. Is it not more valiant to die doing a good deed than to sleep away the end of your life? Let me serve you." I remembered his distaste for my kneeling, so I changed direction. "Or serve me. Not for long . . . just until I find them.

"I love him, Ist." Straightening, I put a step between us. "I love him more than I love anything else. I will barter anything I possess to these creatures if it means bridging the impossibilities between us. Please. Please take me to them."

I clasped my hands together so tightly I feared I'd never be able to break them apart again. Ist hummed, considering. His gaze touched upon Saiyon's ring.

He sighed in a way that deflated him.

"Very well. I will. Take you. To where. I remember. Them."

I could have wept at the response. "Thank you. Thank you." Jubilation pulsed from crown to toe.

Tyu, and especially Zyzi, would not be happy.

"What did your soldiers say?"

He started from the overturned trough he sat on, lifting his ch=in from his palms. "I did not hear you."

"This time." Smiling, I sat beside him, loosening my shawl to better absorb his warmth.

Shoulders hunched, he pressed his elbows into his thighs. "We are advancing."

My stomach tightened. "Good."

He nodded. Stared at the ground.

I swept hair from his face. Reaching up, he clasped my hand in both of his, fingers tightly entwined. "I am trying to believe so."

Leaning against him, I lay my head on his shoulder. "We still have time."

"So little," he whispered, and kissed my knuckles so tenderly I had to bite my tongue to keep my tears at bay.

CHAPTER 13

Zyzi was furious.

But neither would she return home without me, so we prepared the next morning for our journey eastward, Zyzi in bitter silence, me brimming with hope, and Tyu in quiet resignation. I wrote a letter in my sketchbook to mail to the farm if we came across civilization, but Ist seemed certain we would not find any on the route ahead.

We spoke little as we traveled away from the Furdowns that first day. The meadows and prairie fields began to form soft hills spotted with trees, and when we rested, I sketched them on the reverse side of earlier drawings to save space in my book. I drew Saiyon as well, if only to ensure I still remembered what he looked like, though I drew him as the man the war had made him, not the all-powerful god. I *knew* what he was. I accepted it. But I couldn't quite feel it, in my heart. Which was for the better, because Saiyon had never wanted me to see him, treat him, as a deity.

Gods help me, I missed him. I missed him so badly I felt I could bleed from the ache of it.

The second day, Zyzi decided to speak to me again. Not because she forgave me, I'm sure, but because she was bored. Ist listened to our ramblings thoughtfully. Much of the conversation was about our rapidly dwindling supply of food—Zyzi was good with herbs and plants, but she was familiar with little of what grew along our route. However, the next morning, Ist presented us with tubers of all sizes and berries of all colors, some of which I couldn't name. I accepted them with as much gratitude as I could express, to which the godling merely said, "The Earth. Mother. Gives. To those. Who ask."

Zyzi, especially thoughtful as she ate sweet raspberries, asked, "How much farther?"

Ist put his face into the wind, though it did not blow from the direction we were headed. "Two days, I think."

I elbowed Zyzi. "Two days there, and perhaps a week to get home, if we triangulate." I pulled out my sketchbook, where I'd begun to make a map of our journey.

"You assume there will be a road," Zyzi snapped. She opened her mouth to say more, but shut it without speaking. Utter silence descended around us—even the bees and the songbirds had quieted. The morning darkened to a sickly gray, sapping color from everything.

Hugging my sketchbook, I tilted my head toward the sky. Toward *him*, or where he had been. But I could not find the Sun. Icy panic pulsed down my limbs as I searched the sky, Ist grumbling deeply in his throat beside me, Tyu quivering on my shoulder.

A loud burst tore through the heavens, streaking white fire toward the eastern horizon. It rattled my bones. Sang a high note in my ears.

The blue sky returned. Morning light poured over the Earth. Birds and bugs continued their songs as though they had never stopped.

"Satto," Tyu said.

My heart pounded in my throat. "What was that?"

Ist shook his head. "I do not. Know. The war in. The heavens. Has always. Been. Above me." He rubbed his chin. "I did. Not. Intend. For that. To be. Literal."

"The war," Zyzi repeated, shielding her eyes from the Sun, which burned as brilliantly in the sky as it had moments ago.

I swallowed hard. Ist began walking again, and I hurried to catch up with him. "I know the answer," I said, breathless, "but tell me. The

Sun God cannot die. Correct? No matter how the war turns, he cannot be killed?"

Ist nodded. "He is. Immortal."

Nudging my earlobe, Tyu whispered, "Death can be a release, for what those gods do to one another."

She shivered, and my blood ran cold. Allowing Ist and Zyzi to trek ahead of me, I turned back, watching Saiyon as closely as my mortal eyes would allow.

My mind rekindled the memory of him lying on my bed, *cold* and sickly, after reaching his hand through the veil of death and wrenching my spirit back into this realm. And I feared for him.

"Guard yourself, my love," I whispered, sure he would not hear me while entrapped in battle. I rubbed the inside of the ring he'd given me. "Guard yourself, and wait for me."

Nineteen days after Zyzi first told me the rumors of a godling in the Furdowns, we reached the forest where the demons lived.

If one could call it that.

It was a blight, unlike any pestilence or drought I'd ever beheld, either in person or in art. The hills dropped and gave way to a great ashy expanse where nothing grew, and bare, branchless trees spiked the Earth like gravestones. A woodland, once burned, was able to regrow itself, but this place appeared to have been scorched too deeply.

I touched the edge of the scars encircling my torso, and wondered at the metaphor.

"How can anything live here?" I asked, meeting Zyzi's uncertain eyes.

"Hmmm," Ist hummed. "Best you walk. Directly. And let. Them know. You are. Coming."

Both my cousin and I started at the suggestion. "Will you not come with us?" I asked.

Ist hummed again. "I do not. Care. For demons. They feast. On. Godlings. Like me. If there are. Few. I will be. Fine. But many. Would not. Suit us well."

He glanced to Tyu, who shivered.

"We have to return home," Zyzi added, her voice airy. "Somehow, we have to get back home."

My cousin's words struck a sad chord in my chest. Was I so focused on my own goals that I'd overlooked the cost to her? I was eternally grateful for her help and companionship, but I realized that I hadn't expressed it. It was an error I would have to amend, and soon.

"They're here, in this forest?" I asked, scanning the branchless, graphite-like trees.

"They are. They should be."

Clenching my fists, I nodded. "I will go and barter with them, and return here."

"Absolutely not," Zyzi snapped at the same time Tyu jingled, "L'Aija, no!"

I smiled—or tried to—at them. "This is my quest. My deal. I won't risk others."

Zyzi picked at a hangnail. "But . . . they don't eat humans, right?"

She looked to Ist, who confirmed with a nod. That was a relief, at least.

She set her jaw. "Then I'm coming."

"I promised I would not leave your side." Tyu pressed into my hair, considering.

"With flight," Ist offered, "they would be. Easy. To evade."

The little godling took a minute to consider this, then nodded. "I will come."

"Thank you," I whispered, both to her and to Zyzi. To Ist, I said, "And thank you for guiding us."

He hummed and dug his staff into the ashy Earth. "I cannot. Sense. The Earth. Through the. Decay. But I will. Wait for you."

I clasped his three-fingered hand in gratitude, then turned toward the blackened trees and started walking, gaining a little courage with each step. Zyzi fell into step behind me, wielding her knife, and Tyu concealed herself in my hair. My eyes darted from tree to tree, imagining movement that wasn't there.

One might have thought this place would smell of fire, cinders, and smoke, but it didn't. The farther we hiked, the more the scent of sulfur and rot plagued us. It carried a tang my nose instantly identified as *wrong*, and that bitterness clung to the back of my throat even after my body adjusted to the odors.

"Don't agree to anything without consideration," Tyu sang against the shell of my ear. "Listen carefully."

Despite the season, I grew warm the longer we walked, and not just because the way was uphill. Heat seemed to emanate from the dead ground and weave webs between trees—heat like that of an infected wound. Even after two hours of walking, the landscape didn't change. Endless broken-sword trees, endless gray soil. No life of any kind. Not even a fly.

The first hint that we had arrived was a low, nervous giggle off to the west. My heart gave one hard thump in response. I turned but saw nothing. Zyzi's hand came around my elbow, but she continued walking. I shoved down my trepidation as far as I could, cramming it into crags and creases where I could best ignore it. I forced my chin high and wiped perspiration from my brow.

We crested an ashy hill. The demons approached from two sides—north and west—appearing through the broken trees. I counted half a dozen at first, then a few more lagging behind. They were horrible, ugly things. Humanoid in shape, but the similarities ended there. Whereas Pree, Sai'ken, and Kalanakai were abnormal in bizarre and beautiful ways, these creatures were as wrong as the rank air. Most were gray, like the dead Earth surrounding us, and so skeletal their ribs and spines pressed against their skin like piano keys and lute necks. No two looked the same—their features ranged from narrow to wide, hooked to flat, sharp to round. But one thing they all shared was asymmetry. No one demon had a matching pair of eyes or ears. Even the bone structure of their skulls and shoulders didn't match, like they'd been formed by clay in a child's hands. They made me think of raccoons, the way they approached, curious, with wicked smiles on their uneven mouths. Creatures that meant to appear trustworthy but would bite you the instant you got too close.

Zyzi's fingernails dug into my arm. But I was grateful for the pain; it reminded me to stay alert, to stay smart. This was no different than navigating the streets of Algeron at night, or so I told myself.

The band slowed, allowing two demons to march ahead and greet us. The first was taller, with a narrow, malformed head and slanted predatory eyes, the right larger than the left. Two horns protruded from the top of his head, one thick and curled like a ram's, the other narrow and crooked like an old icicle. He had a bulbous turnip-like nose that ended in a point, and pointed shoulders sharp enough to cut. He grinned at me and bowed.

"Greetings." He held on to his *S*s like a serpent would. "You are unexpected." His mismatched eyes drew to my hair, and he licked thin lips. Tyu shivered against my neck, and I reminded myself she could take to the skies any moment. One thing I was certain of, looking at the monsters before me, was that none would be able to follow her. "I am Skall, chieftain of this band. King, if you would."

Several of the other demons snickered.

"This is my compatriot, Kage." He gestured to his companion. Kage had a wider face and long ears, one pointing up, one pointing down, contrasting the large tusks jutting from his mouth, one arcing down, the other curving up. A jagged scar cut through his left eye, sealing it closed, and he had the nose of a pig, with uneven nostrils. Like Skall, he bowed.

"To what do we owe the pleasure?" Skall's eyes slicked over me like oil before passing on to Zyzi.

"I've come seeking your help." I forced revulsion from my face and squared my shoulders. "My sources tell me you may have methods for achieving immortality."

Kage grinned. A few of the others snickered, but one hard glance from Skall had their mouths snapping closed.

"That," Skall said, stepping closer, and I forced myself not to retreat, "is quite the ask."

Zyzi's grip on my arm tightened.

I met Skall's eyes. "Can you do it, or not?"

He smirked. "We can do all sorts of things, but there's a price."

My stomach tightened. Ist had warned me of this. I had been prepared to strike a deal with the demons. But seeing the wretched, corrupt creatures myself bolstered a sort of mental nausea in me. Perhaps I could avoid a true barter.

"I am seeking immortality because I love him, who is immortal." I held up my hand. The demons' eyes immediately went to the ring. Skall kept his features smooth, but Kage's one eye widened. "I met him in the darkness and seek him now in the light. If you cannot respect your god, then you should at the very least fear him."

Kage held up his hands, halting my words. "You make assumptions, human."

Skall interjected, "He is not *our* god."

My courage withered.

Kage put a hand on Skall's shoulder before addressing me. "You can regale us with your love story, dear mortal, but it would be a waste of breath. Perhaps that is how you got this delicious morsel"—he gestured to Tyu, whom he shouldn't have been able to see, and I stiffened—"to accompany you here, but we have no hearts, and thus can scrape no sympathy for you, and especially not for Him." He pointed skyward.

"Only a deal will do," Skall snapped. "We do not give without taking. But we will deal fairly."

Zyzi snorted.

Kage licked his teeth.

I swallowed hard and clasped my hands behind my back, where I could squeeze my own fingers for support without being noticed. "I will listen to your offer."

Skall raised a thin brow, but Kage drew him back, toward the others. They huddled together like wolves around a carcass, whispering to one another, too hushed to be overheard.

Zyzi turned me toward her. "We can leave now, Ai."

"That might be difficult," Tyu whispered.

"Difficult?" Zyzi repeated. "What if we don't like their deal? Will they not allow us to leave?"

"Just as all people aren't the same," I murmured, "surely not all demons are, either." I met her eyes. "We've come this far, Zyzi. I have to hear them out."

I took in a foul breath. We were down one godling, and while Zyzi had some combat skill, I wasn't sure how well we'd stand against nearly a dozen demons. I offered a prayer to the Earth Mother, if She could even hear me through all this ash and filth.

I watched the demons huddle. One lifted its head to glance at me. I tried to fight the stirring of nausea, but the wrongness that wafted from them was like hot breath in an enclosed room.

Finally the party broke apart, and Skall returned to us, with Kage trailing behind. "We have two offers."

"Gracious of us." Kage smiled.

I felt that grin like a spike in my navel.

"First," Skall went on, "would be to trade us the little godling you're hiding."

Tyu squeaked into my hair, and every inch of me hardened into iron. However much I wanted Saiyon, I would not steal the life of another to have him. "No."

The demons frowned and shifted. "Very well." Skall didn't mask his disappointment. "Then you will go to the Yard of Bones."

My gaze shot from Skall, to Kage, and back again. "The Yard of Bones? What is that?"

Kage answered, "It is not far from here." He pointed north. "It is a monument we cannot trespass. You will go on our behalf. Go and bring us back the bones of a godling."

My mouth went dry. "A sacred place?"

Kage shrugged. "It isn't guarded."

"Then why not go yourselves?" Zyzi chimed in.

The two demons exchanged a glance. Skall waved a hand like the question was a bothersome fly. "We can only have the power to grant your wish if we're given the essence of a godling. That, or give us the one with you. Either trade will suffice."

Tyu quivered so violently I had to lift my hand to calm her.

"We'll go." Zyzi met my eyes. Hers were hard but set, reminding me of Kata. "We'll go to the Yard of Bones. One skeleton."

I wondered if she could feel the gratitude rolling off me in waves.

The demons grinned. Nodded.

Zyzi looked at Skall. "Straight north? You'll get nothing if your directions aren't specific."

Skall pointed. "North, around the knuckled hills, straight toward the dip in the far mountains." He again looked at my hair. "That one will sense it."

I waited for Tyu to object. When she didn't, I said, "Very well."

A few of the smaller demons cheered, but Skall merely bowed a second time. "A pleasure doing business. Do not dawdle. My kin and I are . . . hungry."

I stepped back; the demons held their positions. Surely they wouldn't hurt us after bartering with us. Not if they wanted the remains of a godling. Not if they wanted to eat. Still, I descended the hill with one eye over my shoulder before turning northward. They did not follow, but they watched us, ten pairs of mismatched eyes. Even after we crested the next hill and dipped below it, breaking us from the creatures' lines of sight, I felt their gaze. We moved quickly, until sweat poured around my eyes and down the line of my back. Until a sliver of green in the distance marked the end of the demons' territory.

No one spoke until we'd reached it. Wild clover had never been more beautiful.

Finally, Tyu zipped out from her hiding place, flashing colors, twisting and soaring high overhead before returning to my shoulder. "I have never been to the Yard of Bones," she murmured.

Zyzi grasped my hand; her palm was cool and clammy. "Let's go home, Ai."

I came up short. "Home? But the Yard of—"

"Have you lost your senses?" She grabbed both of my shoulders and looked into my eyes. "We're not going to the Yard of Bones!" She glanced beyond me, perhaps thinking a demon might have followed us. "We're going *home*. This is wrong. Tell me this isn't wrong."

I swallowed my fears and set my jaw. "*This* is the only way."

She gaped at me. Released me. Dug fingers into her scalp. "I swear a block of wood is more reasonable than you are."

"The Yard. Of Bones." A familiar voice startled me, and I whipped around so swiftly I nearly lost my pack. Ist approached from the west, leaning into his cane as he walked. "I am not. Surprised. They chose. Such a place."

"You found us." My pulse beat quickly, and hope took root. "I thought you'd left."

He shook his head. "All things leave. An. Impression. On the. Earth Mother. If I choose. To. I can sense. You through Her." He glanced toward the dead forest.

"You know the place?" Zyzi asked.

"It is. A place. Where. The Earth Mother's. Godlings. Take their. Final rest." Ist frowned. "It is. Not. A place. For demons."

"So they said." I glanced to Tyu, who slowly floated back to my shoulder. "Why can they not go themselves? Are they limited to this forest?"

"Limited? No. But only whole. Things. Can visit. There."

Only whole things? I peered past the ashy trees. Was that why the demons felt so wrong? Were they . . . incomplete?

A strange pity brewed in my chest, and I didn't like it.

Ist ground his teeth. Looked us over. Glanced to my ring. After a great sigh, he said, "I will. Show you."

Zyzi stiffened at the same time I relaxed. "Truly? You will?" My heart clenched.

He nodded. "As you said. I will die. In service. To a. Greater. Purpose."

At the same time elation pressed gooseflesh into my unburnt skin, my gut tightened. "But . . . is it not a sacred place? Will I be committing some great sin against your kind if I do as the demons asked?"

Ist tilted his head to one side. "Why would. It be. Sacred?"

The question took me off balance.

Zyzi said, "We always treat our dead with respect."

The godling merely shrugged. "The soul. Is sacred. Not. The body." He turned north and began walking. "Three days. There and back. With work. Included. I would think. I have. Never been. But. I know it."

"Zyzi." I grasped her hand, but she pulled away. "Zyzi, I never meant to ask this much of you." I had no idea how much work acquiring one of these skeletons would be; I needed the extra hands. But this was my quest, not my cousin's, and I could not ask any more of her. "If you want to go home, go home. We'll find a village and an escort if you need. Or"—I hesitated—"you can take Tyu."

The godling fluttered, unsure. "I am charged with watching *you*, L'Aija." She glanced to Zyzi. "But . . . if Ist takes my charge . . . if you will me to attend her, I shall do it."

Zyzi turned away, blinking moisture from her eyes. Words ground like peppercorns between her teeth. "I can't leave without *you*."

"Yes, you can." I planted my heels firmly. "I am a grown woman. I have been for—"

She wheeled on me. "Then stop acting like a child!"

"A child!" I spat. "What part of this is childish, Zyzi?"

She blinked some more. She hated crying as much as I did. And she knew my agony better than anyone else—as much as a bystander could.

She drew in a few deep breaths, and I gave her the space to do so. Ist watched with interest—perhaps he wasn't used to the ways of humans.

Brow tense, Zyzi turned to him. "Can we get there by nightfall if we walk with enthusiasm?"

The godling's thick fingers tapped against his staff. "If we. Travel. Hard. Yes. But I would. Not enter. At night."

"Why not?" I inquired. "Other than the lack of light . . ."

He considered me, as if trying to determine if my question was genuine. Perhaps it had been a stupid one, but I didn't know celestial ways. Not enough. Not yet. "In His. Kingdom. His light. Guides those. Who cannot. See. And thwarts those. Who would use. The yard. For ill."

"But the demons claimed they can't trespass there," Zyzi said.

He blinked his large eyes. "Your under. Standing. Is small. There are more. Than just. Demons. To concern. Yourself with." He glanced at my ring, then gestured northward. "Come. I have. Promised. My aid. Let us. Finish. This so that. I might. Die in peace."

Biting my lip, I followed the godling, nervous energy fueling my limbs. We traveled hard without a word of complaint, and with very few other words between us. I didn't even stop to map our way.

I wondered if Ist, so close to the end of his life, planned to leave the Yard of Bones at all.

The Yard of Bones was the most haunting and mesmerizing place I'd ever beheld. Had I known such a place existed on the Earth Mother, I would have left home long ago to seek it out, to draw it, to make it part of myself. And yet I never would have found it without Ist's help.

He led us to a tight place between hills, opened a door I could not see, and then we were there.

At first I thought snow fell from the sky, only it wasn't true snow, or dust, but flakes of . . . if *light* could be solidified and dimmed to a soft glow . . . that's what it was. Slow, silent, and steady. It coated the ground as well, reminding me of the ash in the demons' forest, yet this didn't cling to the hem of my dress or smell sour. It simply was, and when I tried to cup the substance in my palm, it slipped away like a breath. Like Saiyon's blood had.

Everything was cast in slatish shadows, like we were caught in a space halfway between day and night. Great quartz-like structures rose from the ground like jagged, leafless trees—not enough to make a forest, only enough to stand as sentinels, though I sensed no life in them. When I moved to run my fingers over a branch, Ist said, "Do not. Touch."

So I fought my urge to explore and fell into step behind him, marveling as we went. Tyu floated ahead of us, reverent and hushed. Even Zyzi forgot her anger, staring with an open mouth at the things we passed.

Moments later, I gasped.

A great skeleton lay across our path, larger than any animal I'd ever seen, including the shadow dragon that had attacked the farm. I recognized its rib cage immediately, each rib taller than I was, curving up and inward—pale blue, speckled, translucent. Like tanzanite. The bones seemed to glow from within, or perhaps that was a trick of the "snow" gathered all around it. This time, when I approached, Ist didn't halt me.

I touched a rib. Its stony length was smooth as porcelain. "We could never carry such a thing."

"Fortunately"—Ist led the way around the creature—"Not all. Godlings. Are built. So great."

I glanced at Tyu, wondering how fine her bones must be, if she had any at all. Pulling my hand away, I followed Ist, only to spy an even greater body in the distance, rising up like a mountain, glowing the same way the first had. Something like glass crunched underfoot, and I stepped back to see what looked like a small femur under my shoe. A few other random bones scattered the way.

"Does no one take care of these?" I glanced to Zyzi, who shrugged.

"Why should. There be. Caretakers. When the life. Has moved on?" Ist drawled. "Their spirits. Have passed to. Another. Realm." Pausing, he glanced back at me. "Do you think. The shell of. The Earth. Mother. Is all. There is? That this life. Is the only. Life. To be had?"

I knew of a hereafter—the scriptures mentioned it often, and I had become very familiar with the scriptures over the last year. "It is one thing to be told of another life, and another to believe it."

Ist hummed. "Believe it. Those who. Don't. Are those. Who seek. What you seek. For selfish. Reasons. If that. Had been. Your purpose. I. Would not. Have. Helped you."

He tilted his head, a gesture to keep moving. I followed him dutifully, trying to memorize my surroundings for later drawings.

I *did* believe him. I could believe that these creatures had moved on to another place, even a better place. But I knew it was a rest Saiyon would never be offered, and any hereafter that would claim me would reject him.

After a few more minutes of walking, we came upon a skeleton about the size of a large human man, and it looked intact. The godling had lain here and curled in on himself—herself, according to Ist—and clasped her hands together as if in prayer. I couldn't guess how long ago she had died—none of the skeletons here bore rotted flesh or skin or hair. Each was clean, polished crystal.

I hesitated to touch the remains—it seemed sacrilegious—though I understood godlings did not treat the dead the same as we did. When Ist set his staff aside and moved to collect bones, I knelt beside him and got to work. This was *my* task, and I should do as much of it as I could.

Zyzi held back, perhaps worried someone, or some*thing*, might come by and stop us. After keeping guard for half of the dismantling, however, she took our bags and reorganized them, freeing up hers to carry as many of the bones as it could hold.

"They're beautiful," I whispered to Ist as I continued the macabre work, trying to maintain the mind of an artist so guilt would not chew on me. "Will you lie here, when your time is through?"

He hummed under his breath. "I am. Not. Decided." He popped ribs from the skeleton's spine, which sounded like shattering glass. "I have. Always. Thought to. Rest. In Her. Arms."

"The Earth Mother? Or a lover?"

He smiled at that. "The Earth. Mother. I have. Always. Been. One of. Hers. Even if. She's. Slept. All my. Life."

My fingers brushed up the shoulder bones to the skull, large and pointed into a snout. "How long has She slept?"

Ist handed Zyzi a rib, then paused. "A very. Long. Time. Too long. But I. Cannot. Blame Her. The wars. Hurt. Her soul. I think. And it. Is easier. To be. Patient. With humans. When slumbering."

I nodded, trying to imagine a small race of creatures living on my body, digging into my skin to build wells and foundations for their homes, erecting cathedrals to worship another god.

My mind tried to paint the image as I removed the skull, and one of its teeth punctured my finger. Clenching my jaw, I pulled back to study the wound; it was too deep to ignore, unfortunately. I stared at it, squinting in the dim light. The glimmer in this godling's bones danced around the cut, sparkling in the dollop of blood running down to my knuckle.

Tyu was there instantly, examining the wound, worrying over me. She spun toward Zyzi, who already had a bandage and smudge of poultice ready for her. While I could have easily wrapped the cut myself, this was Tyu's purpose, and I wouldn't take it from her. So I held out my hand as she tended me.

A memory flashed to life.

He asked me to be His hands, Sai'ken had once said to me.

He'd carried me home because Saiyon couldn't.

"Tyu," I murmured. "What did Saiyon—Satto—say to you when he asked you to come here to stay with me?"

She tucked the edge of the bandage in and lifted her blank face to me. Hesitated as she always did when I asked about Saiyon, like she was afraid of saying something she shouldn't.

After a moment, she turned silver—a color I'd never beheld on her. Before I could repeat my question, I heard *his* voice emanate from her body, the silver flickering with each syllable.

"This is more important," Saiyon's voice said, midconversation, and the deep sound of it pierced me. I pressed my hurt hand to my heart. "She is in your care until further notice. See that she has everything she needs. Stave off her pains. Treat her wounds. Keep her safe. Care for her as if she were your child. Your sister. Your lover."

There was a pause, and I thought Tyu was finished, until she pulsed once more. "I cannot be beside her." His voice became quiet and heavy, and behind my eyelids I saw his face, drooped and agonized as it had been in the cornfield. "You must do what I cannot. I am trusting you with my greatest treasure."

A single tear slipped from my eye. I turned my head so the others wouldn't see it. Ist was focused on his work, but Zyzi's eyes were locked on me as she, too, listened to the memory.

Tyu flashed back to her pink, white, and lavender colors. A growing bubble pressed against my chest and up into my throat, but I managed to murmur, "Thank you."

Then I got back to work.

We were in the Yard of Bones longer that I'd anticipated, and the skeleton was heavy. Zyzi and I took turns carrying her bag, and once out, we peeled bark and pulled branches from some trees to make a sledge for everything else. When we were ready to set off, Ist pressed his palm to the naked trunk, and the bark regrew itself. Tyu clapped at the spectacle—it was the happiest I'd seen her since leaving the farm.

Though it had taken us a day to reach the Yard of Bones, it took a day and a half to return to the eerie forest where the demons lived. I insisted Ist stay behind again, because I could not bear the thought of his generosity being repaid by a gruesome demon feast, though I hoped the delivery of the skeleton would turn the creatures' eyes away from Tyu. The Sun was setting by the time Zyzi, Tyu, and I reached Skall, Kage, and the others, backs sore from our load. Tyu, a little braver than before, peeked out from my shoulder to see our path. Zyzi stayed silent, because she had spent the time trying, again, to convince me to change my mind. Every argument she had was reasonable—demons weren't trustworthy, we were taking too much of a risk with their numbers so much greater than ours, the immortality they promised might not be what I'd hoped—but as I saw it, my only other option was giving up on Saiyon, and that I could not bring myself to do.

The demons gaped at us with slack jaws and wide, incongruous eyes and then circled us like predators once we stopped. Zyzi, who carried my bag stuffed with both our supplies, tightened the strap around her shoulder.

I dropped the heavy pack and opened it, the godling's bones glimmering within. Goose bumps rose on my arms, and my burns ached deeply when the demons neared with drooling lips.

"I have kept my end of the bargain," I announced.

Kage nodded, though his attention was on the bag of bones, not me. "Of course, mortal. But we must . . . feast . . . to gain the ability to change you. We don't have magic of our own."

They'd mentioned something similar before, so I believed them. I stepped back, and the moment I did, the demons lunged like ravenous wolves, tearing both Zyzi's pack and the sledge to pieces. I stumbled to Zyzi's side, grasping her arm for support as she squeezed mine. Tyu burrowed into my hair.

The horrid sound of breaking glass, amplified as if by a giant bell, mixed with guttural and smacking sounds so loud I had to plug my ears. I turned away, seeking out the last tendrils of the Sun on the horizon, and gained courage. *I'm coming, Saiyon. Have you been watching me, or is your face turned away?*

I had not seen him since collapsing in the cornfield over a year ago, and my courage faltered. I didn't doubt Saiyon's feelings . . . We had shared too much for that. But he was a god. Eternal. And I wondered, even after Tyu's revelation, if he thought of me as often as I thought of him. I wondered if he'd shared his bed with another star mother yet. I knew he hated that process, that law, but the thought sickened me more than the demons' feasting did.

Clasping my hands together, I brought them to my face and pressed my lips to the ring, still limned with amber. As the sounds of the meal behind me died down, my pulse quickened. It was time. *Finally.* And then I would learn the truth about Saiyon's feelings from *him.*

I blinked tears of anticipation from my eyes as I turned back, still in Zyzi's grip. The last swatch of Sunset colored everything a rusty red. The demons pulled away from their carnage, walking as though intoxicated, their mismatched pupils dilated, their lips, chins, and hands nicked with cuts from the bone shards, teeth glittering.

One of them, whose name I didn't know, looked at me. Releasing Zyzi, I stepped forward. "My end of the bargain is complete. You will—"

"I see it in you," the demon drawled, staggering closer. "The god-ling's essence."

Words froze in my throat as the others turned toward me as well, wetting lips with renewed saliva.

My gaze dropped to my bandaged finger.

My stomach plummeted. I spoke loudly to keep my voice from trembling. "I have fulfilled my end of the bargain! You will use your renewed strength to make me immortal!"

The demon nearest me chuckled. Others staggered close to him, seemingly getting in line to . . . oh gods . . . *eat* me.

"Run," I whispered to Zyzi. I heard her back up, but she didn't abandon me. Tyu slipped from my hair and brightened, meaning to defend me.

My mind spun. I stepped back, mouth dry as unglazed pottery. Skall's eyes reflected the dying light like a panther's.

Predators, all of them. A desperate idea struck me.

I dug my heels into the ground. "I can't give it to you," I told the smaller demon. "I already promised it to Skall."

The demon and a few of his companions stopped in their tracks. Brows lowered, they turned to their leader.

"You made a deal without the pack's consent!" the smaller demon shouted.

Skall hissed. "She's lying!"

"Liar!" screeched another demon.

I backed away.

Zyzi grabbed my wrist.

We ran.

All three of us bolted back the way we had come, following the line the sledge had left in the ashy loam. We didn't get far before the demons took pursuit. I didn't dare look back at them, for fear of falling—the ground was uneven and slick with cinders. We sped downhill, putting a little more distance between us and the demons, but the next incline slowed us down, separating Zyzi and me. Zyzi stumbled on a decayed tree root; I nearly wrenched my shoulder yanking her back up. Another demon bounded after us on all fours, reminding me of a gremlin. Just as we found our feet, he leapt. Tyu slammed into him, knocking him back with a strength that belied her tiny form.

I hesitated. Tyu wasn't immortal. She could be hurt—

Zyzi hauled me away. Human instinct took over, and I ran before the other demons could catch up. Before Tyu's efforts could go to waste.

My thoughts flew back to the farm, to my aunt. Her heart would break if she learned her daughter had died. Died helping *me*, and after all Zyzi had risked to get me this far.

And that was all the demons wanted. *Me*. Or the essence of the godling, which must have entered my blood from that cut.

So at the next rise, I twisted my arm and broke free of Zyzi's grip, causing her to slow. "Go!" I shouted, and took off east, barely able to see in the shadows. I plunged into a copse of dead trees, trying to lose myself in them. My braid caught on the nub of a branch and jerked free just as quickly. One of the demons was right at my heels; I could feel his sour breath on my neck.

I looked down at my hand. Tore the bandage off with my teeth and bit down into the healing wound, opening it up again. *Please work.*

Lunging for a tree, I swung around the trunk, coming face-to-face with my immediate pursuer. I shouldn't have been surprised to see Skall's ugly, pointed face looking back at me.

He leapt for me; I ducked behind the tree, using it as a shield. Grabbed his arm with my injured hand and wiped my blood down the length of it. We wrestled like that, around the tree, him trying to claw at my neck, me trying to bleed. A broken nub in the bark scratched my forearm. Gritting my teeth, I raked my arm over it, tearing the skin for more blood. The tree still between us, I jerked him closer and wiped more blood over his arm.

The other demons arrived. Reversing our dance, I hauled Skall around the tree and used our momentum to throw him back toward his own kind.

They hesitated less than a second before smelling the essence and leaping on him. And when Skall screamed, I emptied the remnants of my stomach contents into the ash. I wanted to cover my ears from the vile, horrid sounds of death and murder, but logic held, and I ripped fabric from my underskirt and bound my hand and arm as quickly and tightly as I could, trying to stifle the blood—the *essence*—as tears poured down my face. My throat and sinuses burned with acid.

The sounds slowly faded. Silence covered the forest as surely as the night sky did, and the light of a half moon on the far horizon shone down on me, pointing out my location to the repulsive creatures that had been my only hope.

When Kage's voice sounded beside me, I jumped, ready to flee. "Sorry about that," he said, crouching only a pace from me. I must have been so fixated on the horrors in front of me that I hadn't heard him approach. But the lust and hunger were gone from his face, and I dared to hear him out.

"They are young," he said with a shrug, "and have little control."

I gaped. "Little control. You think *that* is reason enough? You tried to *kill* me!"

"I did no such thing," he countered, and I could not rebuke him. I hadn't seen him in the following horde, not that I had looked closely.

"Let me make a deal with you. What did you say your name was?"

I pushed away from him, finding my feet. How trustworthy could he be if he couldn't remember my name? "I already made a *deal*, demon. You must uphold it."

He frowned. "Your deal was with Skall, and he is, unfortunately, dead."

Which likely made Kage the new head of the "pack." Anger and revulsion broiled in my gut. "You were there. You partook."

He stood and brushed ash from his misshapen hands. "Even so, we needed our combined power to turn you. With only nine, we do not have enough." He eyed my bandaged hand. "But . . . there is another way. And I am willing to show you, since you are favored by the Sun God."

I dared not believe him. The sounds of Skall's screams still echoed in my ears and pulsed in my injured finger.

And yet I knew no other way to reach Saiyon, save these horrible creatures. And Kage . . . he had been reasonable from the beginning. Calm. More . . . human, than the others.

If I did not make a deal with him, my journey would end here.

I swallowed. "Where are they? Zyzi, Tyu?" I did not want these monsters to go looking for them.

He gestured past the copse. Stepping around the tree that had been my shield, I saw two silhouettes carefully making their way back, searching for me, one large, one tiny.

Relief escaped my nostrils, but I knew I had to act quickly.

Zyzi would never allow a new deal.

Gods, I loved Saiyon so much I would feed these monsters my right arm just to see him again.

"What is your deal?" I whispered. The least I could do was listen.

"There is a sacred place, far from here. A nest where a god was created, that still possesses His powers."

I leaned back, a spark of a memory, of a story told by the hearth, flickering in the back of my mind. "What god?"

"One that no longer lives in the kingdoms you know," he continued, his words careful. "If I take you there, I can use the strength of the pack to convert your mortal body into a lasting one."

I glanced back to Zyzi and Tyu approaching. The other demons seemed to have scattered, nursing odiously full bellies.

"My dear," Kage murmured, "this is the *only* way to get what you want."

I swallowed down a sob in my throat and blinked my eyes. "What must I pay?" I whispered.

He smiled. "Only your art."

That gave me pause. How did he know . . . ?

I touched my pockets. "M-My bag is with Zyzi—"

He snorted. "I don't want your sketches. I want your *art*."

I shook my head. "I don't understand."

185

"It lives within you, much as that essence does." Mention of the essence had me recoiling. "I want your talent. It will power me enough to help you at the god's nest."

I licked my teeth, seeking moisture. "I-I wasn't aware that was something that could be taken."

He shrugged. "The pack will not make the effort without the art. We wouldn't have the strength."

I hesitated. Looked over to Zyzi and Tyu. They were nearly upon us.

My art. My art was such a large part of who I was. Would I even recognize myself without it? But of course I would—I was more than my talents. Art was not kindness and determination and stubbornness and everything else that formed my soul. I did not love art more than I loved Saiyon.

"Talents can always be relearned," he pressed.

I pressed my hand to the Earth, pondering. Rubbed dirt between my fingers. How much could the Earth Mother protect those upon Her, if She slept? Did She even know of the war in the heavens? How much more could I do for my own kind, if I had the strength, longevity, and powers of a goddess? Even if I couldn't end the war . . . I could fight. I could protect. I could challenge. And I could do it at Saiyon's side.

"Isn't He worth it?" Kage asked.

My vision blurred. I pulled my hand from the soil and ran my fingers over the amber band of my ring. It was likely my imagination, but it felt warmer. "Yes."

Kage took my uninjured hand, the one that bore Saiyon's ring.

And just like that, my gift left me.

"Do you know how time works, Aija?"

I lay with my cheek against his chest, tracing triangles over his sternum. "I have a feeling any answer I give would be wrong."

I felt him smile. "Time is like music, playing ever higher and ever lower, and all it affects sings different notes within its chords."

I considered the analogy. When he didn't say more, I propped myself on my elbow and looked at him, hair falling over my shoulder. "Why are you telling me this?"

He cupped the side of my face. "Because if I could stop the music, I would."

CHAPTER 14

"Aija, stop."

His radiance filled my vision and heated me down to my bones. I sat up immediately, fresh tears coming to my eyes. "Saiyon?"

He lingered a few paces from me, yet still his heat surrounded me as a bonfire's would, and I knew he dared not get any closer. His diamond eyes were hard. The light whisking about his person lapped downward, as though heavy.

"You are hurting yourself," he said, his voice powerful yet restrained, and the sound of it fed and renewed every memory of him.

I shook my head. "There is no other way—"

"I cannot be there for you." His voice strained, and I wondered how tightly the chains bound him.

Pressing my lips together, I hugged myself. "Am I hideous to you, with these scars?"

His light flared, making his heat almost too intense to bear. "Do not be foolish."

"You have made me a fool, Saiyon."

We stared at each other, his brilliance hurting my eyes, yet I craved it dearly.

"I love you, Aija," he whispered, and held my gaze. "More than I thought possible. But you pursue what cannot be. You . . ." He hesitated.

I reached for him until his aura scalded my hand. "Don't you see, Saiyon? If I become immortal, I can love you forever. You won't have to lose anyone else."

His entire body tensed. Even his flames seemed to freeze in place. The gold of his skin flickered.

I swallowed at the lump forming in my throat. "You won't have to lose me."

A millennium and a breath seemed to pass between us, between the bond that connected us as surely as his chains connected him to the cosmos. I could not read him, and my heart beat harder, trying to interpret his unrelenting gaze.

He looked away then, at something I could not see, and his light withdrew, like it was shrinking in on itself.

"You have already lost," he murmured. "I see it in you. I was not there to stop it."

I rubbed at a callus on my thumb, created by decades of holding a pencil. "I gave it freely."

"You gave it wrongly."

My blood scorched—not from his heat, but from my own. "Are you so sure, Saiyon? You are tens of thousands of miles away, and your face is turned toward your war. What do you know of what I do down here? How dare you dismiss my sacrifices so easily?"

He turned back to me, as stony as the sculpture I'd chiseled at the Algeron Cathedral. I'd never spoken to him so harshly. Even in the art shed.

"I am hurting," I said, and my voice cracked. "Some of that hurt I can't control. This one, this sacrifice, I chose. I chose it for you. For us."

The flames at his shoulders burned white. "Do not presume it is for Me that you waste what life you have."

A flash of cold shot through my body. I ground my teeth. "If you have time to chide me, then take the time to help me."

He only shook his head. "If only it were so simple." He paused. "I must go," he said with the tone of a prisoner being led to the noose. "Please. Spare yourself."

I woke up overly warm, like I'd slept curled around the hearth. But there was no fire in our camp, and the air carried the sharp chill of autumn. I sat up, blinking in the first rays of dawn. Lifted my hand. The finger bearing his ring was hot, like I'd held it over a flame—

Not a dream, I told myself. *He was here. Somehow.*

But I did not weep. My fingers curled into a tight fist until the ring bit into my skin. Saiyon was a god, accustomed to giving orders and having them followed, but he did not order *me.*

He's hurting, too, I reminded myself, resting a hand on my stomach and the scarred skin over it. *He's worried.*

And I wanted nothing more in that moment than to prove him wrong.

We'd traveled east with the demons for one week, leaving Rozhan behind. To my surprise, Ist had joined us. In the beginning, he'd had to smack a few demons with his staff and restrain others with vines sprouting from the ground, much like the way he protected us from them at night, but they'd learned to leave him be. Kage had barked the order to stand down at them more than once. He, apparently, had better command of the horde than Skall ever did. Still, we trailed the demon pack by several paces.

And so one week passed with no attempts to hurt any one of us—not me or my wondrous companions who still, somehow, accompanied me, pushed by their own loyalties. Now, we were nearly to the god's nest.

I packed Zyzi's and my things. Stewing quietly, *aching* quietly, about the dreamlike meeting I'd just had. I had given my cousin portions of my own rations, set out her bed for her, cleaned up camp, anything I could do to thank her and apologize for the predicament I'd put us in. She was perpetually angry at me, but I loved her more than ever for staying with me, for this would be so much harder alone. Tyu was nothing if not devoted, even going as far as to stand guard of our camp at night. Ist stayed with us, insisting he would not die a liar. But their devotion was not the same as my cousin's. In truth, Zyzi was the closest thing to a sister I would ever possess.

We traveled hard, so I had little time to draw . . . not that I could. I hadn't attempted to, yet. I feared trying would make my sacrifice more real. That it might wound my resolve, or at least make me more miserable as I trekked toward joy. Because truly, I wanted Saiyon more than I wanted sketches and paintings and sculptures. I would erase my name from the ledgers of Rozhan to be at his side. But I'd already given up so much, and waiting for my return payment was a struggle.

The itch was still there. That under-the-skin yearning I got when I saw something new or beautiful and ached to re-create it. Many interesting things highlighted my slog with the demons—red-crowned trees, unusual boulder formations, a fleeing hart larger than any I'd seen before. I itched to re-create them, but the adeptness to do so had left my fingers, and I recoiled from facing what I'd given up. Had I lost my talent before meeting Saiyon, I would have felt ruined. For most of my life, it had been the closest thing to love I possessed. Now, it felt as if I'd been told a family member died, but I had yet to see the body. Had yet to accept it for myself.

Our things packed, I waited quietly for Ist to drop the woody house he'd built around us, the same half-sphere dwelling he coaxed from the ground every night to keep the demons at bay, should they decide to break their pact. They roved at night, I'd noticed. Encircled the camp, played games with one another, murmured in the shadows. Needless to say, I was endlessly grateful for Ist's presence.

I didn't have to wait long; Ist roused and dismissed the stiff vines with a wave of his hand, and Tyu shot into the trees, to stretch her invisible wings, perhaps, or to search for lurking danger.

Kage was waiting for me nearby.

"Nearly there," he promised. He was full of promises, but he had kept the smaller pledges he'd made along the way—guaranteeing breakfast, safety—so I'd rebuilt some hope that all would go according to plan, despite Skall's betrayal.

Adjusting the straps of my pack, I asked, "Why were your men up again last night?"

Kage smiled. "You may bear the Sun's ring, Miss Aija, but we have always been creatures of the night."

I frowned, glimpsing the rising Sun and yearning for him, even while anger, hurt, and stubbornness brewed in my gut. "Do you not need to rest?"

"Our strength comes from others, as you know."

The sound of crunching godling bones still rang in my ears, if I listened long enough to hear it.

Kage peered past my shoulder and frowned. "Again with her? We should leave soon. Have your party ready." He walked away.

Turning, I spied Zyzi, who must have woken when Ist dismissed his magic. She sat on her bedding, legs folded beneath her, hands resting on her knees. She'd started meditating on the first day of our journey with Kage and refused to skip it morning or night.

I walked over to her and knelt beside her. "Kage wants to leave soon."

She hummed under her breath in a way reminiscent of Ist.

I waited a few more seconds before setting my hand on hers. She turned her grip around and grasped my fingers too tightly.

"If you want me to refrain from murdering you," she muttered, "you will let me finish."

I scoffed. "Is that really why you do this?"

"Yes."

Oh. I had thought it a joke.

A few more seconds passed, and she exhaled slowly, opening her dark eyes. "If you allow yourself to be alone with your thoughts, it will bring you peace."

"I'm very good at being alone with my thoughts." And it was true—there was nothing in my mind I feared. During those months of bed rest, I had become very well acquainted with myself.

She patted the bedding beside her, which was perhaps the only friendly gesture she'd made since we set east. I did as directed, adjusting my legs to match hers.

"Breathe in," she instructed.

Behind us, Ist whapped a demon on the head with his staff. The creature must have been sniffing too close again. Ist had to look like a roast turkey to the dark ones, and Tyu a ready appetizer.

"Breathe in," she said.

I closed my eyes and breathed in, then out, listening for her breaths so I could match them. Our environment wasn't perfect for this—the sounds of packing and pacing demons stippled the air—but the more I focused on Zyzi, the easier they were to ignore. In the beginning, my thoughts lingered on the same problems I'd dissected to minuscule pieces, but in time, they began to fade away, leaving my mind blissfully empty.

"Move out!" Kage snapped, shattering the brief reverie. My eyes snapped open to reality, and to Tyu, hovering timidly before me, waiting.

I sighed and stood, lending Zyzi my hand to help her to her feet. She said nothing more to me.

We had a long day of walking ahead of us.

Kage stopped our party the evening of the seventh day, which gave my weary body pause. He never let us camp early. He waited until Zyzi, the godlings, and I caught up to explain himself—we took to walking several paces behind the demons to avoid mingling with them.

"There." He pointed past a wooded area to a great rock jutting up from the Earth, stretching at a diagonal like the Earth Mother's own finger. The rock was slightly red in color. I hadn't even noticed it. My body grew so weary by this time of day that I did little besides look at the ground in front of me. Tyu had even taken to hovering low to stay in my line of sight, holding my skirt with invisible hands to keep me on my path. "There lies the god's nest."

A great sigh released from my lungs, as though I'd been holding my breath these last eight days. Zyzi looked at me, biting her lower lip. Ist hummed with interest. When I placed a hand on his shoulder, he said, "I do sense. Something there."

Even I did. Not magic, or essence, or whatever it was Ist could feel, but something else. Something that tugged on my memory. My heart. "A god truly lived here?"

"Such is the lore," Kage said with a shrug. "But my people have trespassed these lands before. Regardless of how it happened, there *is* power here."

Then it clicked, and I heard Saiyon's deep, smooth voice in the back of my mind as clearly as if he were standing next to me. *The energy of the volcano shook the ground and imploded, devouring most of his mountain, and the lava bled beneath the sea—creating a bridge of molten rock that connected Soolo to the mainland.*

Shivers coursed down my arms. "Soolo," I whispered. Could this possibly be the same place? Was this the nest where the godling Krognik was born, where the warrior Taylain retrieved him?

Hope sparked, bright and painful. *Almost time.* I looked out toward Saiyon, who had begun his slow set. "I'm coming," I whispered.

"Miss Aija must attend alone, of course," Kage added.

Tyu turned tooth white.

Zyzi stiffened. "Absolutely not."

The demon leader raised an eyebrow. "What complaint do you have? We're keeping our side of the bargain."

"Like you kept it before?" my cousin snapped.

"That was Skall's bargain," I whispered. I was so tired. My dress was travel stained, and the pack on my back crushed me like an anvil.

Tyu rushed up to face me, her body inches from my nose. "Do not follow them alone, L'Aija. Let me come with you." Turning to Kage, she said, "I will attend her."

Kage was adamant. "Your essence will interfere. Corrupt the magic."

Tyu didn't back down. "I have been charged by the Lord Sun Himself—"

The demon leader merely shrugged. "Then you doom her to fail."

The pattern of Tyu's colors shifted.

Zyzi squeezed my hand. "Don't trust them."

"What have we been doing all this time, if not trusting them?" I asked. Pleaded, because I *needed* this to happen. I needed Kage to hold up his end of the deal. I needed a victory. "If not *hoping* to trust them?" Scanning the demons, I found the one who had looked at me with such ravaging hunger after delivering the bones. I remembered the sound of Skall's screams. Lifting my chin, I said to Kage, "If the godlings' nature will interfere, why can Zyzi not come?"

"Because another mortal will drain the power." He shook his head. "Mortals are sponges for magic." He gestured to my healed finger. "If two are present, the energy will split, and we will fail."

Ist hummed. "Is the god. Birthed here. So. Different. From the. Earth Mother? He sprang. From Her womb. As did I."

Ist was trying to prove that his magic was similar enough to the god's that he could play witness. My spirit quietly thanked him for it. In truth, I did not want to go alone.

"Not Her womb. Only Her carapace," Kage countered. His stare shifted from me to Zyzi, to Tyu and Ist. "I will settle with you. One of mine will stay behind for each of yours."

Including Kage, eight demons traveled with us, one having stayed in that horrid forest. That would still leave me alone with five of them.

Unease twisted in my belly. "I thought you needed your full number."

He smiled in a patronizing way, like I was a child. "Why do you think we've come so far, mortal?" He pointed to the god's nest. "That *is* the power."

Biting my lip, I glanced back to the others. Already Ist had begun circling his staff like he stirred a shallow cauldron, and vines just like those he grew every night to cage us in began breaking through the ground. Unlike in the demon's dead, rank forest, Ist had power here. He'd said, once, that he could handle a small number of demons. It was being left alone with an entire pack that worried him.

This was my chance. My *only* chance. I had come too far and lost too much not to take it.

"Fine," I said, ignoring Zyzi's sputtering. "But you leave these two." I pointed out the hungry demon, who was one of the weakest-looking ones, and then a larger one that Ist had already put in its place more than once. Hopefully the memory would be enough to make him behave. "The last is your choice."

The demons seethed at being called out.

Kage shrugged. "Very well." He pointed to the demon closest to him, who hissed in displeasure at being left behind.

Tyu, body a bright peach, zipped off toward the trees—but this time she flew over them, skyward, her figure blending in with the firmament. I thought to call after her, but she moved like light. Before my tongue could form words, she was gone.

Her abrupt departure confused me, but at least she'd be safe.

Kage didn't seem to notice, or maybe he didn't care. He raised an expectant eyebrow.

I slid off my pack and passed it to Zyzi. But as I moved to follow, she grasped my wrist and pressed the hilt of her knife into my hand. I wondered if she could feel the punch of my heartbeat beneath my skin.

"I'll follow behind, if I can," she whispered, glancing to Ist.

I nodded. I did not want to risk disrupting the process, but the hard travel had whittled down my strength enough that my fears were beginning to poke through. But if I didn't have this, I had nothing, and I could not accept that. Would not.

Taylain was brave, I told myself. *She climbed this mountain. So can you.*

Not even the gods could spare me from the deep-seated stubbornness born into my blood. Even my pulse seemed to sing, *Kata. Kata. Kata.*

My grandmother would rather die than quit. Now it was time to see how much of her flowed through me.

Slipping the knife into my pocket, I followed Kage toward the god's nest. It was farther away than it seemed. The Earth grew steeper and steeper the closer we walked, until my legs burned and my lungs puffed like a dying fire. I looked up once to see how the Sunlight hit the rock formation just so. It was lovely to behold, yet I recognized something was missing from my reaction to it. Something Kage now possessed, though I didn't understand how.

The rock was not one finger but two; as we climbed around its east side, a second stretch of it extended outward, almost perpendicular to the—

"Sea," I whispered, spying the blue expanse. "We're on the coast."

"Of course." Kage seemed genuinely surprised.

The Sun continued its set as we climbed, climbed, climbed. I hiked up my skirt, not because I was stepping on it, but because the unsheathed knife in my pocket was poking my thigh. I began to worry

I wouldn't have the energy to make it to the top of the formation when Kage stopped us as we reached that second finger, the one that jutted toward the ocean. He gestured to the place where the two fingers met. A large cave greeted us. The demons shuffled about to prepare and light two torches. I held my ground, waiting for them to enter first.

Kage smiled at me the way a parent might smile at a misguided child, then took a torch himself and led the way.

The cave extended inward about thirty feet before dropping off suddenly. The demons walked clear to that drop, holding their torches high, revealing a massive stone chamber of red rock. It looked like the mouth of a great beast. When Kage motioned me forward, I saw its teeth.

The drop was about twenty feet, and the ground below was covered with stalagmites. They fit closely together, barely leaving room between them. They had wide bases and slick, pointed tops, like conical daggers jutting up. A faint *drip*, *drip* sounded as water from the ceiling pattered downward, making me think of saliva.

A godling had been born here.

"There it is." Kage made a wide gesture with the hand that held the torch, causing the shadows to jump and roll. "The god's nest. Here we can use the power of the bones and your art and transform you into what you wish, finalizing our deal."

I pulled away from the ledge, bumping into one of the demons. "I don't understand. How does this work?"

Kage's malformed mouth grinned. "Our magic will change you, and then you must jump."

I tensed and took another step away from the ledge.

"Your body is mortal." He spoke in such a cajoling way, like it was obvious. "You cannot become immortal until you cast it off."

Chills coursed through my frame. "You want me to impale myself."

"I want you to shed your mortal bonds so I can complete our arrangement."

I glanced at the stalagmites. Kage shifted his torch away, like he didn't want me to see too many details.

The demon I'd bumped into wiped his mouth. Was he . . . salivating?

I glanced at my hand, which bore the healing scar from where the godling's bones had cut me. I hid it in my pocket. Felt Zyzi's knife.

This was wrong. Everything in my mind, body, and soul screamed, *Wrong, wrong, wrong!*

Kage must have seen my doubt, for he said, "This is the only way."

I shook my head. Death did not equal life. I had studied every piece of scripture Rozhan had to offer. *Death is not life.*

I backed away. "No. Give me back my art. The deal is broken."

Kage's amiable demeanor cracked. "The deal *cannot* be broken."

A demon grabbed my arm. I twisted, yanking my hand from my pocket and whipping out the knife. Its point sliced through the monster's fingers. The demon hissed. I backtracked, grabbing the knife in both hands, keeping five demons at my front.

"Give it back," I seethed.

Kage's mismatched features warped into something feral. "Oh no, Miss Aija." His voice grew coarse. "You will jump, or we will rip you apart. Either way, that essence is ours."

A sob broke halfway up my throat, escaping my lips like a mew. My hammering heartbeat cursed me with every thud. Had I really thought I could succeed through sheer willpower? I was a mortal. I was *nothing*.

They stalked toward me. I pointed my knife at Kage, then at one of his companions, but I was no warrior. I wouldn't be able to fight them off.

I was going to die.

My knuckles paled around the sheath. The demons began to spread out. They meant to surround me. They—

A sound reached my ears, feather soft. Waves rolling up on shore. The sea.

My eyes stung. I set my jaw.

If I was going to die, I would not die by the hands of gruesome liars. I would not be consumed.

I'm sorry, Zyzi.

I lowered my left hand with the knife. Grabbed my skirt.

Turned and *ran*.

My body was so sore, so tired, but I pushed everything I had into that sprint. Every muscle from working the farm, every spark of stubbornness, every morsel of life, because in a few moments I wouldn't need any of them.

I bolted from the cave, the demons in quick pursuit. My shoes slapped against the red stone as I followed the finger east, out toward the endless sea. I didn't know how deep the water would be below me, or if it even reached this far inland. But it didn't matter. Ocean or stone, the fall alone would kill me.

My last thought before I jumped was a sorrowful one: I'd wasted that which Saiyon had broken law to give me.

The rock gave way, and I fell, the wind rushing up around my ears, deafening me.

I barely registered the way the sky pulsed with light.

I did not reach the ocean.

The ocean reached up for *me*.

It was the middle of the night, my mind just lifting from dreaming, when he murmured, "Part of Me wishes I had stood stronger. Resisted her. Or fallen anywhere else on this world."

His breath grazed my hair. I focused on keeping mine even.

"Then it would not kill Me when I return." His voice was almost too soft to be a whisper. "I cannot bear it . . . and yet I will. I must."

He held me tighter. I feigned sleep. Feigned it for a long time.

This was a confession I was not meant to hear.

CHAPTER 15

For a moment, I don't know how long, everything was cold, wet, and dark.

I woke gasping, desperate for air. My lungs weren't large enough for all the air I needed. I coughed and then retched, bile burning up my throat and splashing on the grass.

Grass?

I tried to focus. To orient myself. My fingers curled around wild grass as I continued to wheeze and gasp, until I could feel the air moving in and out of my chest, my heart rapidly pushing blood through my limbs. Unbound, damp hair stuck to the sides of my face; my clothes were cool and itchy but not soaked.

I'd fallen into the sea . . . and washed ashore? How long had I lain here?

Pushing myself up on shaking arms, I turned over, spying the Sun on the horizon, two-thirds set.

"L'Aija."

I lowered my head to Tyu, who stood on invisible legs on a pebble, lavender swirling through her triangular body. I stared at her for a long moment, blinking salt from my eyes. She was here. She'd come back.

Then she pointed, with a tip of her half-haloed head, toward the sea. And the demigod standing just off the beach.

I gaped. Five paces away, the grass broke into rocks, the ocean lapping against them. In the gentle waves stood a creature shaped like a man, made entirely of the sea—so much so that I could see the expanse of the ocean through his person. He had no definitive features, no ornamentation of any kind. He was water made to look as human as water could look.

Despite all my knowledge of scripture, it took several seconds for my mind to interpret what I was seeing, and then to find my voice. "T-Tereth?"

"Can you stand?" The personage had no mouth, but the voice flowed softly from it anyway, smooth as fine whiskey and just as warming.

It took me three tries, Tyu floating to pull on my sleeve, but I did stand. My pulse throbbed in my scars. I took one stumbling step toward him, then another and another, until I reached the rocks. "You are the demigod of the sea."

He nodded.

"Why—"

"Satto reached out to me, and I answered."

Warmth bloomed in my chest, leaving my hands cold. *Satto.* Saiyon's servants called him that.

If you have time to chide me, then take the time to help me.

Relief and shame danced through my chest.

I glanced to Tyu, who lowered her head. She had known. She had left me to warn him. Lifting a hand, I ran the pad of my thumb over her thin head, a gesture of thanks. Gazing toward the Sun, I would have wept if my body hadn't been so wrung out. *Thank you, my love. Thank you for saving this fool of a woman.*

For I had been a fool. Knees buckling, I dropped to the ground.

Tyu squeaked and hugged the side of my face. The waves surged forward, until Tereth knelt in front of me. When I didn't speak, he said, "What has this mortal woman done, to draw the attention of the Sun?"

I pressed my lips together, holding back a dry sob. I shook my head. Tereth waited, the ocean foaming around his knees.

"I dared to love him," I whispered, and a few stinging tears managed to egest from the corners of my eyes. "The heavens cast him close to my home, and I found him and loved him. But because of what I am, because of what *he* is, we cannot be together." I wiped my eyes with the back of my hand, though the salt on my skin only made them sting more. "I thought to barter with demons for immortality, so I might f-find him again." I swallowed, trying to coax my voice to stay even as humiliation warmed my skin.

A deep rumbling, like boiling water in a cast iron pot, sounded from Tereth's chest. "And they betrayed you."

I nodded. "I beg you not to scold me. I've been significantly reproved." I covered my face with my hands and whispered, "I have lost everything."

I cried, because I was a fool down to my core, and I wept for it. For my choices, for what I had done to Zyzi and Ist and Tyu, for the loss of my art, and for Saiyon, who had warned me of my foolishness more than once yet had still intervened to spare my life a second time. I wept long enough that I expected Tereth to have receded into the waters, but when I finally lowered my hands from my swollen face, he remained there, silently waiting for me to finish.

Were he a mortal man, I would have been embarrassed. But something about him being a celestial entity only made me wonder. And though he did not have eyes as I knew them, it seemed that he studied my ring.

He receded about a foot, perhaps fighting against the tide. "I may know a way for you to achieve what you seek."

My breath caught. My eyes widened, and I did not blink until they burned. I waited for his caveat, or perhaps to wake from my near-death stupor. Neither happened.

Tyu pressed into my hair and said nothing.

"You want this for love, not power," he said, soft as sea foam. "I understand what it is to have a heart so burdened."

I swept a curl away from my face. Scripture said Tereth was the lover of the Earth Mother, which was why he lived so close to Her.

"The only being who can *create* what you desire is She." He lay his hand against one of the rocks, and it seemed deeply intimate. "But She has slept for millennia. You must wake Her. Only She can re-form you into something lasting, if such a thing is possible."

I worked my mouth like a dying fish. "I . . . wake Her? Does She not sleep to hide from war?"

He slumped. "I do not know why She still sleeps. I fear there is something amiss. Something with Her heart, which lies deep in Her center—a place I cannot go, for Her core is fire, and I am not. To attempt it would be to hurt us both. I have searched everywhere else I can reach and come to no conclusion. The meaning of Her slumber must reside there."

"Her core," I repeated, reverent. But how would I trespass such a place when a powerful demigod could not?

I shook off the question. I'd figure it out when I got there. Surely this being would not send me on a doomed mission. Surely there was a way.

He nodded. "Rocks are Her bones, loam is Her blood, plants are Her skin, and fire Her heart." He spoke it like poetry. "If Satto cares enough to turn from His war and call out to me on your behalf, then there must be something exemplary about you."

I wiped a tear from my cheek. "The only thing that might have made me special I gave to the demons."

"Perhaps. Perhaps not. But . . . ah." He reached forward. My instinct was to pull away, but this was the demigod of the sea, who had saved my life and who was, in a way, offering me a new one. So when he took my hand, his touch cool and wet, I didn't pull back. And when something tingled, then burned, in my veins, I held my body still and

205

gritted my teeth, until it flowed into my shoulder and down my arm, dissipating as though it had never been.

"I've taken a godling's essence from you," he explained. "If that simmers inside too long, you'll become just as they are."

My lips parted. The demons, he meant.

"I-I didn't know." Swallowing, I reached for Tyu for comfort and took strength in her papery touch. "They were human once?"

Tereth shook his head. "Not those."

Shaking myself, I forced my mind to think, my will to rekindle, and my body to *do*. "The Earth Mother's heart . . . where is it?"

"Very far from here." He considered a moment. "I can get you close, but the entrance is landlocked. But I will take you as far as I can."

Hope, painful and raw, throbbed between my breasts. "I-I have company. My cousin and another godling." *Oh gods, Zyzi and Ist. Are they all right?* I prayed that my foolishness had not hurt them further—

"Find them and bring them here. You are too fragile for me to carry myself." A tiny seashell floated up his torso. "I will bring a ship for you."

I nodded, numb. "Th-Thank you." I felt a sore on my lips crack. "Thank you for your kindness."

He nodded. "What is your name?"

"Ai. Aija."

"Aija." While he did not express it physically, I detected a smile. "I will be in your eternal debt if you bring Her back to me. My purpose is not entirely selfless."

I did not know how to answer. But there was no need. The water forming Tereth splashed down against the rocks and receded into the sea. The Sun was nearly gone; I forced myself to my feet. I had to find Zyzi and Ist quickly—and pray the demons who'd betrayed me in the cave were not doing the same. Turning, I found the god's nest formation in the distance and oriented myself, pulling on dregs of energy to trek through the scattered wood. I had nothing to build a fire, so I moved quickly, promising my beaten body that we would rest soon. Like in the Furdowns, Tyu guided me, though her directions were little more than whispers.

Despite my losses and my stupidity, my heart beat with renewed vigor. For if Tereth could wait so long and with such devotion for the Earth Mother to awaken, then certainly I could wait a little longer, and work a little harder, to reach Saiyon. I needed only to find the heart of a goddess to do it.

It should have sounded insane, but in that moment, nothing felt more right.

Tyu and I moved swiftly through sparse trees and mossy terrain, but it grew dark quickly, forcing me to take care with my step. Fortunately, I spied a spot of orange in the distance. The demons never lit fires, but Tyu flew ahead to confirm. As I neared, something seized my ankle—a vine sprung up from the Earth. Before I could panic, I heard Ist's voice say, "She is. Here," and the vine released me.

I stumbled into their camp, immediately met by Zyzi's strong embrace. She held me tightly enough to hurt. I squeezed her back. The way she breathed into my hair revealed she, too, had been crying.

I pulled back and studied her face. "Why are you so far south? The demons—"

"They left," she answered, touching one of my salt-encrusted curls. "The Sun burned up the sky, and the three who waited with us ran. What happened on the rock?"

I suddenly felt like I'd swallowed shale pieces. "I . . . They betrayed me."

Zyzi's jaw set.

"I leapt into the ocean. But that flash, that was Saiyon." I recounted in tumbling words what Tyu had done, how Tereth had caught me up, and what he'd told me about the Earth Mother. About my final chance.

Zyzi, eyes bright as they reflected the campfire, dropped to her knees. Ist hummed. I crouched beside her, taking her hands.

"I know what you'll say." My tone took a pleading edge. "I haven't listened to you. Any of you." I looked to Ist, his eyes bright as topaz, and Tyu, who drifted nearby. "I've depended too much on myself. I'm headstrong, and I'm stubborn. But I can't give up now, Zyzi. Saiyon still watches over me, and Tereth himself will take me to the heart—"

"The very gods of the sky and sea bend for you," she whispered. But she wasn't angry. She sounded . . . awed. I gave her time to contemplate, and she took it, Ist and Tyu waiting patiently behind her. "Your will is even stronger than Kata's. Who would have thought it possible?"

A smile tempted my lips.

She sighed. "How far?"

"To the heart?" I asked.

A nod.

"Very far."

Craning back, Zyzi looked at Ist, then beyond him, as if she could see all the way to the farm and Goatheir from where she knelt.

"Let me come with you," she whispered, taking my hands.

"*Let* you?" I repeated. "Zyzi, I would beg you." I blinked tears from my eyes. Gods knew I'd never cried so much as I had this past year.

"I would. Come. And see. My promise. Through." Ist tapped his staff against the Earth. "Show us. Where Tereth. Spoke with. You."

We made torches from the fire and put out the rest, then picked our way back to the coast. I couldn't find the exact spot, but I was close, and we rebuilt our camp beneath a dark willow tree, the sea stretching before us, unevenly reflecting the light of the rising moon. Though I was ragged and weary, I was the last to slumber. Sitting up on my bedding, I stared at the sky and whispered, "Can you not stop this war, my lady? Do you want power so much you would make all those around you suffer?"

The moon did not reply, of course. I hadn't expected her to. But it was as much of a prayer as I could offer.

My thoughts turned to compromise. If I never gained immortality, if the moon would settle for her night kingdom and cease battling the Sun, at the very least Saiyon would have more ability to see me. Not touch me—he could never hold me or caress me, even share a breath with me, as I was now. What we'd had, the *way* we'd had it, would be gone and over, captured in sketchbooks, on canvas, and imprinted in memory and skin. But even if I failed in my mission with the Earth Mother, if the war ended, I could see him, speak with him. Philosophize and weep with him.

It would never be enough, but it would be something.

I woke just as the Sun peaked, to the sound of white water. When I opened my eyes, I saw the waters part not far from shore, and a great, barnacled ship rose from them, its sails long gone, two of three masts missing, its wood warped and water-logged but intact. It was guided not by the winds, but by Tereth himself.

A sunken ship brought to the surface of the world.

I offered a prayer of gratitude to any god that would hear, and I did not stop praying until the ship drew ashore.

"Do I look anything like her? Ceris?"

A subtle curve formed on his lips. "Not at all."

I frowned. I had nothing to prove. Still, try as I might, I could not conceal my disappointment that I did not compare to a woman he had loved.

Saiyon noticed and touched the pad of his thumb to my mouth, banishing the expression. "When you have seen the world, the universe, as I have, you learn how trivial beauty can be. How . . . subjective."

My discontent held strong. "So you care nothing for beauty?"

That curve deepened. "I did not say that." Turning, he looked out toward the stars. "What I mean is that two very different beings can both be enchanting. If not for beauty, I might never have noticed you in the first place."

CHAPTER 16

I'd never traveled the sea before.

It was beautiful.

My mind could not fathom its enormity. Tereth pulled us out into his world until no matter where I turned, I could not find land. Out here, Earth Mother was a blue glass marble, rippling with magic and creatures unseen. The air smelled so crisp, and the sky stretched endlessly. More shades of blue stretched between myself and the horizon than I had ever before beheld. I felt Saiyon's presence on that ship more than I'd felt it anywhere on soil, and I knew he watched me. He had dissuaded me twice now from pursuing immortality, and I wondered what he thought of Tereth aiding me. If it disgruntled him, worried him, or if he, like Zyzi, had finally accepted that I would not give up.

Saiyon himself had claimed love had more power than anything else. I was determined that this time he wouldn't have to love and lose, only love.

The journey was long but full of majesty that inspired me the way Algeron had when I'd first arrived as a young bride. Out of habit, I pulled out my sketchbook and attempted to draw. The rocking of the ship was no help, but I could not create the way I once had. My lines were unsure, my shading nonexistent . . . I *knew* how to draw. I still remembered my lessons and my practice. I still knew the rules. But my fingers had forgotten the ease of shapes and lines and color. It had taken me years to learn those skills; it would take me years to relearn them. Though now, with the impatience of an adult, I feared I no longer had the stamina. So I set down my pencil and flipped back through the pages, finding pictures of my mother and grandmother, of Saiyon, and reabsorbed them.

I had evaded thoughts of Enera, Kata, and Aunt Danika. How angry they would be with me. How desperately worried. My mother would be beside herself, fearing for me. I would be atoning for this the rest of my life. And if my journey was successful, my life would never end.

I thought, once, to send Tyu back to the farm, to have her play messenger. But if I did, she would not find us again, and I would be without my companion. My friend.

Zyzi sat beside me and examined my old sketches. When I reached the back of my book, she asked, "Are you sad?"

I closed the book and glanced out over the sapphire sea. "Yes. But I don't regret it. My choices were not wise, but the demons led me to Tereth."

The sea bubbled beneath us, and I wondered if the demigod was listening.

Zyzi nodded. "How many gifts do you think we'll have to bring home to be forgiven, once this is over?"

I smiled. "Too many. Perhaps Ist could grow us a farm-sized bouquet."

"A bouquet? I'm thinking sugar beets and barley. Because no one is going to forgive us without a lot of sugar and alcohol. Think he's up for it?"

I chuckled and glanced over to the godling, who leaned against the sole mast with his eyes closed. He did not enjoy sailing in the slightest.

That night, the heavens tore open again, right over our heads.

The blasts looked like the fireworks set off over the castle in Algeron on summer solstice, but bigger and brighter. They were loud enough to rattle the ship. I stuck my fingertips in my ringing ears and watched with dread as the sky ripped apart. Our ship veered suddenly, throwing me onto my elbows. Moments later, something large crashed into the sea.

Tereth did not slow down to investigate. Our ship propelled forward, through waters reflecting bursts of Sun- and moonlight alike. I watched, I prayed, and I feared all the night through, until the thunder and colors fell far behind us. The Sun rose late—I had no way to prove it, but I *felt* it—but he still rose, and I finally let myself breathe, questioning him through the ring, asking for assurance of his welfare.

The ring warmed around my finger. I pressed a kiss to its amber line.

Ist, Zyzi, Tyu, and I spent five days on the ship Tereth had pulled from the deep, and on the morning of the sixth, he set us again on dry land wildly unfamiliar to me. Whereas I had boarded in autumn, I now stood in summer. The coast was made entirely of white sand lined with bizarre flora I couldn't name yet still craved to draw. There were violet mountains in the distance, but even from the sea, I could tell they were far larger—newer—than those that lined the horizon from my farm.

Ist hummed nervously as we climbed off the ship and then knelt in the sand and took up a handful of it, letting it run through his fingers. "Will I. Perish. So far. From home?"

"None of us will perish." I grunted as I dropped from the ship's ladder to the ground, feet splashing in a couple of inches of mellow seawater.

The ship floated back, tipping onto its side without the demigod to hold it up, and the water re-formed into the semblance of a man once more. To my surprise, he bowed to me. "There is but one entrance to the Earth Mother's heart, located in the deepest part of the Losoko Canyons northwest of here." He gestured. "It will be a journey. This is the closest I can carry you."

I exchanged a glance with Zyzi before answering. "We will find it. Ist will be able to replenish our food stores. And Tyu has a sense for these things."

Tyu's colors flashed uncertainly.

Brushing off his hands, Ist stood and leaned on his staff. "I am. Too old. For such. Adventures. I have. Realized this."

"Realized it too late, I'm afraid." I offered him a smile, and to my relief, he snorted. Two godlings and two mortals cannot spend nearly a week aboard an empty vessel without growing accustomed to one another.

Zyzi handed me our pack. "Your turn."

I strapped on the bag, the tight skin of my year-old burns pulling as I did so. Looking into the featureless face of the sea, I asked, "How will I report back to you?"

"I will know." His legs sunk into the water. "You have my blessing, Aija. Zyzi, Ist. Tyu." He nodded to them. "Tread carefully. Help Her."

I nodded, and the demigod drizzled into sea foam, floating away on the next sleepy wave.

The sandy beach did not last long.

It gave way to a forest of those strange trees. All their leafy branches jutted from the crown of the plant. Some were of a height with Ist, fat bodied and spiky, while others stretched the height of five men. There were strange animals as well, ones Ist took great interest in. Tyu pointed out a bright flower, claiming one of my burn treatments had come from its roots. The cacophony in the forest was unlike any music, natural or not, I'd ever heard. And as the day progressed, the air grew so humid and hot that I was tempted to cut off my hair and continue the journey naked.

The air cooled the farther inland we traveled, though our movement was slow due to the lack of trails and roads. But on the third day, in the evening, Ist held out his staff and stopped us, his pointing ears flicking.

"Predator?" Zyzi whispered.

He shook his head. "There is. A path. Here."

Tyu flickered and zipped onto his shoulder. "Oh!"

I searched the ground. I was sweaty and itchy and sore, but I could not bring myself to complain. Not with a hopeful end in sight. "Where?"

"A godling. Path." He turned and pressed through the thick foliage perpendicular to where we'd been walking. Unsure, I followed him, and Zyzi trekked behind me. The jungle floor rose, and after a quarter hour the plants around our feet thinned, giving way to dark, porous rock I recognized as igneous—one of the merchants had sold pieces of it in Rozhan, both as decoration and for medicinal purposes. The terrain grew steep, until even Ist panted for air. As the Sunset turned the sky orange, he stopped suddenly and dropped his staff. Holding his hands in front of him, he said, "I beseech. Ye who guards. This gate."

The air crackled, and a godling appeared as if by magic—actually, it probably *was* magic. I gasped, at first thinking the glittering blue creature was Pree. But when she spoke, her voice was distinctly female. "Who passes here?" She paused and stepped forward, examining Ist and then Tyu. "You are not from these parts." Her gaze shifted back to Ist. "Why do you travel with mortals, Earthlen?"

"I have. Taken. Their quest. As my own. We seek. The. Losoko. Canyons. Does your. Path. Lead near. There?"

She hesitated before answering. "Yes. Right through."

My heart leapt. "Truly? Please, godling. Let us pass. It will save us time."

Her attention shifted to me, scrutinizing. "What need do you have for a celestial road—" Her speech froze, and she pushed Ist aside and seized my left hand, bringing it up to her face. I immediately made a fist, fearing she would try to take my ring.

She did not, only studied it. "You are touched by Him." Her eyes lowered. "He gave you those scars."

I jerked back, and she released me. She was not the first to see my scars through my clothes, but the vulnerability of it made me nauseous.

Perhaps sensing my discomfort, Tyu swept back to me. "She is sanctioned by the Lord of Skies."

Zyzi added. "We were brought here by the demigod of the sea to seek out the Earth Mother."

The godling tilted her head. "She sleeps, and only those true in heart can hope to approach Her."

"You speak like. We do. Not know," Ist protested.

"Our journey is blessed by him." I tilted my head toward the setting Sun, though thick trees prevented me from seeing his face. In truth, Saiyon had begged me to stop, but this godling needn't know the details.

Her gaze returned to Ist. "Speak ye truth?"

"Speak I. Anything. But?"

The godling nodded. "Journey onward, brother."

I gestured my gratitude to the godling, who watched us pass and descend the other side of the rock. I halted, seeing where it dropped into a sheer cliff, but when Ist stepped off the black trail, the air rippled silver and green, and he vanished into it. Tyu chirped in glee, beckoning us forward.

Smiling wide enough to hurt, I grabbed Zyzi's hand and followed, vanishing into a portal of the gods.

Many godlings live on the Earth Mother, just as mortals do. Some of them can fly, like Tyu; others are incorporeal and pass through walls without effort. But there are also some, like Ist, who don't possess any special abilities related to movement, and though they live for centuries, traveling becomes bothersome and mundane.

So godling paths were built. Ist slowly explained them to us as we walked through a tunnel that seemed to be made of swirling chips of ten thousand kinds of metal, but when I reached out to touch them, the walls were solid. These paths are unseen by mortal eyes and are built over, under, and through the crust of the Earth Mother. Not only does this make them more direct, but they are also infused with celestial magic, which meant every step we took was *more* than a step. The existence of this wonder cut down our journey significantly.

I wondered if Tereth knew the path was here and had intended us to use it, or if the way was too far inland for him to detect.

It would be a long time before I got the chance to ask him.

When we emerged from the godling path, it was night, and too dark to find our way to the entrance to the Earth Mother's heart. Though I was anxious to search, it would do none of us any good to start that journey now, in our state of exhaustion. Not even Ist knew what to expect once we began our descent, which concerned me . . . but if the way was lethal, surely Tereth wouldn't have sent us. As he'd said, he was invested in our success.

And so we made camp. The night was especially dark, thanks to the steep mountains surrounding us, which shrunk the night sky to a single strip clustered with stars—it seemed there were more stars in that sliver of sky than in all the space over Rozhan. I lay back and stared at them, taking in their beauty, wondering at Saiyon's legacy to have created so many. Wondering at the star mothers. Had they existed since the dawn of time as well, or had the need for their human wombs come later? Such thoughts led me to think of my own mother, and how much I missed her gentle presence.

I didn't remember falling asleep. When I woke to Zyzi preparing breakfast, I thought she'd done so in the middle of the night, only to realize the canyon walls hid the morning Sun. She smiled at me before offering roasted tubers and half a skinned squirrel caught in a trap last night, which she arranged on the plate to form a smiling face. I thanked her and ate as I thumbed through my sketchbook, embracing the pain of loss that came with each picture. I had willingly chosen this, I reminded myself, and I needed to find peace with that. I might have tried some sketching exercises, were I not eager to finish our journey. So I packed up, letting Tyu comb and braid my hair as I worked, and brushed my teeth. Ist explored the area, fascinated by everything he saw—bugs, rodents, rocks. He hummed so loudly he practically sang.

After strapping the pack onto my back, I put out the fire while Zyzi finished her morning meditation. Tyu said, "I sense something. Here." And she tilted her head northwest.

Ist hummed again, closing his eyes. "Yes. I can. Feel it."

We headed north, where the canyon walls crept closer together, sharing secrets our ears couldn't hear. We fell into a single-file line, for the canyon rapidly grew so narrow two women standing side by side would not fit through it. Ist called this a slot canyon, which instantly gave me the image of a giant coin rolling through, and I wondered how long it would take me to draw such a thing.

The canyon narrowed so much at one point that I had to take off my pack and slide through sideways, then remove the cook pot from the bag and heave it behind me. After that, the canyons opened again, wide and nearly circular, like two mountainous hands cupped around us.

I stopped instantly.

Statues filled the way. All kinds of . . . statues.

Tyu shivered and floated close to me. Ist hummed and examined the nearest ones. At first glance they might have appeared as rock formations, but they were too precise, even with obvious erosion. Some were as short as my hip, others twice my height. Many were broken, half-erect and half-crumbled on the ground. Most bore humanesque shapes, which was why I saw them as statues. All of them were . . . strange. Perhaps, had my talent still been with me, I would have been able to determine why sooner.

"What is this?" Zyzi asked, pressing her hand to one of them. "Sandstone?"

"Hmmm no. But I. Do not. Know what. Stone. This is." Ist slipped between two of the creations, picking his way to the back. There was a veritable army in this space. Hundreds of statues, and . . .

"This wasn't made by human hands," I murmured, standing before an intact figure of a height with me, Tyu timidly examining it from my shoulder. Its head was skull shaped, though if it had ever possessed defining features, the winds and rains had stripped them away. It seemed bent over with too many limbs, or perhaps tentacles, trailing on the ground. Almost like a malformed jellyfish—creatures I had noticed, and wished I could re-create, on our journey across the sea. I ran my hand over what might have been the sculpture's shoulder, and that sense of *wrongness* ran up my arm like I'd been burned.

"Is that what you felt?" I whispered to Tyu.

Her head bobbed against my neck.

In response to my earlier statement, Zyzi asked, "How do you know?"

I shook my head, unable to answer. I just . . . knew.

We stepped carefully through the space, the way one might pass through a cemetery. I watched each and every strange statue, trying to imagine them a thousand years younger, trying to determine why they were here. Trying to find a connection between them, but my mind was not sharp enough to form one. When we finally passed the army, we pushed through one more narrow slot—the passage long enough to make me claustrophobic by its end—and were greeted by a smaller opening similar to that which bore the statues, with an even, rocky floor and shale walls so steep no creature could climb them. There was nothing else of note—no insects or animals, no formations, no plants. Only a boulder opposite us, half the size of my farmhouse and shaped like a cherry pit. Ist crossed the short distance to it, then pressed his hands to its surface.

"It blocks. The. Way. On. Purpose. Or by. Accident. I cannot. Tell." He took two steps back, then held up his hand, stalling me and Zyzi from approaching. Digging the end of his staff into the dust, he hunched, his small body trembling with effort.

The boulder creaked.

I rushed to help him, feeble as my strength was. Tyu flew ahead and reached the stone first, pressing with strength that belied her tiny frame. Zyzi took up beside me, gritting her teeth, and shoved her shoulder into the great rock.

Ist's muscles strained beneath his earthy skin, and he planted his feet, pushing into his magic, making the boulder quake as he did. It groaned as it rolled to the side, revealing a path only as wide as the slot canyon we had come from. Ist slumped and Tyu dove for him, grabbing him with unseen hands, her presence and his grip on the staff the only things keeping him upright.

Dropping my pack, I rushed to him, grasping his shoulders before he fell over. I gently lowered him to the ground. "Thank you," I whispered as he blinked rapidly, as though waking from deep sleep.

He nodded once, a simple dip of his chin. "I am. Too old."

"I think you will live another hundred years, at least."

He scoffed. "Only need. One. Moment."

Tyu flew around his head, little sparkles of light in her wake. She'd done that to me in the early days of my recovery. When I was too torn and scalded to move. It was a calming sensation, an energizing one, not unlike Pree's touch had been the night it happened.

For a moment I was there again, bent over in a smoke-filled room, agony blistering my skin, devouring my heart—

The light around us grayed slightly, as it does when a cloud passes over the Sun. Keeping one hand on Ist's back, I peered up, finding the Sun peeking over the mountain. But no cloud covered his face.

A few things happened at once. Tyu slowed. Zyzi startled. A warm glow lit the rocky enclave. Heat pressed into the back of my dress.

My breath caught, as if it knew before I did. Carefully pulling away from Ist, I turned around.

Saiyon looked back at me.

My hand flew to cover my mouth, a sob already working its way up my throat. I had not *seen* him in so long, not in flesh. I stood on shaky legs and approached, until his aura surrounded me, until any closer and I would not be able to breathe in the hot air. Two paces, for a long-legged woman. My heart thumped so loudly the canyon walls seemed to echo the sound until it was all I could hear, all I could feel.

His expression was warm, despite the heaviness on his brow. "Aija."

I swallowed. "Saiyon."

His diamond eyes flickered to Zyzi, Tyu, and Ist, who gripped his staff and stood so he could bow, then to the narrow entrance to the Earth Mother's heart before returning to me. He breathed out through his nose, transporting me, momentarily, to midsummer.

"You are a stubborn woman," he said.

I smiled. "You say that like you're surprised."

"I am not." His hand twitched, like he meant to reach for me, but he must have sensed the intensity of the heat between us; I already bore as much as I could. His hand remained at his side, though I craved his touch almost enough to risk being burned again.

"I am afraid for you," he whispered, brow lifting, "but I will not hold you back any longer."

My spine straightened.

"I have spoken with Tereth," he continued, so softly I didn't think the others would be able to hear him. "If there was ever a way, this is it." He ran a golden, blazing hand over his golden, blazing beard. "I am sorry."

I couldn't tell if my eyes teared—if they did, the heat evaporated them too quickly. "I'll find it, Saiyon."

His head tilted to the side, and he looked at me so tenderly I was transported again to my room in Rozhan. To late nights and whispered conversation. To his deep-golden skin lit by a single candle. To his hand in my hair as he whispered secrets and desires and fragments of promises, for the chains forbade him from lying.

There was no fire, no smoke, no pain.

I breathed deeply, trying to root myself in the present. Trying to ignore the slow tearing in my chest, like I was a canvas being rent across the weak patches holding it together.

He spun his hands together, much as he had when he created my ring. "I will help you," he said. I heard Zyzi's footsteps behind me, though she didn't get as close as I did. Between Saiyon's fingers formed a delicate chain, not unlike the ones that bound him. He broke it into three pieces, which looped together to form three necklaces. A nod from him had Tyu zooming over to collect them—and I envied her that she could be so close to him. That she in her deceptively delicate form could touch him when I could not. When Tyu dropped them in my hands, they burned, but only for a moment before cooling to the temperature of my skin.

"Those will help you endure the heat of the Earth Mother," he said. "Her heart is made of fire, and no mortal can trespass it otherwise."

I gripped the chains, hope burning up my throat like acid. "Then . . . this will let me touch you?"

The weight returned to his brow, and my hope extinguished. "If such a thing were possible, My love"—his eyes dropped to where my scars lay beneath my clothes—"I would have given one to you that very night."

Rip, rip, rip.

"The Earth Mother's heat is an Earthly heat, like that of your hearth. Mine is celestial. It is not meant to be borne by mortal creatures."

Pressing my lips together, I clutched the chains in my fists, trying to tame rising emotion.

"I want you to succeed." His voice carried like smoke. Heat swirled around me, stirring my skirt, pressing in on all sides as if embracing me. "You must succeed, for if you die . . . I would not recover."

The words slammed into me, not because they were poetic or declarative, but because *Saiyon couldn't lie.*

I saw, in my mind's eye, the cracks in him. Not from the strains of his bonds, but from a heart just as broken as mine. A heart that no symphony of time could heal.

Still, I whispered, "Can you make such a claim? You are immortal."

"But I have been chained for My entire existence, and I love so few things." He inched closer, and I held my breath, enduring the heat. So quietly I knew only I heard it, he said, "Come back to Me, Aija."

I gripped the necklaces tighter. "I will."

A soft whistle touched the air, and a being I did not recognize materialized beside Saiyon. He seemed to be made of stone, yet no two rocks touched; they were held together by some sort of magical air, giving him the form of a slender human. I startled but did not retreat.

"Satto," he murmured, oblivious to the rest of us, "we must hurry."

I let my shoulders slump. "The war continues."

Saiyon's posture drooped to match mine. "We are trying to pull away from here," he explained, "but the moon will not leave the Earth Mother's side. She uses the goddess as a shield." He looked downward, at his feet, which did not quite touch the ground. "It would benefit the universe in more ways than one if you were to wake Her."

"I will." My resolve cemented, looking into his hopeful eyes.

Turning to the godling—demigod?—Saiyon nodded, and the creature warped away as quickly as it had come. Then Saiyon held his breath, his body darkening to a blacksmith's red, and his heat pulled back even further. It seemed to hurt him, but he stepped forward, leaving less than a pace between us. He leaned down as though to kiss me.

Pulse racing, I tilted my head toward his. The heat grew stronger, stronger, until it was almost unbearable—

And it vanished all at once. The Sun God was gone, leaving me cold and yearning. Even my scars seemed to pull skyward, searching for their maker.

I wiped a single stray tear from my cheek before turning to the others. "Put these on," I said, holding out the slender chains of beautiful white gold. Zyzi, wiping the back of her hand over her own cheeks, took one without a word.

Ist, hobbling over, said, "He is. Intense."

I smiled, slipping my own necklace on. "He is." I turned to Tyu. "He only gave me three. Can you endure Her?"

Even if I'd had a fourth necklace, Tyu would not be able to wear it—her own head didn't touch her body. She'd have to carry it.

She studied the entrance. "I am not like Ist. I am of heavenly make." She glimmered lavender. "But I do not know the Earth Mother."

Leaning forward, I pressed a kiss to her half halo. "I would not risk you. Would you stay here and guard the way? Ensure nothing foul follows us?"

She flickered white, unsure.

Ist, pointing his staff to me, said, "I'll guard her. With my life."

Tyu's flickering slowed. She nodded. "Two days, L'Aija. If you do not emerge in two days, I will come for you. And if you perish, I will not live long."

Gooseflesh waved over my skin. "Saiyon would not be so cruel—"

"Not from His actions. I would not forgive myself."

Pressing my lips together—I was so weary of weeping—I cupped the side of her tiny head. "Take care."

She nodded.

Ist, Zyzi, and I turned toward the dark, narrow entrance to the Earth Goddess's heart.

As one, we approached.

I entered first.

"I've never seen you like this. So light." My mother dried off another bowl from the sink. "Despite everything, I want him to stay."

Turning toward the fire, I murmured, "I want him to stay, too."

CHAPTER 17

For the first mile, everything was simple, dark, straightforward. I could barely detect the decline in the rocky ground. The tunnel never varied in shape or size; it hovered a few inches over my head, and if I stretched out my arms, I could easily touch both walls at the same time. We had no need for a torch, for the chains Saiyon had gifted us glowed without heat.

After a mile, everything changed.

Everything.

The ground was no longer ground. The walls and ceiling were no longer rock. There was no distinct line separating the Earth I knew from this place I didn't understand. My feet continued true, but there was nothing beneath them that I could see. Nothing but flashes of light in teal and chartreuse, studded on occasion by skeletons I could not identify. Not godlings, for their bones were nothing like the luminescent crystal in the Yard of Bones. These were the remains of mortal beasts, mortal mollusks, mortal *history*, lodged deep beneath the Earth where no man would casually find them.

The light spiraled the deeper we went, curling up and around us, between our legs and whispering through our hair, like it was alive. Another hour, and new, vibrant lights joined it—pinks and reds and violets and yellows in patterns and shades I marveled at—spectacles that would be just as impossible to re-create as Saiyon's eyes, even if my artistic talent returned. Puffs of glitter rose up from the non-floor like snow would fall from the sky, dissipating where it touched us. I slowed to gape at it and grinned at Zyzi, whose mouth was wide open like a child's.

Deeper and deeper we went, until I lost all track of time. I'd been walking for an hour, a week, a year. Veins of gold and ore flashed past us without any stone entrapping them. My feet passed over uncut gemstones without ever touching them. Bubbles of light, some the size of my thumbnail, others the size of my head, floated lazily around us, and when I touched one, it popped into a cloud of vibrant color, clinging to the air like it didn't want to fade.

The air grew warm, and then hot, and our necklaces glowed brighter. The temperature never surpassed that of a brilliant summer day, though it was certainly enough to make Zyzi and me sweat. Ist merely hummed, popping bubbles with the tip of his staff, whistling when light danced around his feet.

It was in a breath between songs that I heard it—a faint drum echoing around me, almost imperceptible. Holding up a hand to quiet Ist, I listened.

Two steady beats.

A heartbeat.

I jumped like fire coursed through my veins. I tried to quicken my pace, yet it seemed I could not move any faster, no matter how hard I tried. The pulsing grew louder the closer we got, until it was no longer distinct beats but a thrumming melody unlike any song mortals could create. I felt its cadence in the marrow of my bones and tasted its harmonies in the back of my throat; they had replaced the air and I breathed them in beat with the goddess's heart. We pushed forward, the colors brightening, the music intensifying, the walls that weren't there *shifting* until up was down and left was right, until there was no direction at all, and we walked on nothing and passed nothing and *I could see Her soul—*

I opened my eyes, though I didn't remember falling asleep. Whether it was sleep or merely unconsciousness forced upon my mortal mind because of its limitations, I didn't know.

The first thing I saw was the fine chain around my neck, glowing brightly, yet with a heavenly softness that didn't hurt my eyes. The next thing was Zyzi leaning against me, still slumbering, breathing deeply.

Then the great heart not ten paces from me.

I stared at it, fragments of thought slowly piecing themselves together. It was the height of a man and breadth of an ancient tree. Igneous, like the rocky ground we had followed to find the godling path. Sliced through it were veins of molten rock, radiating not unlike my necklace. Gold, ruby, and topaz. *And fire Her heart,* Tereth had said, and I knew that without Saiyon's intervention, I would have burned up long before reaching this place.

Ist was already up, if he'd even slept, and stood before the heart. Carefully laying Zyzi down, I stood on shaky legs and reverently crossed to him.

Ist had set his staff on the ground at his feet.

"All my. Life. I have. Never seen. Something. So. Remarkable." His voice was breathy, lightened by awe. "I can die. Fulfilled."

I placed a hand on his shoulder. "Do not die yet, my friend," I whispered. It seemed wrong to be any louder than that.

I could still hear the melody of the Earth Mother's heart like a faraway thing, despite standing beside it. I lifted a hand to touch it. Hesitated. Glanced at Ist.

He nodded, and I let my fingertips graze a dark piece between ruby veins. I expected it to be hot—I expected it to burn me—but it wasn't. It was lukewarm to the touch. As I traced the heart down to the next vein, I had the distinct impression that it was not Saiyon's necklace that prevented my skin from blistering. No—the goddess's heart was *cold.*

But not entirely.

I thought of Saiyon on my bed, the grayish tone to his skin, the *coldness* of it, after he'd wrestled me from the claws of death. Had the Earth Mother broken a law as well? Yet this didn't seem the same. There was still warmth here . . . but if Her heart was supposed to be fire, something was wrong.

"Why do You sleep, Earth Mother?" I whispered, pulling my hand back and circling the heart. "Why do You let mortals tread where they should not?"

"Perhaps. She is. Conscious. Of us," Ist suggested, bowing. "Perhaps. She senses. The chains. We wear."

I touched the glowing gold against my collar. His suggestion made sense. The Earth Mother and Saiyon were allies. I'd read that again and again in all the scripture and scrolls I'd studied.

Circling the heart once, twice, I pulled my memories from my apprenticeship under a Rozhan scholar—a competent and stern woman who let her husband take credit for everything she created, believing a male name would open more doors for her and see a higher price for her wares. Kage had taken my talent, but my memories were intact, eroded though they were. But I could hear her voice in the back of my head. Hear her corrections, her stories. I tried to see the heart as she might.

My eyes followed the fiery webbing, searching for a pattern yet detecting none. I counted the igneous sections. Examined the stony chamber we stood in, which was not unlike the beginning of the tunnel that had led down here. There were no lights, glittering ash, or colorful bubbles. Only the heart and its muted light, dampened song. I was no musician, but I listened to the harmonies, trying to detect a sour note, but my ears picked up on nothing.

Zyzi still slept. Crossing over to her, I shook her shoulder. "Zyzi," I murmured. "Wake up." I needed all the help I could—

I could—

I'd turned back to the heart, my hand still on Zyzi's sleeve. I don't know how I saw it. Perhaps it had to be regarded from that exact angle, or it could be that Ist was right and the Earth Mother was conscious of us and wanted me to know. But there was a sliver of black too dark to match the rest of the heart. Pulling from Zyzi, I crept over to it, nearly lying on the ground to better see it, my necklace illuminating the spot.

A gouge, about the length of my forearm and half as wide. Reaching up, I touched the impression, and the quiet song shuddered.

My muscles slackened. "There's a piece missing."

Ist shuffled over to me. "Hm?"

"A piece missing." I pulled back, knelt. Ist must not have believed me, for he crouched and prodded the area as well, humming low as he did.

I rubbed my hands together, suddenly feeling cold. *Her heart is broken, too.*

How could I find the missing piece of Her heart? Who possibly could have taken it? Or had it been *lost*? The Earth Mother was said to have slept for thousands of years. It could be anywhere . . . including the heavens I could not breech.

My hope cooled and shrunk, and I tried not to collapse around it.

Zyzi stirred, and Ist, bless him, went to her, allowing me to stare at the missing sliver a little longer. Allowing me to organize my thoughts.

I did not know what had happened to the missing piece. I did not know where to start searching.

But I knew with an innate certainty the Earth Mother would not wake unless I returned it.

I was disoriented when I emerged into the Losoko Canyons, like my body had returned to the world I knew, but my mind was still trapped far beneath. It was daylight, and I was turned around, unsure of whether it was morning or afternoon, today or tomorrow—but Tyu rushed to me, checking me over for injuries, and the promise she'd made assured me that less than two days had passed. The others recovered more quickly than I, for soon Zyzi was bearing our pack and pulling me from the rocky wall I leaned against, guiding me like I was a child. I listened absently to her conversation with Tyu and Ist as we walked, Zyzi releasing me only when we had to fit through the tight slot canyons.

"We could start here, first," she suggested. "That dark rock doesn't seem native to this place. It would stand out."

"A stone. Among. Stones. But who. Would leave. Such. A prize. In. The dust?"

Tyu buzzed about, searching the area regardless.

"How could we possibly track such a thing?" Zyzi asked. "Are there . . . songs or folklore, about a missing piece of heart?"

Ist shook his head. "I know. Of none. That are. Aware of. The reason. For. Her slumber."

"Perhaps there's some sort of magical residue. Tyu, do you sense anything?"

The tiny godling flashed a deep purple—negative.

"I likewise. Do not. Sense. Anything. But you may. Be right." He climbed over a cluster of rocks. Zyzi released my hand so I could pick my own way. Another short slot canyon lay ahead. "I may be. Disoriented. From the. Journey. Hmmm . . . We should. Sleep soon."

"It's midday."

Ist didn't bother checking the sky. "Is it?"

Turning sideways, I sidestepped through the narrow slot in the ancient rocks, following them, barely cognizant of my own movements. The conversation came to a sudden halt, and when I emerged on the other side, I immediately understood why.

The statues.

I'd forgotten about them. We'd retraced our steps to the gorge that housed that bizarre, weathered army. Seeing them again was like jumping into a winter pond. Wordless, Zyzi and Ist began to make their way around, but I approached the first cluster of statues, bypassing broken ones to a figure that looked more whole, upright and beaten down by wind and rain.

I pressed my hands to it, and that *wrongness* shuddered up my arm once more.

"Ist." I didn't take my eyes from the statue, but Ist came to my side.

"Why?" I asked, slowly pulling away. "*What* is wrong with these?"

Ist frowned and studied the statue. Put his hand right where mine had been. Hummed so low I almost couldn't hear it.

Then he closed his eyes as if in prayer, ears twitching on occasion. I stepped back to give him space, but he didn't move. Seconds passed, then a minute. Peering over him to Zyzi, I shrugged, unsure what was—

"There is. A heart. Inside." Gravel churned in his voice as he retreated from the strange formation.

"A heart?" I whispered.

He nodded. "A shell. Of one. From. What I. Can sense."

Something about that sparked in the back of my brain. *Why does that sound familiar?*

Zyzi approached, Tyu close behind. "It's not . . . *alive*, is it?" She leaned away from the thing like it might come alive and seize her at any moment.

"No. I don't. Suppose. It ever. Was." He lifted his head. "None of them."

I turned away, biting down on my knuckle, thinking. *Heart.* A shell of a heart. Wrongness and a heart.

Heartless.

Heartless.

And suddenly I knew, like a goddess had opened up my skull and dropped the information in. I knew, and it struck me so forcefully I said his name aloud.

"Kage."

The others stopped midconversation and turned toward me. "What?" Zyzi asked.

I met their eyes. "Do you remember when we first met the demons? Kage said he had no sympathy for my story because he *had no heart.*"

Ist tilted his head. "I do not. Understand."

I paced between the statues, wringing my hands for no reason other than to burn energy. "There's this idea in art called negative space. Where you draw what isn't there."

"Ai . . ." Zyzi trailed off.

I dismissed her with a slash of my hand. "Imagine a cup on a table. You don't draw the cup or the table, but the space around it. The *inverse* of the subject." I stopped near the statue I'd been studying. "The demons have bodies but no hearts. These creatures have hearts, but no bodies."

"Opposites," Tyu chirped, floating to my side.

I slapped the statue. "They were *created wrong*, don't you see? Created as though something, some*one*, had only a portion of the ability to create. And who is the goddess of creation?"

Zyzi's expression slackened. "The Earth Mother." She spun, taking in the statues with new eyes. "You think these were created . . . not by Her, but by the missing piece?"

I nodded, eagerness bubbling beneath my skin.

"Hmmm . . ." Ist stood very close to the statue, studying it. "An. Interesting. Theory. But who. Would have. Tried. To make. Such. Vile. Things?"

Kage's words en route to the god's nest sang through my mind. *You may bear the Sun's ring, but we have always been creatures of the night.*

Leaning back, I peered up into the heavens, trying to see beyond the blue veil of daylight.

"The one who started all of this," I whispered. "The only being it possibly could be."

The moon.

PART 3

In the darkness, with my face buried so firmly against his neck so that he might not hear me, I whispered, "I love you."

CHAPTER 18

I sent Tyu heavenward the next day; she had reached Saiyon once, when the demons cornered me at the god's nest. She could do it again—or so I hoped. But Tyu returned a few hours later, saying simply, "He is not there."

So we set up camp, not willing to leave our evidence behind. I climbed out of the canyons. It took me the rest of that day and the next, but I did it, leaving Ist and Zyzi to sniff out more clues. Tyu attended me, refusing to be parted from me a second time. I needed to be in a place where I could feel the Sun on my face, where he could see all of me. I twisted my ring back and forth, flickering it between black and amber, wondering if it would draw his attention.

"Saiyon, I need your help." My instinct was to speak softly, as in prayer, but I needed to be heard. "I can't do this next part on my own. Please. Come to me one more time."

I pled to the skies until the Sun was nearly set, then traced my way back to my companions, only to repeat my efforts the next day.

"As soon as your war allows," I said, lips to the ring. "You, or someone you trust. Can you hear me, Saiyon?"

We needed to start our journey back. We needed to report to Tereth. Zyzi reminded me of this when she brought me meals Ist had coaxed from the ground. I agreed. We needed to do all of those things. But not as much as we—I—needed that missing sliver of heart.

I repeated my efforts the third day, and the fourth.

On the fifth, at Sunset, he came to me.

The Sunset was glorious. Clouds ribbed the sky, reflecting shades of orange, pink, blue, and violet from horizon to horizon, like something conjured only by the hands of a master artist. I was about to turn back for camp, having determined to set out on the godling path, when he struck the mountain like a lightning bolt and blazed before me. The sight of him took my breath away every time, and renewed that dull ache and sharp wanting that lived in my core.

Tyu immediately bowed.

"Forgive me," Saiyon said, pulling back the flames licking his skin until his face strained. "I came as soon as I could."

I took the cadence of his voice and wrapped it into a delicate coil, storing it away so I could remember it when missing him became unbearable again, because I knew it would. "There is nothing to forgive."

He hesitated a beat, studying my face. "The heart?"

"It's missing a piece."

I'd surprised him.

"The heart is . . . not cold, but not as warm as it should be. A piece about this large is missing." Holding up my hands, I illustrated the size. "I believe it's in the moon's possession."

A spark of blue flame coursed over him. "Of course it is." He shook his head. "What leads you to believe this?"

I told him of the statues in the canyon and my conversations with Kage. I thought he might soar away to see for himself, but he did not. He believed my every word.

He looked away. Folded his golden arms. "It isn't safe."

Firm, I said, "Life isn't safe, Satto."

He glowered at me when I used that term.

I smirked.

He sighed. "Do not pretend to lead a normal mortal life."

"I don't intend to lead a mortal life. Can you take me to her?"

He mulled it over, and I could tell by the flicker of despair he hid that I had convinced him. "I cannot take you *to* her—were it so easy, this war would be over. But I can send someone to help you." He glanced over my shoulder.

"The others are beyond the ridge, at camp."

He nodded. "He can only take *you*."

Tyu chirped weakly.

I bit my lip. Then I would have to say goodbye to the others, for a time. Set a rendezvous point, unless they wished to wait for me. But no, it would be better for them to take the godling path back to the coast. Tereth would help them. He still awaited our report.

"Where?" I asked. "When?"

"I will send him here, as soon as it is safe for him to move." His gaze traced my face, my neck, my torso, stopping at my burns, which had always been visible to those of celestial make. His features drooped and contorted, like I'd pressed a dagger into his gut.

I hugged myself. "Saiyon, it isn't—"

"I do not want you hurt further, Aija," he murmured.

I waited until he met my eyes. "Then we are in agreement."

He paused. Nodded.

I hadn't realized night had descended until he disappeared.

The next day, I pulled out my sketchbook as I waited.

I flipped through my old pictures, both the ones I'd sketched quickly and those I'd spent more time on, trying to walk myself through the steps, to remember the weight of pencils and charcoal in my hand. Then I turned to a blank page and started from the beginning: shapes.

Everything is made of shapes. Humans are circles and triangles and rectangles, slowly pared down, bent, and smoothed to look like heads, necks, torsos, and limbs. Animals are much the same way. Mountains, riverbeds, Sunsets—everything can be broken down into shapes. This is one of the most basic principles of drawing.

My shapes were awkward, like I'd been given the hands of a child. But I drew them, lightly, then darkly, over and over and over again, reteaching my fingers the rudimentary skill. If nothing else, they were a distraction from Zyzi's anger and Tyu's sorrow—neither had been happy to hear they couldn't accompany me on the next leg of our journey. *I* wasn't happy with it, either, but I understood how much Saiyon and his godling risked to aid me.

I drew and drew, shaped and reshaped, waiting. I did not try to pull the shapes together to create something more; I knew that would only frustrate me. So I kept adding to their numbers. Circles, squares, rectangles, ovals, pentagons. Filling one page, then another, and another.

I had been expecting Pree, or perhaps Sai'ken, but the godling who came to me late that afternoon was an entirely new being, a creature of darkness and shadows who, like Tereth, lacked distinctive features. His silhouette was more avian than human, and he shrunk as he approached, until he was only the size of my hand.

"Aija," he said, his voice melodic as he regarded the others like a startled songbird might.

I set my sketchbook aside. "Thank you for coming. What is your name?"

His shadows shifted. "Better that you don't know. Do not mention me, if you're forced to speak to anyone. Tell them only that you found the godling path. Speak kind words of the moon—that will get you far."

Tyu flickered shades of violet. Zyzi toyed with her knife.

I nodded slowly. How dangerous must this mission be for him, if he could not even risk giving me his name? I took a moment to consider. "You work for both of them, don't you?"

The godling hesitated. "My allegiance is where it should be. Come."

He started up the canyon, giving me little time for farewells. I embraced Zyzi tightly, refusing the knife she offered me. I wanted this mission to be peaceful, and I doubted a simple knife would help me against a demigoddess. Tyu hugged my cheek; Ist clasped my hand.

Taking a deep breath, I hurried after the nameless godling, until we topped an incline open to the sky.

Turning back, I felt him scrutinize me. "You'll need to remove those."

Unsure of his meaning, I looked myself over before touching the ring on my finger and the necklace. "But—"

"You should be, generally, overlooked," he explained. "The moon has many mortal followers. But those things will stand out. Mark you as the enemy. You will not get far."

Biting my lip, I removed the ring—I had not once taken it off— and then the necklace. I waved, and Tyu rushed over, reverently accepting the jewelry without word. And they were *only jewelry*, or so I told myself. I had already made far greater sacrifices.

The godling led me across the ridge in silence and opened a purple-and-gray portal ahead of us. I followed him inside, biting down on a gasp at the sharp burst of cold. I'd expected something like the other godling path, but my organs shifted like I was falling. It was closer to the sinking I'd felt after being stabbed than anything else in my experience, and the similarities immediately jolted me with horror. There would be no gods to save me this time if—

The cold dissipated. I did not *land*, but ground solidified under my feet so suddenly that my knees buckled, sending me toppling forward onto my hands. My godling companion stood at my side. He did not touch me, but waited for me to orient myself. As I rose to standing, I took in our strange surroundings.

We were in some kind of desert, and though I had not seen all of the Earth Mother, it did not look like something She might have grown.

It was flat and porous, brown—but that might have been the shadows. The entire thing was caged in by faraway mountains on all sides, making me think of the shell of a tart. Those mountains were haloed by light, perhaps Sunlight, but I was unsure. The rest of the sky resembled a night on the Earth Mother, though a little too light and a little too blue to pull it off. Void of stars.

The godling pointed ahead. I wasn't sure which direction, or if the cardinal points had any meaning here. "Walk toward that dip in the ridge. See?"

I squinted and scanned the ridge three times before I saw what he referred to. "Yes."

"Stairs will appear. Don't wander off. If any beings speak to you, tell them your words are for her only."

I swallowed, searching the way. There were no other land markers that I could detect. "What if I get—"

I turned, but my guide was gone.

"—lost," I whispered. I shivered and hugged myself, though it wasn't cold. Neither was it warm. It just . . . was. I moved my thumb to my ring to steel myself, only to remember it wasn't there. Breathing deeply, I relaxed my shoulders, straightened my spine, leveled my hips. *So close, Ai.* I had to remember that. I was *so close.*

So I started moving. I had nothing with me, save some tubers in my pocket, and I nibbled on them as I walked. Not so much because I hungered, but because I needed a distraction. My chewing was the only sound in this vast place, and my gaze shot about me, wondering if anyone would question me. My companion had made my mission sound so simple, yet if there was one thing I'd learned in my time communing with gods, it was that nothing celestial was ever simple.

The land around me seemed unchanging, to the point where I began to worry that some magic had me walking in circles, unable to move forward. But I kept my focus on that dip in the ridge and walked on, determined to reach it, wondering how long it would take. What if that godling did not understand the way of mortals? A woman could easily starve out here. Dehydrate. Break an ankle and have no one to help her—

I shook myself. *Focus.* Walk.

Perhaps two hours later, I saw what had to be the staircase, though I did not appear to have come any closer to those mountains. Floating rocks, cemented to the air itself. Brown, flat, raising upward into that unnatural blue. So high I should have noticed them earlier . . . if they had been there. They very well may have simply materialized when I crossed the right spot.

Glancing around, I put one foot on the first stone, which hovered roughly a foot above the ground. It didn't budge. I stepped onto the second, and the third, placing my foot evenly in the middle of each stone, unsure whether it was possible to fall off, and not daring to try.

I was about twenty stones up when I saw a figure descending—a sizeable, broad-shouldered creature with six arms and a large white chin. I was out of breath when we met, but I tried to hide the fact.

He regarded me. "A mortal. Where do you travel?"

I swallowed, trying to keep my tongue moist. "My words are for her only."

He nodded, accepting this, and slipped past me. There should not have been enough room for him to do so, yet he did, as though he'd phased through me. I dared not look back or slow my steps, in case he paused to watch me. I did not want to appear suspicious.

Eventually, however, I had to stop. Sweat beaded at my temples, and I shook the bodice of my dress to cool my skin. The stairs seemed endless. I still could not see their end, and when I looked back, I could not quite see their beginning. I did not look long; the high suspension made me queasy. My burns had begun to ache as well, and I wondered if they would give me away. Yet surely the godling who had brought me here would have warned me, as he had with the jewelry. Either way, I could not remove my skin.

Licking my teeth and pretending I didn't thirst, I picked myself up and climbed. I wondered if there was a trick to these stairs, and one who didn't know it would walk forever. Had the godling forgotten to tell me? Perhaps if I focused on—

Cold.

It enveloped me entirely, stealing the breath from my lungs and, for an instant, the beat from my heart. Black engulfed my vision. I blinked, then found myself on my knees against dark glass, shivering, though the icy sensation had dissipated. Rubbing warmth into my hands, I lifted my head, realizing that I'd been placed in a position of humility. Whatever power had brought me here intended for me to kneel.

The room, for lack of a better word, was in shambles. Pillars were broken in half or leaning precariously. Splintered glass and rubble framed the floor, like it had been pushed out of the way but not yet discarded.

"She is, indeed, a mortal," said a woman upon a cracked glass throne some fifteen paces from me. She lounged to one side, elbow propped on an immense armrest. Her skin was the palest I'd ever seen, so much so it was luminescent. Her hairline was high, giving her a large forehead over small, intelligent eyes. Her nose and mouth were small as well, her cheekbones sharp, her hair blacker than any dye humans could create, and it fell behind her slick and straight. Her clothes were gauzy, and while they bore no embroidery or jewels, the way the iridescent fabric folded and coiled made them look ornate. "But why would he bring a mortal here?"

I stood slowly, studying her. Trying not to stare at her most prominent features.

Her scars.

They pocked her like a plague. Scars on her forehead, her cheeks, her neck. Any part of her the clothing didn't cover was tarnished by them, scars like shadows and craters and valleys, blue and violet and gray.

Cold washed through me anew when I realized whom I must have been speaking to.

Moon. And the damage to her palace . . . This must have been from the war.

Shadows on either side of her throne shifted, and I realized they were entities of some sort. She had not been speaking to me, only about me, to these creatures. Pushing off the armrest, Moon sat up straight and regarded me with a look of boredom. "Well? Will you keep me guessing, or must I speculate on our mutual friend a little longer?"

"M-Mutual friend?" I croaked.

"Ghethren, you fool." She spoke like we were old friends, inclined to tease each other, but there was no humor in her eyes.

I stared, mouthing the name, trying to place it.

Frowning, she turned toward one of the shadows. "She hasn't gone mad already, has she?"

Her dark eyes returned to me, studying me. Then she stood. She was small in stature, yet her presence was so commanding she seemed the largest thing in the room. "I've suspected him for some time. But he will be dealt with."

A shock zipped up my spine. *The godling.* He hadn't told me his name. Had he been spotted helping me? Had he been followed? Had *I* been followed? Was that how I'd come to be here?

Setting my jaw, I grounded myself.

"But what was he doing with *you,* I wonder?" she asked, nearing me. "I didn't think he cared for mortals."

"I'm here to speak with you, mistress," I said, and Moon stopped mid step.

"She *does* speak." Her laugh was more of a titter, laced with condescension. "And whatever need do I have for another groveling mortal?"

I met her eyes, trying not to let their black depths unnerve me. "I've come to barter for the heart piece."

I didn't specify the Earth Mother. I was about to, but the look of shock on the demigoddess's countenance told me at once that I needn't bother. She had not expected me to say that. She had not expected me to *know*.

Without looking back, she said, "Leave," and the shadows departed. In their absence, the round throne room brightened to silver. Pillars lined the far side, and between each glowed more of that empty night sky. Empty of any hint of Saiyon.

She stepped closer to me, until there were roughly four paces between us. "Who *are* you?" It was a demand, not a question.

"My name is Aija of Rozhan," I answered. "I have traveled a long way for this audience."

"Rozhan," she repeated, the name apparently interesting to her. Her mind was working, but she didn't reveal her thoughts.

Knowing I could not bully my way to what I wanted, I bowed. "Please, mistress. I beg that you return what you stole. I will—"

"Ha!"

My tongue fluttered to a halt as I peered up.

Moon clapped her scarred hands. "*Stole.* So presumptuous." She whipped around, the fabric of a cape and long train billowing behind her as she stalked back to her glass chair. "The Earth Mother *gave* it to me, stupid child."

She startled me from my bow. "Gave it? Why would She—"

"You are not the first to barter with me." She spun back before reaching the throne, studying me anew. "Your *Earth* is a coward. She *gave* me a piece of Her heart in return for peace." She scoffed. "And I agreed. Who does not want the power of a goddess? The power of creation?"

Her countenance tightened into a vile expression that made her truly ugly. "But it didn't work." She shrugged. "She didn't keep Her end of the deal, so I didn't keep mine."

I shook my head. "Why not return the heart piece and speak to Her of it? She's not awake enough to—"

"*Silence.*"

The word hissed through the chamber like a viper's warning. I closed my mouth so quickly my teeth clacked.

She scowled a moment longer before lowering onto her throne. But I knew what the demigoddess didn't say. I'd spoken with the demons and seen those crumbling statues. The Earth Mother *had* kept Her side of the agreement. Moon merely didn't have the capacity to create the way Earth Mother did. She wasn't strong enough. Or as Saiyon might have said, that had never been her intended purpose, and even a god cannot reorder the workings of the universe.

Our eyes met. She pressed one hand over a large scar on her cheek, hiding it.

"But who *are* you, Aija of Rozhan?" She spoke as if she had not just rebuked me. "Enlighten me, so that I might decide what to do."

I swallowed, trying not to let fear overwhelm me. If Moon chose to harm me, even kill me . . . I had no allies here. "I am a farmer's daughter. I was an artist most of my life, until I traded the skill away."

"An artist?" She perked, and a wicked smile pulled at her mouth. "How interesting. Anything of note?"

I debated the wisdom of telling her, but I felt sure she'd detect any lies or pandering. "I worked on the Sun's cathedral in Algeron."

The smile fell. "Is that so? I've seen it. Garish thing."

I did not respond.

She leaned on that armrest, considering, and I did not interrupt her. After several minutes, she said, "Let me strike a deal with you, Aija."

Those words stiffened my muscles. Memories of Skall and Kage were still fresh.

"Create an image worthy of *me*, and I'll give you the thing you seek."

My jaw fell open. I did not have my talents anymore. She knew that. Yet . . .

"You're in earnest?" I asked. It would be hard. I would have to relearn everything . . . Perhaps I could enlist some of my friends from Algeron. I could direct something grand, a mural, perhaps—

"Of course I am." She sniffed, offended.

I still knew the *principles*, didn't I? Surely I could manage it . . . for *him*, I could manage it.

Treading with care, I asked, "How much time would I have?"

She smiled sweetly. "As much as you need." Taking up her skirt, she tore off a piece. "I'll make a contract."

I eyed the fabric as she began to write, using nothing more than the tip of her finger.

"I will provide everything you need," she said. "But the art must be to my satisfaction."

I nodded. "Might I return to Algeron, to—"

"No." Her voice was hard. "You will complete it here."

Goose bumps rose on my arms, but I had little to barter with. So much for enlisting my colleagues. "How do I know you will not renege on the agreement?"

She scowled. "If you think so little of me, we don't need to *make* an agreement."

I licked the inside of my teeth. "But the Earth Mother—"

"*She* promised me the power of creation. What She gave is not true creation. She is a liar." Her voice was stony and dry. She met my eyes as if daring me to look away. Then she added, "Even goddesses and demigoddesses are bound to a higher power."

A loophole, then. I don't know if her agreement with the Earth Mother had been written or spoken, but Moon had clearly found a loophole.

I couldn't let her do the same with me. And I couldn't walk away. To do so would be to end the journey and accept defeat.

I squared my shoulders. "Then I will have your word that no harm will come to me during my stay, and that I will be returned safely home when the work is finished."

She considered for a few heartbeats. "Very well." She wrote more, then crossed the room, bringing the contract to me. The writing was in Rozhani, and the letters glowed as softly as her skin did. I reviewed the document twice. She had written it precisely. Art to her satisfaction, completed in her domain, any pertinent supplies pertaining to tools and mediums I needed provided by her.

"Sign it, Aija of Rozhan," she said impatiently, slipping a crown of silver light over my brow. "I will not part with the heart piece any other way."

I could do this. One way or another, I could do this.

Lifting my index finger, I signed my name: A-I-J-A—

The moment I lifted my hand from the fourth letter, the throne room warped around me, blurring into shadow. Wind rushed at me, tearing at my hair and clothes, stinging my skin. I tried to scream, but the sound didn't come. Cold seeped into my blood, and that sensation of falling overwhelmed me, shifting my organs nearly to the point of pain—

And suddenly everything was still. Black. Dark. I could not see my hands in front of my face. I could not see *anything*, even the strange crown Moon had placed over my forehead.

"Welcome to Oblivion, foolish mortal," her disembodied voice echoed. "Or did you not know all darkness belongs to me? Now you'll see what happens to those who dare accuse me."

I reached out for her but felt nothing. Nothing ahead of me, behind me, above me . . . only darkness. My heart raced until I couldn't feel the space between beats. Until it filled my ears and my head with frantic drumming—

"When you're ready to die," her fading voice whispered, "take off the crown."

And she was gone.

What if it's true?
What if I can't go where you are?

CHAPTER 19

The contract had said the moon's domain. Not the moon's *palace*.

She was right. I *was* a fool.

I should have demanded clarification, but I hadn't known enough about the heavens to know this place even existed . . .

Did *I* still exist?

I cried. I screamed into the darkness. I ran and fell into nothing and ran some more, but there was no end. *No end.* No light. No doors. No sounds.

Later, *much* later, I would learn about my prison. Oblivion is the space beyond the made universe, not in distance but in *sense*. The darkness that crested its edges and its in-betweens. And Moon had trapped me in a pocket of it, stitched away from the rest of existence.

My own personal hell.

Time passed. So much time passed, or maybe it simply held still. My thirst vanished. I didn't hunger. I didn't need to relieve myself. I was unsure if this was the working of Oblivion or the enchanted crown snug against my skull. All I knew was if I took off the latter, I would die, and it would all be over.

I walked and walked and crawled and walked, but the darkness had no end.

After that, I lay . . . floated . . . existed, for what felt like an eternity. I had been tricked. Was escape even possible? The more the darkness enveloped me, the more time passed, I realized no one would ever find me, not even Saiyon. I would never see my mother or grandmother again. I would never return to the farm or feel the wild grass between my toes. Zyzi . . . How long would she wait for me? Too long. I'd probably ruined her life as well as mine.

Ist would pass on, as well.

I hadn't realized those goodbyes . . . all those goodbyes . . . would be my last.

And Saiyon. *Oh, Saiyon.* He would search for me and fail. I'd taken off my ring. I would have shattered his hopes as surely as I'd shattered mine.

He didn't have the option of removing a crown.

I wept. Oh, how I wept. I wailed like a madwoman, shrieked like a demon, fought like a feral beast. Over and over again, until I was beyond spent. But my rest was no different from my wakefulness. Dreams couldn't find me in that terrible place.

After . . . there was no point in delineating time. *After,* I tried to consider the stipulations in the contract. Remember what I had read. The moon had to bring me supplies, and she couldn't *physically* harm me, but the art . . . she had to approve it. Even if my talents returned and were amplified, I couldn't create in this darkness. And if I did, what would keep Moon from deeming even the most beautiful creation unfit? She bore no chains. She would keep me here until I truly lost my sanity and killed myself.

Did my life have no path that didn't lead to pain?

My mourning warped into a vicious cycle of sorrow, denial, anger, numbness. I moved through the steps again and again, that last step— numbness—growing each time. Until I was as numb and lifeless as those statues in the Losoko Canyons.

But.

Oblivion could not suck away my memories. I thought of the statues, and I thought of *my* statues. The ones I had created in Algeron, the ones I'd created for clients, the ones I'd created for myself, tracing all the way back to my youth. I thought of the shape of my masters' hands, the wetness of the clay, the feel of a knife gliding through it. I remembered, and my fingers twitched, trying to mirror what I saw behind my eyelids.

I thought of paintings. Of the night I'd attacked canvas in my bedroom, slashing at Saiyon's chains the only way I knew how. I considered delicate portraits painted with the finest brushes—likenesses that could fit inside a locket or pocket clock, then great murals spanning entire walls, entire ceilings. I remembered layers and blending, stippling and scumbling.

Remembering wasn't enough to rebuild what I had lost. But it did chip away at the darkness and give my mind something to cling to. It helped me find myself.

Moon was bound by her agreement, regardless of how she'd skewed the terms, so finally, *after*, I called out to her.

When she arrived, what I had once seen as a soft glow beneath her skin appeared as radiant beams, and I turned away from her, my eyes watering. I had been too long in the dark . . . but oh, how *wonderful* it felt to *see*.

"I need materials," I said, far too shaken by misery to remember politeness. "I need a sketchbook and an array of pencils. Several candles and means to light them—"

Moon tittered. "Have you learned nothing, Aija of Rozhan? Only celestial light can exist here."

I glowered at her. "Then bring me a godling who glows as you do."

Her slender frame bucked with laughter. "My creatures are not *pertinent supplies*. They are not tools of art."

Which meant the contract would not force her to provide them. I ground my teeth. I hated her. I hated her voice, her cruelty, her every ugly scar. And yet I did not want her to leave. My soul was desperate for light. For company of any kind.

The sliver of rationale I still possessed whispered my project would have to be a sculpture. In the darkness, I'd be able to feel the bumps, divots, and ridges created in clay—something that would be impossible with sketches or paintings. Before I could make a new request, however, Moon spoke.

"I know who you *really* are." She walked on nothing, cutting through the blackness casually. "I've done some sleuthing. You're His lover."

Every muscle I had tensed into steel.

"A mortal lover, of all things!" She truly thought it hilarious, the way her laughter rang. That, or she was a fantastic actress. Her grin pulled at the deep scars in her cheeks, making them look like they pierced all the way to her tongue. She circled me. "Yours is that little farm my scouts found Him on. How quaint. I should destroy it."

She paused, smugly staring at me. I swallowed the fight rising in me, glad I'd not yet lost it to the numbness. I had no power here . . . but *memories* reminded me of our interactions in the throne room. Of that one self-conscious gesture she'd made.

So I stared at her scars, the ones pocking her forehead. Smile wavering, she covered them with a pale, equally scarred hand.

I met her eyes. "Regardless, you must uphold our bargain." I swallowed. "I will need clay. A lot of it. As much as you can bring me." Because I would make mistakes. Because I had to relearn. "And a set of sculptor's tools—"

"Do you know"—her voice lingered just above a whisper—"how many lovers our dear Sun has taken?"

She was fond of interrupting me. In halting my words, I'd bitten my tongue.

"So many." Her grin slowly returned, and she lowered her hand. "Gods, demigods, godlings . . . He takes them and uses them and discards them as He wishes. The galaxies are scattered with them. But mortals are His favorite."

My hands tightened into fists. "Stop."

"Because there's no mess after, you see." She began pacing. "He adores the star mothers. Collects them by the dozens, takes His pleasure in them, and sends their corpses back to the Earth—"

"Stop," I growled.

"He kept one, for a while." She shrugged. "Eventually grew tired of her as well." She spun on her heel, dark eyes sparkling. "Even I've shared His bed, though admittedly I wasn't impressed—"

"Shut your godsdamned mouth, you rapacious whore!" It took all my willpower not to charge her and wring her neck, for while our contract guaranteed my welfare, it did *not* guarantee hers.

She smirked, but anger tightened her brow. "Hit a sour note, have I?"

I let every drop of disgust I had contort my expression. "You disgrace him so easily, and yet you would be swallowed by this darkness if not for *his* light." My nails carved new lines into my palms. "You should keep more mortals in your pathetic court, *Demi*goddess. Perhaps we could teach you how to lie convincingly."

Her smirk shrunk as her lips pursed, and her eyes glimmered with murder.

Despite her vileness, I was sorry when she left. I did not want to face the darkness again.

But the moon was not entirely unbound by laws, for *after*, I stumbled on blocks of clay, their scent so familiar I wept over them, and fumbled around until I found a belt of sculptor's tools, which I tied around my waist so I would not lose it.

And I got to work.

I threw the ball of clay into the black, never hearing it land.

Clay stuck to my hair as I dropped my head into my hands, breathing deeply to keep ahold of myself. I knew the basics. I should be able to enact *basics*. But I'd never learned them in the dark, and my hands were clumsy. Even without sight, I knew my every attempt to sculpt her was wrong, wrong, *wrong*.

Despair rose in me. I hated it. I didn't want to succumb to it, but it was so tempting. So *easy*. If I let despair take me, I would eventually cycle into blissful numbness, which was the closest thing to contentment this terrible cage could give me.

So I gave in. I cycled, for a time.

After, I found myself and approached the clay once more. The texture of it between my fingers was both relaxing and maddening. I sat before it, curling my legs beneath myself, and closed my eyes, though it made no difference whether they were shut or open. I took a deep breath, and—

Wait.

I remembered this.

If you allow yourself to be alone with your thoughts, Zyzi whispered, *it will bring you peace.*

"It only brings me insanity," I complained to the darkness, but I forced my shoulders to loosen, my posture to relax. In my mind's eye, I sat on wild grass and smelled a newly extinguished fire. A thin wood surrounded me. A periwinkle sky.

Breathe in, Zyzi instructed.

I did. I inhaled until I could feel my breath down to my pelvis. I listened for her breaths, and after some time, I *heard* them, like she was sitting next to me, just on the other side of this block of clay. I listened to her, and I matched my breaths with hers, letting my mind and body unwind bit by bit.

And then, *after*, alone with my thoughts, I began to remember things I'd once thought lost. I remembered my tutor's callused hand enveloping my small one, guiding the knife through the clay. I remembered the way I threw it down to remove the air. I remembered warming it in my hands. I remembered the layers.

I remembered Skall. Kage. I remembered how clever they were, twisting words and promises, traveling to great lengths to get even the slightest taste of godling essence. Doing whatever it took to achieve what they wanted. Hadn't I been like that once?

I remembered Tyu. Her unrelenting dedication to me. Her determination to see her task through, even when it got hard.

I remembered Tereth. Not merely his goodness to me, but his patience. Sitting there, breathing, I was awed by his patience. He had been waiting *thousands of years* for his love to wake, and still he waited. I had not spent even a fraction of that time yearning for Saiyon.

And I remembered Ist.

All things. On the Earth. Mother. Leave an. Impression. On Her, he said. *Her body. Is formed. By them. By us.*

Impression.

I lifted my hands and touched my own face. Could I start there? Soften the clay enough to take an impression of my own face, then alter it to match the moon's? Her features were smaller, save her forehead, but it would give me a place to start. I desperately needed one.

Opening my eyes to the darkness, I dug my hands into the clay and worked.

Moon appeared, searing my eyes with blessed light.

"What is it now?" She folded pocked arms tightly across her dress. In Oblivion, her regal clothing did not flow and billow as it had in her throne room. It hung limply from her, a rotting husk.

I want light. I want to remember I can see and hear. Remember that I'm human.

But I knew better than to say those things.

"I need plaster." *Need* wasn't precise, but it might prove useful for the impressions I was making . . . and I wanted an excuse to see her. To see *anything*. Her light was Saiyon's light, so in a twisted way, every time she illuminated the black, he was with me. "There are a few variations—"

Moon left, and I crumbled in the consuming darkness, wishing I were clever enough to make her linger.

After, I had my plaster.

I worked.

I failed.

I worked.

I failed.

I pressed my fingers into the crown and nearly tore it from my head.

"I do have a war to deal with," Moon said when she came next, holding some sort of glimmering baton. She didn't sound angry, merely annoyed.

I took my time speaking, soaking in her light, letting my eyes adjust, reminding them what they'd been created to do. She moved her weight to one leg and put a hand on her hip, waiting, but did not berate me for my hesitance. I wondered if she knew why I basked in her glow, or if she simply liked being appreciated.

Finally, when I felt more myself, I said, "I need to touch your face."

Moon pulled back, nearly dropping that baton in her hand. In that moment, she looked a girl of sixteen, small and vulnerable. But the appearance of innocence evaporated, leaving narrow eyes and a curling mouth. *"Why?"*

I gestured to the clay and plaster. "I have to work in the dark. I can't use my eyes, only my hands. I need to know what your features feel like."

Her frown deepened. Turning away, she traced one of the larger scars on her forehead, then caught herself and whipped her hand away.

"Or you can provide me a light." Doing so might require her to remove me from Oblivion, but I did not pin my hopes on that option.

She twitched. Did not answer right away. I didn't mind—the longer she took, the longer I had her light with me. I looked over my previous creations, seeing their flaws. Had I my talent, I might have finished by now. Working in the lonely dark would have been a challenge, but at least my fingers would have some deftness, my heart some confidence.

Saiyon rose in my thoughts, as he often did, but I pushed him away. First, because thinking of him now only made me miserable. Second, because I feared his enemy would sense my thoughts and torment me for them.

I almost asked about the war, but when I looked back, seeing her curled in on herself, so childlike, I . . . I *felt* for her. I despised myself for feeling anything but hatred, but pity scratched at my ribs.

Pressing my lips together, I approached her. She shrunk back, fearing my touch, but I did not reach for her. "I have scars," I whispered, putting my hand on my abdomen. "Godlings have seen them through my clothes, so I imagine you can, too."

Her dark eyes flicked to my midriff.

"It hurt, when it happened." I spoke softly, carefully, like she was a bird liable to be startled away. "They still hurt, sometimes."

Slowly, so slowly, her eyes rose to mine. For a heartbeat, I saw the immortal soul trapped within her pocked body. I saw buried vulnerability and sorrow. I saw *humanity*.

Then she blinked, and it was gone, replaced with a darkness more complete than that which surrounded us.

"Are you trying to *empathize* with me, mortal?" Her voice was hoarse and sharp. "Your life is less than a breath compared to mine. Your pain is nothing."

I kept my silence.

Growling low in her throat, she looked away. Hesitated. "Very well." She sounded defeated. Perhaps her thoughts had turned toward the contract—she had agreed to provide me with pertinent supplies, and what was more pertinent than her face? Or, perhaps, I had reached her. "Hurry up and do it."

My legs shaky, I crossed the distance to her. She held still, waiting, but did not meet my eyes. I closed mine—that was how I was to work. Gingerly I felt her hair and hairline, her wide forehead, her brow, eyelids, nose, cheeks, mouth, jaw, and chin. My hands quickened over her larger scars. I feared angering her.

When I was done, I thanked her, which made her regard me with suspicion once more.

Then she left, and the darkness returned.

I called on Moon more than once. I would forget the shape of her chin, or the height of her forehead, or the thickness of her neck. Even when I was sure I had it right, I would call on her. Not only to double- or triple-check my efforts, but because madness stirred at the fringes of my mind, and the only thing that kept it at bay was Moon. Her voice, her presence, her light.

She didn't always come right away; she was fighting a war, after all. But she would come eventually. Always with a gripe and a complaint, but more and more, they seemed halfhearted at best.

I remembered my mother. Her soft words. Her meek soul. And however it hurt, I remembered Saiyon. His calm demeanor, his diplomacy. I tried to channel those qualities to soften my edges and mute my frustration.

"You seem tired," I said once as I inspected Moon's hands, though I had no intention of re-creating them. Outside of the face, hands had been the hardest thing for me to learn, the first time.

She frowned at me. "Of course I'm tired."

I nodded, not meeting her eyes. "How long have you fought him for?"

The joints of her fingers stiffened. "I have fought far longer than your kind can remember. I have fought for everything I have."

Loosening my grip, I looked at her. "Is what you have not enough?"

"No." Her answer was quick. Final. Then, so quietly I don't know if she meant for me to hear, she said, "Nothing I do will ever be enough."

"Make it quick," Moon snapped. I hadn't heard such venom in her voice for . . . a long time.

I blinked rapidly, trying to adjust to the sudden appearance of silvery light in the endless dark. I stumbled over a plaster mold and shattered it. My heart leapt into my throat until I realized it was one of my failures.

I didn't take the time to pick it up. To see exactly what I had done amiss. Moon never let me use her light for my work.

"What's wrong?" I asked, squinting.

She sneered. "I have a vexatious mortal who thinks I serve her every whim." She straightened, every part of her rigid, and hissed at me to get to work.

It was an intimate thing, really, to touch her as I did. I suppose we'd grown used to the process, because she didn't so much as flinch when

I traced my thumbs over her cheekbones, closing my eyes to memorize the height of them. The deep divot on one, gained from another of her ancient wars.

"Are you . . . losing?" I whispered. She didn't like it when I pried.

She growled. Stayed silent for several minutes. Then said, "I lost a good soldier today." Her voice grew thick, then loud, like she was forcing herself to push through the emotion clogging her throat. "Someone . . . important to me."

My hands slowed. "A godling?"

She wrenched back. "Obviously. I wouldn't care if I lost a mortal." She looked away. "Even if I have so few."

I nodded, keeping my hands to myself. "I knew a woman in Algeron . . . She worshipped you."

Her face flicked to mine.

"She had a little room in her house hung with white ornaments. No windows, no candles. She thought it would be disrespectful to let in more light than necessary." It had been more of a nook than a room; she hadn't been a wealthy person. I'd seen it by accident. She had a bad leg, and I'd come by to deliver a basket of vegetables on behalf of her daughter, who was my neighbor. So many in Rozhan, on the entire Earth Mother, worshipped Saiyon, even after the moon's temporary victory. Many considered it blasphemy to do anything but.

Moon chewed on the inside of her cheek. "I don't believe you."

But she lingered a little longer, silent, and I told her everything I remembered of the woman and the nook before she grew tired of me and left me to Oblivion.

I was close. I wept as I worked, because this was the best piece I'd ever created. To my hands, it felt . . . real. Like *I* was inside the clay, and with every careful stroke of cutter and brush, I revealed a little more of myself. A strange sensation began to bloom in me, like the first crocus of spring. It *hurt*, but gradually I recognized it as hope.

Then my hand slipped, and I crushed the flower completely.

The nose was ruined. I fumbled for it, trying to feel the nostrils, the bridge. Trying to put it back together. But the more I tried, the more my clumsy fingers destroyed it, until it was little more than a hump of clay, and—

I clutched the spearhead tool in my fist and lashed out at the sculpture, shrieking as I did, cutting through it from crown to neck. The clay resisted my strike, as if to stall my hand. I had lost much, but I had not yet lost my strength, and the blow carried true.

After, I panted, hands on my knees, wheezing like I'd run the length of Rozhan. *Breathe*, Zyzi chided me, and I tried. Gods knew I tried. Inhale, exhale. Inhale, exhale.

After, I straightened, regret rooting my feet to Oblivion. I reached forward, feeling the gouge with trembling fingertips, following it down the bust I'd spent so long creating. I could have fixed the nose, had I any peace left in my strained mind. *I could have fixed it*. I could have—

Wait.

My hand trailed down the gouge again.

Wait.

I pressed my fingers into it, widening it.

My skin began to itch.

I gasped.

How long since I'd felt *this*? This want, this *need*. The itch to create, the spark of an idea, the eagerness to see it through. Not since before the darkness. Not since before I met Moon.

I had a vision. It came to me as a candle lit in the darkness, and I knew what I wanted to create. What I *craved* to create.

It would not be easy. Anything but.

Carefully, so carefully, I lifted my smallest knife and cut.

When Moon appeared again, she said nothing, only regarded me with irritation. Were she mortal, I was sure a vein on her forehead would be throbbing.

"I need to touch your face again." This was . . . I couldn't recall how many times I'd asked. I did need to, though I also found myself craving her light more and more.

"Really." She folded her arms. "*Again.* Just end it, Aija of Rozhan. Why suffer longer than you must?"

I winced at those words, for they had crossed my mind on multiple occasions. All I needed to do was take off the tight circlet on my head, and I would have peace.

I shook myself. "Please allow me."

Groaning, she stepped forward. I closed my eyes and rediscovered her features. This time, I explored her scars.

I was only on the third one when she slapped my hand away. "What are you doing?"

I blinked. "I'm—"

"He isn't looking for you," she snapped, and I reeled back. "If you're biding your time thinking He'll save you, He won't. He isn't even *looking* for you."

Once, such comments would have rolled off my shoulders. At most, made me angry. But Oblivion had broken down so much of who I was, tears instantly came to my eyes.

She smiled at them, but there was no joy in her countenance.

Swallowing against a lump in my throat, I said, "I need more supplies."

She groaned. "What now?"

"Gemstones. Cut and uncut. Rubies, sapphires, diamonds—"

She snorted. "I can't be won over with such embellishments. They mean nothing to immortals."

I pressed forward. "Mother-of-pearl, if you will. Gold leaf and silver shavings."

"Think you'll build a throne to yourself here?" She chortled. "Aija, Queen of Oblivion."

I bowed my head. "Please."

That word rankled her. I don't suppose she heard it often.

As always, she vanished, and later my wandering hands found barrels and chests full of precious things, far more than I could possibly use.

After, I called on her again to take measurements.

In truth, I used her glow to separate gold from silver, emeralds from topaz, and built in my mind how I would re-create the vision in my mind, one clumsy step at a time.

After.

After, I finished. I worked with a painful slowness I never could have tolerated in my days as an Earthly artisan. I made more impressions. Morphed the countenance of my own face into hers. The act made me discover our differences, and our similarities. I forgot I had sight at all. I pressed and poked and sliced clay. Carefully utilized my plaster for longevity—I would never dare to chisel something like marble in this place. I placed delicate pieces of gold leaf fragment by fragment with tweezers. Sorted stones by size and shape and fit them together like a puzzle.

After, I called on her, and she came, standing with her eyes rolled back like she was annoyed by the prospect of another prodding of her face.

"Come," I said, and crossed the nothingness of my new home. My heart beat rapidly in my throat. I had not yet presented the demigoddess with *anything*, and if she refused this, my sanity might finally slip. I had given it all I had. There was nothing left within me.

Seeming more curious than anything else, Moon followed me, her halo of silver light testing the shadows. I brought her to a pedestal—another of my requests—and laid eyes on my own creation for the first time.

I bit down on a gasp.

It looked . . . right.

It was a bust of Moon, down to her shoulders. Her hair was slicked back, her skin the pale color of plaster, her head tilted as though looking toward the heavens. And her scars. I'd included *every last one* of her scars. I knew the depth, length, and breadth of all of them, and had not left out a single one.

But the bust gave an impression of the scars being fresh. Newly cut, and in their depths were peeks of precious things. Flayed flesh lined with gold leaf; parted skin revealed clusters of gemstones and slivers of seashell. It was the visage of a marred and damaged woman who bore beauty within her, and every time someone or something hurt her, more of that beauty bled into the world.

Because in spite of everything, the moonlight had always been a beautiful thing.

I turned toward Moon, ready for her criticism, her cold laughter, but she merely stared at the bust, her mouth slack, her eyes wide, her body still. Her luminous clothing fell heavily over her narrow shoulders. She touched one of the scars on her cheek.

She shook her head subtly, and I knew I had failed. My chest seemed to cave in. I touched the crown on my head.

Seeking to defend my work, I said, "I-I meant to—"

"*Quiet,*" she snapped, cold and faint. Her jaw set. She took a step toward the bust. I was sure she would destroy it.

But she lifted her hand to the same scar on the bust's cheek, touching the inlaid emeralds there.

I held my breath.

After, she said, "Just go."

I wasn't sure what she meant. The only way I could leave was to remove the circlet keeping me alive. "I—"

"*Go!*" she screamed. She threw her hand out, and I reeled back, thinking she meant to hit me. But a puff of whiteish light formed in her hand, and suddenly there was a long rock there, dark and porous as igneous, with the slightest carmine vein on its edge.

The heart piece.

She threw it at me.

"Leave," she whispered, resigned.

I stepped away from her, thinking to leave her with her tangled emotions.

And stepped onto a patch of familiar, moist loam.

It was the moment dawn was supposed to break the sheet of night. I did not need to look at my grandfather's pocket clock to know this—I felt it in my bones. All farmers did, and I supposed I'd been back on the farm long enough for it to seep into mine as well.

I didn't want to rise. I was too hot under this blanket, pressed against a body too warm to be mortal. Yet I wanted to absorb every bit of the moment, all the sensations I could never hope to re-create with charcoal, clay, or brush. The smell of his skin, the clarity of my mind, the syncing of our hearts, like we'd always been half of something greater, and the universe had only now dared to fit us together.

So I lay there, memorizing, drifting in and out of snoozing, in and out of sluggish thoughts that melted into fragmented dreams and back.

I don't think I was dreaming when I heard him murmur, "I love you," quiet and careful, just the way I had done it hours before.

CHAPTER 20

I stood there for a long time, eyes staring, heart thumping, limbs twitching. It would have hurt, were it day. My eyes had been steeped in darkness for so long. But I had returned sometime in the night.

I stared at the same spot of brightness in the sky, utterly dumbfounded. The same star. It took too long for my mind to process, *This is a star.* Finally, I looked at another star. Then another, and another. I took in the whole night sky. No moon. New moon?

Then I looked at the horizon, and I jumped, thinking the darkness of the distant mountain line was Oblivion chasing me. I hit my backend hard when I fell.

Grass.

My fingers coiled in short, cool grass. I stared at it nearly as long as I'd stared at the star.

Then I bawled like a newly born child.

I cried before I really knew why I was crying. I pressed myself into the Earth Mother, absorbed Her chill, dug fingers and toes into soft, moist soil. I cried until I was spent all over again. Until I was—

—thirsty?

Trembling, I touched my forehead, feeling a dimple where the moon's crown had once rested, but it wasn't there.

I was . . . home.

And it was . . . spring?

It had been fall when I left home with Zyzi in search of Ist.

I lay back, staring at the stars, breathing in fresh air, listening to tired crickets, and thought of my cousin.

Of breathing.

I dove into my memories yet again, this time with my eyes open.

And remembered myself.

It took a bit of time for my mind to function properly after that, but I'll tell you what happened with clarity.

I was in Rozhan, very close to my family farm. My heart leapt at this, and at the prospect of seeing my family, but I knew the heart piece I'd brought with me belonged on the other side of the world, and even with Tereth's help, it would take me weeks to return it.

In the morning, I sat up and watched the Sun rise, weeping yet again at the beauty of it. Though I'd yet to realize it, I would never be able to hold back tears as easily as I once had. For better or for worse, that part of me had broken.

"Saiyon," I whispered to the morning, but he could not hear me. I no longer wore his ring. He didn't know where to look for me, and my voice blended in with the voices of the billions of mortals who lived in his kingdom.

But I had done it. I had survived. I was home.

And I had the heart piece.

Tucking the rock into my bodice, I gauged my location, slow to remember. My mind wasn't at its best that first day. Then I pointed myself toward the farm and reached the cornfields by noon. I shuddered at the sight of them, their baby plants only to my calf. I touched each one I passed, marveling at the leaves, at *life*, at home.

My grandmother's murmuring as she shooed away chickens bolstered my heart, and I ran for the first time in six months, desperate to see her face. The sight of her struck me as a sudden wind. She'd aged.

And when she saw me, she screamed. Screamed and threw the pail she'd been carrying, wailed my name and ran faster than I'd ever seen her run to cross to me. She threw her frail arms around me and squeezed me with a strength that belied her small frame, and I wept into her hair and shook in her embrace.

"Child! Gods burn you, you foolish child!" Pulling back, she took my face in her hands. "You're so thin! Gods burn you! Where have you been?"

"The god's nest, and the Losoko Canyons—"

"What are you babbling about?" Tears glimmered in Kata's eyes, and she embraced me again. "Without even writing! We've wasted away worrying about you, with only a godling to tell us you were gone—"

"Godling?" I spoke into her neck.

"Searching for you. They're all searching for you. And Zyzi, trapped on the other side of the world—"

News of Zyzi weakened my knees, and I nearly collapsed right there. I only found my strength because Kata faltered. She could not hold me up. "She's all right?"

Kata pulled back and looked over my face. Cupped my cheek. "I don't know. We haven't heard anything recent. But you"—she blinked rapidly—"you're home."

"I'm home," I repeated, and my eyes moistened. Embracing Kata again, I breathed in her smell. Waited until I was steady to release her. "Where's my mother? And Danika?"

Kata jerked away from me, looking at my face like I'd lost my mind. "Danika! Why would Danika be here?"

I chewed my lip. "If she weathered out the winter . . ."

Kata placed a rough palm against my forehead.

271

Grasping her wrist, I gently pulled her hand away. "Kata, how long was I gone?"

Confusion warped her face. "That's why they came looking for you. The godlings. Fool girl, He sent godlings searching for you, and you weren't here."

A chill cut through me. "H-How long?"

Swallowing, my grandmother said, "You and Zyzi left eighteen months ago. How could you not know?"

Strength left my legs. I dropped to my knees. Heard my grandmother's voice like a distant thing, and when I didn't respond, she ran off.

Eighteen months. I'd spent nearly a year and a half trapped in Oblivion.

My mother's cry broke through my shock. I looked up to see her—she'd lost so much weight—barreling toward me. We collided, and she knocked me onto my back, sobbing into my neck until I thought the guilt would consume me as ravenous termites.

But I embraced her anyway, like she was my own child, and together we mourned all the time we both had lost.

Zyzi had never come home. Saiyon's servants had visited her, but six months had passed since those servants last brought news to the farm, and so I had no promise that Zyzi was still well, or even still alive. All I knew was she'd been in the canyons back then, on the other side of the world, waiting for me. Whether Tyu had returned to the heavens, or Ist had lived long enough to accompany her, remained unknown.

Yet I felt in my gut that she was alive. Our families had speculated far and wide about our demise, and my mother and grandmother listened intently as I recounted everything to them, even my most foolish decisions.

"You have to go back." My grandmother touched her chin; a slight tremor had built in her hands while I was away.

Enera gaped. "Go back? No!"

"I must return it." Clasping Enera's hand, I lifted the slim, rough rock. Even detached, that hint of ruby vein still glowed.

My mother looked at the rock with swollen eyes. Snatched it from my hand. Stood. Raised it over her head like she might cast it through the window.

"Mother!" I burst to my feet and tried to wrestle it from her.

"This thing is driving our family apart!" she screamed.

"This *thing*"—Kata's sharp voice slid between us—"is Aija's fate, not ours!"

My mother and I both froze. While Enera did not release the heart piece, she turned to see her mother's face.

"Or did you forget"—Kata's words were ice, though her expression was familial—"that *our* god fell to *our* farm, lived beneath *our* roof, and chose Ai for Himself?"

A shiver vibrated between my shoulders. So much time had passed . . . even *I* had nearly forgotten.

Thank you, Grandmother.

Enera pressed her lips together. She lowered her hand, but I did not take the heart piece until she offered it to me, refusing to meet my eyes.

I grasped the rock and held it close. "I can't delay. Not if Zyzi, Tyu, Ist, and Tereth are waiting for me. Not if Saiyon still waits."

My mother sniffed. "You name divinities like they're cousins."

I smirked, and she, too, fought a smile.

"Three days." My grandmother did not suggest it; she demanded it. "Three days before you leave. You will give us that much."

And I was in such a fragile state I did not fight it, and neither did Enera.

It took more than three days.

Despite my relief at being returned home, despite my joy at being with my family and the victory of reclaiming the heart piece, I was broken.

I saw Oblivion in every shadow. Heard it in every pause between words and sliver between breaths. For the three days Kata had demanded, I couldn't sleep. I'd forgotten how to, for the moon's crown had taken away the need for rest—the need or ability to curl into unconsciousness and forget. It wasn't until utter exhaustion claimed me that I slumbered, only to have nightmares of darkness.

One would think such a dream wouldn't be so bad. Nothing attacked me. Nothing hurt me. It was simply waking darkness. Complete, impenetrable darkness. And I woke again and again, sweating and panting, only to panic at the natural darkness around me. Like I couldn't wake up.

My mother started sleeping with me.

Food was hard as well. I vomited my first meals, my stomach unable to keep them down. Despite the hunger that racked my body, I had to start with little sips of broth, like a convalescent, because my body had forgotten how to eat. I lost a lot of weight the first three weeks, until my stomach readjusted. It took a little longer for my bowels to catch up.

I knew I had to return to the Losoko Canyons, yet I was also objective enough to realize I wouldn't make it in my present form. I couldn't camp if I couldn't sleep through the night. I couldn't hike if I couldn't hold down larger portions. But neither could I sit still.

So I worked. I sowed and weeded and watered. I took the sheep out and repaired the chicken coop and led Vine down to the water. I split wood and nailed shingles and mucked stalls, reteaching myself to farm. Reteaching myself to be *human*, and to be free, and to be myself.

Every day I called to Saiyon, pleading for him to find me, to *see* me. But I no longer had my ring, which was what he'd always used to track me. I'd been away from the farm so long he wouldn't think to look. If he still searched for me at all.

Thoughts like that triggered the darkness that had coiled into a tight ball in the back of my mind, so I avoided them. But when the darkness leaked out, when work could not keep it at bay, Kata read to me and my mother sang to me. I clung to their voices, to their presence, and wept for every reason and no reason at all. Slowly, so slowly, the darkness became manageable. The nightmares dwindled. My body regained its weight and remembered its strength.

Three months after returning home, I started a new sketchbook.

The next day, I packed a new bag and headed south.

Kata did not like physical affection, but I embraced her tightly before I left. Deep in my soul, I think I knew it would be the last time I saw her. I think she knew it, too.

My grandmother was too old to travel, so my mother came with me. We'd made an uneasy agreement that she would see me as far as the Furdowns before heading back to the farm. Kata needed her more than I did, though I was uneasy at the prospect of traveling alone.

The Uwad River, where we got all our water, and where I'd first found Saiyon, crossed back on itself farther south. So we were crossing it for the second time when a voice so deep I could barely discern it called out to me. At first, I thought it was merely the sound of white water, but there were no rapids in sight.

My mother grabbed my arm when a bulb of water, about the size of a cow's head, poked up from the surface.

"You have drunk of these waters before," it repeated.

Putting a hand on my mother's shoulder to calm her, I bowed to the godling in the water. "I have. My family has farmed these lands a long time."

The bulb rose higher, until it reached about Ist's height. It seemed to be studying me. "You bear His mark."

I touched my scars through my dress. "Can you speak to him? Satto? Can you send a mes—"

But the bulb broke apart, splashing back into the water, and though I called out to the magic in its depths, nothing responded to me.

It would be a long journey, and that was assuming I could get Tereth's attention once I reached the coast. I felt confident I could—after all, I carried a piece of his lover with me. But then I thought of demons, and wondered what other things might sense the powerful magic with me and want it for themselves.

"We'll have to sleep one at a time," I murmured as the prairie rose into a mild hill. "We need to keep this safe."

My mother nodded. "Did you bring the knife?"

My grandfather's favorite blade. I touched where it rested in my belt. "Yes. I—"

Weightlessness engulfed me.

My body seized, panicked. *Oblivion.*

But darkness never came. Only light. Light, light, and more light.

I wasn't falling, but . . . *flying*.

The world fell apart around me, shifting into crystalline pink walls that were not really walls, more like figments of the imagination half-realized, and circular windows that peered out into a sky so clustered with stars there seemed more stars than night.

And there, standing before me, was Saiyon.

I gasped. The sight of him shocked me dumb. Had I so easily forgotten his face? For it seemed as new to me as the night I'd held a candle over it, beholding his features for the first time. His radiance enveloped me in celestial warmth; his ethereal clothing floated softly around him, like he stood in water, and his diamond eyes were brilliant and wide.

"Aija," he whispered, and stepped closer to me. Closer than he should have been able to step—I half realized my body had crystalized to mimic the strange walls, like I'd grown some sort of astral armor.

I blinked. Shook. Lifted a hand to touch him—I got within six inches of his skin before it began to burn. Closer than before, but not close enough. "Saiyon—"

He dropped to his knees in front of me. I gaped; someone gasped. I noticed in my peripheral vision that we were not alone. My mother had not come with me, but some sort of godling stood nearby, and—

"I have searched *everywhere*." The hoarseness of his voice made me think of a dry summer, of parched grasses and dark-brown grasshoppers. "All over the Earth Mother and through the heavens. I have men and godlings searching . . . searching . . ."

He shook his head, like he couldn't believe I stood there, though he was the one who'd swept me up. I wondered if this was his home, his palace, a place for him and his servants to reside, a pocket of heaven all his own.

I knelt to better see his face. Wanted to touch him so dearly a sob worked up my throat, but I managed to dam it halfway. Still, my voice wavered when I said, "The moon tasked me with creating her likeness. She sent me to Oblivion to work—"

The fire that always licked his skin flared and burned white hot, enough so that I had to shuffle back from its heat. I suspect the thought of hurting me was the only thing that pushed Saiyon to temper it to a bright yellow. *"What?"*

I shook my head, trying not to dwell on that darkness, because I had not yet overcome it. Even then, it edged the corners of my mind. "It is done. I'm free."

Rage and sorrow warred in his gemlike eyes. "It is not simply *done*."

"My Sun," a soft voice said behind me. The godling who had gasped treaded carefully toward us. "She is not a star mother. She cannot be here—"

"Leave." He did not shout, but the command was so intense it reminded me again of a lion, this time stalking its prey. Saiyon's smoldering gaze did not leave mine as the godling vanished without complaint.

"It is done, and in the end, she was merciful," I whispered, shivering despite the heat. Dark tendrils caressed my thoughts. Focusing on Saiyon's light, on being *here*, they slowly receded. "She freed me and gave me this."

I pulled the heart stone from my bodice and held it across my palms. I didn't need to explain—Saiyon's shifting countenance said he knew exactly what it was.

He reached for it, withdrew his hand. Such was the dance between us, always. "You did it." In that moment he looked . . . young. "You amazing, incredible woman . . . you did it."

I smiled at him, his fire burning away unshed tears. "I did it."

He bowed his head. "But this trespass is not forgiven. Moon will answer for it."

I moved to cup his face; his light simmered down to a deep red, allowing me to get within a few inches of his jaw. But even here, with whatever magic encapsulated me, I could not touch him.

The darkness lapped again, this time carrying a briny salt, one that had haunted me on and off in Oblivion. In truth, it didn't matter, but . . . I wanted to know.

"What darkens your gaze?" Saiyon's voice was near a whisper, and he searched my face like my soul was a book he could thumb through.

"This war"—I treaded very carefully, my pulse quickening—"is . . . is it a lovers' feud?"

He blinked, genuine surprise raising his brow. "Lovers' feud?"

I nodded. "Moon said . . . she said she'd once shared your bed."

Vibrant orange burst from him, and I leaned back from the heat. His voice was deep and dark when he said, "I have never touched that creature."

And Saiyon could not lie. It didn't matter—I *knew* it didn't matter—but relief blossomed like a lily inside me, and the darkness receded.

He reached into a pocket—not of his clothing, but of the air, like the universe itself opened for him. From it he withdrew a few gold chains and a familiar ring: a thick gold band with a black line encircling it.

My lips parted. A lump rose in my throat at the sight of that singular piece of jewelry. The token of him I had carried for so long. That I'd had to leave behind when I entered Moon's kingdom, along with the necklaces that had allowed me to trespass the Earth Mother's heart chamber.

He could not place it on my finger, so he released it, and it floated toward me as if on water. I took it, surprised by its heat. I swallowed hard as I returned it to my hand, but the lump stuck. The necklaces he laid at my feet.

"I might not have found you, even if you'd kept it." He met my eyes through pale, gilded eyelashes. "Oblivion is . . . endless."

He spoke like his throat had tightened, too.

Steeling myself with a deep breath, I twisted the ring so that the black line turned amber. "Thank you."

He nodded.

I drew two more breaths to calm the emotion threatening to leak into my voice. Picked Zyzi's, Ist's, and my necklaces from the floor. "Tereth—"

"Is well aware." He gestured to the heart piece still in my hand. "He, too, has searched for you."

The lump grew. "I must return to Her." I hefted the heart piece before slipping it back inside my dress with the necklaces, my voice little more than a croak. "I must return this. Can you take me?"

He scanned my face back and forth like I was a book being read. "I can. I will. I would not have you go alone."

"Your war—"

"I cannot trespass so deeply into the Earth Mother even if there were no war." His features softened. "Tereth would not like it, even so."

My lip twitched.

"But your cousin resides in the south of Helchanar."

My heart jumped.

"I have spoken to her more than once since your disappearance. I will take you to her, and together you will make this journey. But you must go quickly." I retreated, and his colors brightened. "If the moon was willing to release you, if she showed *mercy*, she will not conform to it long. I have known that creature for millennia, Aija. She is cold and vindictive. She will see your freedom as a mistake and seek to correct it by whatever means necessary."

"Then let us move swiftly, and turn her face from me. Just . . . let me say goodbye to my mother."

He nodded, and the battle in his eyes gave way to sorrow—a sorrow so deep and evocative I longed to draw it, though it would take me years to remaster the skill.

And just like that, I stood on wild grass again, my mother startling, her gaze shooting past me to the presence I felt at my back. Tears filled her eyes. "No. Not already."

I wrapped my arms around her and squeezed until my muscles trembled with the effort. "I will see you again. I promise." Pulling back, I pressed a kiss to her cheek. "I don't know what is in store for me, but I will do everything I can to see you again. This is not goodbye."

Enera cupped the sides of my face. Tears lapped over her eyelids, and my own eyes stung. "Only farewell for now. Again."

I kissed her other cheek. "For now. Only for now." My lips quivered when I smiled. "Saiyon will see you home safely."

She shook her head. "Sometimes I wish you'd never found Him by the river."

I jolted. "Mother—"

"But I'm glad you did," she whispered, and stroked my hair. "I'm glad you did, if this is a happy ending for you. But only if this is your happy ending." She drew in a shuddering breath. "That's all a mother wants for her children. Happiness. Just never thought it would take so much . . . effort."

I laughed, the sort of laugh that borders on crying. She pressed her forehead to mine, and we shared breath for a long moment before I clasped her hand and stepped back.

My mother let go first.

Light—burning tall, bright, and harmless—engulfed me, and when it dissipated, I was in a strange country thick with green forest, chilled by the shade and the absence of the Sun God, standing before a humble lean-to held up with vines and thatched with straw, lines strung every which way to dry herbs and clothing alike. A dark-skinned woman with curling hair carried a yoke laden with heavy water pails, which fell off her shoulders the moment she saw me. A chirp sounded within the lean-to, and from the thick of the forest, an aged and bent godling called my name.

Alive. All of them, alive.

And together.

"Satto," he said, holding up a finger. "Sun, of course. Tayo."
He raised a second and third finger. "Mendas, Sandas..."

"How many names do you have?" I marveled.

He considered for a moment. "Ninety ... eight, I believe."

I whistled. "And 'Saiyon' is your favorite?"

"'Saiyon' was My first. It is the most ... personal, to Me. Few know it."

My brow lowered. One of his own golden eyebrows crooked upward in response.

"When you first woke," I explained, "you gave us that name. Yet it's ... sacred, to you. If that's the right word."

He nodded.

Impatient, I pressed, "And?"

His lip quirked. "And I knew who you were the moment I woke, though I'd never seen your face from so intimate an angle."

My cheeks warmed.

Reaching forward, he tucked hair behind my ear. "Even then, it was the name I wanted you to have."

CHAPTER 21

Saiyon gave me the rest of the evening—for it was evening in Helchanar—and the following night. My mind was hurried, eager to finish my task, but my soul needed my cousin.

I did not tell Zyzi, Tyu, or Ist the details of my time in Oblivion. Zyzi was my confidante—she always had been—but I was not yet strong enough to relive those dark times still so deeply rooted in my soul. I would, someday, when the darkness was not so thick, and my hope not so fragile. I answered Zyzi's questions as best I could, and she was satisfied enough.

She, Tyu, and Ist had settled in Helchanar last spring, after camping for months in the Losoko Canyons, awaiting my return. Ist had fought off the end of his life to wait for me and help Zyzi, because he had promised to see this journey through. I could not fathom that these three would be so dedicated to my cause, so patient as to endure a strange land and distance from family for nearly two years. My heart broke for their love for me, again and again, until I knew I would not recognize it as mine when it became whole once more.

"He came twice," Zyzi said as the fire burned low, casting her tiny hut in hues of red and gray. We both sipped chamomile tea, mine weak, as my mouth was still getting used to tasting things again. I'd told her about my mother, which led to the subject of Saiyon. "Once, a week after you left, then again maybe four months ago. The first time He was worried. The second time . . ." She sipped her tea, thinking. "All of this makes me see the celestial sphere differently, Ai. I always saw gods and their ilk as omniscient, terrifying beings, wise and farseeing." She considered again. "That is not to say He isn't those things, but . . . if my mother went missing for so long, my father would be beyond distraught. Her loss would consume him. And that agony is not something reserved only for mortals."

There, beside that tiny fire, I sobbed into Zyzi's lap, not truly understanding why.

We packed the next morning. Ist was notably slower; he would be about 826 years old now. Tyu, at the ripe young age of sixty-six, accompanied him, her tiny body lifting one of his arms with celestial strength. Zyzi was nearly thirty. I had spent my thirty-sixth and thirty-seventh birthdays in Oblivion. It seemed like someone had gathered the chords of time like sheet music and torn a page free. Those years were a melody that would be forever lost to me.

I wondered if this was how the star mother Ceris felt when she'd been displaced in time. When I got the chance, I would ask Saiyon for the fullness of her tale. I was beginning to think we had more in common than I'd originally imagined.

About two hours after dawn, Saiyon's presence again lit the forests of Helchanar, and the urgency in his voice echoed in my chest. "We must hurry," he said.

He swept us up in his light, and when it dimmed, we stood at the entrance to the Earth Mother's heart. The great stone moved by Ist had been replaced, perhaps by some godling servant of Hers. Thankfully, Saiyon rolled it aside with a wave of his hand; I feared Ist's heart would give out if he tried to do it himself. Shaken by the thought, I put an arm on Ist's shoulder.

As I lifted my face to thank Saiyon, however, he suddenly buckled, as though he'd taken a blow to the gut. The Sunlight pouring into the canyon flickered. I ran to him, but without that crystalline shield, I couldn't get close.

Panic shot through my bones. "Saiyon, what—"

"Go," he urged, looking up through golden hair. "I will be fine."

Tyu fluttered around him as I glanced at the sky, and though I could see no explosions or unusual striations of light, I knew his other half had been struck. The battles had not ceased during my time away. Moon had kept busy in between our visits.

Tyu shook her flat, half-haloed head. "He must return. I will guard the way."

My feet rooted to the Earth, but Zyzi grasped my hand. "Let Him go."

I met Saiyon's gaze one more time before he flashed away.

"It is. Time," Ist said with a nod, leaning on his staff. "Lead the. Way."

Pulling in a shaky breath, I ensured we wore our god-made necklaces and that the heart piece was still tucked into my bodice—it made divots in my skin that mimicked my burns—and led the way into the wondrous tunnel down to the Earth Mother's heart.

The journey was just as I remembered it, the heart and its stony chamber unchanged. Pulling the heart piece from my bodice, I half expected something to happen—the heart to shudder at its proximity, demons to barrel in and stop me, the moon to appear and sweep me away. Nausea overwhelmed me at the sudden thought that Moon might have tricked me—that perhaps this wasn't the heart piece at all, and it had always been her purpose to see me fail.

I could not survive another failure. Perhaps that was why the Earth Mother had slept so long—She, too, had taken Her fair share of loss. Of heartbreak.

I approached the heart. Knelt. Felt the warm stone for the crack. It seemed the right size. Before I pressed it in, I rested my forehead against a topaz vein and prayed. "Please accept this. Please help us."

Surely if anyone could grant me what I wanted—if anyone could end this war—it was the Earth Goddess.

Holding my breath, I reached down and pressed the rocky piece in place. It slid in smoothly, like it belonged.

For a heartbeat, nothing happened.

Then the entire room began to quake.

Zyzi shrieked; Ist ground his teeth and said, "There is. Great unrest. In the. Earth."

"*We* are in the Earth!" I cried, stumbling away from the shaking heart. Debris rained from the ceiling. "Earth Mother, please! Help us!"

A stone the size of my head ripped loose from the ceiling and landed at my feet.

"Godsdamned goddess!" Zyzi spat.

I grabbed Ist's staff and jerked him toward the tunnel, the only escape we had. Zyzi followed close on our heels. The sparks of color there, the bubbles of light, took on darker hues and spun around us violently, blurring into one another. Ist's hand found my forearm, and I felt his power course through me—

I spun through weightlessness, unsure if I fell or flew.

Then a *crash* like a bursting mountain rang out around me, making my ears sing, and rocks, boulders, and sand rained around us. I called out for Zyzi, but if she answered, I did not hear her. Shrinking in on myself, I used my free arm to protect my head.

The cascading rock stopped, leaving only that high-pitched note in my ears. It faded slowly, and I coughed, daring to lift my head as dust clouds gradually dispersed.

Had I ever attempted to depict the Earth Mother during my artisan days, I never would have gotten close to Her image.

She stood before us, twenty feet tall and radiant, surrounded by an aura as vivid as Saiyon's, but Hers was olive green and smelled of sage and freshly cut grass.

She did not take a humanoid form, as I might have imagined, but had a head and face like a deer's, with gentle down over large, dark eyes and long, deerlike ears. Antlers rose from Her head, if I could call them that. They looked more like winter trees, extending nearly as high as Her body was long, forking over and over again, glistening in the way of the godlings' remains in the Yard of Bones, but with the same topaz vibrancy as the veins of Her heart. She had a long neck and body and stood like an animal with four legs, but Her hind ones were hidden by a thousand coiling, flowering vines, with blossoms every color of the Sunset and more. She had at least four tails that shifted as another god's clothing might, soft and foxlike. Her front legs were similar to a bear's in thickness and strength, but the joints were more like a horse's, and both ended in wide bird's feet, three long toes on either, each toe tipped with a formidable talon.

Tyu was there, tucked into my side, her head bowed low.

The Earth Mother regarded us for but a moment before lifting Her head. I heard Her voice more as a rattling in my skeleton than a sound—low and resonant, in a language I did not understand, but I thought I heard Tereth's name in its song. Surely the being who stood before me was not the Earth Mother in Her entirety, and She merely split herself as Saiyon did, for all the planet was Her domain, Her body. She closed Her eyes, and I knew elsewhere She reunited with Her lover. I felt an intruder for witnessing even a reflection of such an intimate moment, and yet all the awe and terror radiating through me would not allow me to move away.

I had stood in the presence of Satto himself, been imprisoned by the moon, and ridden the waves of the sea lord, and yet I had never been more intimidated by a being than I was of Her.

After several minutes, Her focus fell to our group. She shrunk before my eyes, until She stood at seven feet instead of twenty. It seemed an invitation.

One of you has restored Me, She said, Her words reverberating in my jaw and shoulders. She beheld Ist. *You are one of Mine.*

Ist nodded. He struggled to his feet; Zyzi and I both rediscovered ours so we could help him, Tyu taking up her place beneath his arm.

The Earth Mother glanced at Zyzi, then shifted Her gaze to me. Paused. *You have been marked.* She took in the ring on my hand.

"I-I've come to plead with You." I dropped down to my knees. It felt wrong to look Her in the eye, and wrong to look away. "Please, Earth Mother. I have traveled . . ." My throat squeezed. "So . . . very . . . far, to speak with You. I have confronted the moon and retrieved Your heart pi—"

Neck bending, She loomed closer, and my words turned to dust in my mouth. Her head hovered two yards from mine. *I can see the emptiness where you sacrificed, dear child. And the lingering darkness in your eyes. Did she keep you in such a horrid place?*

I swallowed, unable to answer.

She pulled back. *She did not use My gift wisely.* She closed Her eyes. *I can feel her deviations upon My skin.* Her eyes opened, regarding all four of us once more.

Thank you, for awakening Me. I would not have thought it possible for such a feat to be accomplished by the hands of two mortals, a servant of the Sun's court, and an ancient godling. She nodded to Ist before turning back to me. *What is it you seek?*

I felt so foolish asking that I nearly didn't. But I had not come so far and lost so much to set my desires aside.

"I wish to be immortal," I whispered. When She showed no response, I added, "Tereth said if any might accomplish it, You could. I-I . . . I love him, Your Grace. The Sun God. He was struck to Earth during the war and came to my farm . . . but with his powers restored, he had to leave . . ."

She nodded. *I see. The marks make sense now. And the ring.* She hummed deep in Her throat, the vibrations rumbling through the Earth. *I would not have thought . . . but Saiyon is always full of surprises.*

I should not have been shocked that She knew his first name. For all I knew, She was older than he was.

I will consider your plea, She said. *But I must first speak to Him. If you are genuine, I see no reason to withhold this from you. You and your friends have done much good today.*

I nodded and blinked back tears. My heart leapt so painfully it stole my breath away. "Th-Thank You. But he . . ." I swallowed, trying to open my throat. "He was hurt, before leaving us. The war—"

Is ever ongoing. She huffed through her nostrils. *I am not surprised. We will wait.*

At that, the ground opened up, and the goddess dissipated into a cloud of spores, spiraling into the crack until She was gone.

Ist knelt beside me and bent his head in prayer.

Tyu, bright and pearlescent, swept around the rocky alcove, singing loudly in a language I had never heard.

Zyzi, breathless, leaned back against a fallen boulder and said the vilest curse I'd ever heard from her lips.

I laughed, and just as with my sobs the night before, I did not entirely understand why.

Saiyon came that night.

I had just drifted off to sleep, huddled with Zyzi for warmth, when his light descended upon the canyon. I started awake, but Ist, Tyu, and Zyzi slept beside me as though comatose. Before I could rouse them, the Earth Mother's voice rattled through me. *I have kept them slumbering. Come. I will speak first with you.*

Rising, I crossed to Saiyon's glowing form, just as stricken by his presence now as I had been earlier. As if all this time he'd been a figment of my imagination, only now become real. He smiled warmly at me, and from the dust rose spores of light, coalescing into the same great deerlike figure as before, except this time She loomed closer to six feet. Perhaps She did it to avoid the appearance of lording over the Sun God, despite his standing in Her domain. As always, I had to keep my distance from him, and I felt the separation keenly.

It seemed a single day had passed since he'd lived on the farm. Since I'd sat on the roof with him and gazed at the stars. Since I'd listened to his stories. Since I'd lain with my head against his chest. Since he'd shattered the shell around my heart and pulled me from the throes of death and showed me what love meant.

Only a day, and yet all of eternity.

The goddess regarded him with a tip of Her head. *Saiyon.*

He returned the gesture. "Talanlaeleel. It is good to hear You again."

I exhaled at the lovely, musical quality of Her name, and dared not repeat it.

She smiled. *This mortal woman has laid a claim on You.*

I flushed at the directness of it, but Saiyon merely bowed his head. "She has it."

Would I ever stop crying?

His answer appeared to please Her. *She has asked Me for immortality. I can do this.*

My heart leapt into my throat and beat faster than a humming-bird's. And the expression on Saiyon's face . . . the greatest artist in all the chords of time could never re-create it. The youthful openness of his eyes, the soft parting of his lips, and the subtle flare of his nostrils. The way the light *shifted* in every facet of him, creating new colors this world's light could not interpret. And that radiance . . . that smoldering radiance just beneath his skin that I could somehow see, perhaps the same way he could see past my clothing to my scars. In that flicker of hope, I beheld Saiyon's very soul.

Tears poured over my cheeks. My heart swelled until my body nearly burst with it.

But—the Earth Mother looked him squarely in the eyes—*do You want this?*

"More than anything."

My head was light as a samara on the breeze; my body flashed hot and cold in anticipation. I wanted to touch him. *Needed* to feel his strength under my hands, his skin on my cheek, his lips on my lips. Hear his voice in day and dark. I wanted to make him laugh and dive into his tales, his memories. I would have sold my mortality for nothing more than to embrace him right then. To bury my face into the side of his neck and smell the depth of summer. To feel *home*.

"I love her," he continued, looking at me. One of his flames crept across the ground toward me, illuminating me, warming me. "I have loved her since before she knew Me. I have feared and yearned for her like I have for no one else. I have been incomplete since our parting. If she could be pulled from the chords of time"—his voice grew weak—"I would never ask for anything more."

New tears traced the paths wended by the old.

She nodded. *I will need Your strength.*

"I will give it."

I found my voice. "Y-Your war. Your soldiers."

The Earth Mother regarded me. *She knows I am awake. She will not strike. Not yet.*

She meant the moon.

Earth Mother took a step away from Saiyon and toward me. Looked me up and down. *I didn't ask your name.*

"Aija," I whispered. Then, stronger, "Aija of Rozhan."

Aija of Rozhan. I give you the choice to keep a sliver of your mortality.

My breath caught.

This will require you to be renewed by Me every millennium, but I do not see why we should not be allies.

I searched Her face but found no guidance there. "Why?"

She tilted Her head like it was obvious. *Because then you could bear children. But if you do not wish it—*

I didn't hear the rest of what she said. My mind had hooked on to *bear children.*

Bear children.

With Saiyon.

And our children would be . . . stars.

I glanced to him; his eyes were round and full of wonder. When they found mine, I saw hope too bright to be restrained in their depths. Hope I mirrored.

We could have a family.

The law of the star mothers would be fulfilled. There would be no more star mothers, other than me.

"Yes." I sounded winded. "Yes, please."

She nodded and pulled back, Her glow intensifying.

"Wait."

She regarded me curiously.

"Ist," I said, glancing to his sleeping form. "Ist . . . Can You do the same for Ist? He is near his death, and—"

Aija of Rozhan. She regarded me softly. *I know all who are made of Me. That is not what he wants.*

"But—"

You are shortsighted. This realm is not the end. He is ready to go.

I looked at Ist once more. Pushed back against a lump in my throat. Nodded.

I will have to remake you.

I turned back to the goddess.

It will take time. Much time, in the mortal sense.

My gaze shifted between Her and Saiyon, then back to Her. "How much time?"

That is yet to be seen.

Saiyon lifted a hand toward me. "Aija—"

"I'll do it," I assured him. "But let me say goodbye. Please."

Earth Mother nodded, and Zyzi, Tyu, and Ist roused.

I ran to Zyzi first and threw my arms around her. "It's time, Zyzi. She's going to change me."

Though my cousin's arms embraced me, I felt her body slacken.

"I don't know how long it will take," I whispered, tears pressing into her shirt. "But if I can see you again, I *will* see you again." Pulling back, I took my grandfather's knife from my belt and pressed it into her hands. "Live your life and your truths. And take care of them for me."

She hugged me again, her grip suddenly tight enough to hurt, and she wept into my hair. "You sure as the hells better see me again, Aija. And if you think our mothers won't whip your backside just because you're an immortal . . ." She sniffed. "I want your happiness above anything."

"I don't deserve you."

"Yeah, you don't."

I laughed, and it hurt. I bequeathed all my art to her, other than whatever pieces my mother and Kata wished to keep for themselves, so that if times grew lean, she would have something to sell . . . and something to remember me by, though I knew even through a million lifetimes, neither of us would ever forget the other.

Next was Ist, who agreed with the Earth Mother about his fate. "But thank you. For thinking. Of me." He grew a delicate pansy from the Earth and tucked it behind my hair, and I kissed his head. He had launched us on this journey, and without him, I would never be standing so near the end.

Finally, Tyu, who sparkled a deep violet. I cradled her in my hands and pressed a kiss to her tiny halo. "You have fulfilled every promise," I whispered.

She hiccupped. "I will wait for you, L'Aija."

Wiping my eyes dry, I turned from my companions to Saiyon, who looked down at me with such love in his eyes my spirit threatened to unravel.

"My mother," I whispered.

"Is home," he said. "And well."

"Zyzi—"

"I will see her returned safely."

I nodded. Rubbed my throat. "I don't know how long—"

"Aija." His warmth enveloped me as he floated closer. "I will wait for you."

I nodded and wiped away new tears. Laughed. "I will wait for you, too."

I'd waited so long already. I could wait a little longer.

When I stepped away, the olive glow of the Earth Mother surrounded me, bundling me like an infant in a swaddle, or a butterfly in a cocoon.

When darkness overtook me this time, I did not fear it.

"I wish I could see the world as you do. Every continent and island, sea and ocean. To think there is so much flora and fauna I don't even know. So much we haven't discovered. I heard there is an ice cap on the top of the world. Is that true?"

"Yes." Saiyon smiled softly. A faraway look shone in his eyes.

"What are you thinking?"

Two heartbeats passed before he looked at me. "How odd your wish is. Before, I had wished to see the world as you do."

I poked his shoulder. "Now you have."

"But only the smallest part of it." He ran the pad of his thumb over my knuckles. "And I will never truly see it as you do. At least, not in the Sunlight."

CHAPTER 22

Ten Years Later

Light cracked through my eyelids.

I breathed, and it was . . . different.

Something around me, some sort of translucent chrysalis, fell away, followed by the tumbling of a quartz chamber—a dome? Had the Earth Mother erected it to protect me?

How much time had passed?

I sat up, my body surging with a peculiar alertness, black smoke puffing around me. I looked again—not smoke, but my hair. Hair darker than obsidian, billowing around my shoulders like steam. And my skin—I raised my palm to better see it. I had sketched this hand dozens of times in my life—it was *my* hand, only . . . changed. My nails were as iridescent as seashell nacre, set in skin deep as onyx and glimmering with hints of opal, which intensified in the lines of my palms. Closing my fingers, I marveled at strength that went beyond muscle and bone, a strange fortitude no mortal thing could emulate. And my chest, my heart, radiated something difficult to explain without using the language of the gods. Perhaps . . . if temperature came in threes, that would suffice. It was not hot, not cold, but that indiscernible third. A curious and astonishing kinesthesia that seemed to double with each breath.

Rise, Aija.

I looked up and saw the Earth Mother looming over me, just as beautiful and bizarre as She'd always been, Her many tails swirling about like hungry snakes. I rose, and I felt the pull of muscles differently. I wasn't hungry. I wasn't tired. I wasn't confused.

I *was.*

And when I stood, light rimmed my vision. I looked down.

My scars. My scars had not left me—the Earth Mother had said I would keep part of my mortality. But now . . . they *shone.*

Mouth agape, I touched the radiating band of light encircling me, my ebony hand passing through magenta and cyclamen, violet and aquamarine, cyan and chartreuse. The lights shifted when I did, soft and radiant, and I wondered at them.

In that moment, I saw—*felt*—all the good I could do, the power I could lend, the fears I could allay. Like the world was my canvas and I was paint that would never fade or crack, that could unleash beauty in all its forms. Beauty that could ease hurt and nourish the downtrodden, inspire minds and assuage anxiety.

Beauty—power—that could stymie war itself.

Earth Mother stepped forward and clothed me in shale and silver, then hung a pearl circlet on my brow. *A gift from Tereth,* She said warmly.

I touched the pearl. Wondered again at the light in my middle, the billowing smoke of my hair. In a bead of silver, I saw the reflection of my eyes—their taupe color was the same, but the whites were brilliant, like they weren't white at all, simply *light.*

"Is . . . it done?" I whispered.

Her deerlike muzzle dipped. *It is. You are neither godling nor demigoddess, young Aija, but something else entirely.*

Emotion pushed against my chest like a too-deep breath. "Immortal?"

Another dip of Her head. *So long as you wish it.*

Turning from Her, I looked up at the sky. It was morning, but the Sun had a grayish cast to it. It wasn't bright enough. Fear spiked through my center, and my lights flashed cobalt in response. "Is he—"

He is immortal, as well, She assured me with the softest smile. *The war continues, as it has for millennia. Kefrani's pride is strong, but even she grows weary of endless struggle. She has lost many. Already she has moved her battle deeper into space, for fear of My intervention.*

I turned back to Her. "Kefrani?"

The name of the moon. Her first. I wonder that she does not use it anymore.

I thought of the moon, of her self-conscious fingers tracing her scars. Of her wide eyes taking in the sculpture I had made. Did it still stand?

"How long?" I whispered.

Ten years. Not long.

The number gutted me like I was a pumpkin. To think that someday I might also think a decade was short. "Zyzi, Ist—"

Zyzi returned to her village, as promised. She spoke as a patient mother to a child. *She does well there. Ist has joined the hereafter.*

Indigo banded me at the thought, but I remembered he had wanted to move on. He had been tired of this life, and I had been small minded in my understanding.

I could no longer be that.

Your grandmother as well. Her passing was peaceful. Your mother lives.

I startled upright, and the lights in my midsection swirled. "How could You . . . ?" My throat squeezed. "Tyu."

Yes. I felt more than saw Her smile. *She checks on you, every year's anniversary. And, dear child, I am aware of all who live upon My skin. Even those who are not of Me are Mine.*

"They all leave their impressions," I whispered, remembering the critical lesson from my deceased friend. One that had seen me through the darkest time of my mortal life.

My *mortal* life.

Because this new, wondrous opportunity was the start of another existence entirely. My *immortal* life. Perhaps it was an effect of being remade, or merely a lag from my long hibernation, but it dawned on me clearly then, what I was. *Why* I was.

I still had a heartbeat, and it pounded strong in my chest, brightening the colors slashing through the onyx of my body.

The want to do, to help, to succor pulsed through my veins, but there was something I had to do first. Something that tugged deep inside.

Saiyon. Saiyon was waiting for me.

I opened my hands, relearning them. It seemed the body of a celestial could still tremble with emotion, though where my mortal palms might have sweated, my immortal flesh remained dry. I closed raven fingers into fists, testing my new strength. "Thank You. For everything."

She nodded. *Return in one thousand years, and I will renew you.*

I looked toward the heavens. "How do I find them?"

You need only follow the destruction. Be wary, young one. Immortality will not guard you from danger, nor from pain.

I turned, taking in the canyons around me. They were unchanged. "Which way?"

You are more than you were, Aija, once of Rozhan. She smiled in truth. *Go.*

I licked my lips, a mortal gesture, and stepped toward the heavens. And flew.

The skies parted for me, until they were no longer blue but indigo and black, dotted with millions of stars. I marveled at them, at the distant spirals of cloud and color, at glowing worlds suddenly within my reach. And I itched to behold them, to draw them, and I felt in my fingers the yearning that had never left me.

I looked, and I saw the destruction: bits of rock without orbit, broken blades, and scattered light. I listened, and I heard the blasts, not unlike those that had torn through the sky as Tereth carried me and my friends across his seas. I turned and followed it, my hair smoking behind me, my light guiding the way. I flew through rings of asteroids and unmade things. Felt the eyes of stars young and old watching my path. Dust and orbits parted. The sounds of war grew louder, until I could smell them—sulfur and iron and fire.

There. From Earth, with the best telescope, it might have seemed a cluster of stars, but I beheld two celestial armies filled with creatures as fantastic and unfathomable as my new body, wielding weapons of metal and ivory, bursting with light and shadow, zipping like comets through their carnage. They were not like human armies, garbed in liveries and armor, lined up shoulder to shoulder to crash evenly into one another. These were far smaller, for one godling could wield the power of ten, if not one hundred men. The sides were blurred with little distinction, for in heaven, soldiers could not only attack from the front, side, and behind, but from above and below as well. Each warrior was distinct, yet each was part of a greater, powerful whole, led by—

Far to the right, the subtle, pale glow of the moon as she watched her minions attack. Far to the left, the golden brightness of Saiyon, leading a far larger defense.

Saiyon. *Saiyon.*

I watched from a distance, my body blending in with the universe around me, trying to determine my way. But I was still newly made then, and did not fully understand the ways of gods.

But then a shrill cry rang through space, and soldiers on both sides retracted, regrouped. Moon's dwindling warriors flocked to her, readying for her next command.

At a cry from the moon, the warriors of the night charged.

No. I would never have him, not truly, as long as this futile war continued. This realm was no longer unknowable—it was mine, too. I had claim to it.

And I remembered I had once been a woman who took what she wanted.

Zipping forward at the speed of thought, I emerged onto the battleground, the moon's army charging me from the front, the Sun's from behind—

"Stop."

The command washed out from me, and not merely in speech. It exhaled as a living thing, as *power* as strong as those who had made me, for both the Earth Mother and the Sun God had merged their magnificence in my creation. My colors blazed and spiraled, and had I mortal eyes, they would have blinded me. Darkness lashed out like fire, highlighting the magnificence of the Earth Mother's work, and the charging godlings slowed, unsure of what I was, what I could do, and whom I fought for.

I felt Saiyon's eyes between my shoulder blades. I felt them like twin candles grazing my skin, and my every part burst alive at the sensation. But I could not turn now. Not when war orbited me. Not when the moon loomed before me, and I remembered what the Earth Mother had shared.

Kefrani's pride is strong, but even she grows weary of endless struggle.

I leveled my gaze with hers. "Moon," I called, voice carrying despite the distance between us. "Kefrani."

Her eyes widened. Holding out a hand, she stalled her soldiers and floated closer, becoming larger as she did so, until she was far larger than myself. But I knew Kefrani. She had been my only companion for eighteen months.

Behind me, I heard *his* soft voice utter my name, heard the hopeful recognition lacing it. *Aija.* It nearly broke me anew. My immortal heart remembered all the fissures and cracks it had earned in its mortal life, and his voice caressed each and every one. I longed for him, but I had to be cautious.

"You dare call me by that name?" Moon asked, but a glimmer of youth sliced through her features as she, too, recognized me. "You! You are she."

Her expression was a mix of so many things it would take at least a dozen paintings to capture them. Anger, sorrow, shock, joy. I clung to the last: *joy*. Had my art, feeble as it was, made such an impression on her?

Had Saiyon been wrong in thinking she might attempt to revoke what she had given me?

"I am she," I confirmed. "Call off your war. It is pointless. You know this."

Anger warped her softer features. "How dare you—"

"You know the universe better than I do." I spoke softly and reached for her. Clasped her hand. She pulled away, but my fingers held strong—fueled with a strength that now rivaled her own. "You know you cannot displace him."

Silver flashed around her scars. "I don't need His throne. Only His influence."

"Is the night sky not enough?"

"No," she snapped.

I looked into her eyes, and I saw something there I had not before. Something that I understood all too well.

"You are lonely," I said.

I expected her to jerk away, but her hand went completely limp, and I knew I'd guessed right. All her worshippers, all her warriors, and Moon was lonely, locked away in her throne room with only shadows for company. Forgotten by many of those on the Earth Mother. So lonely she would lock away a talentless mortal under the ruse of a contract, hoping that mortal might call out to her so that she, too, might have someone to talk to.

"Thank you," I said, and caught her by surprise. "If not for you, I would never have known him." I tipped my head behind me but still did not dare look at Saiyon. Not yet. "But you rail against that which cannot be, and all the world suffers for it."

Now, she did yank away. "You know nothing."

"I know loneliness. Both he and you have given it to me."

Kefrani frowned.

A thought crossed my mind, stemmed from the memory of Moon's visits in Oblivion. She had never made me wait long when I called upon her. The contract had never said she couldn't leave me waiting.

"I will visit you," I said, and her face went slack. "I will come to your side, not as a prisoner, but as a friend. You can tell me what I don't know. Your wishes and passions, your sorrows and defeats. I will listen to you. I can be your companion, *without* the compulsion of a contract."

She hesitated, searching my eyes like I was the trickster. I opened myself to her, showing her my thoughts, my heart.

Her gaze flicked to my scars.

"Or," I added, "you can continue fighting, and lose more of those who care for your cause . . . and who care for *you* as you are."

Several seconds passed before she lifted her chin. "I will have you always. *Then* I will halt my army."

I shook my head, and she scowled. "Not always. Everything I have sacrificed, I have done for him." Finally, I dared to look back. Saiyon was an army away, but my immortal eyes saw every facet of his face, his parted lips and diamond eyes, heavy brow and slack jaw, the shock and hope at war beneath his skin. I smiled at him, and my radiance brightened, mingling with shades of rose and periwinkle. For me, the time away from him had been moot. For him, it had been ten years. "To have *him*. I cannot sacrifice him as well."

For me, that was law.

Moon reeled back. "No, I—"

"A season," I pleaded, turning back to her. "A season for every rotation of the Earth Mother, I will reside in your court, at your side.

Beckon to your wishes, balm your hurts. I will create for you, I will dine with you, I will fly with you."

She hesitated.

"Now?" she whispered.

My heart stretched and twisted at the thought of waiting even longer to be at Saiyon's side. It was early spring in the Losoko Canyons. "Soon," I reasoned. "I'll give you winter."

"I want summer." Her tone took a cold edge, and she looked past me to Saiyon when she said it. The Sun was always strongest in the summer.

But she was nearly convinced, so I nodded. "Summer."

She scanned my face, raising her hand as if to summon something . . . but then lowered it instead. "As you said, Aija. No contract. I want to trust you, so I will. But if you don't come—"

"I will come," I promised.

She pressed her lips together. Nodded. And with a glimmer pulsing from her skin, she called back confused—and some relieved—soldiers, and retreated into the depths of the sky, to the folds of a kingdom cloaked in night.

I watched her ascent so long that when I turned around, *his* army had dispersed as well. Some vanished from this edge of the heavens; others lingered at a distance, leaving nothing between us but empty space against the star-pocked heavens.

Flakes of golden ash fell from his eyes as he slowly, so slowly, neared. "Is it really you?"

I smiled, shimmering violet and gold. "Saiyon. My love."

We came together close, closer, ten paces apart, five, two. His heat surrounded me like that of a warm hearth, but it did not hurt me, and all my soul leapt with unbreakable hope. My band of colors burst alight, until even those on Earth would see them in the midday sky.

Saiyon, trembling, held out his hand to me.

Shaking, I reached out and took it, the contact of his skin racing through me, whistling in my ears and pumping through my heart, heady and powerful and eternal.

His fingers closed around mine, and he pulled me into him, his strong arms encircling me and mine encircling him, and I wept for the first time in my immortal form. I buried my face in his neck and I wept, holding on to him like I would lose him again if I didn't, our lights burning and churning together.

"Divinity should not weep so easily," he whispered, his own eyes pressing golden ash into my hair.

I dared to release him just enough to kiss him, to remember him.

Then, at that moment, I didn't have words to describe that kiss. But now, with the benefit of time, I can.

It was as two asteroids colliding, the impact rippling through space. Of a meteor burning through atmosphere. Of nebulous storms popping and sparking. Like a new cosmos was born in that moment, a universe all our own. And the universe, and all the worlds that were and are and will be, revolved around us, for truly no love in all creation was greater than ours.

And the war ended. Three months of the year she spent beside Moon, and Sun sorrowed for her loss, but rejoiced at her return. The law of the star mothers was fulfilled, and Aija and Saiyon's children filled the night sky, banding across it to guard both kingdoms.

The lights of Aija's victory can be seen by mortals at night. At least, they can by those on the northmost reaches of the Earth Mother, save for when she enters the realm of night. And so men, inspired by the dancing glow of the skies, gave Aija her second name.

The Northern Lights.

ACKNOWLEDGMENTS

I didn't originally plan this book. *Star Mother* was meant to be a standalone, but once I reached its end, I knew I needed another story. I knew Saiyon needed a happy ending. And I'm so grateful to everyone who helped me create it.

First, of course, to my ever-supportive, ever-self-sacrificing husband, Jordan Holmberg. He is my time giver, my brainstorming partner, my alpha reader, my everything. Literally the best partner I could ask for. LOVE YOU, JORDAN.

Many thanks to the next closest thing I have to a spouse—Caitlyn McFarland. She is a great, honest sounding board and read through my outline for this book so I'd have fewer things to fix after it was drafted. Also, we have a podcast called *Your Mom Writes Books*. You should check us out. :D

I'm so very grateful to my editor Adrienne Procaccini, who picked up this book and has been so supportive of me and my stories, and to my "foster" editor Lauren Plude, who took up the *Star Father* mantle with great enthusiasm. And of course, to my editor Angela Polidoro, who gloves up and sticks her hands right into the rank guts of nearly every book I've written. (And it can get messy, ha!)

Huge thanks to my alpha and beta readers: Tricia Levenseller, Rachel Maltby, Whitney Hanks, Leah O'Neill, and Rebecca Blevins.

They read some of the roughest stuff I have and still talk to me afterward. I really should pay them or something (hopefully they don't read that).

Finally, as ever, praise God and praise Jesus, for all that is good in the world and good in my life, and for the angels seen and unseen that buoy me and mine.

Cheers.

ABOUT THE AUTHOR

Charlie N. Holmberg is a *Wall Street Journal* and Amazon Charts bestselling author of fantasy and romance fiction. She is published in over twenty languages, has been a finalist for a RITA Award and multiple Whitney Awards, and won the 2020 Whitney Award for Novel of the Year: Adult Fiction. Born in Salt Lake City, Charlie was raised a Trekkie alongside three sisters who also have boy names. She is a proud BYU alumna, plays the ukulele, and owns too many pairs of glasses. She currently lives with her family in Utah. Visit her at www.charlienholmberg.com.